DIETER SCHLESAK is a German Romanian poet, novelist, and essayist. He is a member of the German PEN Center and the PEN Centre of German-Speaking Writers Abroad, and has received scholarships and awards from numerous organizations, including the Schiller Foundation and the University of Bucharest. Schlesak was born in Transylvania in 1934 and has lived in Italy and Germany since 1973.

JOHN HARGRAVES has taught German literature at Yale University and Connecticut College. He is the author of *Music in the Works of Broch, Mann, and Kafka* and has translated works by Hermann Broch and Elias Canetti, among others. His translation of Michael Krüger's novel *The Executor* was awarded the Helen and Kurt Wolff Translator's Prize. Hargraves lives in Manhattan and Connecticut.

THE DRUGGIST
OF AUSCHWITZ

THE DRUGGIST
OF AUSCHWITZ

A DOCUMENTARY NOVEL

Dieter Schlesak

TRANSLATED FROM THE GERMAN
BY JOHN HARGRAVES

PICADOR
———
FARRAR, STRAUS AND GIROUX
NEW YORK

www.picadorusa.com
www.twitter.com/picadorusa • www.facebook.com/picadorusa

For book club information, please visit www.facebook.com/picadorbookclub or e-mail marketing@picadorusa.com.

Illustration credits: pages 9, 86, 239: Schindler-Foto-Report; pages 18, 35, 37, 118: Yad Vashem/Wallstein Verlag Göttingen; pages 19, 26, 124, 162: Hessisches Hauptstaatsarchiv Wiesbaden; pages 128, 134, 150: Dieter Schlesak; page 345: National Museum Auschwitz-Birkenau

Designed by Jonathan D. Lippincott

The Library of Congress has cataloged the Farrar, Straus and Giroux edition as follows:

Schlesak, Dieter, 1934–
   [Capesius, der Auschwitzapotheker. English]
   The druggist of Auschwitz : a documentary novel / Dieter Schlesak ; translated from the German by John Hargraves.— 1st American ed.
   p. cm.
      Includes bibliographical references.
      ISBN 978-0-374-14406-7
1. Capesius, Victor, 1907– —Fiction. 2. Pharmacists—Romania—Sighisoara—Fiction. 3. Auschwitz (Concentration camp)—Officials and employees—Fiction. 4. Nationalsozialistische Deutsche Arbeiter-Partei. Schutzstaffel—Fiction. 5. Concentration camp inmates—Poland—Oswiecim—Fiction. 6. World War, 1939–1945—Atrocities—Poland—Oswiecim—Fiction. I. Hargraves, John II. Title.
PT2680.L43 C3713 2011
833'.914—dc22

                                                                    2010038536

Picador ISBN 978-1-250-00237-2

Originally published as *Capesius, der Auschwitzapotheker* in Germany by Verlag J.H.W. Dietz

First published in the United States by Farrar, Straus and Giroux

First Picador Edition: February 2012

10 9 8 7 6 5 4 3 2 1

CONTENTS

EDITOR'S NOTE

Dieter Schlesak's *The Druggist of Auschwitz* is unique for the way that it blends its fictional narrative with actual testimony from the Frankfurt Auschwitz Trial (which ran from December 20, 1963, to August 10, 1965) and interviews with survivors, guards, and administrators—including Victor and Fritzi Capesius—conducted by the author himself. This English edition follows the typography of the original German edition, which differentiated the fictional from the nonfictional, or documentary, elements by using italic and roman typefaces. The italicized sections of the book correspond to the fictional narrative constructed by Schlesak; the roman sections are those in which Schlesak is quoting either from the transcripts of the Frankfurt Auschwitz Trials or from his own interviews. We would also like to note that the quotations from Schlesak's interviews have been edited by him and reflect the sentiments and ideas expressed in multiple conversations rather than direct quotations from a single interview.

THE EYEWITNESS

I

They are herding us toward the showers. I see a long trench blazing with flames, I hear screams, children crying, dogs barking, gunshots. I see leaping shadows, half hidden behind the high flames. Smoke, ash, and the smell of burnt hair and flesh fill the air. "This cannot be true," cries someone near me. Women, children, and invalids are chased, alive, into the flames by German shepherds. A wave of heat, then shots. A wheelchair carrying an old man plunges into the flames; a shrill cry. Small babies, white as lilies, trace an arc through the air as they are catapulted into the fire. A boy runs for his life, the dogs chasing him; he is pushed into the flames. His scream hangs in the air. A mother nurses her child at her naked breast. She and the baby fall into the inferno. One swallow of mother's milk, for eternity.

Adam saw it, Adam knows it, he knows something we do not know, something we will never know.

But he survived it.

Even he doesn't know what the dead know.

He feels the guilt of the survivor.

Writing helped him survive. He wrote *there*, and he wrote in German.

Adam: I am a German; it was they who made me a Jew. German is my mother tongue. When I couldn't go on, when it became so unbearable that all I wanted to do was to jump into the fire with my fellow sufferers, into that pit of burning human beings, then I gave it all to German, my mother tongue, as if only she could heal this, she alone. Here, read it: I cannot forget. And he handed me one of his pages, covered with tiny script.

But life must go on, he continued. And stared straight ahead. When he enters the room, you feel only him, he fills up the room, the whole house; his presence changes the space around us. No one speaks, everyone is silent, when he enters the room.

This is Adam, who was *there,* a member of the crematorium Sonderkommando, a man who has something within him we cannot comprehend: Adam is alive, he exists, *really.* I could look him in the eye, touch him, eat and walk and talk with him, feel his silences, his descent into himself, his way of being there and yet not . . . not there, like being dead, and yet still living . . . at those trenches . . . back then. Then? But they are here, now, they will never go away . . .

·

Adam: Then suddenly—I never felt anything like it before, how can I even describe it?—I separated from my conscious self and changed over to the "other" side; I felt a strange sympathy with that SS man performing his difficult, murderous work in that almost unbearable heat . . . We looked at each other: this, THIS, it cannot, it must not, be happening. But it is! It's real!

So Adam, the last Jew of Schäßburg, wrote. I had visited him at his home, and now, after leaving him, it felt like a final farewell, because he is old and sick. But I can still call him on the telephone, twice a week, and there are numerous letters, actual letters, and he gave me his diary, his "little rolls," just copies, of course; and even though his head is like a death's-head, with black, deep-set eyes, I can still reach him. His heart is damaged, and his broken bones never healed properly; they still ache from the icy winters in the camp (down to minus 37 Celsius), painful rheumatism, pneumothorax, and he has only one lung left (tuberculosis has calcified the other one), but he is alive, not dead like all his friends, his wife, his children, his parents; Adam is alive NOW . . .

•

He embraces his dead wife every day, he says. And there is something that permeates everything, gets into the earth or the floor, the flowers, the grass, the trees, the light gets grayer, still this deep-seated fear, it hollows out everything from inside, this fear: *Adam: There are black beasts inside me, I hear their harsh, malicious laughter whenever it is quiet. Grim animals sitting in my rib cage. They crouch there, ominous, their wings folded back, or they cower somewhere hidden in my innards, so I can no longer dare seek refuge inside myself. Something uncanny is there, in the darkness inside me. I seek shelter outside, beside myself with fear. When I take strong pills, the pills themselves settle briefly in the fragile tissues of my brain, and dream my nightmare, until I awake with a start, hunted, chased into another dream . . . till suddenly it all dissolves, and then my arms turn black, and my wife who was turned into ashes THERE dissolves into grayness, the room, the walls crumble, not in glowing light, no, but into a gray nothingness, a dreary morning of ashes, everything crumbling into ashes, ashes . . . Everything dissolves, the world now just a huge void, a gap . . . and then I wake up, as I did every morning at four, with whistles shrieking, commands shouted: Get up,* Aufstehen! Fertigmachen!! *Get up, you swine, up! And I am back at the camp, as always. And then I know everything else was just a dream, a kind of holiday.*

All that matters are the people we know and once knew, the living and the dead. And we speak for the dead. We live for them. Perhaps they have opened up a way for us to reenter that realm, a realm whose forgetting made these crimes possible in the first place. They are the only reality left. Those who know it, those who were part of it. For me, everything else is gone.

Adam's experiences cannot be told in words: *It's like that for us all, Adam says, we who went through it, we come from another world . . . An abyss separates us from you, a sort of vacuum of horror, it has to do with naked life itself, and little to do with the abyss between perpetrators and victims; unless, perhaps, everyone who does not know, or still thinks the way they did, is one of the perpetrators! For everything on earth has changed since THAT!*

And he quoted a poem of Paul Celan, speaking to himself softly, very softly, for now it was the dead speaking, the victims, the murdered ones, it seemed, coming from beyond the border back to us, the living, as if wanting to give us hope and comfort, because everything was different now, because that old death no longer existed, because we didn't need to fear it anymore, for now THEY were actually there, quiet, hopeful, but barely audible: *If there can be any sense in the death of millions of victims, it would have to be in the sheer crazy hope that a crossing has opened on the frontier between life and death. Celan: "In the mills of death you grind the white meal of promise, / you set it before our brothers and sisters / we shake out the white hair of time . . . and let something now come which never was before! / Let there come a human being from the grave."*

Adam's tiny rolls of paper, which looked like miniature papyri written in German, contained things that even he had forgotten, indeed, that he had to forget, so he could go on living. He pulled out these rolls, as if they were the witnesses, and not he, as if it had all started with them . . . He took them hesitantly from the ancient, beat-up desk, tentatively, as if they didn't belong in the everyday world, things that could not be seen or felt, like copies of burned Torah rolls . . . that was how he touched them, these yellowed paper rolls . . . lying in his open hands . . . He bent over them . . . sniffed them . . . then held them out to me . . . as if he wanted to tell me something that was impossible to impart in any other way . . . and no, they didn't smell like old paper . . . They still had smoke, ash, and the smell of burnt skin on them . . .

I hear Adam speaking, I hear his telephone voice, telephone conversations that went on for hours . . . I hear his tape recorder voice. And I hear his "real" living voice, slightly nasal, quiet, deliberate. And of course, he always spoke in German, German words, German sentences. Once I had asked him how he could possibly bear speaking German after "that." At this he became very angry, he shouted: *But it was these SS guys who wanted to turn me into a Jew, before that I didn't even know I was a Jew—I was a German with this language I had babbled even as a baby. It comforted me, this language, it wept within me, this, my language. I clearly heard its weeping when these human animals—they did come from Germany, yes, they were "Germans," but could not speak proper German—when these animals would shout their false "German" phrases, these analphabetics who could only bark German like dogs. I refused: I was the German, and they were the animals, clearly, and they did not succeed in making me a Jew. I am a German AND a Jew, a gift*—he laughed bitterly—*may it remain part of me and all my feelings, my very existence, my poems and diaries, these un-Germans and murderers cannot be allowed to win, even afterward, and claim that THEY stand for what is "German."*

But where is Adam? Was it a dream, Adam's existence? No, we breathed the same air in his house in Schäßburg, his home, we spoke with each other night after night in this quiet small town. The little "rolls" were there, too, I could touch them, they seemed to glow, to burn up, fire without ash, but I could read what they said, it's right *there*, forever, the horror of the experience can never be erased, it is burned into us who read it, shuddering; and in none of the documents, none of the other reports, does it reach out to us, as it does here, and become a nightmare.

Day after day I read them, but would break off, again and again, would think I was dreaming, and then, after many sleepless nights, I had become someone else, someone who was continuing this writing; it was as if the writer who could put that reality down on paper was only now appearing, as it took shape from behind a thick fog of knowing and forgetting. And now, here it is before you, entire, in your life, but so *late*! I kept hearing Adam's warning words: *You have to do something, you must help, the world coming after us must know it as exactly as possible.*

Perhaps the immediacy of the horror in these rolls is because Adam wrote it down while experiencing the horror, he wrote it in THAT unfathomable nightmare that was Auschwitz, in all its inconceivability still THERE, finding direct expression in the German words of a Jew, amplified, still echoing down to us today. The other eyewitnesses did not report their experiences until testifying at the trial twenty years later, often halting, weeping, or writing it down . . . This was the painful experience of Ella Salomon, a teacher, and her mother, Gisela Böhm, a pediatrician, both of them from Schäßburg.

•

Ella Salomon: "We were witnesses in Frankfurt in 1964 at the Auschwitz trial and with the aid of tranquilizers, and with microphones in hand, we testified before a large audience, among them sociologists, students of law and other fields. They got their *lecture* from living witnesses.

"It was very difficult for us to be among the people of this, the enemy's land. Every stone made us weep, every word hurt. We were badly burned children.

"The women from the former resistance movement had prepared a reception for us at the airport in Frankfurt. They all embraced us warmly right after we landed. One of them was Emmi Bonhoeffer . . .

"My interrogation in the courtroom lasted over an hour; my mother's took two hours. Emmi and some of the Marian nuns were present. It was very heartening to see them there, because Attorney Laternser, Capesius's defense lawyer, treated us in a very derogatory fashion. He bombarded us with mis-

Ella Salomon (left) and Gisela Böhm, at the entrance to the Gallus Court Building, Frankfurt am Main, November 16 or 19, 1964

leading, confusing questions. When he asked me about my tattoo number and I said I no longer knew it by heart, he gave me a look of scornful disgust. And on top of that, the next morning the *Frankfurter Allgemeine* reported that I had been theatrical."

Or the other witnesses in the chamber during the Auschwitz trial: the audience at the trial sat there, numb and wide-eyed with horror, looking at the woman in the witness chair. She had just described in a calm voice the torturing of prisoners in the notorious "Boger swing," and at that point, words failed her. In halting phrases, she told how one day fifty children, aged five to ten, were brought into the camp on a truck. "I remember a four-year-old girl . . ." Her voice broke off then, and her shoulders began to heave; as the witness wept despairingly, numb horror spread through the courtroom . . .

Adam: You see, although I had been called as a witness, I could not go to Frankfurt because of serious illness and constantly recurring health problems at the time resulting from my experiences in the camp. But others did it for me . . .

I told Adam what had moved me, and asked him why the horror of reading his ashen script had affected me so deeply, differently than other reports from hell.

You know, that's not quite right, he said. I am not talking about feelings, even from the abyss, but about these unimaginable realities, especially at those trenches . . . "Small babies, white as lilies, trace an arc through the air as they are catapulted into the fire . . ." As I just now read *what I had really* experienced *back then, I was convulsed with horror, and I was back in that very condition that I had, thank God, forgotten about . . . But it was that way, just that way . . . Many of my fellows have related the same unbelieveable cruelties, just think about Filip Müller, or about Dov Paisikovic in the Sonderkommando, or about Gideon Greif's book,* We Wept Without Tears. *Or the book by Mengele's assistant, Dr. Miklós Nyiszli. And one thing you mustn't forget: May and June 1944, when our fellow Transylvanian Jews were dying in the gas chambers, the most horrendous May in human history, when up to twenty thousand human beings, not soldiers in huge battles, but month after month, day in day out, from morning to evening to night, girls, women, babies, children, and old people, suffocated screaming in the gas chambers. Even for Auschwitz this was the absolute peak!*

In a period of about nine hundred days over six hundred death trains arrived at Auschwitz, with over a million Jews, and approximately twenty thousand Sinti and Roma [Gypsies]. Day after day, night and day, the SS was carrying out mass extermination. Most of the victims went straight to the gas chamber. Twenty minutes after the Zyklon B was inserted, the doors were opened, and the prisoners ordered to clear out the bodies found up to two thousand naked corpses all tangled together. Babies, children, sick people, trampled to death on the floor; that's where the gas got to first. Above them the women, and on top the strongest men. To save money, mostly they didn't throw in enough Zyklon B, so that the killing could take as long as twenty minutes while the weakest lay at the bottom in their final agony. For each gas chamber of two thousand people, they used sixteen five-hundred-gram canisters. Each canister cost five reichsmarks.

It was the "last hurrah" for these, the greatest executioners of the last thousand years, and it went on till November 1944. Up until March 1944 the Jews of Hungary and Transylvania had lived in a protected enclave. Till March the higher Hungarian military had shielded their Jewish citizens, they called them up as laborers into the army, and even Horthy protected them; there were 795,000 Jews in Hungary and Transylvania. You know, after the Vienna Treaty in 1940, northern Transylvania was declared part of Hungary. So everyone was spared until March 19. But suddenly Hitler no longer trusted Horthy, because he had begun negotiating with the Allies. So on March 19, German troops marched into Hungary. And Eichmann came to Budapest. He decided immediately: all the Jews of Hungary should be exterminated in a Blitzaktion.

And on May 4, 1944, they convened a conference in Vienna to set up the schedules for the transport trains . . . And from there it just proceeded like clockwork. All you have to do is check out the "Kalendarium" of Auschwitz at the Fritz Bauer Institute in Frankfurt am Main.

Adam showed me the text excerpt from his extensive archives, and read:

A conference was convened in Vienna on May 4, 1944, to set up the schedules for the transport trains that were to deport the Jews from Hungary. About 200,000 Jews were to be deported from ten camps in the Carpathians (Zone I); in the Transylvanian Region (Zone II) there were located around 110,000 Jews. From mid May on it was arranged that there would be four transports a day from these regions, with 3,000 Jews each.

May 9, 1944: As a result of the speeded-up preparations for beginning the extermination of Hungarian Jews, Rudolf Höß, the highest-ranking officer of the SS garrison at Auschwitz, ordered that the unloading ramp and the rail line into the Auschwitz II-Birkenau camp, as well as the three train tracks on the ramp inside the camp at Birkenau, be finished as quickly as possible, and to get the as-yet-unused incineration ovens in Crematorium V into working order, and to excavate five trenches (three big ones and two smaller ones) for burning corpses, to renovate Bunker II for use as a gas chamber, and to dig even more incineration trenches by the bunker, and to construct barracks for the prisoners to undress in. In addition, Höß transferred the chief officer of the subcamp Gleiwitz I, Hauptscharführer Otto Moll, back to Auschwitz, and appointed him the commando leader of all the crematoriums, and gave him responsibility for all outdoor incineration of the victims killed in the gas chambers. Höß also ordered reinforcement of the Sonderkommando used in the crematoriums, and also of the "Canada" Sonderkommando, which was to sort through the prisoners' plundered possessions, directing that additional prisoners be assigned to these units.

Everything was kept secret. Even the courtyard in Crematorium III was hidden from prying eyes by a screen.

Moll also ordered that tables and benches be built in the yard at Crematorium IV, as he realized that it was impossible to fit the masses of condemned human beings into the gas chambers simultaneously. For those waiting victims the tables and benches served as an additional undressing area in the open air, since the locker room inside the crematorium was not big enough for the countless numbers of doomed men, women, and children.

In Capesius's documents this description of the extermination process was found:

The apparatus of extermination ran smoothly. The staging and running of the transports was carefully prepared. The camp commanders were notified of the arrival of a transport via telegrams and radio messages, and they would then give further instructions to the detention camp leaders, the Political Department, the office of the SS garrison doctor, the truck drivers' unit, the guard detachment, and the work deployment office. Each one of these units involved with the "handling" of a transport had a specific duty roster for its "operation" [*Einsatz*] in "special actions" [*Sonderaktionen*] on the unloading ramp . . .

2

Ella Salomon: "For us it all started on May 26, 1944. With deportation. You were allowed to take fifty kilos. In a cloth sack. No suitcases. The ghetto was to be cleared out on May 26. At five a.m. Everyone took along food and their most valuable possessions. Jewelry. Medications. And Mama even took her doctor's satchel and instruments. Deportation. Final. Everyone crying. All the shutters closed, the streets completely empty. All you heard was the masses of people, the clattering of their shoes on the pavement of the ghetto.

"In a stinking cattle car, with over eighty people crammed in together, shocking scenes were playing out: two young women were going crazy. There was no food or water. People were drinking urine. Other prisoners were pulling or prying out their own gold teeth, in exchange for water. The guards (at first Hungarians, but after crossing the border, SS men) took the teeth, but didn't bring any water. During the transport the few possessions we had were taken from us by the guards.

"Cattle would have been given water on the journey, but we were not. The car's huge iron doors were kept locked. There was a gap in the door of barely a few centimeters. The air that came through this gap had to keep eighty-four people alive!

"For four days and three nights we never saw God's sky above us. We could only relieve ourselves inside the car. The situation was intolerable. Some people lost their minds. A middle-aged woman lay beside me. Her hair turned white overnight.

"The memory of two little twin girls will never leave me: On the second morning of the journey, I held them by the arm and climbed with them up to the narrow opening in the car, so that my little travel companions could get some air. They were nine years old, pretty, healthy, and very smart. They bombarded me with questions the whole time, questions I could not answer for them. They were the daughters of Dr. Mauritius Berner. I met their father later in Jerusalem. But the girls went up in smoke. I can still feel them today . . . their warm bodies in my lap."

•

Dr. Mauritius Berner: "Outside, the locks and chains are taken off, and the door opens. A huge crowd of people is moving forward outside, and on the opposite track there is an empty freight train parallel to ours, and we walk in between. By the cars of the train next to us there are huge masses of suitcases, thousands of pieces of luggage in unimaginable disorder, and we cannot comprehend what it means, where are we, what has happened, why this picture of total devastation?

"As we look up ahead between the two pairs of tracks, a few hundred meters off, we can see two factory chimneys of an unusual type; flames several meters high are shooting out of them, columns of fire. Disoriented, we want to know where we are. The first minute we have the feeling of being in a bombed-out station; that would explain the huge mass of luggage lying about in such confusion. The huge columns of flame coming out of the chimneys, in the early dawn light, make me think we are in some mine or ironworks, or the entrance to Dante's Inferno. Clearly we are going to have to work in a mine or an ironworks, I tell my wife, but that doesn't matter, I quickly add, the main thing is, the five of us will stay together, the work can be ever so hard, but we won't let anyone separate us. But then we haven't time for any more comments, white-and-blue-striped zebralike creatures silently start to force us forward with sticks, while snatching our luggage from out of our hands. When we struggle to keep these last bits of our belongings, they reassure us that we just have to leave everything here for the time being, everything will be delivered to us afterward. We still try to resist, to defend our last possessions. But a few steps later, a German soldier comes up to us and explains that we have to leave our luggage. We give in, lay our luggage down by the cars, and I say to my wife, No matter, the main thing is that the five of us are together. At that moment, though, a German soldier steps in again and blocks our way: 'Men to the right, women to the left,' he says, and in an instant I was separated from my wife and children. We move forward in parallel, but separated from one another. The crowd carries us forward. Suddenly I remember the half bottle of water we saved from yesterday: I still have it. I push my way through the rope separating us and give the water to my wife. As I am being shoved back my wife calls out to me:

'Come, my darling, and kiss us!' I run back over to them, I kiss my wife and my children, with tears in my eyes and my throat tightened up with grief, and I look into my wife's eyes, wide, sad, beautiful, and filled with the fear of death. The children look on in silence, following their mother. They could not comprehend what was going on here, and just let themselves be pushed along by the crowd of people streaming behind them. A soldier pushed me to the other side of the line, and we were separated: I couldn't even give them a word of comfort, or send them an encouraging look from behind. One more minute, and they were gone from my sight.

"I, too, was forced ahead by the moving crowd, and we came into a wider area—where the view was no longer hemmed in by the two parallel stopped trains. Soldiers and those creatures in stripes sent us here and there, and ordered us into columns.

"And then, I hear: 'Doctors, line up here!' I go there, where other colleagues are already gathered, wearing Red Cross bands on their sleeves. The crowd presses sluggishly forward beside us, men on one side, women on the other.

"Meanwhile we see that everyone is filing in front of a tall German officer wearing gloves, who, with a gesture of his thumb, sends people to the right or to the left, thus separating family members who want to walk together. We also notice from far off that he directs the older, weaker-looking people, and mothers, to one side, and younger, stronger people, men, and some women to the other. Those who refuse to be separated from their older parents are loudly reassured that the separation is necessary, because there were still ten kilometers to go on foot, and the old, the weak, and the children would be transported by motor vehicle. Once there, everyone would be reunited.

"And there are trucks there as well, and a small car with the Red Cross insignia next to the tracks, so we can see that there really are vehicles available waiting to transport the weak and the sick. And we hear that the sick are being delivered to a nearby hospital. Reassured, everyone goes to the right or left, confident they will see one another again soon.

"Then the officer who separates right from left comes up to our group. He asks each of us very nicely where we had done our university work, and if any of us were sick or tired, since the camp was still ten kilometers off, so if any of the 'gentlemen' preferred, they could switch to the other side, he said, where they would be transferred by motor vehicle.

"One of our group, the pharmacist Kőváry, immediately switches to the other line. Meanwhile we explain to the officer that our documents and our medical diplomas are still in our luggage, lying next to the railroad cars. 'Can't we at least get our diplomas?' 'Of course,' replies the officer, after a brief moment. 'Certainly, you will be needing your diplomas!' We rush back to the cars and eagerly search for our bags. I locate mine, and bring back my diploma and other documents with me. Then I go back to my group. Then all of a sudden, in a line of women that had just been separated into right and left, I spot my wife with the children. I go up to the German officer and ask him to allow my wife and children to stay with me. I base my argument on the fact that I, too, am a doctor (since we doctors have been placed in a separate group, I conclude that we will be working as doctors) and that I have three children, two of whom are twins, who need special care. 'Twins? Call them back,' the officer says. I run happily after them, calling my wife and my children by name. They turn around, and I run after them and bring them back. The officer takes us over to the doctor performing the selections and informs him that the two children are twins. But the second officer doesn't even look at them; he waves a hand dismissively and says, 'Later, I don't have any time right now.'

" 'They will just have to go back to the group you took

them from,' says the officer. And then, in Hungarian: 'Don't cry, your wife and children are just going to take baths, you'll see one another again in an hour.' "

•

Ella Salomon: "There were eighty of us in the railroad car on the transport to Auschwitz. I had Dr. Berner's twins on my lap. I love children. I was telling these children stories, because I wanted to make the journey easier for them. We sat as close as we could to the slit in the side of the carriage, to get air."

Presiding judge: "Had you known the defendant Capesius before you were deported to Auschwitz?"

Salomon: "Yes. He came into my father's waiting room, my father called me, and said, 'Your pharmacist uncle has a present for you.' He gave me some blotting paper. I was twelve or thirteen then. Capesius was sweet to me. Then I saw him again in Auschwitz. Before that I also saw him in

The ramp at Auschwitz-Birkenau

Victor Capesius (far left) with the daughter of Gisela Böhm, Ella Salomon (second from left), at the swimming pool at Sighişoara, 1928–29 (Private collection, property of Gisela Böhm)

Sighişoara at the swimming pool. At home I have a photo-graph of him with us."

Presiding judge: "Do you know what happened to Dr. Ber-ner's twin girls?"

Salomon: "I never saw them again. I met Dr. Berner in the men's camp at Birkenau. He told me he never saw his wife and children again.

"On arrival in Auschwitz the transport was inspected by a commission. The prisoners would be asked whether they could walk or not, in which case they would then go by car. Since I was tired, I wanted to ride, and had a big argument in Hun-garian about this with my mother, who was of the opinion that I should definitely walk. Among the commission mem-bers I recognized Dr. Capesius, the pharmacist from Sighişoara, and I was so surprised to see him there."

3

Göppingen. Beautiful area. In the distance, the Drei Kaiser-berge mountain. Like many of his compatriots, Capesius did not go back to Transylvania after 1945. A court in Kolozsvár had sentenced him to death. Was he homesick? Yes, he was homesick. I was at Capesius's home, at "Vic's," as my mother used to call him. I was paying him a visit in Göppingen. And he was happy to have found a fellow countryman; he would have been risking his life to go back home to Transylvania.

Capesius was Mother's dancing-school partner during her high school days in Sighişoara; the heavily built SS pharmacist, the man from the ramp, so frighteningly close at hand? He and his wife greeted me as a compatriot, almost touched to see the son of their old friend from back home standing before them. But I felt a cold shiver run down my back, and I had to conceal my trembling hands after they had clasped them warmly. I spent several days with them, the last time just before his death in the 1980s.

He managed to survive in Germany. In the Auschwitz trial he was sentenced to nine years, and he served the time. Now he was free, but he was marked by all the things he had gone through.

Capesius: "Yes, when you see suffering like that, it is so depressing, it makes you sick to your stomach. You really feel like puking. At first. Then you get used to it."

Capesius said this in Göppingen, as we were walking home from the Marktapotheke, his pharmacy business. And his wife, Fritzi, walking beside him, short and frail with rimless glasses and intelligent eyes, corrected him softly in her Viennese dia-lect whenever he had a memory lapse or began to stutter: this bulky old man who when called on to testify in the Frankfurt courtroom had been nervous and distracted, could not give a coherent account of events; he had made a poor impression on the court, was often absentminded, with a slightly foolish smile on his face.

.

May 1965. *Dr. Victor Capesius:* "Mr. Chairman, last Monday I was in a state of nervous tension, because from early that morning I had thought that I would be called to testify, but then that did not happen until the afternoon. That made me a little confused later on, and people have criticized me for smiling, quite unconsciously, the whole time. I certainly did not feel there was anything to smile about, and can only explain this by saying that I was in solitary confinement for over four years. This, plus all these people here, and all these electric lights, distracted me, and so I mostly couldn't concentrate on my answers."

His dark glasses and his formal dark suit did not reduce his sense of insecurity. Something like an internal fog—as if he had chronic sinusitis—was oppressing him. He was just not there, and had no idea how to focus his thinking more sharply. For a minute I feel sorry for him, tormented by his own helplessness and clumsiness, by his being the insecure provincial that he was. These two old people look on me as one of "them," a compatriot, and they are touched. And Frau Capesius, the doctor (they first met in Vienna when she was in medical school), looks at me searchingly through her thick glasses, just as she did long ago, when I came into the drugstore; my father was buying cough syrup for me. Frau Doktor was a person who commanded respect; she spoke German with a proper accent, so you sort of looked up to her—she sounded like she came from "up there." But she had spent her whole life in Transylvania, and in Göppingen she was homesick for Sighişoara. Both old people mixed up the names of cities, said Hermannstadt when they meant Stuttgart, where they often went for concerts and lectures in the Haus der Heimat, or said Kronstadt (Braşov) when they meant Munich.

Capesius: "Most of them were condemned after the war."

"So they were hanged . . ."

Capesius: "Yes, right after the war. Dr. Fritz Klein, too."

"Where was he from?"

Capesius: "Kronstadt . . . Zeiden. And Klein was in Auschwitz. And he was an Obersturmführer. By that time he was fifty-five years old, and didn't actually have to join the military. But he did.

"And so Fritz Klein did his service as Mengele's subordinate in Birkenau, following Mengele around during the selection process, actively participating in all that, and so on, sometimes Mengele did it, sometimes him. And then comes this one doctor from Târgu Mureş with his twins. And Klein hears him say, they're twins, they're just now taking them off, and so Klein says: Twins? Where are they? And then he ran right over to Hauptsturmführer Mengele, who was two levels higher . . ."

"Everybody knows him, he was really well-known."

Capesius: "Well, sure, because everything in Auschwitz was all about that. Because the Americans eventually got all those studies, all that genetic research . . . research on twins and genetics . . ."

Frau Fritzi Capesius: "Identical twins, that was his area of interest."

Capesius: "And the Americans paid the Poles a lot of money for all that, since that was really an important matter, as there was no other place where you could just perform research like that, no problem . . ."

Frau Fritzi Capesius: "Horrible . . ."

Capesius: "Well, sure." (Pause.) "And Mengele then waved them aside, since they weren't identical. And then Klein comes

back, and gives the doctor from Târgu Mureş a pat on the
shoulder, and says, okay, let them go, you'll be back together
again in an hour . . .

"He drank, too, Fritz Klein. A lot. He was mostly drunk.
And the word was, that, like Dr. Rohde, he just couldn't take
the realities of camp life. But I kept my distance from him."

(Capesius saw Dr. Mengele several times a week on the
ramp with the Transylvanian country doctor Fritz Klein. He
described the SS doctor and mass murderer with fussy bureaucratic precision.)

Capesius: "Mengele was five feet, four and a half inches tall,
had a short, straight nose, freckles, and piercing dark brown
eyes, hair parted to the left. Mengele was of medium build,
wiry, athletic, and looked a lot like his Gypsy forebears, probably back when the Mengele Works was still just a blacksmith
shop. Mengele was a stickler about doing things legally, and
acted impulsively."

The most irritating thing about Capesius that one could
not ignore: that soft, strained, yet casual-sounding voice in a
Transylvanian accent; I am convinced that in the camp he had
had a commanding voice, but then had undergone a personal-
ity change in his fall from commander to prisoner, such that
he now sounded like a befuddled, whining old man. When my
mother heard his voice on tape, she said, surprised, "Vic was
an educated guy, just listen to how he sounds now, he's definitely gone soft in the head."

He was better in writing, even if he still made a lot of mistakes, and his handwriting was crabbed and small, and would
probably tell a graphologist a lot about his emotional poverty
and his immaturity. Still, he could be unbelievably precise
about appearances, especially, and was at his best when recall-
ing figures, names, titles, places, and physical sizes, like the
cold bureaucrat and head of personnel he was. Here is how he

described Mengele in his notes from prison: "Dr. Josef Mengele, Ph.D. And M.D., aka 'Pepo' (birthplace Günzburg on the Danube, March 16, 1911), was the 'Chief Doctor' in Birkenau. He drove an Opel. His father before him was the owner of the Mengele Works, which manufactured farm vehicles like the 'Unimoc.' Mengele was in Auschwitz from January 12, 1942, and from January 5, 1943, in Birkenau BIIe. He was particularly aided in his 'camp work' in Birkenau Crematorium I by a Jewish doctor, Nyiszli Nikolaus (Miklós), from the Romanian town of Großwardein, and this was later made public by this same doctor, first in Paris, and then later in *Quick* in eleven articles running from January 15, 1961, to March 26. These articles contained much that was true, as well as much exaggeration and downright fiction."

4

Paul Pajor: "It was a Sunday. First the order was given: 'Women and children up front, men to the rear.' But everyone wanted to stay with their families. Prisoners in zebra-striped uniforms were there, and I heard one of them whisper to someone, 'Give the kids to the old women, young women keep separate.' We men lined up in rows of five. When I got to the front, I saw an officer pointing people to the left and right. An old man was standing in line in front of me. When I got close, I recognized the officer immediately. I couldn't believe that it was him, but then he spoke to me in Hungarian: 'Aren't you a pharmacist?' I answered, 'Yes, I am, I am a pharmacist.' He asked again, 'Don't you have a pharmacy in Oradea?' When I said yes to that, too, he motioned with his head for me to go to the right. I heard him say, almost as if to himself, 'Yes, on the corner.' After that, I never saw this man again. This officer was Dr. Victor

Capesius. I got to know him prior to 1940. At that time he was the chief sales representative for Bayer and visited us frequently. He came into my drugstore several times, was always quite nice, chatted with me while his driver arranged his sales displays of Bayer products. Sometimes, he would say: 'I will leave you some Bayer packing paper, so you won't have to lay out anything for things like that,' and so on. When he spoke to me on the ramp, I knew for sure that it was him."

Magda Szabó: "I had my sister-in-law's little child with me. A prisoner asked me if that was my child. I said no. He said, 'Hand it over!' So I did. Than an SS officer came up to us. He spoke Hungarian, and so perfectly. He said the camp was still a long way off, and if anyone felt sick or weak, they should raise their hand and they would be driven there in a truck. Later, when we were taken to the camp, we only walked a few minutes. The officer was Dr. Victor Capesius. At that point, I still didn't know him, but he is the type that's easy to recognize, he has a red face and doesn't look German. When I heard him speak Hungarian to us, well, that made me so happy."

Judge Hotz: "You have described the officer's face. Did he have a nickname?"

Szabó: "We called him 'Mopsel' (tubby)."

•

Marianne Adam: "Standing at the head of the 'selections' group this time was a portly SS officer, his face red from the heat. He would invite the girls, in his cultivated Hungarian, to move to the left: 'Oh, you must be tired, you've worked hard. Here with us you will rest and regain your strength. This is a rehabilitation camp.' A lot of people back then still didn't realize what Auschwitz really meant: that every word was a lie. They believed whatever the cheerful, red-cheeked officer said; they marched off in rows of five, and once on the other side, they went right into the gas chamber. He motioned me, too,

Victor Capesius, Frankfurt am Main, 1960

to the other side. But I was lucky: I pretended not to hear him, and walked following my fellow new arrivals—into life! The officer did not insist that I move to the other side, since at the moment he was occupied with those who were already destined to die. So I stayed alive."

5

Adam Salmen's diary: It gets into you, into your pores. Day and night, train cars rolling, rattling, whistling, people streaming from the cars, bodies crammed together . . . Young Tadeusz Borowski from Žitomir and Warsaw, like me, is part of the commando squad "Canada." * *That morning the command was at four a.m.: "Canada squad, fall in! Now! A transport!" March through the gate in rows of five. Hands on our pants seams. "Caps off!" The still sleepy SS man counts off the people on his clipboard: one hundred. Every few meters an SS guard with an automatic pistol. Gray, numb masks, not human beings. March past Camp BII, to Section C, now vacant. The Czech camp. Quarantine,*

---

*"Canada," the rich storehouse of prisoners' personal effects; an *Effektenlager*, or storeroom for effects.

from gray to green: apple trees, pear trees, the infirmary, the cordon of guards, then the road, at double time. The ramp, under trees. Birkenau. The train station. Huge stacks of matériel, mountains of tracks, sacks of cement for construction. Trucks. And, soon, living "human matériel." Human beings, made of flesh and blood, children, cries, memories, feelings. Nothing, I think: now, all that's left is their bodily material, to be disposed of like refuse. SS guards all around, a cordon surrounds the ramp, sweaty faces, canteens, "Comrade drink!" One of the SS guards says, in broad Bavarian dialect: "Comrade, you got a drink? It's hot today." In the shadow of the embankment, the "Canadians." There, the advance workers are on the ramp, they divide the people up, groups are forming, one to open up the rail cars, one for unloading, and the third with the movable wooden steps. Motorcycles droning, fat SS junior officers, silver insignia in the sunlight, shiny boots, chubby-cheeked faces red from alcohol, some of the SS ranks with briefcases, others holding thin, flexible switches, riding crops demanding "flesh, flesh," as one of them says with a mocking laugh. Shabby wood barracks for those on duty, the "students' fountain" there, mineral water or gluhwein *in winter. "Heil Hitler," then handshakes, showing letters, photographs, stories, girlfriend or wife, and almost all of them have children. They play with their whips, making them whistle through the air. Gravel crunches underfoot, just like home.*

The various ranks of SS officers and men have fixed assignments: they observe the selections at the ramp, they receive the transport documents from the transport leaders, they divide up the deportees into men, women, and "unfit for work" (old, sick, children), get the terrified, disoriented people to line up in rows of five, and "select" them, they confirm "delivery" of the death train and tally up the data on "transport strength" (head count) . . .

I see the pale faces behind the barred windows of the cattle cars, double-"secured" with barbed wire, exhausted from lack of sleep, disheveled, frightened women, men, looking like a miracle [to us]: they still have hair. And I hear how things seem to be boiling over in the car, hollow knocking against the walls and cries of "Water! Air!" Their open mouths, dark holes, breathing, gasping for air as if drowning. And then the revolted expression on the face of the giant SS junior officer, camp leader, probably, one more drag on his cigarette, throws it away, signals to a guard, who shoots off a round on his automatic pistol, making a brief clatter over the row of cattle cars. Then deathly silence.

6

Roland Albert: "Yes, it was Pentecost—right? Odd, but was it the Angelus I heard, maybe a bit late, ringing in the nearby village church with its pointed steeple? I could certainly see the train arriving. From the watchtower, where I was on duty, I could also see two friends from the old country, our Sighişoara druggist Dr. Capesius and the doctor from Zeiden, Dr. Fritz Klein, as they performed their 'selections.' And later on, I had to do ramp duty, too. I didn't like doing it. But I had to. Orders are orders. And I had to look on, as somebody with a shaved head ran straight into the barbed wire. But otherwise I escaped into books, mostly Hölderlin. Before I got promoted, while I was still an ordinary soldier, I had to do sentry duty a lot. I was always screwing up on watch. There was often thin, blue smoke coming out of the kitchen barracks, and from the crematorium, clouds of thick, black smoke, dense, roiling clouds of smoke. So they weren't just burning up dried out, skinny 'Mussulmen,' but new arrivals. The wind kept the smoke blowing down onto the camp, and the thick swirls of smoke floated down over the barracks. It smelled greasy and sweet, and made you want to puke. I can't forget it. Even today I can still feel that taste in my mouth. When I was on watch duty in the big tower, I looked down onto the two double tracks and a rail switch, and in between this long ramp. All the trains drove slowly in, backward, as if they were creeping. From the bend in the tracks, I saw freight cars, and a trainman at the taillight waving his arms, leaning way out."

Roland couldn't see everything on that day. He did not see that twenty-four-year-old Ella Böhm (called Salomon after her marriage), who, half fainting of thirst and suffocation, was supporting her mother: "But I could hear the trains whistling like back home in Sighişoara, like the whoosh of the light rail train to Hermannstadt: the long, drawn out, piercing whistle of the locomotive, thick clouds of smoke, like in a dream . . ."

•

Adam: It was May 29, 1944. Six a.m. Pentecost, the quiet holiday. Trucks are being stationed beside the closed doors. And we hear an SS lieutenant yelling: "Anyone who takes gold will be shot!" And I think, gold? They have brought everything they own with them, is that why they have to die? Here, everything is naked, out in the open. In the camp, there is abundance again. The kitchen is richer, soups, bread soups, even soups with specks of fat, goose fat, preserves, fruit, slivovitz, gold, jewelry . . .

I am standing next to Borowski. We hear the bolts rattling. Open cars. I see the fresh air rushing in, almost knocking the people over. They are having trouble breathing.

They pant for air. People amid suitcases, packages, satchels, bundles, rucksacks, bags, and they among them. Their life, they hoped to bring it with them, they had been told that there was a "new life" to be built, in a camp ghetto, with their fellow prisoners. Books, papers, jewelry. The doctors had all brought their instruments with them. Enormous amounts of medicines. They were supposed to lay everything down in a pile beside the cars. Lay them down carefully, not throw them. A woman bends down one more time over her bag. Then the thin switch of an SS man whistles *across her face, a thick welt, and blood. She falls to the ground with a loud cry. A disheveled little girl starts to cry and yells, "Mamele, Mamele, Mamele!" Pocketbooks, with banknotes, gold, watches, jewelry falling out of them. Jars of marmalade, put-up fruit, sausage, Transylvanian salami, sugar scattered around like snow. The crowd tramples over it all. Whipped on by the words "Schnell! Schnell!" they are forced to double-time it; women are screaming, children are crying, and everywhere the whistling sound of whips and the shouting of the SS. Past the doctors doing the "selection." And there, they can even see the stocky figure of Capesius, the druggist from Sighişoara. The people walk slowly past him in single file, a gesture of the hand to the left, to the right. Those at the left are picked up in trucks. The old, the weak, the sick, the children, the crying, shrieking babies; endlessly the trucks, one Red Cross truck (how reassuring, here, then, they take care of you!) behind them, the Red Cross emblem, otherwise the symbol of salvation; Thadeusz sees it, too, I see it, and we both think the same thing and talk about it. That calms the people down somewhat, even while the truck holds the poison Zyklon B for the gas chambers. And we, ourselves, have to push the people, everyone in the Canada commando separates the doomed from those chosen to work, sixty "pieces" per truck, after sixteen trucks we've done the whole thousand. A young, clean-shaven SS man makes a mark in his notebook with each truck. "Okay, move. Bewegung! Get going." German is the language of hate here. German is the executioners' language, every "und" and every "oder" hurts like the lash of a whip. Orders in German, like shots, that kill!**

•

Innsbruck, May 1978. We are standing in the rain by the car. Raindrops on Roland's bald head. Once we are in the living room, he points to the bookshelf where Hitler is now absent, but he says, "I was the first in Sighişoara to read *Mein Kampf.*

*Cf. both Kielar and Borowski.

But in the library at Innsbruck I read a lot of mathematics and biology, and then 'the classics.' " His primary interest was poetry, he said, especially the "divine Hölderlin." And he talked and talked. "My mother, your aunt Cecilie, could yap away for hours, like a machine gun," he said, laughing. Roland's laughter soars through the sparsely furnished apartment like a colorful bird.

Roland Albert: "So I have to say, I liked being a soldier. And I would have stayed a soldier, if we had won the war." "How come a soldier?" "Well, for one thing, being a soldier is a profession where you have the most free time. That attracted me." "There you could read poems, you could pursue your artistic leanings . . ." "Yes, I even served guard duty and had my knapsack filled with poetry. You know. I was constantly derelict on watch." "Even in Auschwitz?" "Yes." And he laughed his castrato laugh. "And I was just an ordinary soldier for two years." "But you were an officer there." "Yes, but only later on, after '43." "You were a lower-ranking officer until '43?" "No, I wasn't. I am one of the few who was promoted to officer directly from the ranks." And he laughed again, oddly feminine, and in a muffled coloratura tone: something nervous, even hysterical breaks through the satiny tone, like an imp giggling. Shrill, raw, rash, naïve.

"Till May 1943, when I was still just a private (in May I was promoted to officer), I still had to do watch duty, and I looked down from above on this teeming mass of people. And often, then, I would quickly look at a book. Lines on a page were like protective walls. I thought about religion class. The religion class that I had to teach mornings at the German school. One day, school. One day, watch duty. It was Babel there, and there was a prisoners' Esperanto, too . . . forty languages? German gone to the dogs. Had to keep a low profile . . . for them I was the *esesmani* from the *blockfihrerstuba* beneath the tower, so they said."

·

Adam: They are herding them into the shower rooms. I see a long trench blazing with flames, I hear screams, children crying, dogs barking, gunshots.

·

Roland: "Strange. I often thought about religion up there in the tower. Which Psalm will we go through tomorrow?

"German Christianity?" *(Like a shock wave, the horror of the night plants itself in the heart.)* "How could I tell the children that there is neither God nor salvation?

"But what am I saying? I thought that then and I think so now. And the other guard with me certainly noticed that I turned away, that I didn't want to see what was happening *down there*, I just didn't look . . . but I did see everything, I had to see everything . . . but just thought about something else . . . like what I was going to cover in school with the kids, oh, they were sweet, obedient children in the Auschwitz German school. And so I will talk about the Führer that God sent us, I thought back then, to calm myself down. God had taken all responsibility away from us in this millennial breakdown, this fall from heaven, that we experienced there. A great time, but a dreadful time."

7

Adam Salmen: Tadeusz, my "Canada partner," with whom I was forced to work on the ramp in those days, had a completely different view of all this. He committed suicide after the liberation, only twenty-nine years old, he couldn't take it on the outside; the memory of it killed him.

Tadeusz Borowski: "I wanted to run away, but the dead were lying all around. Lined up in rows on the gravel, on the concrete edge of the railway platform, in the cars. Children, ugly naked women, contorted, convulsed men's bodies. I ran as far as I could. Someone struck me with a riding crop. Out of the corner of my eye I saw the SS man screaming furiously. I tore myself loose and disappeared among the fat 'Canadians.'

"Finally I was able to crawl down the embankment. The sun had sunk down close to the horizon, its fading blood-red light flooded over the ramp. The shadows of trees had lengthened, the cries of human beings sounding louder and penetrating farther in the quiet evening air. A gentle silence slowly descends on the world.

"Only here, underneath the tracks, is it possible to gauge the hellish confusion up on the ramp. Two people have fallen to the ground, arms grasping each other in a last desperate embrace. He had dug his fingers into her body, his teeth tearing her dress apart. She groans loudly, letting out short, hysterical cries; not until she is kicked by a hobnailed boot is she still. The two are pulled apart like pieces of wood, and they are driven onto the truck like cattle to be slaughtered.

"Four prisoners are lifting the huge, bloated body of a woman. All four are sweating under the heavy burden; they curse and kick at the children in their way. There are children everywhere, they run around like lost dogs from one end of the ramp to the other, searching and whimpering, crying and screaming. The men catch them, grabbing onto them wherever they happen to catch hold, by the head, the neck, the hands, and throw them up onto the truck. The four 'Canadians' can't lift the woman's corpse. They bring on reinforcements; at last the heavy body can be thrown up onto the truck with those still alive, and the dead, who will go together into the ovens, and the children, who continue to scream and cry."

·

Adam: The really hellish things only started after that, when we had to empty the wagons carrying the dead, the dying, the crippled, and the sick, those who could not give any more, those who

were no longer "selected." And this was the job of the "Canadi-
ans." A one-legged girl is carried past by two prisoners; they hold
her by both hands and her one leg. Tears are running down her
childish face. "Oh, that hurts, hurts, hurts!" She is tossed up
among the bodies and the half-dead living on the truck, crying
with pain. She, too, will be burned, together with the dead. And
a beautiful clear starry night blazes above it all.

One hour ago, there had been a great crowd of people. Over
there, where the chimney is smoking, that is where the children
and the old people, the older men and women, are made to suf-
focate, screaming, in the gas chamber.

Only one hour ago, the selection was still going on.

Tadeusz and I were met by a stinking, sweet wave of air com-
ing from the railroad cars. A mountain of human bodies. The
bodies were inextricably tangled together. The pile was no longer
moving, but it was still steaming.

"Unload them!" sounded a voice harshly behind us in the
dark. The SS man materialized out of the night. On his chest was
hanging a handheld searchlight. He shone it into the car inte-
rior. "What are you hanging around for? Start unloading!" He
swept his blackjack over our backs. I grab the hand of a corpse,
and the fingers clamp onto my hand like a vise. With a scream I
tear myself loose and run away.

Tadeusz: "My heart is beating like a hammer, my stomach
is turning, my knees are giving out.

"I rolled myself underneath a cattle car and threw up.
Then, shivering, I climbed back down the embankment.

"I lay on cool, hard steel and dreamed of returning back to
the camp. I dreamed of my bare, naked wooden cot without
even a straw mattress, I dreamed in fragments of dreams that
one dreams along with the few friends that will not be gassed
tonight. All at once the camp seemed to me like a haven of
safety, of security. It is always the others who die. We ourselves

somehow keep on living, we always still have something to eat, the strength to work, a house, a home, a girl . . .

"The lights are shimmering, the stream of humanity keeps ceaselessly flowing by, fevered, dulled, numb. These people really believe that they will be starting a new life in the camp, they prepare themselves for the bitter struggle for mere existence. They do not know they are about to die, that all the gold and all those jewels they so carefully and anxiously hid in the seams of their dresses—they will never be needing them again."

•

Adam: Once everyone was gone from the ramp in Birkenau, Tadeusz Borowski has to go into the cars. A gaunt, pockmarked SS Scharführer orders him: "Move! Clean it out!" He can still see the great cloud of dust behind the last truck taking the people to the gas chamber.

Selection at the ramp

Tadeusz jumps into the first railroad car, but recoils at what he sees: lost watches, urine, feces, paper, pocketbooks, clothes, the little children trampled and suffocated, with huge, swollen heads and bloated bellies. With trembling hands he carries them out into the light. "Like chickens, two in each hand!" He takes them to the truck with the dead bodies.

He leans back against the car. He is very tired.

A friend, Henri, a French prisoner, wakes him up: someone is pulling at his hand: "En avant! Get down off the tracks!" He raises his eyes, a face is floating in front of him, all blurry, then coming back, growing bigger and bigger, gets more transparent, gets mixed up with the trees, gets as long as their trunks, God knows why all these beasts are black all of a sudden. He has to blink his eyes hard a few times: Henri.

"So, Henri, are we good people?"

And now the real work of the "Canadians" starts. The goods of those who are just entering the gas chambers get thrown onto trucks, suitcases are piled up, a few things sorted out, some things slit open and rummaged through, "just for fun," or to look for alcohol or perfume. Tadeusz wrote it all down later. But everyone wrote under the threat of death, it was punishable by death to be caught reading or writing, but everyone knew that sometime later they would have to bear witness: We simply dump the perfume bottles onto ourselves. One of the suitcases pops open. Suits fall out, clothing, shirts, and books. Something heavy, wrapped in a cloth, rolls up to my feet. I pick it up and unwrap it: two handfuls of heavy jewelry, rings, bracelets, necklaces, diamonds, gold . . .

"Right here," says the SS man, and calmly holds out his open briefcase to me. It is full of gold and brilliantly colored stones, together with all kinds of banknotes in foreign denominations. He closes the briefcase and hands it to the officer. The officer walks off with it.

Members of the "Canada Commandos" sorting victims' luggage

With the Hungarian transports at Pentecost, so many people and so much wealth arrived at Auschwitz that Hans, the Kapo of the "Canada" team, became the most popular man in the whole camp. Even the camp "senior member" Danisz played up to him, smiled at him, and Jupp, the camp Kapo, was suddenly his best friend, walking around arm-in-arm with him. Hans gave gifts to everyone, beaming with pleasure. But that only lasted a few weeks, until the Hungarian and Transylvanian transports started tapering off, and finally stopped altogether. The ramp was totally empty again. And Hans was forgotten. Nothing normally considered human mattered there, nothing but simple survival: the others lived through the deaths of victims forced into the gas chambers, who could take nothing with them, as they died naked of suffocation, because the soup from the camp kitchen was slightly thickened by the uneaten food that was brought here by the doomed. These soups stilled their hunger at least for a while; the deaths of others meant hope and a longer life for themselves, especially for the prisoners, as absurd as that sounds. For they, too, had become dehumanized, not just the perpetrators.

Borowski is tired and he keeps waking up at night: he sees a truck loaded with bodies, bodies dragged up, bloated cadavers, cripples, paraplegics, half-suffocated victims thrown on top. This mountain of dead people moves, groans, cries. The driver starts moving, an SS man yells: "Halt!" They are dragging an old man in a tuxedo, dragging him along the ground. He is wearing a sling on his arm. His head bangs rhythmically along the ground. The old man first whimpers, then whines, "I want to speak with the commandant . . . I want to speak with . . ." He is tossed onto the truck with the other dead bodies. And the SS guy yells to him: "Shut up, man, in a half hour you will get to know the all-highest commandant! But be sure and say Heil Hitler to Him!"

Tadeusz nearly passes out as two men carry up a child, a girl, one legged, tears covering her little face.

•

Victor Capesius: "Between May 14 and July 7 of 1944, thirty-four trains with 288,357 Jews arrived from northern Transylvania and Hungary, who all went through the selection process on the ramp; of that number, only about one third were declared fit for work and saved. Children below the age of fourteen did not fall into this category. Starting in 1943, many people from Transylvania and the Banat were assigned as guards at the camp. But they were always just bodyguards."

•

Dr. Adrienne Krausz: "I was deported to Auschwitz in June 1944 with my parents and my sister. We arrived early in the morning—it must have been between three and four a.m.—the lights were still burning. Both my parents were doctors, and so they had known Dr. Capesius from back home; as a sales representative for the IG Farben Works he had often made sales calls on them in their office. When my mother saw the officer carrying out the selection process, she said, 'Well, that's Dr. Capesius from Klausenburg over there.' I think he recognized my mother as well, because he waved at her. My mother and sister were sent to the left by him, into the gas, but I went to the right and I survived. Later I met a friend who had been with my father during the selection. He told me that my father had said hello to Capesius and asked him where his own wife and eleven-year-old daughter were. Capesius supposedly answered: 'I'm sending you to the same place where your wife and daughter are, it's a good place.'"

Presiding judge: "Did you see Capesius in the camp anymore after that?"

Krausz: "Yes, I saw him again that same day. We were brought to the baths, our hair was shaved, we showered and dressed again. But while we were still naked standing in line, Dr. Capesius walked through. I was standing next to Frau Stark, an elderly woman who had also known Dr. Capesius from back home. She spoke to him, and asked, 'Doctor, what will happen to us?' or something like that, I can't remember exactly anymore what it was. He pushed her away, so that she fell down on the slippery floor. That was the last time I saw Dr. Capesius."

8

"Frau Weiß, the Jewish woman from Sighişoara," I heard my schoolfriend Gernot Wagner say, "was a colleague of mine in the porcelain factory in Sighişoara. She was shy, but always nice. All I knew about her was that she was Jewish and had been a prisoner at Auschwitz; her husband, too, who was then director of the Sighişoara Bread Factory, had been in Buchenwald. It may have been in 1962, when quite coincidentally I was standing next to Frau Weiß's work station, when the morning break began, right at ten. That was the moment when all the grinding equipment (there were ten double grinders) was turned off. And in this moment of sudden silence, we all heard the boss in the next section yelling loudly at one of the workers. Frau Weiß started suddenly, and said, in Romanian, '*Vai parca il aud pe lagerführer*' (I thought I was hearing the camp leader). We were picked up in Klausenburg in 1942. Father, Mother, and we three girls. At first we were brought to Dej to work in a brick factory; then we were locked into cattle cars, everyone given a piece of bread and a bit of margarine. After a horrible three-week trip, we arrived on the Jewish ramp at Auschwitz. My parents went straight into the gas. We girls went to work.

"At first we had to 'take a bath,' naked, of course. And afterward we had to stand in line and be 'inspected' by an SS man. One of the women prisoners had a scar from an appendectomy operation—she was immediately sorted out for the gas chamber, and another, with a scar on her arm, likewise.

"But the worst thing was the morning roll call. We were chased out of our bunks at five in the morning, and we had to stand outside until nine, summer and winter, without moving. We had to 'learn' that even the dead were expected to report for roll call, we had to carry them out there, and after standing there for hours with them, we had to bring them back to the barracks, and keep doing this until they were registered as dead and brought to the crematoriums. They mostly stank horribly and at night we had to sleep next to them. We were not human anymore. Our only thought—our only wish—was once again to be able to cut into a loaf of bread and slice it up from one end of the loaf to the other.

"The fact that I survived at all I owe to the workers in the factory and also to an SS officer who came from the Banat. They repeatedly smuggled bread and other food to me."

.

Ella Salomon: "From the station we marched several hundred meters till we reached the bathhouse. We had to take our clothes off outside in the open air in front of the bathhouse, keeping only our shoes on. We were then led into an anteroom in the bathhouse and then we had to take our shoes off. After waiting around for an hour they took us one by one into a shower stall. Then we went into a large shower room, where we could wash up with soap. Although earlier they had told us that our clothes were being cleaned and we would get them back again, in the bath we were given other bad clothes and wooden shoes.

"The water was hot. Afterward I had to wait outside in the open and wait for our friends. And then, still naked, we were sent into a little room to a barber. He shaved off every hair on our bodies. We had lost every sign of our identity. We had nothing, we were nobody. But still inside of ourselves, the 'I' was still there, that self with which we tried to resist. But at that moment, the tragic situation became clear, and many could only resist up to this point. Without their hair, the most different-looking women were transformed into mere bodies, all the same. Indistinguishable. Facial features seemed to dissolve, to be replaced by a vacuous, emotionless expression. Something strange was happening, as if all of us together possessed just *one* unattractive body—something radically altered the relationship of the number of individuals and their aggregate physical size; all at once we occupied less space. We were an insignificant mass. Had we lost our aura? The psychic extension of the individual seemed no longer there. At the same time, a burden had seemingly fallen away, the 'I.' No history, no past, no name. Girls who had been constantly crying up to then could hardly stop giggling, and laughing at these comical figures, their girlfriends. They would call them by name, as though they were somewhere else, amazed that such a faceless body would then

respond; a kind of hysteria broke out, laughing, piercing screaming, yelling, wild hugs, too; many hid their faces in their hands,
rolled around on the ground, yelling and screaming.

"As we called it in the *lagerszpracha* (camp language), or
krematoriumsesperanto, we were now *cugang* (*Zugang:* arrivals) and the whole situation was *die aufnama in den stand
lagru*, the *aufnamowanie* (reception into camp), and in the
process everything that made us human beings was taken
away: civilian clothing, personal articles, even our hair and our
names. In any event, we were now just *numery*. Yes, too, we
had to fill out the German *personalbogen* (personnel form), in
which we had to tell them the number of gold and platinum
teeth, fillings, and crowns we had. And then came the *kwarantena* (quarantine) with its endless *apela* (roll calls). And the
tresura cugangow (training of new arrivals), which thank God
we didn't have to do completely, just a few days, since Dr.
Capesius or Dr. Klein had spoken for us. But others had told
us about how they had been abused. My Polish bunkmate in
the *koja*, from whom I also learned the *lagerszpracha*, or else
I would not have been able to make myself understood (though
she also spoke a little German), told us dreadful things as we
lay in our bunks at night.

"The bunks were triple-decked, no straw mattresses, no
blankets, nothing. We had to lie on bare boards. Around eight
of us had to share one bed, later it was ten, even. It is hard to
imagine how we all found room. It was only possible if you lay
on your side. We cuddled our bodies up together just like
spoons in a drawer. When one person wanted to turn over,
when her foot or arm had fallen asleep, then all ten had to turn
over.

"Before daybreak, really still the dark of night, we would
hear the horrid words 'roll call!' The truncheons and prods
were set in motion right away, and we were hounded out of

our beds—beds?—bunkboards into the cold winds of dawn. We were made to assemble again in rows of five, and stand and stand. There was no mercy. Whoever collapsed was left there. Three, four hours this torture would go on, which they called 'roll call.' Then the SS would arrive, to count us off. But before this happened, the *Blockältesten* (highest-ranking prisoners) would torture us almost to death. Every day, for example, the *Blockältesten* would punish us in the following way: we would have to kneel for hours in the pouring rain in rows of five, holding a brick in each hand. Naturally this completely bloodied both knees. Many got sick, got pneumonia, and died. But no one cared.

"The dreadful supper rationings were repeated. We stood in line again, for a disgusting, revolting grass soup 'seasoned' with pebbles.

"The hours-long roll call was done regardless of the weather: whether the heat was in the nineties or the cold in the minus thirties with cutting winds that went right through your whole body, we had to bear it, teeth chattering. But no one gave a damn.

"The roll call also served the purpose of checking on our physical condition. People slowly shrank, gradually got smaller and smaller. Those who were only skin and bones, people called them 'Mussulmen'; they would be thrown out, and we knew what they were being thrown into!

"We so feared this Mussulman look, which we equated with death, that we did everything imaginable to avoid it. We slapped our faces, to make our cheeks turn red, and we wolfed down all our food, even the most revolting bits. Some prisoners would stuff their clothes with something. And at every mealtime we would fight one another for the more nourishing thicker liquid at the bottom of the soup pot.

"And I can still hear the noise, the yelling, the most obscene swearing, and the words they would shout before the morning *apel: 'Schnell! Schnell! In finfe austellen!'* (line up in fives), and then that *'Micenab micenauf'* (Caps off! Caps on!) or the singing. I slowly got to hate these folk songs that I had once liked back home, and which the Saxons* used to sing. Once I had to watch, and Magda Szabó was there, too, when a poor, emaciated Hungarian woman (nearly a Mussulwoman by now herself) had to take *fünfundzwanzig* (twenty-five) with the *pejcz* (whip) on her naked buttocks, screaming with pain each time; she could barely count off the blows, as required—once when she forgot, the blow was repeated. Another time a woman was also laid out on a bench, not tied to it, she had to hold herself on, only her head was held by two women prisoners, I saw it: stroked by one of the women holding her, while the *gumiknypel* (rubber truncheon) whistled through the air down onto her naked thighs and buttocks, which after this treatment were just a shapeless bloody mass of flesh, and she just lay there, gasping, unable to get up.

" 'Selections' were carried out during roll call, sometimes by Dr. Mengele or by the female wardens. I can still remember by name SS Chief Warden Mandl and a beautiful warden called Grese.

"Those women prisoners whose names had been written down for liquidation were then led by the senior officer to the gas chamber . . . [long pause].

"The whole purpose of these concentration camps, this murderous madness, was death. Already by the fall icy winds from the Russian steppes cut into your face. While it was still dark as night, at five a.m., that's when we had morning roll call . . . that's when they called out numbers and you were put on work teams and sent down to the brickworks, singing the whole time: we

*The Siebenbürger Sachsen, or Transylvanian Saxons, the ethnic German natives of Transylvania. —trans.

had to sing this song: *'Seht, da kommen die Juden her, aus Paläs-tina mit dem Holzgewehr, keine Angst, das schießt ja nicht, weil es vom Juden ist, Jude wolle wallera'* (Lookie there, the Jews are coming from Palestine with their wooden guns, never fear, they cannot shoot, because it was made by a Jew, a Jew, hey hey!), and we had to march to it, and woe to anyone who didn't sing along. For then you would feel their rifle butts."

•

Adam: Later we learned there were some who resisted, like Zofia, a beautiful young Pole who fought back, a wonder of a person: just keep yelling back. And then would come her punishment; mostly she was laid out on a bench and whipped. But she never cried out. She fought to keep her dignity. And she did, for months.

But the worst of their methods of compulsion was language: right on the camp gate the cynical motto ARBEIT MACHT FREI and the way the commandant or the camp leader referred to us as recruits. After all, it's a concentration camp, a murder mill. And then this induction process, this reception madness where your own clothing is taken away, put into bags as efekty, the re-moval of all personal effects, the personnel sheet, the bath, the head shave. And then the kwarantena.

I tried to "save" my beloved German language. For German was despised. All the prisoners lived in an extreme situation that was defined by the German language. Communication with guards basically took place in German, camp mail had to be written in German (just to make censorship of the mails possi-ble), in every block you were constantly reminded that it was re-quired to speak German. If you didn't know German, survival was just about impossible.

•

Ella Salomon: "Soon we began to be tormented by an animal hunger, and all we talked about was set tables covered with the finest dishes, our favorite foods. When we crept out at night to wash, we heard chewing sounds all around us: our fellow prisoners were dreaming they were eating their favorite dishes.

"It started around that time: every morning—those terrible mornings!—the SS duty officer or even the head SS officer would ask the doctor as he came into the block, whistling: 'What's new in the monkey cage?'

"We had a young, beautiful woman in the block, but very pregnant. We had unanimously decided to hide her with some straw that we had found on the floor of the block. I told her to make herself as small as possible, because the straw we had wasn't quite enough to cover her completely. Then she would be invisible. I started to cover her, it was urgent, because otherwise she would have had to report for roll call, and her 'sin' would be found out, if not today, then tomorrow. While I was feverishly working at this, a high-up SS officer poked me from behind with his stick. I recognized the druggist Capesius from Segesvár [Sighişoara], my mother's hometown. In his day he had been a sales rep for Bayer products; when I was a girl he often came to my parents' office practice. Smiling in his phony way he would give me a pencil or a pad of paper. In school I was very proud of my Bayer pad.

"But now, he pushed me aside and swept the straw away from the pregnant woman with his stick; I never saw the expectant mother again."

.

Adam: This is the daily routine: Wake up at five a.m., with police whistles. Make beds, military style (blankets must be stretched exactly over the straw pallets). Wash up (of course only a few sanitary installations are available for many thousands of inmates). Eat "breakfast."

Fall in, rows of five. How long roll call takes varies greatly, depending on how fast attendance can be taken.

The inmates must march off in step to the music of the camp orchestra. The workday, as a rule, is eleven hours with a half-hour midday break.

Work of returning inmates is checked.

Eat supper. Nine p.m. bedtime; it is forbidden to leave the barracks.

I have started writing down the day's events on pieces of paper, in tiny script, at which I am now expert, and storing them in an old tin can that I bartered for at the flea market. It's amazing how the "organizing" works, even bribing the SS, so that shady deals from outside and smuggled goods from area residents are easier and easier to get through the inspections at the gate. This stuff winds up in a melina, *a hiding place; mine was a hole in the ground beneath the wall where a brick was missing. I would just take out the newly made brick to get to the hole. In the "special operations squad" (Sonderkommando) it was even easier, I just hid the can underneath the heap of bodies, let one of the dead victims hold it, whose face I made a point of remembering. Macabre, yes, I thought so, too, but such things don't bother us after a while; rather, I thought this would let the poor devil live a little while, in me, in my memory. Thus I have kept a whole gallery of dead faces within me. Every day, another one, as if they, too, were witnesses along with me. Well, they can sure keep a secret, the poor, the departed, the murdered.*

9

Adam: I came, together with Dr. Otto Wolken from Vienna, to Auschwitz I, that is, the Stammlager or main camp of Auschwitz, in 1943. The way from the railroad station into the camp was rather long. We were accompanied by SS guards, who came up to us on the way and asked, "Have you got any money? Have you got a watch? Hand it over, you can't keep it anyway, everything will be taken away from you. Give it to me, and I will help you in the camp!" There were also some people breaking their backs with their heavy luggage. Dr. Wolken was unusually observant, his description is more exact than mine, so I took his down into my diary. In the Auschwitz trial he repeated it:

Dr. Otto Wolken: "And then we got to the camp. We marched in through this gate. From a block to the left we heard waltz music, the band was rehearsing. Indeed, we had no sense that we were entering a hell, it all looked so nice and peaceful. We were brought to a block, and then were told: 'Everyone undress!' Everyone was given a sack. 'Please put your personal effects in this bag.' Carrying these bags, we then went to the so-called Political Department. We handed in our bags and were given a tag with a number. We were told to keep the tag safe. This was important: we wouldn't get our things back without the number. Then we were brought into a wash-room, a big room with concrete floor, puddles of water on the floor, water dripping from the showers. We went in. At first we were around eighty or ninety people, then more and more.

"It was around noon when we came in, and hour after hour went by, and more and more naked figures came in. We were tired, we could not stand up any longer—we had already been traveling without food or water for a day and a half. And so we all just sat down on the floor, in the puddles, we didn't care, and we kept waiting and waiting. We were waiting at least for someone to give us a bit to eat. All we could do was try to catch some of the dripping water in our hands. Then it was night. We were driven out of the block in the dark and assembled on the roll call square. We had to stand there all night. It was a very cool May night, with wind and cold rain drizzling down on us. We stood and stood and stood, until morning.

"In the morning, they began shaving us. The hair from all over our bodies was more ripped off than shaved; there was no soap. We were flayed, not shaved, and then smeared with the famous lice disinfectant Cuprex. Then we learned for the first time what 'camp' really meant. When we came out of the shaving room, we had to climb onto a small pedestal. An SS man stood in front to check that we were properly shaved. If we were not, we were beaten and chased back, even though we were not the shavers, but the shaven. Only after we found favor with them were we allowed to shower and go out the other side into an open yard. And there we stood for hours, until everyone had made it through this procedure.

"Then we finally entered a block. Prisoners were standing there, each had a pile of clothing in front of him, and they threw us each a garment: 'Here you go, custom made!' We got shirts. I got a child's shirt, the sleeves only reached my elbows, I couldn't button it in front, it was too small. Then I got a pair of trousers which would have fit a giant. I had to wrap them around me four times to be able to walk without tripping on them. After this 'outfitting' we then had to go back to the Political Department. And only then did we learn what the little number tags, which they earlier had given us for our clothes, actually meant. We had to show them the tag, roll up our left sleeve, and we got our numbers tattooed there. The wardrobe tags contained our future number! It was now clear to us that we were no longer human beings, but just numbers.

"There's not much to say about the quarantine period. We had to spend the whole day in a narrow yard between two blocks. There they lifted up two concrete covers, around which they had put up wooden scaffolding: this was the latrine for the whole group, some eight hundred people. Everything took place in this yard. In the middle was this wooden frame, and anyone needing to relieve himself would just sit on or stand on this frame, depending. And it sometimes happened that someone sitting on the one side would find himself being 'washed' by someone standing on the other.

"Well, such conditions encouraged even the Blockältesten

to rebel. They were just corpses on holiday, anyway. They were beaten up, pounded to a pulp, and if they were tired at that point . . . the process of dying was taking too long. When, despite the brutalities and all the other pointless work, there were still too many prisoners left alive, the camp doctor would make an appearance. And would fulfill this function in a more elegant manner. He comes, stands there, and whether winter or summer, he says: 'Strip completely naked! Fall in for roll call!' Then he walks through the ranks, and selects with a wave of his finger who is to be 'promoted' from life to death. But the selection process was not carried out with great precision or fastidiousness; a selection of five hundred men was finished in five minutes. It was simply if they didn't like the way someone looked—some wound, some kind of disfiguring scar, scabies, a boil, anything was sufficient reason to be sent to the gas chamber. We did our best, we put some rouge on them, I did as well, for as long as I served in the first-aid station, we did everything possible to make them look good before the selection, so they would pass.

"Then there was a long break. Everyone was too busy with the transports from Hungary and didn't have enough time to worry about the camp."

•

Adam: I was able to earn a large number of assignments in the camp, and was constantly switching around; this fit my curiosity and my restless nature. Unfortunately, toward the end, as a punishment, I was assigned to a Sonderkommando, but before that I had been a "doctor," a "plumber," a secretary in various barracks, and I think I have Langbein to thank for joining the resistance group known as Kampfgruppe Auschwitz: as a go-between and a "delegated" messenger he sent me all over. While I was still working in the registry office dealing with the Toten-bücher, or the books for death registrations, I met Dr. Berner, whom I had known earlier; he was working in the "Canada" area and with his connections was able to get me into the "Canada" property warehouses, too. In the quarantine camp and the hospital I worked with Otto Wolken, who wrote everything down, kept a diary, in order to give an exact account of these crimes, to keep them from being forgotten! And I copied his reports into my little "rolls" in case his notes got lost. But we both lived until the liberation on January 27, and he was able to dig up his buried notes again.

•

Dr. Otto Wolken: "I have already mentioned—in regard to the selections—that the Hungarian transports brought about a huge change in the whole business. Suddenly the Eichmann 'travel agency' was back in business, and day after day four, five, six, some days even ten trains arrived in Auschwitz. There was a lot of activity on the ramp. Thousands upon thousands of people were gassed every day.

"The Hungarian Jews selected for work went to the former Gypsy camp, empty since they had already been liquidated. They were 'billeted' there, as I have said, at 1,000 to 1,200 per block. The Hungarian women went to Camp BIIc. And there they were billeted at up to 2,000 per block, so that they had to sleep in two shifts—one at daytime and one at night. Some new blocks were constructed as quickly as possible in Section BIII, the camp to the right of the central camp, and the women were transferred there. The inmates referred to this part of the camp as 'Mexico.' It was called this because the women there were sometimes totally naked, or sometimes dressed only in shirts. They often were taken into the 'sauna' for bathing, and they just wrapped around themselves whatever quilts they had found in the transports. Most of these quilts were very bright in color: yellow, purple, red, green. The women just wandered past the camp road, wrapped up to their heads in these quilts. This multicolored image elicited for some reason the idea of Mexico.

"And these women happened to be walking by our camp. My friend Adam, who comes from Transylvania, too, was moved almost to tears by them, and tried to find women he knew among them. And this camp road, which led right by our camp—we had a clear view onto it—was still important for us, because we could see the various activities going on outside. We could observe when they had selections in the women's camp, BI. And when these women were loaded onto trucks and brought to the crematorium—mostly to Crematorium IV or V—these transports drove along the edge of our camp and then at the upper end of our camp turned the corner onto the road to the crematorium. We stood at attention for roll call. And outside the trucks drove off with naked, screaming women. They were crying out to us men, they hoped for help from us men, their natural protectors. How they cried! We stood there, paralyzed, shivering, and just looked at them. A motorcycle driver at the front, then a truck, after that another SS man on a motorcycle, and another truck, and so the column passed by.

"One day we were witnesses as one of these women jumped down from the moving truck. The SS officer driving the motorcycle behind, shot her, the next truck was stopped, the body thrown onto it, and the drive continued. And at the end of this column was the truck from the Red Cross. But it did not carry any sick people; it had poison gas on board. A shocking and scandalous misuse of the international sign of humanity."

•

From the very beginning, the SS regularly take sick and exhausted inmates from the camp to the gas chambers in the crematoriums. Mostly these inmates are the so-called Muselmänner *(Moslems). In the whole camp, the selections preceding these gassings are the most feared. For not just the totally weakened inmates fall victim to these selections, but thousands of others who are only slightly ill or are even healthy. Dr. Otto Wolken was present on some occa-*

sions. He told me: "The Jews have to leave their block and fall in for roll call. They are counted. Then they must completely undress, even when it is 30 degrees Celsius below zero. And now the SS doctor walks up and down the rows. Whoever looks too weak to him, or too frail, anyone wearing a bandage or having a boil, he gestures to stand on that side where those who are shortly to meet their deaths are assembling. Often, even an obvious scar or scratch is enough to be selected. The numbers of those selected out are noted down immediately, the total number in every block is recorded, so that no victim is lost."

Often it is Dr. Mengele and also Dr. Fritz Klein who perform this executioner's work. People say that Klein always volunteered whenever a doctor was required for such selections. And those sorted out by him for special processing are all crammed together in a special block freed up specifically for the purpose. He supervises this, too. Kapos and the SS take care of the "shit work," as Capesius puts it.

·

Dr. Otto Wolken at the trial: "Often up to a thousand victims stayed there, mostly one or two days. To prevent their fleeing, all their clothing except for their shirts was taken from them. A guard was stationed in front of the block. They were given some food, but they were no longer given rations of bread and extras such as sausage or margarine. After two or three days these selectees were mostly totally worn out by hunger and their long wait for death and were apathetic. Late in the evening, as a rule, they were then loaded into trucks—eighty per truck—and taken off to the gas chambers. And during this process the SS allowed itself a little 'fun' with them, with beatings and shootings."

·

Adam: For us Sonderkommando prisoners who were forced to receive the victims, often selected by Klein, Mengele, and Capesius, and to accompany them into the changing rooms, the en-

counter with these naked, emaciated creatures was a horrific nightmare. Of all that I have been through, the worst was when they brought women in from the camp. They brought them in a dump truck, and women were standing naked on the loading surface—in front of the crematorium the women were simply dumped out of the truck—where they fell alive in heaps, like trash, onto the ground. And then they threw them into the gas chambers. To me this was unbearable! The SS knew that those people brought in this manner clearly knew that they were about to die. Why did they have to be brought in on a dump truck and dumped out like coal? . . . To this day that is my most horrible memory, for these women had already been through so much in the camp—the beatings, forced labor, hunger, exhaustion—only to suffer such a death at the end. I found this much crueler than when a person came into the crematorium, undressed there, not knowing what awaited him, and then was gassed, thinking he was entering a shower room. The pious chronicler Lejb Langfuß, who had to work in the death zone for almost two years before his own murder at the end of 1944, showed me his secret notes. We both had a common hiding place for our written testament of horrors; I included his in my "rolls," in case his should be lost. In a document titled "The Three Thousand Naked Women" he described the womens' and girls' last moments:

The truck stopped, the tarpaulin cover was taken off, and they began throwing off this mass of human beings as if they were gravel being unloaded onto the highway . . . The ones who were thrown down toward the end began to work themselves free from the heap of bodies, to stand upright and try to walk . . . They were shivering, they were shaking terribly from the cold. Slowly they dragged themselves to the bunker that they were meant to think was a dressing room, into which a staircase led down as into a cellar. The rest of the women

were led by commando staff, who ran upstairs quickly
and picked up the unconscious ones, those victims who
had been left without help . . . Many of the women
could no longer walk on their own, so the commando
people would pick them up in their arms and carry
them down. And they knew that this bunker was the
last step leading to their death. Still they were very
grateful; they expressed their thanks with a pleading
glance and a shivering movement of the head, while
indicating with a hand gesture that it was hard for them
to talk. They took comfort in seeing the tears of sympathy and the expression of sorrow . . . on the faces of
those taking them downstairs. This direct physical contact with the victims, who knew that they were about
to be murdered, tormented the men horribly.

*Langfuß recorded conversations the doomed women had
among themselves and with the Sonderkommando prisoners, as
well as the reactions of the men:*

As he looked at the wasted, skeletal figures of the women,
one of the men felt such despair that he started to weep.
And one young girl cried, "Look, this is what I see just
before I die: someone, at least, with a look of sympathy,
tears shed for our terrible fate . . . and I thought we
would be leaving this earth like abandoned orphans.
Among all these gangsters and murderers, I see one person before I die who still feels." She turned to the wall,
leaned her head against the stone, and started to sob
quietly, yet with wrenching poignancy. She was deeply
moved. All around us most of the girls standing or sitting kept their heads bowed, in stony silence, gazing
with utter loathing on this wretched world and especially on us.

•

Capesius in Göppingen: "According to the technical design the crematoriums were capable of incinerating 4,756 bodies a day. But this was really only a theoretical value, which included time for maintenance and the cleaning of the furnaces. In fact up to 5,000 corpses were burned per day in Crematoriums II and III, and up to 3,000 in Crematoriums IV and V. The capacity of the pyres by the bunkers was unlimited. In the summer of 1944 during the deportations of the Hungarian Jews, the SS took over the operation of Bunker II again. In this period up to 24,000 people per day could be killed and incinerated. The ashes of the dead were used as fertilizer on the fields, for filling in swampland, or were simply dumped into the neighboring rivers and ponds. Mostly into the Soła River, which flowed right by."

•

"My children were always finding ways to amuse themselves. Whether turtles or martins, cats or lizards, there was always something new, something interesting for them outside in the yard": thus wrote the camp Commandant Rudolf Höß in his report for the Polish judges, before he was hanged at Auschwitz in 1946: "In the summer, my children would splash about in their little pool in the yard, or in the Soła. But the thing they liked the most was when Daddy went swimming with them. He had little time to play with his children . . . I believed, always, that I had to be on duty all the time."

LATRYNA

Adam: Ella, whom I can now meet with in Section C, said today she had been made the "shit mistress" of the Womens' Toilets. She says it's totally crazy . . . this thing they have about cleanliness in the middle of all this shit, "echt deutsch," *so German: always talking about shit, they even use it as their major swear word.*

This exaggerated way they harass you about cleanliness in the latrines. They're obsessed with these shit brigades (szajsbrygady), *these shit columns* (szajskolumny), *and shit commandos* (szajsko-manda) *led by shit leaders, shit masters, toilet masters, shit Kapos, it was all out of proportion, yet even in these dreadful conditions so typically German, so "echt deutsch." And there were these toilet wardens for cleanliness, too, but whose main job was to make sure no one sat and crapped on the seats reserved for the block seniors or the Kapo.*

Men or women, it made no difference. With "Mussulmen" and "Mussulwomen" the distinction lessened, was annulled: any sexual differentiation or even attraction was erased.

I saw one poor devil drown in the latrine; for the amusement of the SS the Kapo played this game of "Shit to ten, with bath." The Kapo led the prisoners to the latrine, long trenches beneath a board set up over them, with round holes where ten prisoners could sit. The Kapo would count and all the prisoners had to be finished by "ten"; whoever didn't would fall into the trench of shit and go under. Only the lucky ones were pulled out by their comrades and led to the hand pump.

But in the summer, another game: lice-hunting in the sun; lice were the "blondies" and fleas were the "brunettes." Yesterday it was horrible: ice and cold, but we were ordered to hand in our ragged clothing and wait; naked and shivering, the prisoners stood out in a snowstorm. The camp was so infested with lice that we said, At night the blankets walk by themselves. And ten of the weakest were stretched out in the yard, frozen in the snow. No one was allowed to bring them back inside.

I'm writing this now, on the same day. Now, I can still believe it. It's impossible to write it down later. And no one would believe me. And even German is wrong. Only the obscenity of the lagerszpracha *can reproduce it correctly. And the filth, the insults are so humiliating, language is the deepest indicator of spiritual destruction.*

10

Adam: As punishment I was transferred out of "Canada" and onto the Crematorium Sonderkommando; that is hell itself. It was called the "ascension-commando," and every one of the four hundred, later eight hundred, Jewish inmates assigned to it was sentenced to death from the get-go: the commando was liquidated every three months. We all knew that. And we lived in Block 13. Block 13 was totally isolated from the other barracks; the yard was surrounded with a high wall. The entry gate was almost always locked and watched by a sentry. This was usually a powerfully built inmate armed with a truncheon. Just imagine it: the barracks, which the four hundred men of the Sonderkommando were forced to share, were about 40 meters long, 10 meters wide, and 2.6 meters high. The only openings for light were little slits in the roof and the two entryways.

Every barrack was divided into eighteen boxes. Right next to the entry, two of these boxes served as hutches for the orderly room and the block senior inmate. In the last two boxes by the back entry were two buckets into which we relieved ourselves. The last cots on the right side of the block had been set off and reserved for the sick. As a rule there were as many as eight hundred people housed in these barracks. So our "accommodation" was downright luxurious by comparison. For example, Filip Müller shared one of the upper (and therefore most desirable) bunks with "only" two colleagues: Stanisław Lankowski and Daniel Obstbaum. Not only that, but we could make mattresses and second blankets for ourselves from the garments of the people murdered in the gas chambers, to which we had access.

Cleanliness and order inside the block was the responsibility of the so-called Stubendienst, or fatigue duty. This was a privileged position. The prisoner assigned to fatigue duty spent almost the whole day in the barracks, and performed no difficult physical labor. Two brothers, Abraham and Schlomo Dragon, were assigned to fatigue duty along with four other prisoners. They cleaned and fetched the daily ration of soup and bread for all the inmates of the block from the camp kitchen.

The bread was of miserable quality, and the soup consisted mostly of water, with rotten vegetable scraps floating in it. While the majority of prisoners in Birkenau got only this to eat, the prisoners of the Sonderkommando could often afford to skip it.

Along with the two Dragon brothers, Schlomo and Abraham, I was part of the fatigue duty group and so I didn't have to work outside and see the terrible things happening there daily, let alone participate in them.

But our fellow sufferers told us everything, when they came "home" from "work," and every day there was something terrible to report. They talked about the transports, and where they had come from. Schlomo and I mostly sat together, and we kept talking about what they said afterward; we could not get over how our comrades reported it, they seemed tired and numb; they sounded like robots as they spoke of screaming, of scenes that no one who hadn't been there could believe: "Today there were kids, there were people from Cluj or Oradea, from Paris or Athens, today lots of little children, today a transport from Holland. The people didn't know what would be happening to them; all of them were horribly afraid. And then, when it happened, they yelled at first and resisted; after all, they had just come from their normal lives, were well-nourished, in good clothes, and totally unsuspecting. They resisted, but it did no good." And every day, there were new stories, new chapters in this idyll of death.

In May of '44 the "Hungarian action" began. From this point on, a thick cloud of smoke hung over the death zone without interruption, and the penetrating smell of burning human flesh hung in the air. Day after day, on average up to six

RSHA transports arrived, with deported men, women, and
children from Hungary and Transylvania.*

•

Dr. Fritz Klein from Zeiden: "Whenever transports arrived at
Auschwitz, it was the doctors' job to select out those who
were unsuitable or incapable of working. This included children, older people, and the sick. I had seen the gas chambers
in Auschwitz, and I knew that those whom I selected had to
go to the gas chambers. But I only acted on orders. All orders
were delivered orally, only . . . I never protested against people
being sent to the gas chambers, even though I did not agree
with it. You can't protest when you're in the army.

"It was not pleasant to take part in the inspections of the
deportees, as I knew that the persons selected had to be sent
to the gas chambers. Women who got pregnant in the camp,
and thus became unfit for work, were likewise sorted out in
later inspections."

Klein was sentenced to death in the Bergen-Belsen trial in
Lüneburg by a British court and was hanged in Hameln on
December 13, 1945. The last photo shows him in a shirt, look-
ing thin and vacant. Still living, yet already dead.

II

I saw one photograph that I found chilling. The pharmacist
keeps it in his black document portfolios. Of all things, one of
these Hungary transports was photographed by the "records
department" of the camp Gestapo, and one of the photogra-
phers was Bernhard Walter, who, Capesius said, had been a
photographer in civilian life. Familiar faces from home. Grand-

---

*Reichssicherheitshauptamt, or Reich Main Security Office, the department re-
sponsible for the deportations. —trans.

mothers, "nanas" with babushkas on, mothers, children, some crying, some silently holding on to their mother's hand. One who looked exactly like my nanny, Erszi. *Istenem, hova menjünk,* oh, my God, where should we go, she seemed to be saying.

Shortly after they became photographic images, their bodies became ash. I see their faces before me now; they look at me from out of the book, *Das Auschwitz Album.* Lilly Jakob-Zelmanovic Meier found this record after her liberation, in an area near the Nordhausen concentration camp. She presented the album as evidence in the trial in 1964. Close-up images shot in the peace of early morning, during the arrivals on the death ramp. One girl is looking at me: her round face, her teenager's full mouth . . . These dark, black, brown eyes gaze anxiously, proudly, but all of them endearingly; they are standing before a strikingly alien background with train tracks, freight cars, and large piles of baggage lying about everywhere, and these spruce uniforms, these grotesquely puffy jodhpur pants and boots, and in among them, the blue-and-white-striped prisoners . . .

•

Adam: You have to imagine it, this idyllic scene. The gassing detail: children hanging on sleepily to their mother's skirts. Mostly it's the fathers carrying the babies, or pushing them along in baby carriages. One hundred meters along the black cinder pathway, strips of grassy lawn, trees left and right. Then a gray iron grating, fifteen steps down. Down. Then they see the sign reading BATHING AND DISINFECTING ROOM. *And they calm down again, and go down the steps. The two-hundred-meter-long room is harshly illuminated. Much larger than the locker rooms in our gymnasiums. Rows of benches, clothes hooks with numbers. Signs in many languages: tie your shoes together, hang them with your clothing on the hooks, remember your number. That has a calming effect, too. Yes, that, too: typical German orderliness, they all think. Yes. Soothing. But there has to be order, because the bombed-out citizens of the Reich need clothing badly.*

*Then comes the command to these frightened people: strip
naked. Naked? Everyone is horrified. Chaste girls and women,
grandfathers, fathers, children, do they have to see everything?
Everyone blushes with shame and fear.*

*There was a young girl from the Transylvanian city of
Klausenburg (Kolozsvár in Hungarian) called Ilonka. Everyone was really good at pretending, just to maintain calm; we
were so darn kind to them. I can still remember, everyone was
scared stiff, no one could cry or laugh, everyone was impassive.
Me, too. The kids were singing and playing ball. A girl from
Bistritz had been in German kindergarten and sang: "Susie,
little Susie, now what is the news, the geese are going barefoot,
because they've no shoes, the cobbler's got leather but his last he
can't use, so he can't make the geese any shoes."*

*The spot was so pretty between the grass and flowers. But then
that stairway down. And horrible . . . how they all had to strip
completely naked . . . what can I say? After, as Ilonka described
it, she was probably the only one who survived the gas chambers:*

"Slowly, very slowly, Daddy took off his tie, his coat, and
folded it up carefully as he did at home, first the shirt, yes, his
chest all hairy, I'd seen him in summer when we went swimming, with his black fur. But Mama took her hat off first, and
straightened her hair. She still smelled of perfume, oh, she was
pretty. And then I didn't look, while Daddy slowly slowly pulled
down his underpants . . . *that* I didn't want to see. No, I undressed myself, rather, and turned my back on him and on
Mama, too. And then held my hands in front of my little bushie,
which no one had ever seen, not even Mama. I didn't want to
look at Granny and Grandpa either. The people in striped suits
spoke Hungarian to us, reassuring us that we were just going to
take baths, and you can't do that with your clothes on; they
wanted to help Grandpa with his clothes, but he proudly refused any help, after all, he was no kid, no baby, he could still

dress and undress himself, and Granny did, too. There were two lame people next to us who couldn't do it alone; they took the help. The little children were undressed by their parents, lots of babies crying. I saw three pregnant women, one right behind us, one two rows back, and one to the right; they undressed almost proudly, displaying their fruit, for they were two not just one, giving the world something that men could not give. In this place, only male guards and male prisoners in striped suits, not a single woman, just four SS men and the striped suits. And when we were all undressed—we had never seen one another naked like that before—I noticed the SS men opening both halves of a heavy doorway at the end of the room . . ."

A short SS man in the Gallus Courtroom in Frankfurt gave his testimony, hesitantly: he had first learned about the gassing sites as a driver. His name was Hölblinger: "I was a standby driver, drove the medic truck used in prisoner transports."

Presiding judge: "And did you drive at night, too?"

Hölblinger: "Yes, whenever the Jewish transports arrived at the ramp in Birkenau. I had to drive the medics and the doctors to the ramp. Then we drove on to the gas chambers. When we got there, the medics climbed up on ladders; they kept their gas masks on up there, and emptied out the canisters [of Zyklon B]. I could see the prisoners undressing; they were always very calm and unsuspecting. And it went very fast."

Presiding judge: "How long did the gassing take?"

Hölblinger: "About a minute. When the gas started, you could hear the horrible screams. After a minute, everything was still. The medics brought the gas in tin canisters."

Presiding judge: "How were the victims brought to the gas chamber?"

Hölblinger: "Jews who could not work were brought in trucks to the gas chamber. Five or six trucks were used for this; they were driven back and forth repeatedly."

Presiding judge: "Were the bunkers illuminated with vehicle headlights?"

Hölblinger: "Yes."

Prosecutor Kügler: "Was the defendant Klehr chief of the SDG*?"

Hölblinger: "I don't know. We just called them the Gas Fritzes."

A fellow SS officer once drove with Hölblinger to the killing site.

Acting Judge Hummerich: "Were you ever part of a gassing detail?"

Böck: "Yes, there was one night when I drove there with driver Hölblinger. A transport had arrived from Holland; the prisoners had to climb down from the railway cars. These were the better sort of Jews, some women were wearing Persian lamb coats. They had come in express train cars. Trucks were standing ready for them, with wooden steps next to them, and the people climbed into the trucks. Then they all drove off. Nearby, in the area that had once been the town of Birkenau, there was now only a very long farmhouse, and next to it, four or five large barracks. Inside these barracks people were standing on huge piles of clothing stacked up on the floor. The block leaders and one junior squad leader carrying a stick were there. Hölblinger said to me, 'Now let's go over there.' There was a sign: TO THE DISINFECTION ROOM. He said, 'Now they're bringing kids, too.' Then they opened the doors, threw the kids inside, and shut the doors again. You could hear horrible screams. An SS man went up on the roof: the people screamed inside for ten minutes. Then prisoners opened up the doors. Everyone was jammed together in a huge jumbled heap. It was horrible. The bodies were loaded onto a ladder truck and driven off to a trench. The next ones undressed in the barracks first.

---

*Sanitätsdienstgefreiter, the SS corporal of the sanitary service.

"Six trucks were used for this detail. Mercedes trucks with trailers. I was supposed to drive as well, but I refused.

"In the beginning, the gassing was done in the small crematorium.

"At that time Grabner was picking up the transports at the train station, about forty or fifty Jews per trip. 'Come on, now, let's go, get those clothes off!' He said that in a very friendly, intimate way. Then an SS man climbed up on top. You could hear screams all the way to our billets."

Prosecutor Kügler: "When were these six trucks procured?"

Böck: "Around spring of '42, when they really got going with the gassings. They were heavy trucks, five to six tons. The guys that took part in these details had ten or twelve bottles of schnaps in their lockers."

12

Roland in Innsbruck: "Well, we had to take breaks, too. To rest. To forget. Maybe on Sunday go hunting in the Beskidy mountains with our cavalry captain. And then my wife would have the Sunday roast hare for us in the oven. See that smoke? You were always smelling that sweetish smell. Burnt flesh. Burnt skin, burnt hair."

•

Life continued for us in Sighişoara, too. The smells in the courtyard. The blackish pavement was hard, when you fell down, your knee would bleed. "Maybug, maybug, fly away home." May. Birds migrating. *Der Mai ist gekommen / Die Bäume schlagen aus . . .*

On the wall to the right of Grandfather's room we had a picture hanging: a huge golden field of grain with Jesus and the twelve apostles among the red poppies. And evenings we said our prayers:

Ech bän klien
Menj Herz äs rien
Und nemest sal drän wunnen
Alz Herr Jesus elien.
I am little, my heart is pure,
and no one shall dwell there
but Lord Jesus alone.

After every little fright in the endless night would come the morning, God's heavenly morning with coolness, the morning sun beaming on the garden beds, always fresh dew on the flowerbeds; you could run through the grass in bare feet.

And Uncle Roland comes home on leave, sits in the parlor, and laughs, then he plays a Schubert song on the Bechstein, and sings along. And everyone applauds. And on Sunday he wants to play the organ in church. And now, after so much time, I can hear him again—he must now be long dead:

Roland: "It was strange how the Sonderkommando had to trick them . . . Many women hid their babies under the piles of clothing. The Sonderkommando were really on the lookout for that, and worked on the women until they were convinced, and would take their child into the gas chamber with them . . . Strange . . . The little kids whined mostly because they weren't used to taking their clothes off like that with so many people around, but when their mothers talked to them enough, or the Sonderkommando, then they calmed down and walked, as if it were a game, into the gas chamber, teasing one another, a toy under their arms. I also noticed, you know, how the women who either guessed or knew what was in store for them, even with the fear of death in their eyes, could summon up the strength to joke around with their kids, to persuade them it was okay. One woman, as she walked by me, came right up to me and whispered, pointing out her four children, who were walking hand in hand so the littlest ones wouldn't trip on the uneven pathway:

'How can you bring yourself to do this, to kill these beautiful children? Have you no heart at all?' One man hissed at me as he went by: 'One day, Germany will have to atone for murdering the Jews!' His eyes were blazing with hatred . . . Occasionally while undressing the women would start screaming, it was absolutely bloodcurdling, tearing out their hair and acting like madwomen. They would quickly be taken behind the building and shot in the back of the head with a handgun. Sometimes, too, at the moment when the Sonderkommando left the room, the women would figure out what was about to happen, and screamed every curse in the book back at us . . ."

•

Adam: You can imagine that many have asked themselves how it was possible that these people did not resist, that they walked like lambs into the gas chambers. But there is an explanation: most of the people who went from the ramps into the crematorium were simply not aware that they were walking into gas chambers, and so they didn't resist. But even those who did know, or guessed, that a horrible death awaited them, went into a kind of paralysis. It just seemed totally impossible to resist at all. Think of the masses of humanity who walked on foot into the gas chambers, women, old people, children, young men. Every act of rebellion only resulted in dreadful beatings, even for the children. The pain, the humiliation of it all. And I believe that most of those who could have resisted did not so as to spare their children, their wives, and old people this further suffering. So the SS was able to force hundreds of thousands to go, like sheep to the slaughter, into the gas chambers.

I often was forced to look on. We had to do everything they told us. The SS Germans did it all. "Move! Now! Into the showers!" they would shout, no, bellow, and the crowd would push, like one huge organism, into another blindingly illuminated hall; Ilonka was pushed and dragged forward, she lost sight of Mama and Papa, Grandma and Grandpa, she called out to them, in vain:

"When I was in there, I noticed that there weren't any benches or hooks, in the middle of the room just columns, and they had some kind of sheet-metal tubes, with little holes all over them, the walls were very rough and coarse, cracked and bare and horribly cold, icy cold, deathly cold, but there were actually lots of warm showers and hot-water pipes just like at our swimming facility back in Kolozsvár, except everything here was bigger, much, much bigger. And such a sharp smell in the air, I thought I would smother with all these people breathing and murmuring and shouting."

A truck has driven up, the truck with the red cross on it. The Red Cross? Dr. Capesius and Josef Klehr get out. Klehr has four green tin canisters in his hand. They both cross over the green strip of grass to the gas chamber, climb up onto the roof, put on their gas masks, and then Klehr lifts up the little trap door, but only after Capesius has given him the order to do so, because it has to be an SS doctor who gives the killing orders. Klehr breaks the seal on the canister, and shakes out the coarsely granulated contents, a violet-colored, crumbly mass, into the opening. The Zyklon B.

Böck, SS man, trial witness: "After the entire transport—it may have been around a thousand people—was inside, the door was shut. Then an SS man, a squad leader, I think, came up to our medic van and took out a gas canister, and with the canister he went over to a ladder going up the building to the right of the gate. He was wearing a gas mask, I noticed. When he got to the end of the ladder, he opened a circular tin seal and shook the contents of the canister into the opening. I could clearly hear the rattling noise as he banged the can against the wall to empty it out. At the same time I could see brownish dust coming up out of the opening. Whether or not this was gas I can't say. In any event I saw clearly that he only emptied one canister. When the SS man closed the little cover

over the opening, an indescribable screaming could be heard from the room below. I simply can't describe how these people were screaming. That lasted about eight to ten minutes, then everything was quiet."

A young SS man, who had to come along for "training," holds his hands to his ears in horror as the noise and the screaming start. They wait another five minutes after throwing in the prussic acid; just as if they were on a regular cigarette break, they light up and climb down back into the truck. After another twenty minutes or so one of the commandos or the SS men turns on the electric ventilation system. And the gates are opened. In the meantime, some of the Sonderkommando have loaded up all the clothing from the changing rooms onto trucks and driven off to the disinfection station.

•

Roland: "On the one hand, I am quite sensitive, but on the other, it was there I found out that I am actually tougher than the so-called 'robust' types. That I can tolerate and see things that make other people faint . . . I don't know, in any case it helped me to survive."

"But did you then . . . have any contact at all with . . . this . . . with the . . ."

"With the exterminations?" Long pause. "Hmmm . . . I . . . we had to see a lot of things," said Roland. He says this with a different, harder, more distanced tone of voice, as if he were talking to someone he didn't know at all.

•

SS member Böck in the Auschwitz Trial: "You could still see a bluish cloud hovering above a giant tangle of corpses. The bodies were knotted up with one another to the point that you couldn't tell which limbs went with which bodies. For example, I saw one of the victims had poked his index finger several centimeters into the eye socket of another. From that you can judge how dreadful the death agonies of these people had been. You cannot describe these scenes with words. It made me so sick I nearly threw up."

•

Roland: "Intolerance had never really taken root with us back in Transylvania. What I am trying to say is that despite differences in social rank, we always retained a certain tolerance back home. Our pastors in Transylvania often got along very well with the Jewish rabbis. They kept up friendships. I remember that Professor Schotsch was good friends with Rabbi Beislieb, who lived next door. And my parents were good friends with the Rippers, a Jewish family in Sighişoara, and I myself also had good Jewish friends."

•

Adam: When we opened up the gas chambers, we Sonderkommando always pulled our gas masks on, since otherwise the gas still remaining among the bodies caused the most horrible coughing attacks and choking fits, even in small amounts. We carried water hoses as we entered the chamber of horrors, which was flooded with harsh light. You can hardly imagine what we saw before us: at first I covered my eyes, I didn't look, I just sprayed the hose with my head turned away. But I could still see: the bodies were not scattered throughout the room, but towered up in a pile to the ceiling, for the Zyklon B with its poisonous gases first started at the floor level and then rose . . . So the unlucky victims trampled over one another: the higher up they could get, the later the deadly gas would reach them. A horrific struggle for two more minutes of life. But they trampled on their parents, their husbands, and children in vain: none could escape death by suffocation, not one. So at the bottom lay the children, babies, and old people, and on top of them the stronger men. And they were all clutching one another tightly, their bodies covered with scratches, blood running from their noses and mouths. Their faces were bluish, swollen and disfigured beyond recognition. And yet among the bodies we would

occasionally recognize someone, relatives or acquaintances. Some-
times even a brother, a sister, a mother, children . . .

Adam needed a break, I could hear his quiet voice say:

TENEBRAE

Nah sind wir, Herr,
nah und greifbar.
Gegriffen schon, Herr,
Ineinander verkrallt, als wär
der Leib eines jeden von uns
dein Leib, Herr.
Bete, Herr,
bete zu uns,
wir sind nah.
. . . Es warf uns dein Bild in die Augen, Herr.
Augen und Mund stehen so offen und leer, Herr.*

•

So we stationed ourselves, wearing rubber boots, in a circle
around the mountain of bodies, and almost like firemen of death,
we trained a strong stream of water on them, for death from
poison gas causes a violent reflex emptying of the bowels; then we
had to separate the convoluted bodies from one another. I have
forgotten how it feels to be doing this. Thank God, I can't remem-
ber. This is just my head repeating it, just words . . . and after this
"work," this tearing apart of hands, arms, bodies, we often had
to pry them apart, sometimes brutally with crowbars . . . Only two
of us were capable of this, we would look away as we did it, avert
our eyes from this second death . . . Then we would each tie a strap
around our arm, attaching the other end to the arm of a body, and

---

*Tenebrae: Lord, we are near. / Near, and touchable. / Touched already, Lord /
Grasping one another, as if / the body of each one of us / were your body,
Lord. / Pray, Lord, / pray to us / we are near. / Your image was cast into our
eyes, Lord. / Eyes and mouth are so open, so empty, Lord (Paul Celan).

drag the slippery bodies through a channel of blood to the elevator in the next room. There were four large freight elevators there, each could hold up to twenty-five bodies: an elevator operator would come when the bell was rung and take the lift up. Then the incineration room. Huge double doors opening out. A commando to drag the bodies. Again, these straps pulling them up to the ovens.

Long lines. The children and babies. The injured ones, bleeding from their noses and mouths. And the worst, when they were still alive . . . some of them doomed to be burned alive, those who spoke or blurted anything out were simply burned alive. Their horrific screams . . . could still be heard in the furnace on the iron rack.

These long lines all had to be "processed" first. Human hair is valuable. We knew it was used as igniters for bombs, detonators for time bombs. It was cut from the women's heads, blond, black, brown, red, gray, oh, a lot of gray hair. Later the order came down that only young hair was to be cut. Old hair wasn't even good enough for mattresses. And then the specialists, who operated mostly on the older and elderly ones. Oral surgeons, famous dentists, eight professionals. During the Hungarian transports, it took more than just eight. They could hardly keep up with all the gold teeth they had to "harvest" with crowbar and pliers. Then a bath in hydrochloric acid to remove the bits of flesh and bone. There was a box with an opening in the top, rings, bracelets, watches, necklaces were thrown in. The crematoriums yielded eight to ten kilos of gold every day.

•

According to Capesius, these men belonged to the Sonderkommando that ran the crematorium: "Kaduk, Unterscharführer, as of November 1942, until the end of 1942 he led the Sonderkommando with Moll, Otto. Moll, Hauptscharführer, born 1915, executed in Landsberg, May 28, 1946, sole commander from May 8 to July 29, 1944 (thus, during the Hungarian transports!), short in stature, blond with a round chubby face full of freckles. Brutal."

Adam: He took a crying child that had been found alive underneath a heap of bodies in the gas chamber, and threw it screaming into the sizzling fat of the burning trenches.

Capesius: "The deputy was Sommer, Karl, SS Unterscharführer, sentenced to death November 3, '47.

"Muhsfeldt, Erich, SS Oberscharführer. Leader of the new Crematorium I . . . Executed in Kraków, December 22, 1947.

"Keim, SS Unterscharführer, 1944 commandant, Crematorium III; Gorges, Johann, called Hans, SS Oberscharführer, commandant, Crematorium IV, born December 1, 1900, lived until his death in Trier, Kirchstrasse 1.

"Other Rottenführers and Oberscharführers in the crematoriums were Grauel, Erich; Eidenmüller, Heckert; Hollander, Kurzius; Seitz, Steinberg Otto; Voss, Graf Otto; Bedarf, Waldemar, disinfector of personal effects in 'Canada.'

"Klehr, Josef, the leader, poured the Zyklon B pellets himself into the gas chambers, or supervised it."

One person looked down through the hole from above, not a voyeur; it was his charge to observe their final agonies. This was our Dr. Capesius, our "Vic." He didn't sing along. He was unmusical.

•

Adam: Unbelievable things also took place in the changing room. On October 23, 1943, 1,800 persons arrived from Bergen-Belsen. Almost all of them had foreign passports, mostly South American ones, and they thought they had bought their freedom and were headed for Switzerland. Then this indescribable disappointment and their resistance, too.

In the Frankfurt Trial, October 16, 1964, the eyewitness Arie Fuks describes this event as follows: "We had two transports, from Riga, I think, in between. And another one from Warsaw. Yes, it might have been then, when the camp marshal from Camp D was killed, Schillinger. The night when he was killed."

Prosecutor Kügler: "Were you present when Schillinger was shot?"

Witness Arie Fuks: "No, he was shot in the crematorium, in the anteroom, which we called a bunker. We heard about it twenty minutes afterward on the ramp, from Unterscharführer Effinger."

Prosecutor Kügler: "And what did he tell you?"

Witness Arie Fuks: "At that time he told us that the woman's name was Plotka."

Prosecutor Kügler: "She arrived with a transport."

Witness Arie Fuks: "With a transport from Warsaw. She was a professional dancer or something. And so he said to her, 'Take your clothes off!' She said, 'I have never undressed in front of a man.' So then he took out his pistol and threatened her: 'If you don't take your clothes off, I'll shoot you.' She was so quick, they say, that she grabbed the pistol out of his hand and shot him. And there was this other Unterscharführer, a really fat guy—I can't remember his name—she shot him, too, in the leg."

Adam: Filip Müller and David Nencel, members of the Sonderkommando then, were eyewitnesses; they, too, have described all this in detail. The notorious SS Obersturmführer Hößler, well known as a skillful liar, was able to get half of the doomed prisoners to undress, and they were immediately shoved into the gas chamber. But the other nine hundred or so victims refused to undress. They brought out the truncheons and started beating them all. In all this chaos, one single, very beautiful young woman, a dancer from Warsaw, started to undress right under the lustful ogling eyes of Unterscharführer Schillinger, ostensibly because he had threatened to shoot her if she didn't.

David Nencel, who was standing very near the young woman, saw it all:* "The woman was undressed, she took her under-

---

*Cf. Adler, Langbein, and Lingens-Reiner.

pants and threw them in the SS man's face. I think she did that to protect herself. I said to her in Polish, 'Run away, don't be afraid.' If the SS had understood what I told her they would have put a bullet in my brain. I think at that point the woman started the whole thing—she probably shot the SS guy with his own pistol. Then the lights went out. Then they drove all of us in the commando out of the room. It was just like the front line: they pulled out machine guns from above and killed them all in the changing room. I was there myself. And then the SS ordered all the Sonderkommando prisoners to leave the room. The SS came running up just like they were at the front—with machine guns and things like that. The people were murdered in their clothes, they weren't yet undressed . . . They began their resistance by refusing to undress. I don't know what the other Sonderkommando prisoners did, but I told these people then that they were going to die. I said that to them—if the others did or not, I don't know. But for the SS the problem was that they refused to undress. The only one who undressed was this one woman. She was a very beautiful woman. To judge from the photos we found later, she must have been a dancer. This woman came with her jewelry and her things—these people at first didn't know where they were going."

•

*Zalmen Gradowski**: "And then there were the brave actions of a heroic young woman, a dancer from Warsaw, who grabbed the revolver away from Oberscharführer Quakernack from the Political Department, and shot the camp marshal, that notorious bandit Unterscharführer Schillinger. Her action inspired the other courageous women and they started striking out at the SS, throwing bottles and similar objects at these wild beasts, these uniformed SS men."

*"Hefte von Auschwitz," Sonderheft 1, Oświęcim, 1972, p. 98f. "Das Verfahren: Auschwitz in den Augen der SS." *Der 1. Frankfurter Auschwitz-Prozess*, p. 40166.

But not just the SS was surprised; this sudden revolt scared the Sonderkommando prisoners, too, when the lights went out.

Adam: At the same moment the door was bolted from outside. So now we, too, found ourselves in a pitch-dark room. The dramatic events we had just seen left no doubt in my mind that things would come to a bad end.

Filip Müller of the Sonderkommando: "The darkness paralyzed us. I felt my way along the wall to the exit. Most of the Sonderkommando guys had gathered over there. I stood together with my comrades at the door. A man near us, who obviously had noticed we didn't belong to the transport, spoke to us in the dark. He wanted to know where we came from. "From the death factory," someone answered. The man was about to say something, but suddenly the door was thrown open. Harsh searchlights blinded me. Then I heard the SS man Voss shout: "Sonderkommando get out!" We rushed through the door, and once we were outside we ran upstairs out to the yard. In front of the door to the changing room two machine guns had been set up. Searchlights were set up behind them. SS men with steel helmets were lying there, ready to use the machine guns. A horde of SS thugs was running around the yard. I was just on my way to the incineration room when Camp Commandant Höß got out of his car."*

•

Capesius: "I can only say: I knew Dr. Nyiszli well, I had known him when I was a sales rep for Bayer in Transylvania. And he had to do horrible things there with the Sonderkommando; it was a miracle that they didn't bump him off for knowing too much. But Mengele needed him. One time, he told me, Klehr, who was in charge of the gassing commando, came barging into his room, and told him in a very excited way that a girl had been found still alive beneath the mountain of bodies in

---

*Cf. *Der Auschwitzprozess.* Das Verfahren: 97. Verhandlungstag (05.10.1964).

the gas chamber, that she was still moving. And Nyiszli went running with his doctor's bag into the gas chamber, and right there next to the wall—still half covered with bodies—was this girl, naked like the rest, but wonderfully beautiful, like an angel breathing her last—lying there . . ."

Adam's diary: And such a thing had never happened before; the Sonderkommando were all aghast, horrified, even Klehr. After freeing her from all the bodies, we brought the fifteen-year-old girl into the commando's changing room, and gave her three injections in the arm to revive her. And her body was ice-cold, covered with a coat. Hot soup and tea from the kitchen. Then a coughing fit, as with chills, thick wads of phlegm coming from her lungs damaged by the gas. She started to get some color. Life came back. She looked around, confused.

The girl revived gradually, lifted up her head, her arms, then she grimaced, she started crying, a few phrases of Hungarian, she grabs Nyiszli by the coat, hangs on to him, frantically, tries to sit up, he lays her back down, a nervous collapse, lies back exhausted, breathing hard, and then a choking cry. A silent, dry crying, no sound, no more sobs. And Nyiszli starts talking to her, Hungarian, familiar sounds. Thawed out, first words: Hát jövök. *I came with my parents from Kolozsvár. Then she drinks tea, greedily. Beef consommé, too. Sleeps a bit.*

But then Muhsfeldt comes in, checking. Sees her. The girl on the bench. Nyiszli alone with Muhsfeldt. Talking. But Muhsfeldt first shakes his head. "Here there is no help." He wanted to take the poor girl into the anteroom of the incineration chamber. After everything she had been through, standing there . . . waiting . . . and then to get shot in the back of the head . . . Still, and I don't know if it is true, because afterward no one heard anything more about her . . . some people maintain that she was saved, like by a miracle, that she was allowed to leave with the construction brigade . . . Was she the only one of all those millions to survive death in the gas chamber?

THE AUSCHWITZ DISPENSARY

I

Capesius: "I was at the Auschwitz concentration camp from February 12, 1944, to January 1, 1945. On February 10, 1944, I was detailed to Auschwitz by Sturmbannführer Lolling, since the pharmacist at the SS dispensary there, Dr. Krömer, had become ill. On February 12, 1944, I reported to the garrison doctor, Dr. Wirths, at Auschwitz. Dr. Krömer received me in the SS dispensary. Then he went into sick bay and died on February 18, 1944. I was appointed to succeed him and on the same day was transferred to Auschwitz.

"I made an attempt, through the help of my friend Sturmbannführer Dr. Becker, who had influence in the Berlin medics' station, to be assigned to Dachau or Berlin, but I was unsuccessful.

"The SS dispensary was located in a brick building outside the main camp area of Auschwitz. The building had a ground floor, a second floor, and an attic. The dispensary was on the ground floor, where there was also a room in which the medications and equipment arriving on the ramp at Birkenau were sorted through. Sometimes there were medical instruments as well. These items were meant exclusively for prisoners. This task was my responsibility, but the actual work was performed by the Polish inmate pharmacist named Sikorski.

"The garrison physician and dentist were also located here. On the second floor was the SS infirmary with beds for SS patients. The attic was used to store medications that came from the ramp at Birkenau.

"I had about twelve prisoners working for me in the SS dispensary. Except for the bookkeeper, all the prisoners were pharmacists of various types. I took over almost all these prisoners from Krömer. At the moment I cannot recall any other prisoners' names working there.

"I was housed in a wooden barrack near the Auschwitz train station. This barrack was near the officers' mess.

"My job as *Apotheker* was to order the medical supplies needed for SS personnel and prisoners from the central medical station in Berlin—by this I mean the central station of the Waffen-SS, which was housed in a bread factory, rather than the army's medical station—and I had to order supplies for the main camp at Auschwitz and all the auxiliary camps, including Birkenau and Monowitz.

"Furthermore, I frequently had to pick up medications from the ramp at Birkenau with a medic truck. I would go with a driver and two prisoners to the ramp at Birkenau, where a pile of cases and instruments was waiting to be picked up. A uniformed soldier would turn these materials over to me. It was not always the same man. He was not in SS uniform. We always referred to these men as 'SD' [Sicherheitsdienst: security police]. Receipts were not issued.

"Occasionally one of the Oberscharführers working for me would perform this function for me. It could be that one of them was named Jurasek.

"What I really mean to say is that we rotated this assignment among us.

"The SS dispensary was in the infirmary barrack, on the ground floor of the block. I myself had a large room, also on the ground floor, with three tables. In this same room was the bookkeeper, a prisoner who kept the accounts and maintained our files. In another room on the ground floor, the prisoner pharmacist Sikorski worked with five pharmacists and druggists. There were also two rooms in the basement, one where medicines were kept and another containing wicker-covered bottles of alcohol. Temporarily we also kept twenty cartons with two thousand cans of DDT there (for delousing)—sent to us by the Red Cross.

"There was a shower in the basement, and a barbershop on the ground floor. The attic was sealed. There we presorted and stored the luggage of those doctors and pharmacists arriving in the Jewish transports.

"I took inventory of the dispensary immediately, as it had not been turned over to my command in an orderly fashion. I poured the contents of any containers that bore a coded number or an illegible label out into a zinc vat. Anything still in its original container, or whose pharmaceutical effects were especially powerful, or whose effects I was not completely sure of, I kept in a large white crate in the basement. This crate was secured with two locks. The SS dispensary I was in charge of was the main dispensary for the whole Auschwitz camp. The separate auxiliary camps had their own prisoner dispensaries, and these gave us monthly supply requests. The prisoner pharmacists in these dispensaries generally came to get their medical supplies and drugs from us, accompanied by inmate physicians. Those camps without their own prisoner dispensaries sent their inmate physicians to us monthly to pick up supplies. There were also external camps that supplied their drug needs themselves.

"The dispensing of drugs and medications in the main SS dispensary was performed by prisoners Sikorski and Strauch. The latter was a pharmacist from Oppeln. He also dispensed medications by individual prescription to SS officers and NCOs.

"There were other SS personnel in the dispensary besides me. From May to August 1944 I had the assistance of an SS pharmacist, Lieutenant Gerber. He did not report to me, but directly to the garrison doctor. He worked independently, as did I, and represented me in my absence. After the opening of the SS military hospital in August 1944, he took over the SS dispensary in Birkenau until December 1944.

"I had other SS assistants: an Oberscharführer, Kurt Jurasek; a university-trained pharmacist; and a Rottenführer. These men were also responsible for supervising the prisoner pharmacists."

•

Capesius in Göppingen, near Stuttgart, his home after the war: "By the time I arrived on February 12, 1944, for them the war was already lost, and for me as well. Sikorski said that the boss had said, Look: today *you're* in here, and tomorrow, maybe it'll be *us*. The war can no longer be won. 'The boss said' . . . Yes, that was me."

"Wouldn't you have been afraid to say things like that, there?"

Capesius: "Not to him."

"He was a pharmacist, a prisoner working in the dispensary?"

Capesius: "Yes, and his father before him had been an apothecary for the czar.

"In any case, the man (Krömer) had been shot because of his defeatist talk; he told all the new arrivals: Your eyes will pop out of your heads, this is Sodom and Gomorrah. There's another expression, something about the underworld, some kind of quote people use when things are so bad they can't get any worse . . ."

"Apocalypse?"

Capesius: "No, no that . . ."

"Inferno?"

Capesius: "Yes, 'the Inferno in the underworld is nothing compared to this,' something like that. And he had a very early SS membership number, from the first year . . ."

•

Witness for the prosecution Jan Sikorski describes the dispensary thus (June 19, 1964, in Russian): "Krömer was lying in the hospital at Auschwitz for some time, in the SS hospital. And after that Dr. Capesius arrived."

Presiding judge: "So that was the end of '43."

Witness Jan Sikorski: "Around the end of '43. Or maybe . . . yes . . ."

Presiding judge: "Who else was employed in the dispensary then besides you and Dr. Capesius?"

Witness Jan Sikorski: "Dr. Capesius, he was the head of the dispensary. And an SS officer, I think his name was Gerber. He was from Alsace. He spoke excellent French and had been in the French army. Then he was captured, and as a German he then became a member of the SS. There were lower-ranking officers, too. But no pharmacists. Those were Jurasek, Dobrzanski, and there was one more. In the army, not the SS. He was called Frymark. He had had a cigarette shop on Alexanderplatz in Berlin. He told everybody about it.

"And then prisoners, are you interested in them, too?"

Presiding judge: "Yes, we are interested in the prisoners, too."

Witness Jan Sikorski: "Besides me there was a German Jew from Silesia working there named Strauch. He had been a school chum of the pharmacist Krömer before the war. There was also a bookkeeper named Berliner, an old man. And two women from Hungary, I only know their first names, Piroska and Éva. And then a well-built, good-looking young pharmacist from Transylvania, Grosz, also a Jew. And also a Greek, Aaron was his name. And another Hungarian, a big fat guy, Altmann. I think he was a wine merchant by profession. From Poland there were two more druggists, Prokop and Jozef Gorzkowski from Kraków. And two more pharmacists, Szewczyk and Swiderski. There was also a short, young assistant, Sulikowksi. He was a colleague of my brother's, that's how I knew him.

Jan Sikorski, Frankfurt Am
Main, June 19, 1964

"People spoke in Polish, Russian, Hungarian, but also German and Yiddish, and also this special prisoners' language, the so-called *lagerszpracha* of Auschwitz . . . Our pharmacist Capesius, the boss, acted as though he wasn't listening when his prisoners were talking *lagerszpracha*. No, no, he didn't do anything bad. Just followed orders. Capesius had a good reputation with the prisoners. He was an objective person."

Presiding judge: "Now, tell us, please, sir, what was your assignment in the dispensary?"

Witness Jan Sikorski: "I was a kind of *Oberhäftling,* a supervising prisoner. In this commando. The commando was too small for a Kapo. Sometimes they called me that, Kapo. In the morning I had to collect the names of the prisoners and write them down on a piece of paper. And I had to bring them all through the gate to work.

"Then I had to register all of them, register that I had brought them to work, and then each of them went to his own job.

"Then I received all the orders from the camps. And filled them. And then I sent them out to the individual camps."

•

Notes of the attending judge from the fifty-seventh day of the proceedings (June 19, 1964). Statement of the witness Sikorski, formerly a prisoner pharmacist, regarding the defendant Dr. Capesius:

Sikorski: "One day, some can openers with prongs arrived from Berlin. These were to be used for opening the canisters of Zyklon B.

"The first shipments of Zyklon B came to the dispensary. They were kept in the basement to the right where there was another small room, which was locked. The cartons with the Zyklon B were stored there. But the gas was there only a short time. Dr. Capesius said once that he wanted nothing to do with it. He wanted to return the gas to the administration. I heard that lower-ranking SS officers had driven specially to Berlin to pick up the Zyklon B. It was in brown cartons. I never saw the canisters until after the war, in the Auschwitz Museum. It was also said that Zyklon B was stored in the theater building. But I don't know if that was right."

Upon questioning, the witness explained: "Dr. Capesius knew about the Zyklon B."

When asked how he knew this, the witness said, "He had to know what was in the dispensary. You couldn't get anything done without him knowing. Dr. Capesius was business-like."

To the question who had the keys for a) the basement, b) the theater building, and c) the small crematorium, the witness explained: "The head of the dispensary held the keys for these three spaces. He never gave them out himself; this was SS officer Jurasek's responsibility. Dr. Capesius kept the keys in his desk drawer, as far as I can remember. The SS officer had to ask him whenever he wanted the keys."

Capesius sat at his rickety old desk and filled out request forms. Were they orders? What was he ordering? What did he do all day? Did he sometimes open up the drawer where the keys for the Zyklon B were? Did Klehr, the head of the gassing squad, pick him up in a medic truck?

.

Judicial interrogation of the defendant Victor Capesius (December 7, 1959, Frankfurt am Main): "Question from the court: Was this bunker the former crematorium?"

Capesius's answer: "I do not know, nobody ever told me that. In any event, the storage room or bunker space where these Zyklon B canisters were kept was never my responsibility, nor was giving them out."

Further question: "Besides the building in which it was housed, did the SS dispensary have any other places in the camp to keep its supplies?"

Answer: "Yes, directly across from us in a bunker [the old crematorium]. The following things were stored in this bunker: urns, whether full or empty I don't know; petrol; creolin; carbolic acid; calcium chloride; and possibly other liquids in wicker bottles. These were all supplies for the camp dispensary, which was also my responsibility. These materials were used to supply the various camp dispensaries of the outlying camps."

Further question: "There was no Zyklon B stored there?"

Answer: "Our camp storage rooms in this bunker did not take up the entire storage capacity of the bunker: perhaps only half of the entire bunker."

.

Testimony of witness Ignacy Golik, also a prisoner employed in the SS hospital: "Around fall of 1942 or spring of 1943—I can't recall the exact time anymore—I observed from the second floor of the SS infirmary a long line of prisoners from Birkenau marching to the small crematorium [the old crematorium]. The prisoners were accompanied by an SS guard detachment, about company strength. There were some two hundred prisoners . . . They were led through the gate into the crematorium and assembled in a courtyard fenced off by a cement wall.

"Then I saw how the prisoners were forced to undress. They didn't do this voluntarily, but only when the SS men began beating them. Then they marched the naked prisoners in rows of five into the crematorium. At the same time four or five medics climbed up onto the crematorium roof and tossed the contents of the Zyklon B canisters down into pipe spouts built into the roof as gas intakes. As far as I can recall, each medic had two canisters. They all wore gas masks.

"As described earlier in Section D VII 4, near the crematoriums were larger and smaller sized trenches dug into the ground, as incineration pits. The gassed victims' corpses were burned in these trenches. Sometimes human beings were shoved alive into these pits, if for some reason it had not been possible to bring them into the gas chamber.

"One case especially has stayed in my memory. It was probably May or June 1944: an older Jewish woman had been selected, but not her daughter. The daughter would not be separated from her mother, and then Klehr brought both women from the disinfection station as stragglers directly to the pit and pushed both women into the fire alive."

Witness Edward Pyś, formerly a prisoner in the SS infirmary, testifies: "Once, in summer or fall of 1942, I myself was an eyewitness to a gassing in the old crematorium, which was in the immediate vicinity of my workplace.

"They yelled at us, If any of you dare to look out the window, you will have to go into the crematorium, too. When the barrier was closed off, two or three trucks covered with tarps drove up to the entrance of the crematorium. In the trucks were male and female persons, probably Jews, still in civilian clothing, not yet in prisoners' uniforms, and they were forced to get out of the trucks in front of the crematorium.

"When the security police Koch and Theuer started introducing the gas, someone started the motor of a truck in front of the crematorium and ran it at full speed for about a quarter hour. Although the crematorium was sealed off, almost airtight, the noise of the motor could not drown out the cries of the people in the gas chamber. From my observation post, where I watched from behind a shuttered window, it sounded like the screaming of wild beasts; there was nothing human left in that sound. If I hadn't known that there were people in that crematorium, I would never have believed that these screams came from human beings. This dreadful screaming lasted a few minutes."

•

Judicial interrogation of the defendant Victor Capesius (December 7, 1959, Frankfurt am Main).

Question: "Are you aware of what was stored in the other part of the bunker?"

Answer: "No. Somebody told me there had once been an incineration section in the other part."

Question: "So, was the old crematorium there, then?"

Answer: "That's not what I was told. When I arrived, the bunker was just used to store supplies."

Question: "You said earlier that someone had told you that Mr. Klehr had stored Zyklon B canisters. Can you say where he kept them?"

Answer: "No, they only said, very mysteriously, in a bunker."

Question: "Was that perhaps the remaining section of the bunker, in which you kept the supplies you mentioned above?"

Answer: "I can't say.

"I took care of the prisoners who worked for me in the

dispensary to the best of my abilities. I made arrangements to have meals cooked for them in the attic, and got food supplied for that purpose."

Adam's response: Ridiculous. This is probably post-traumatic amnesia. Our Vic was so horribly stressed in Auschwitz, our SS major, that of course he had to forget it all. And naturally, forgetting is a good idea. He was a decent man, always. And, as your uncle Albert says, he expanded his dispensary staff like crazy, to save as many as possible. And he was a "businesslike" man, as his prison employee Sikorski testified.

2

DR. VICTOR CAPESIUS (FROM TRIAL DOCUMENTS)
Born February 2, 1907, in Reußmarkt/Transylvania. Currently resides in Stuttgart West, Bismarckstrasse 48. Married to his colleague Dr. Friederike Capesius, a half-Jewish woman from Vienna, with whom he has three children ranging in age from seven to thirteen. Wife and children still lived until the beginning of the 1960s in Sighişoara, Romania: the family was only reunited after twenty years of separation, and this only for a year, since Capesius was arrested in December 1959 and lived another ten years apart from his wife and three children. Annual income in 1943 was nine thousand reichsmarks. His net worth of twenty thousand reichsmarks was lost through the occupation of Romania. Member of the Waffen-SS from August 1943 to May 3, 1945. Sturmbannführer from November 9, 1943, to May 3, 1945. Court-martialed and sentenced to death in absentia in Klausenburg (Kolozsvár), 1947.

Son of a physician and public health officer. Proven Aryan ancestry going back to the eighteenth century.

(Ancestry certificate? Yes.) Attended the German gymnasium in Hermannstadt (Sibiu) and Schäßburg. Baccalau-
reate (*Abitur*) 1925. Studied pharmacy in Klausenburg.
One year army service in the Romanian army as a pharmacist, rank first lieutenant. But was relieved of duty
after only one month to study chemistry in Vienna
1931–1933. Received his doctorate, January 30, 1933.
Until August 1943 he worked for a subsidiary of IG
Farben in Romania, calling on physicians' offices, mostly
in Transylvania and Bucharest. At the outbreak of the
war, he was called back to duty to his Romanian unit in
Cernavodă, where he directed the hospital dispensary
of the Romanian army. Promoted on January 24, 1942,
to pharmacist, rank captain, in the reserve. But was
again given leave to resume his civilian job as a representative of IG Farben on June 16, 1942. Was called
up again on August 1, 1943, but this time, due to the
Berlin-Bucharest accord, joined the German Waffen-SS.
Assigned to the Central Medics Camp, Warsaw Branch,
with simultaneous rank assignment of Hauptsturmführer (captain) in the Waffen-SS.

Besides his promotion to major, there is another significant
gap in his official vita, namely, his positions at various concentration camps: Dachau, Sachsenhausen, and, at the end of
1943, or as he maintains, February 12, 1944, Auschwitz, where
he assumed the direction of the SS medical dispensary, or was
assigned to do so. Sikorski, the Kapo of the dispensary, said in
court it was the end of 1943. On January 18, 1945, Capesius
managed to flee to Berlin, and then probably with Himmler,
Höß, and other high-ranking SS officers to Schleswig-Holstein,
where he was captured by the British and released again on
May 23, 1946. He lived in Stuttgart West, Bismarckstrasse,
under his real name, and began studying electronics at a tech-

nical college there, since he could not find a job on account of his having been in the SS. In the summer of 1946 he was recognized by a former prisoner in Munich and arrested by the American military police. But the investigation got bogged down, and on August 2, 1947, the court for detention cases, Camp 74, decreed that he had broken no law, and he was free again. He started to work again in a pharmacy in Stuttgart, and on October 5, 1950, he opened up his own business, the Marktapotheke in Göppingen. And after that, a cosmetics shop in Reutlingen. By 1958, the era of the "economic miracle" (*Wirtschaftswunderland*) in Germany, he was grossing 400,000 deutschmarks a year.

There is a legitimate question, which was asked in the trial: Where did he get the means to open his own pharmacy? He answered that he had nothing to reproach himself for.

The witnesses for the prosecution of course gave very incriminating testimony against him, as did the prisoners who had worked in the SS dispensary; the possibility that he escaped from Auschwitz in 1945 with assets stolen from the murdered victims cannot be ruled out. The question as to how far Auschwitz and its crimes extended into the postwar economic boom times of the fifties and sixties is a deeply shaming one. The scandalous conduct of the Swiss banks, who would not release the money of the murder victims, is a part of this shame. Money doesn't stink? Not even of ashes and smoke?

•

Letter of Ferdinand Grosz, a prison employee at the camp dispensary, to Hermann Langbein (Vienna):

> I was born in 1912 in Lunca de Jos (Transylvania) and graduated from university in Bucharest in 1935. Until I was deported I worked in Târgu Mureş, in the pharmacy of a certain David Johann, who was a good friend of Victor Capesius. Every time Capesius came

on a sales trip for Bayer to Târgu Mureş, he would
spend hours in our pharmacy. My acquaintance with
Capesius dates back to then.

When I was deported in June 1944, I was sent to
Auschwitz, where I was tattooed as prisoner number
A-13864. First I worked in the Palitzsch sand pit, then
on the stables commando, then from October 1944
on the dispensary commando of the SS infirmary. I
got this position as a protégé of Capesius, whom I had
met by chance. The infirmary Kapo there was Karl
Lill; the Kapo of the dispensary department was a
Polish pharmacist whose name I can no longer recall. I
worked there until the camp was evacuated in January
1945, and had an excellent opportunity to get a closer
look at Capesius's activities.

I can confirm that he was on duty at the "ramp"
two to three times a week, and that his work there was
not dispensing medications but with carrying out the
"selection" of the arriving transports.

As far as medications were concerned, his only
interest in them was to have us all inspect the
prisoners' jars of creams and tubes of toothpaste for
hidden jewels. He came to us daily to check up on
whether we had found anything. Just in those months
that I worked in the infirmary he collected huge
quantities of jewelry, which he viewed as natural and
proper income for himself.

In 1947 Capesius sent his brother-in-law from
Sighişoara (Schäßburg) to me requesting that I fill out
a statement confirming that he, Capesius, had saved
my life in Auschwitz.

I threw him out. Even though by accident or
coincidence he had saved my life, one must not forget

the gassing of those many thousands of human beings he had selected for extermination, a crime which can never be atoned for.

Târgu Mureş, November 21, 1962.

Capesius's response: "I never had any involvement of that kind with jewelry. By October of '44 there were no longer transports of this type. After my departure on August 25, 1944, I of course no longer was picking up luggage myself; that all continued as it did in my earlier absence. Moreover, by October, when Grosz came to us, that was all over, and Grosz worked in Sikorski's room, I think, where there were no searches done such as he described, since that was a clean room. And even with Prokop I never took any jewelry.

"I never asked anyone for a good-conduct certificate, not even Fritz Strauch, who would have been the most likely possibility. My wife never wrote me about it. I never gave her Grosz's name."

3

Adam: I was not in the SS dispensary every day, either. Langbein only took me along for a few days to his office, which was in the infirmary; I was often out on dangerous duty with the Kampfgruppe.* Langbein's seat as Wirths's secretary was quite near the SS dispensary, and it was in Langbein's office that I met Dr. Wirths, who seemed very friendly and affable, and right off the bat recited a poem by Eichendorff—Langbein had introduced me, somewhat jokingly, as a poet . . . But Langbein reassured me

---

*The Kampfgruppe Auschwitz was a resistance organization within the camp that tried to send out information about what was happening in Auschwitz. —trans.

afterward, and said that Wirths was not a monster, and knew the score. They all wished to be considered "cultured," to show their artistic sensitivity. Mengele, especially, you know, often had the orchestra play for him. They played in this building, too. Here, too, we often saw your musical friend SS Roland, who would be working the ivories over with his stubby fingers. He liked Schubert songs most of all—but unfortunately he would sing along. With particular gusto: "The Linden Tree," and the whole Winterreise cycle. But Capesius was completely unmusical and hummed along loudly with everything. Even Fritz Klein avidly sang old army songs from the Kaiser's era, with accordion accompaniment. Klein was a dreadful anti-Semite, but otherwise a good guy, a "poitash." But it's incorrect to say that all the inmate pharmacists in the dispensary were as happy working for Capesius as he asserts. Take the Hungarian Ferdinand Grosz from the David Johann Pharmacy in Târgu Mureș, for example, which was where Éva came from, too. Grosz only arrived in Auschwitz with the Hungarian transports at the start of June, but Capesius didn't bring him onto the SS infirmary staff until October '44. Young and handsome, Grosz hated his boss and later gave seriously damaging testimony against him. The same was true of Márton Lázár from Târgu Mureș, who worked in the same area as Sikorski, and was engaged to Éva Bárd. But with him that was understandable—you could ascribe his dislike of Capesius to jealousy. And then "Grandpa" Josef Groszkowskim (known as Yuyu), who was way over sixty, came from Katowice, and Capesius even visited his wife once there. You have to imagine this scene: an SS Sturmbannführer comes by to say guten Tag *to a family whose husband and father has been deported to a concentration camp and who fear for his life; picture, then, how this man in full SS regalia tries to reassure these people, how they all look at him a bit askance, not knowing quite how to react, but still compelled to offer him a chair, and even a cup of tea, the wife with eyes red from weeping, and then her desperate questions, and his hypocritical friendliness, once more this collision of normal everyday life with all that an SS uniform symbolizes, and in fact IS. Hell itself. Capesius would try to "make nice" with people in his chummy way, as if nothing at all had happened, as if everything were completely normal, right up to his famous statement, "You're just going to have a shower, you'll see one another again in an hour," which he made on the ramp to Dr. Schlinger, whose wife and children were going straight into the gas chamber. Right there you can see how completely he could repress things, as if everything were totally normal and okay; and yes, on top of it all, our doctor was also in love; he seems to have been smitten with the young Jewish pharmacist Éva Citron Bard from Târgu Mureş, who was just twenty-six at the time, and he only thirty-seven. He would likely have known her earlier, perhaps she had been his lover: for during his pretrial confinement in Frankfurt he complained, talking about sexual deprivation, which had never been a problem in his SS dispensary since the "crew had been quite mixed." There had been rumors back then, and even Wirths knew about the liaison between the major and the Jewish Hungarian woman. And after all, he himself knew something about "Jewish passion," and even spoke admiringly of it to Éva: Wasn't his wife from a Jewish background? Capesius had first gotten to know young Éva in the pharmacy near the gates of her native town; later on, between September 3 and September 9, 1944, the "kindhearted doctor," in uniform, even, had paid a call on that very same Apotheke am Stadttor, reassuring everyone that Éva was all right. Târgu Mureş belonged to Hungary; the front ran in the vicinity of Sighişoara, which was already under Russian occupation. And Romania had declared war on Hungary and Germany. At that point in September 1944, Capesius could no longer visit his own family in Sighişoara—it was so near the border it already was part of Romania—so he visited Éva's pharmacy in Târgu Mureş instead. One thing is correct: he held a protective hand over his personnel . . .*

Capesius: "Yes, Dr. Wirths wanted to reduce the size of the dispensary and have all those 'who knew' gassed, but I was pigheaded about it, and kept them working on all kinds of pointless projects, just to keep the people busy, and thus save them. So I had them go through the three cardboard suitcases again, which had been sent to us earlier from the 'Canada' warehouse—or maybe it got here from someplace else—reinspecting them several times starting in October [these suitcases were full of complete sets of dentures, still with pieces of flesh clinging to them] to see if any of the metal remnants were usable. So in this way I had a policy of 'full employment.'"

Adam: Still, a lot of witnesses have doubts: isn't this another of the druggist's typical defensive statements? He was an absolute genius at turning everything to his own advantage . . . In this regard, he never ran out of ideas. Especially the matter of these mysterious suitcases, which aroused a totally different suspicion in most of us, as did those "metal remnants" . . . I can't say much there. And beyond all that, dear man, I ask myself: How can I, how can you, who knew the man and his wife so much better, maintain that sometimes, perhaps, he even deserved to be defended? Yes, the jury in Frankfurt found him guilty of making money off the property stolen from the gassed victims, which is morally reprehensible, of course, and indicates a really shabby unconscious; the investigation was quite exact and painstaking about details, but there still is the question of resentments, of hate-driven exaggerations, traumatized witnesses with fantasized stories, for none of them was really "objective"; those people testifying in Frankfurt were horribly injured and psychically damaged!

Most witnesses held the opinion that the selections were more of a sideline for Capesius, an alibi, so to speak; his main reason for going to the ramp was to pick up these suitcases with valuables in them, which speaks of a particular insensitivity and a brutality of soul.

Capesius himself said in Göppingen: "Supposedly these suitcases were sent to us, or to Dr. Schatz's dental unit, for the gold teeth to be melted from their mountings, and used in new prostheses for prisoners, but given our equipment this was totally impossible. And the suitcases we kept with clothing ended up benefiting a lot of people, before the final dissolution of the camp in January '45, since things like that were distributed; the suits, which were too small and till then not used, were particularly useful to the women in the stone block."

Adam: Remember, even this stuff had been plundered from the gassed victims, including the suitcases! Éva once recognized a suitcase and burst into tears, for the little suitcase had belonged to her beloved cousin Erszébet from Târgu Mureş. A sick, fragile girl . . . and they all looked at her, as everyone knew that in Auschwitz the sick were gassed.

Capesius: "I often took such clothes with me in the fall when I went hunting in the Beskidy mountains, and gave them out to our Polish beaters and their children, with whom I was very popular, and their children were also treated in the SS dental unit."

•

Jan Sikorski in the Auschwitz Trial on his boss, Dr. Capesius: "Dr. Capesius often drove to Birkenau and personally brought back suitcases. I don't know whether he participated in the selections. I was not present on the ramp with him. And no one in the camp ever told me anything about it. Dr. Capesius went to the ramp, completely officially, and picked up the trunks, which were then brought to the sorting rooms. Prior to then, medications and instruments were always being stolen in 'Canada.' The dispensary got only the very worst. For that reason, Dr. Capesius went to the commandant's office and got official permission to collect the suitcases himself.

"Dr. Capesius was a good boss. He took care of his inmate workers in the dispensary. For instance, he once traded to get potatoes for his people."

But at another hearing, Sikorski testified quite differently. He gave very incriminating testimony, saying that Dr. Capesius had misappropriated the gold that had been extracted from the teeth and the dentures of the gassed victims.

Sikorski: "On the building's ground floor, where the SS dispensary was located, stood trunks filled with teeth. These trunks were still there on January 15, 1945, but there was no more gold in them.

"The teeth were sorted by an inmate named Sulikowski. He did this for Dr. Capesius. The first time they turned up, Dr. Capesius showed them to me. The first time I counted fifteen trunks. How many there were later, I don't know. They stood there for one to two months. I think the trunks were brought from the crematorium. We knew then that generally these things went into the crematorium and were melted there. Once some inmates showed me gold bars of six to seven hundred grams each, made from the melted gold fillings and teeth. I assume that some friend of Dr. Capesius had given him these things. These suitcases looked just like the ones with the medications in them. Where Sulikowski melted the gold down, I don't know. It was a sideline for the boss.

"One time I arranged it so that Dr. Capesius was able to trade three or four liters of alcohol for a brooch from a prisoner."

Former inmate Wilhelm Prokop, a druggist in the dispensary, had even worse things to report: "Capesius impressed me as the kind of man for whom a prisoner was simply a number, and just there to be liquidated. In the attic of the dispensary there were at least fifteen suitcases that were overflowing with gold teeth extracted from dead victims' mouths, still with bits of flesh adhering to them. A horrible stink. Capesius would walk up to the suitcases, stoop down, and run his hands through this vile-smelling stuff. He would pull out one denture, hold it up, as if he were trying to estimate its value. I ran away."

Former inmate Yakoov Gabai from the Sonderkommando said in an interview: "There were two guys from Czechoslovakia, the so-called dentists, they yanked the gold from the victims' mouths. They were actual dentists . . . there was a large crate there, into which they tossed the gold. A large box, a cubic meter in size, with the word 'Germany' printed on it. They threw the gold teeth in there . . . Every week a German would come, or two, a major or lieutenant colonel, officers, they would open the crate and take whatever they wanted, no controls."

So forcing all those herds of people into the gas to die screaming in those cement rooms served this purpose, too: to make their killers rich.

Adam's diary: The gold was supposedly intended for the Reich. Sometimes I have to wonder: If our druggist did not do the selections, as he maintains, but only confiscated medical supplies on the ramp, then where did all these trunks of valuables in the attic of his dispensary come from?

4

So, about Dr. Victor Capesius. He sold me peppermint cookies when I was a kid. That was in his pharmacy, The Crown, the oldest pharmacy in Sighișoara. It's located in the big market square, which today is called Piața Hermann Oberth. I was seven then. I asked for a "Haumichblau" ("Beat Me Blue") for five bani. These Haumichblaus were supposed to be good, someone had said. He laughed at me, said "Haumichblau," and laughed.

After the war Capesius lived in Stuttgart and then in Göppingen. I first visited him and his wife in May 1978 in Göppingen. I was shocked by the swanky neighborhood he lived in, and I thought: How unscrupulous, he probably enriched himself from the valuables of those poor people who were gassed, from property that was looted from the victims, and possibly from their gold teeth as well. Where else would he have gotten the money for the pharmacy and the cosmetics shop?

Testimony of W. W. Prokop: "Working in this dispensary I got to know Capesius as a person who was always trying to turn the huge Hungarian transports to his maximum advantage. One day I was sorting out medicines in the attic storeroom when Capesius appeared. He previously had charge of the suitcases kept up there, which had belonged to the abovementioned prisoners. Capesius brought these suitcases himself from the camp at Birkenau. [Is that why he was on the ramp so often, and in the crematorium?] I paid attention to his activities during my shift. I noticed how Capesius separated out the valuable objects and expensive items, packed them in the best leather suitcases, and took them with him later. Capesius suddenly saw me watching him, and then he turned to me and said more or less this: 'Prokop, it's up to you how long you survive. You have seen nothing; but if you did see something, well, that event can hit at any time, that end which is in store for you anyway.' So right away I knew that if I told anyone a thing about it, I was lost. We had to sort medicines in different rooms anyway. In one room I noticed twenty-five to forty different bags with thousands of individually extracted teeth and whole sets of dentures. These teeth came from the jaws of gassed inmates, often with bits of gum and bone still clinging to them."

When he was being held for questioning, and later during the time he served in prison, Capesius tried again and again to reconstruct his biography, to bring clarity to his vagueness, to illuminate his memory, because now so much depended on it—his freedom, his life. But he had no connecting thread, no arc, no context. Naturally Capesius has no feelings of guilt or denial or revulsion about the things he had seen and participated in, the things he HAD to do; he remembers only the command, the squad, the assignments, the date, the number, the calendar. He recalls only unambiguous and graspable bureaucratic details: he had a sense for these things, these for him are reality. Everything else is nonsense, he said, "fiction." No, he was never even just a simple party member or a National Socialist. But neither was he the opposite; there was no secret "no" inside to guide him, as it did many others. Businesslike, yes, he's certainly that, to excess, but cold; it's things he loves, and they him. And he has a feeling for them. He has no need of ideas—other people have those. He privately makes fun of them. What counts is only that which actually happens, sometimes mysterious, threatening, too, like the trial now. What is important is who gets what, and that's determined by power and money and connections, and he once had all that, but not anymore! He didn't want to follow that thought any further, not even now.

5

Accessory Prosecutor Ormond: "You were in Auschwitz three years and never got beyond the rank of SS Sturmmann?"

Huley: "I could have made the rank of Blockführer, if I had been so inclined. But you could conduct yourself in such a way that you would not get promoted to Blockführer."

Dr. Ella Lingens, the only German (Austrian) physician inmate, said during the trial:

"I hardly know a single SS officer who could say that he

never saved anyone's life. There were few sadists. No more than 5 to 10 percent were compulsive killers in the clinical sense. The rest were completely normal people who well knew the difference between good and evil. They all knew what was going on there . . ."

Presiding judge: "You mean to say that everyone in Auschwitz could certainly decide for himself whether he was good or evil?"

Dr. Lingens: "That's exactly what I mean to say."

•

Adam: It is clear that Dr. Capesius never cared about what happened, about the horror, the mass murder, or even his own role as a murderer—all he cared about was saving his miserable little life, his own skin. In the trial he even tried to use the terror of the camp as a defense. That was the reason he got such a severe penalty, a punishment that would continue on even after the sentence was served, for the crime was too great, the crime was greater than the punishment.

Frankfurt am Main, January 24, 1962. *Question from the court:* "While you were in Auschwitz, did the events taking place there ever seem to you to be illegal?"

Answer of the defendant Capesius: "I grew up in Transylvania with a great respect for all things German. At home my parents always looked to the German state as a model. My father especially was constantly saying that Germany was the model of order and the rule of law. Given this attitude, I assumed as well that what was going on in Auschwitz was legal, although it seemed to me to be cruel. Moreover, my upbringing in Transylvania led me to believe in tolerance toward other nationalities, for here we grew up with five different ones. Specifically Romanians, Hungarians, Germans, Armenians, Gypsies, and Jews. Including the Germans, that's actually six nationalities."

Question from the court: "Did this attitude toward the

events of Auschwitz apply to the killings in the gas chambers after the selections?"

Answer of the defendant: "I never assumed that anything like that would be possible in Germany without the appropriate law. Moreover, I want to mention here that I was never hostile toward the Jews. To the contrary, in the opinion of witness Sikorski and also of SS Oberscharführers Jurasek and Dobrzanski, I always treated the Jews too well compared to the Poles."

Question from the court: "Did the thought never occur to you that there was a discrepancy between the existing regulations and laws and the extent of the killings taking place in Auschwitz?"

Answer of the defendant: "Inwardly I object to any concentration camp of the Auschwitz type. But I had no power to change the conditions there. Moreover, I did try to get transferred out of Auschwitz. And also, I stated that I objected when I was supposed to be assigned to the selections. I have described the details earlier."

Defense Attorney Laternser: "In this manner, this pharmacist came into the proximity of this major crime of Auschwitz. Should a defendant such as this, whom rumor also accuses of enriching himself from inmates' property, not be defended with particular care?"

The Frankfurt court needed almost two years, and used thousands of pages of notes, witness examinations, and visits to the scene; care was certainly exercised, and it pronounced its verdict: guilty.

In this case the issue was not whether the perpetrators had to obey orders or not, whether they were ordered to perform "ramp duty" and to send many people including children to their deaths—which Laternser even turns around when he uses the phrase "selection as salvation" from death, that is, saving a precious few by sending them into the work camp instead of the gas chamber, when Hitler, after all, had ordered the extermination of *all* Jews—no, the issue here is the attitude, the morality, the awareness of injustice, even the conscious-ness of guilt, which Capesius utterly lacked. He vehemently denied ever having done selections. He lied. All the witnesses clearly refuted this assertion. Dr. Lucas, who very probably also carried out selections, not always having been able to avoid it, was acquitted, as was Dr. Münch, by a Polish court, no less, because they not only put up moral resistance to the machinery of murder—which required much spiritual strength, courage, and morale—but they also condemned this machin-ery in the trial.

6

Adam: It wasn't until after the end that the shame of it over-came us. We had been too numb, too exhausted. After the selec-tions, the beatings on the scaffold, seeing women's naked buttocks being hoisted up and displayed like a vile, pale star, shimmering, wasted. And now we were supposed to live with this guilt, which others had loaded onto themselves. And even if you have gotten out, you never really escape. Even the victim is not spared, it had all actually happened, had been our experience . . .

So, yes, the pit, the abyss between the two "places" called Auschwitz, was so deep, so enormous, that Adam knew noth-ing about the perpetrators and their lives in their cozy houses: with holidays, birthdays, Christmas . . . and Roland and Cape-sius shutting their eyes to the horror of the barracks, the gas chamber, and the hunger cells. It wasn't until the end that this glass-and-concrete wall suddenly shattered.

And remembering it again, I can hear Roland's voice, sound-ing so unctuous and preachy: "You know, what made the stron-gest impression on me didn't even happen in the camp, it was on the evacuation march afterward in March 1945. I see it now before me, I can see this man—one of my inferior officers, Schmidt was his name, from Stuttgart, a totally brutal guy, so he was often decorated. I think he even had the Iron Cross second degree. I can see him with his iron helmet, saying, cold as ice: *'HEY, You!'* During a 'rest break,' pointing at an Italian boy, around twenty: *'Get over here, NOW!'* Everyone knew what that meant. And I saw and didn't believe my eyes: the youth started to blush red as a turkey, this violent, sudden flush of shame . . . I had never seen a human face turn that red before. It was on the death march of 1945," Roland went on, "all the other times I looked the other way when my men would shoot prisoners. Usually they were singled out completely arbitrarily! But on that beautiful spring day, as the trees began to bud, the birds were chirping, that day, I couldn't look away, the blush on the young prisoner's face was like fire, it spread out everywhere. And when the shot rang out, they all flinched. I flinched, too, even though I was usually pretty hard-boiled. It's so up close and personal, being 'selected,' being 'called on' like that. Like being called on in school, woken up, made to face the truth, all eyes on you, but being called on to die . . . ! Imagine it, being selected, being called on for your own death, eye to eye with your killer, the marksman of your death."

Adam spoke often of that shame, that all-encompassing feeling after the liberation of January 27, 1945. *Joseph K. in* The Trial, *as he died like a dog, was it only his blush of shame that would outlive him?* said Adam.

And Roland when I visited him in Innsbruck: "Actually, I don't like to talk about it." But then suddenly the words came spilling out, as if he had just got his wind back, or was speaking from some Beyond:

"I might possibly write about it someday, you know. There are so many perspectives, you know, unh . . . unh . . . unh"— he was almost gasping—"that haven't been sufficiently explored in the whole thing."

"Like what, for example?"

"Well, for instance, how humanity really flowered there, in the midst of all that misery."

"Human solidarity, you mean?"

"No, I don't mean solidarity. No, I mean humanity itself, individual instances of it. If you know what I mean."

"You mean among the prisoners?"

"Among the prisoners and also between the prisoners and the guards. Which was forbidden, you know."

Adam: That was mostly in the crematorium, there were almost no guards there, nobody checking up on you. It was sort of like a club. Yes, we even sang together with the SS men, and ate with them. They actually seemed all right! In the face of death and the gas chamber and the ovens! Except for Moll, of course, he was a madman and a sadist. And we were always making deals with the SS men. Even with the officers. A regular business! Still, the Ukrainian SS men were horrific.

•

Roland: "Yes, humanity, on a small scale. Take our Dr. Capesius. He liked people, was kind. He tried, he, unh, expanded his staff in the camp dispensary totally unnecessarily, in order to save as many as possible, and in the trial no one gave him credit for that."

"He was accused of having played a role in the selections."

"Yes, he did it, but he did it to get people out, to save them."

"But he maintained he had never done selections, that he had been confused with Dr. Klein from Zeiden . . ."

"I don't know what to say to that. Of course, it's easy to accuse people who are already dead, and he was really the first victim."

"He was executed . . ."

"Yes, but completely innocent, you know. If you had known Klein . . . Of course he was also a Transylvanian. For him, people were people. He even sat down with the Jewish prisoners and drank coffee with them. And he was arrested for it, you know. He was a human being. He was kindness itself. He only wanted to help."

•

Adam: The prisoner doctor Nyiszli from Transylvania, who, as you know, was Mengele's right hand, his slave, and whom I often saw with the crematorium Sonderkommando, and whom I also visited in his autopsy room, describes Dr. Klein, on the New Year's morning in '45, somewhat differently:

Dr. Nyiszli: "January 1, 1945, arrives, as we waver between doubt and hope. New Year's morning! Snow everywhere, as far as you can see, endless white covers the landscape. I take a short stroll in the crematorium yard. The growl of a heavy truck interrupts the stillness. A few moments later, the big brown prisoner transport truck of Auschwitz camp, which the inmates call 'Brown Toni,' drives through the gate.

"A high-ranking SS officer gets out. I recognize him and give him the proper salute. It is Dr. Klein, an SS doctor, one of the bloody, sinister figures of the Auschwitz concentration camp. There is a prison in Block 11 of the camp. He is bringing a hundred victims from there.

"'I am bringing you a New Year's job,' he says to Oberscharführer Muhsfeldt, who has come running up in such a state of inebriation that he can hardly stand. He really had celebrated his New Year's Eve well. Maybe it was his own funeral party. I can see he is not pleased to be getting a bloody assignment on New Year's Day.

"The hour of death has come for one hundred Polish Christians. The group is all men. The SS sentries lead them into the empty room next to the furnace room. There they are ordered: 'Undress immediately!' Dr. Klein strolls around the yard with Muhsfeldt. I go into the undressing room and interrogate the men.

"One of them tells me he kept a relative in his Kraków apartment for one night. The Gestapo declared him to be helping the partisans, and court-martialed him. In Block 11, he was awaiting his sentence. He thought he had been brought here to wash up and that he would then be sent out on forced labor. The poor guy. His death sentence has already been pronounced—that's why he was here!—they just haven't told him. Another one ended up in the camp prison because he had bought a pound of butter without a coupon. That was his entire crime. The third one had accidentally wandered into forbidden territory—so they made him a partisan and a spy. I hear similar things from all of them. Small misdemeanors, unfounded accusations, brought them to Auschwitz.

"In 1945 there was no longer a Sonderkommando, so the SS sentries had to bring the victims themselves to stand in front of the Oberscharführer's rifle.

"More noise from the truck engine. Brown Toni pulls up once more, with new victims. A hundred well-dressed women get out. They, too, are forced into the undressing room, and they, too, are forced to take their clothes off. One after

Fritz Klein standing in a mass grave after the liberation of Bergen-Belsen in 1945

another, they are brought out to stand in front of Muhs-feldt's weapon. They, too—Christian Polish women—are be-ing made to pay for their small infractions with their lives.

"And burning the bodies: this, too, is done by the SS men. They ask me for rubber gloves to perform this task. Dr. Klein has left, after he has ascertained that all two hundred victims have been killed.

"There is no contradiction between the order of Novem-ber 17, which forbids all forms of death by violence, and today's action: today was merely the carrying out of the court-martial's verdict, namely, executing partisans! Who was this Dr. Klein who lived with Capesius in the 'doctors' barracks'? And who supposedly 'shielded him from guilt'?"

Capesius describes Klein in his notes from prison thus: "*Height:* 174 cm, exactly the same size as Mengele, whom many Jews described as tall, because he was slim, whereas Klein was big-boned and bloated from drinking. *Weight:* 85 kg. *Hair:* thick, bristly hair, a crew cut, which Klein tried to comb back, so he used a lot of pomade on it. His hair, and his hairline, too, were very much like Prosecutor Grossman's, likewise the color of his mustache, while his hair was quite gray, though not as gray as my hair is today. *Eyes:* deep-set, small, but alert and shining eyes, with eyebrows like attorney Hummerich's. His eyes were always watering a little. *Nose:* a long, straight nose, but knobby, not red, more liverwurst color. He always wore a pince-nez, like Himmler, but with nickel frames. He always carried a handkerchief folded into a 5 × 10 cm rectan-gle. He never unfolded it, but I noticed he always refolded it so the outside stayed dry, because he used it, not to blow his nose but to dab away the tears. Without removing his glasses he would dab underneath the lenses with the handkerchief and his index finger, every ten or fifteen minutes. [In his crabbed hand: "In the Belsen book, he is just skin and bones"!] *Shoe size:* 41–42, relatively small. He always wore SS boots and woolen underwear, two layers, even, from fall to spring. *Voice:* Klein sang first tenor, and he would sing Hungarian songs dating from his days in the Austrian Imperial army; his voice was as high as Pepi Becker's, who likewise had been an Imperial army volunteer in the First World War and knew all the songs.

"The SS soldiers described him as polite, never or rarely using a harsh tone. Klein always rode a bicycle or drove an ambulance truck, since he couldn't ride a motorcycle. Baretzki recalls that Obersturmführer [first lieutenant] Klein was the only officer who always came to the camp on a bicycle, dismounting and properly showing his ID, even when he was waved through.

"When he was speaking dialect with me, his conversations often began with the exclamation '*Off, Off,*' or '*Vai, Vai,*' or '*Yai, Yai,* Vic.'* Whether he was talking about the harsh German laws with respect to the Jewish question, or about other problems. Klein was fifty-five then and often emphasized that he could be my father, and he did take a fatherly interest in me, although I avoided him because of his drinking schnaps and the aura of Auschwitz around him. I looked for company with the Rump family (Rump was the pharmacist for the town of Auschwitz) or on the Stoffels' estate in the Beskidy mountains, to get away from the concentration camp atmosphere, which had an unambiguous smell when it got foggy in early spring or late fall, even if you didn't see anything in particular in Auschwitz."

Klein seemed to want to continue observing the Hippocratic oath in the beginning. One female inmate-physician even said: "Dr. Klein, an older man, seemed not to know exactly where he was in the first few days. When he entered the

*Transylvanian dialect, meaning sounds of lament. —trans.

block, he introduced himself to me with a handshake, and explained that the conditions in the block were dreadful, and that he would try to get a place for the older sick prisoners, at least, that had more humane conditions." Was that comment reported by the officer who accompanied him? The next day, though he continued to be "polite and accommodating," and was the only SS doctor in the camp who never yelled, he was acting more like an SS man, and he was one of the most unpredictable "selectors" in Auschwitz. But he could be reasoned with; he gave explanations for his actions even to the female inmate doctors. Still, the Viennese prisoner doctor, Ella Lingens, an "Aryan," knew about the relationship between the Gestapo man Draser from Hermannstadt (Sibiu, Romania) and a Jewish woman, but she didn't dare ask Klein for his help to protect the woman. When she asked him how he felt about his Hippocratic oath, Klein supposedly said: "Out of respect for human life I excise an ulcerated appendix; the Jews are the ulcerated appendix in the body of Europe." And once he mercilessly "selected" an orphaned fourteen-year-old Jewish boy with a carbuncle on his neck, and when the boy began to bawl and howl and beg for his life, he just answered that he was not sending him to the gas chamber, but to another hospital "where it's very nice."

His inborn Nazi convictions totally blinded him. And at age fifty-five, he certainly had not needed to volunteer for the SS.

7

In his cell Capesius has great trouble reconstructing his "case"; after all, it is a complex process of remembering, of witnesses' accounts, deeds, dates, but for him it is all about his own little nothingness, his own ego, and saving his life; the millions of dead are just a detail. This pathetic excuse for a human being! The only thing guiding him—this is plain from his whole defense and the trial documentation—is this attempt to extricate himself, to talk himself out of his crimes with lies, inventions, and exculpatory witnesses, if necessary.

A tissue of lies: reset dates, forged stories, and fake alibis, and bribes, too, for the exculpatory witnesses! Over and over again, nothing but dates and numbers for a defense, never an awakening, never any self-reflection: morality, guilt, conscience. Just like Auschwitz itself, a void. Can you learn anything from a void?

This lonely man in his cell, the same thought keeps rising to the surface of his mind: it can't be real, this thing that has happened to him—now the trial is even a greater evil than Auschwitz itself, than the gas, the Zyklon B. He knows that he played a role there, a few times, yes, he knows it must be right, after all, he remembers it—it's just that he can never admit it! It was orders, you do it *automatically . . . you're just a tiny cog in this machine, this giant factory of death*. It's as if he only knows now what had been done: Was it he who had done it, too, or had he been someone else?

And Roland had also said something like that: someone else—not he—had done all that, what he had done, or rather, what had he *had* to do, a split person, an Auschwitz-being. Roland: an Auschwitz-creature. Victor Capesius? They do it, they did it, and even today, they don't know it?

Sure, it's all correct, what the witnesses at the trial had said about him, Capesius remembers that, but he just cannot admit it. Maybe he hears the witness Dov Paisikovic talking, sees it all in front of him like a film:

Fifty-third day of the trial (August 6, 1964). *Presiding judge:* "And where did your transport come from?"

Translator Grünblatt: "Where did you come from?"

Witness Dov Paisikovic: "From Munkács ghetto."

Presiding judge: "Where?"

Translator Grünblatt: "Carpatho-Ukraine."

Presiding judge: "Where did you work?"

Witness Dov Paisikovic: "In the Sonderkommando."

Presiding judge: "And did you once work in the so-called Bunker V?"

Witness Dov Paisikovic: "Yes. Bunker V was more outside of the camp, in the woods."

Presiding judge: "In the woods, toward the woods. And what sort of house was it? Had it been a farmhouse earlier?"

Witness Dov Paisikovic: "Yes, with a straw roof."

Presiding judge: "Straw roofed, a former farmhouse. What did you have to do there? That was not actually a crematorium, so far as I have heard, but actually just a gas chamber, where the people were gassed."

Witness Dov Paisikovic: "We arrived there at the farmhouse. From the front we saw nothing. And then the Hauptscharführer came on a motorcycle and said: 'Here you'll get something to eat, but you'll have to work.' Then we walked around to the other side. And there, we saw Gehenna."

Translator Grünblatt: "Hell."

Witness Dov Paisikovic: "A hell on earth."

Presiding judge: "And just what did you see? What was there?"

Witness Dov Paisikovic: "There we saw pits dug into the ground, around thirty meters long. And in those pits wood was burning, with some kind of accelerant. Not gasoline, something else . . . Wood and something else, gasoline, not gasoline. Naphtha or diesel fuel."

Translator Grünblatt: "Naphtha or petroleum."

Witness Dov Paisikovic: "Kerosene . . ."

·

Witness Filip Müller says: "Women with their kids in the little woods by Crematorium IV. They didn't seem to suspect what was awaiting them. They looked exhausted and only concerned about their children."

In contrast to them, the Sonderkommando inmates were aware of the horrific situation these people were in. Filip Müller, who at this time was working as a stoker in Crematorium IV, described how the victims were kept waiting in these summer days of 1944, often for several hours, waiting for their deaths.

"More than anything else, in that summer heat it was thirst that tormented them and brought many of them to the point of desperation. All they could think about was when they would get something to drink; they seemed incapable of thinking about anything else . . . The people were standing about a hundred meters from the pits. In between there was a screen about ten feet high that blocked their view. In front of them SS sentries were standing with loaded guns, to prevent any of them from coming too close and seeing the inferno through slits in the screen. Behind the screen raged a hellish fire. It flared up into the sky like a huge torch, leaving a gray-black cloud hanging over the countryside, visible from far off.

"The crackling, hissing, sizzling of the fire was the horrible musical accompaniment to this inferno. But these people could never have imagined that the dense smoke and the clouds of ashes that darkened the sun, the huge fire that raged behind the barrier blind, and the sweetish smell penetrating the air came from the incineration of thousands of murdered human beings, who a few hours earlier had suffered the same fate that was now in store for them."

•

Presiding judge: "So you first came to Bunker V and what was your assignment there?"

Witness Dov Paisikovic: "Dragging the bodies to the pits."

Presiding judge: "And then there were others who threw them into the pits. And the bodies were burned in the pits?"

Witness Dov Paisikovic: "Burned."

Presiding judge: "[Pause.] Now, where did you go in the evening when you were done?"

Witness Dov Paisikovic: "At night on the first day we went to Camp D, Block 26. The number was tattooed. From there we went to Block 13."

Presiding judge: "Now, tell us about the people who came together with you. Were they all able to do this? Or were there different ones for whom it was too brutal, some who could not endure it?"

Witness Dov Paisikovic: "There were many who jumped into the pit, who jumped into the fire . . . on purpose."

Presiding judge: "Out of sheer despair at what they had seen?"

Witness Dov Paisikovic: "Yes . . . couldn't go on any-more . . . Many were still alive . . ."

•

Adam: While the pyres burned continuously behind Cremato-rium IV, hundreds of doomed men, women, and children were waiting in front of the extermination site. They were standing or sitting in the little wooded area on the grounds of Crematorium IV. There is horrifying photographic documentation of these vic-tims taken as they waited. In the summer of '44 a member of the SS photographed the arrival of the Hungarian RSHA transports, and of the victims at their different stations. With these pictures he assembled an album of 185 photographs for his own private use. The album was discovered by accident by Lilly Jakob Meier, a Hungarian Jew who herself was deported to Auschwitz, shortly before the end of the war. Now known as The Auschwitz Album of Lilly Jakob-Zelmanovic Meier, *these pictorial documents are among the most important evidence about the deportation and extermination of the Transylvanian and Hungarian Jews.*

Waiting for the gas chamber in the notorious "Little Woods"

It was unimaginable, what my sufferering comrades told me (the words of Morris Kesselman, a colleague of Dov). It was inconceivable what happened there—simply beyond the realm of possibility. Everything was much more horrific there—the SS men would grab the children and throw them alive into the burning pits. The SS men were especially merciless here. It all took place outside, in an open field. There was no pretense of "showers." Most of the people had to undress in the open . . . and then—I saw this myself—the situation got to the point that the children started crying. And so then the SS men grabbed all the children and took them off—to calm things down again, you could say. The mothers could not see what was happening to their children, because the burning trenches were hidden behind the barracks. Then the SS men just threw the children, alive, into the fire.

SS Hauptsturmführer Moll . . . It wasn't enough for him to murder Jewish men, women, and children in the gas chambers . . . He personally took naked women up to the trenches of burning

bodies, so he could see the unfathomable horror in their faces . . .
before he shot them from behind with his pistol and pushed them
into the pit. Some he pushed in alive.

•

Presiding judge: "Yes. And were you also present when the
transports came in and the people were taken into these so-
called changing rooms?"

Witness Dov Paisikovic: "I was there many times."

Presiding judge: "You have said you have no names. How
many people, then, were then taken into the gas chamber?"

Witness Dov Paisikovic: "Approximately three thousand.
But not all at the same time. The undressing room could not
hold so many at once. And they all undressed in there."

Presiding judge [interjecting]: "Yes. And what happened
with the ones who had already been brought into the gas
chamber?"

Witness Dov Paisikovic: "They waited until the others were
finished."

Presiding judge: "And how long did it take, then, until this
gas chamber was completely filled with people?"

Witness Dov Paisikovic: "Two hours, it could have been."

Presiding judge: "And what were the people told was going
to happen to them?"

Witness Dov Paisikovic: "That they would be going into
the baths."

Presiding judge: "They would be going into the baths."

Witness Dov Paisikovic: "Yes."

Presiding judge: "And did they also believe that? Or did
they resist, was there any fighting or any kind of . . ."

Witness Dov Paisikovic: "There were somes cases when people knew something. But mostly they didn't know anything."

Presiding judge: "Yes. And were there also people who did
not want to go in, and who resisted?"

Witness Dov Paisikovic: "Those they pushed in by force."

Presiding judge: "So once they were inside, they must have noticed at least by that time that no bathing was happening here. Or did they still not notice?"

Witness Dov Paisikovic: "No, inside there were these . . ."

Presiding judge [interjecting]: ". . . showers."

Witness Dov Paisikovic: "Yes, these showers. It was set up like that so that when somebody came in, he wouldn't know that this was a gas chamber. It was sort of . . ."

Presiding judge: "And so what approximately was the longest time? At the outside."

Witness Dov Paisikovic: "The longest time—it could have been twenty minutes . . . shorter time—five, six, seven minutes."

Presiding judge: "And then the gas chambers were opened up?"

Witness Dov Paisikovic: "Opened, and the ventilators turned on immediately."

Presiding judge: "Now you say, 'The doctor gave the order.' Did the doctor first ascertain whether the people were dead?"

Witness Dov Paisikovic: "I don't understand."

Translator Grünblatt: "Did the doctor first check to see that all were dead?"

Witness Dov Paisikovic: "No, he didn't have to check. On the door . . . there was a window, and . . . the window, he peeked through it. He just looked. He wasn't in the gas chamber. The man who dumped in the gas was the one wearing a gas mask."

Presiding judge: "Did it sometimes happen that people were not dead after this gassing?"

Witness Dov Paisikovic: "There were many cases of that."

Presiding judge: "And what happened with these people?"

Witness Dov Paisikovic: "They were shot."

Presiding judge: "And who did that?"

Witness Dov Paisikovic: "SS."

Presiding judge: "SS. And you know no one from the SS except for Moll?"

Witness Dov Paisikovic: "Not by name. I know Steinberg by name. And there was another one, whom we called 'Holländer.' I don't know if that was his right name. And there was one other, whom we called 'the Red.' He was all red in his . . . face."

Presiding judge: "And have you also known instances when little children were still brought into the gassing rooms when they were already full?"

Witness Dov Paisikovic: "Yes, children were thrown in, over the heads of everyone."

Presiding judge: "Thrown in over everyone's heads? Have you also seen children being killed in other ways?"

Witness Dov Paisikovic: "Yes."

Presiding judge: "What was done with them?"

Witness Dov Paisikovic: "There were instances where an SS man would take a child from its mother, and give it a piece of sugar or a bonbon, are they called? And then he took the child by the hands. And under the eyes of its mother, he would smash the child against the wall."

Presiding judge: "Under the mother's eyes?"

Witness Dov Paisikovic: "Under the mother's eyes."

Presiding judge: "[Pause.] And so when the people arrived in the transports, how were they unloaded?"

Witness Dov Paisikovic: "On the ramp."

Presiding judge: "Yes. And they went from the ramp onto trucks."

Witness Dov Paisikovic: "Only those who could not walk went on trucks."

Presiding judge: "The ones who couldn't walk."

Witness Dov Paisikovic: "Yes. Old people."

Presiding judge: "And so how were they unloaded from the trucks?"

Witness Dov Paisikovic: "They were, how do you say, dumped out. It was the machine that dumps, that spills things out."

Presiding judge: "Yes, and if the people then held on to the truck, what happened to them then?"

Witness Dov Paisikovic: "They were shot in the hands."

Accessory Prosecutor Ormond: "Sir, you were, as I have heard, present at this trial once earlier, before you were named as a witness. At that time did you recognize anyone among the defendants?"

Translator Grünblatt (Yiddish): "During the trial in Frankfurt before today, have you seen any of these [unintelligible]?"

Witness Dov Paisikovic: "[Pause.] That one over there."

Presiding judge: "Yes, go over there and point him out to us."

Accessory Prosecutor Ormond: "[Pause.] And who is that?"

Witness Dov Paisikovic: [unintelligible]

Accessory Prosecutor Ormond: "Whom else do you recognize? Perhaps the defendants should rise. He doesn't know who is a defendant and who is a defense attorney, your honor."

Presiding judge: "Please do so. [Pause.] The first one? Who is that, then? You don't know. [Pause.] This one, yes."

Speaker (not identified): "Whom?"

Presiding judge: "Capesius. You have recognized the defendant Dr. Capesius. What can you say about him?"

Witness Dov Paisikovic: "He was a doctor and once he came to the crematorium with the Red Cross truck. Then he sent the driver back for another gas canister, because one was missing. It was him: there is absolutely *no chance* that I am mistaken on this."

Defense Attorney Laternser: "Will you describe the incident precisely?"

Witness Dov Paisikovic: "The man came once with the Red Cross truck into the crematorium. And was over on the other side, where the gas chamber was. They threw them in from the other side, not where . . . they threw them in from underneath. The man said: 'Where is the canister? Where is the

Zyklon?' The driver brings one canister. He says: 'Where is the second one?' He says, 'I brought only one.' So he yelled at him and sent him, once more . . . to get a canister."

Presiding judge: "Please. Yes. And then, when he was there and had sent for the second canister, were there people already in the gas chamber, being gassed?"

Witness Dov Paisikovic: "The people were in the gas chamber, not yet gassed."

Presiding judge: "Did he come there alone with the Red Cross truck, with the driver, or were there others there, too?"

Witness Dov Paisikovic: "The SS were there, too. The man, and our Unterscharführer, Steinberg. Unterscharführer Steinberg had the gas mask. And he dumped the gas pellets in."

Presiding judge: "How often did you see Capesius at the crematorium?"

Witness Dov Paisikovic: "Many times."

.

And in his cell in the Hammelgasse prison, Frankfurt, Capesius is reproaching himself for answering the prosecutor's trick question, instead of ignoring it: Had it been one or two or more canisters of Zyklon that he ordered? And had he gone with the ambulance to the gas chambers? He should have said he believed that he had never been there.

8

Capesius in Göppingen: "And I couldn't forget them, those people who had journeyed here from home to accuse me; they were foreigners, they had been bought off, it was a conspiracy, they had to slander me, to make Communist propaganda; otherwise no one would have let them travel anywhere! A Communist plot against me, after all, they all came from the Communist East! I was handed over to them, and they finished me off!"

He started feeling sorry for himself, weepy, as he had as a child. And in school. He was so softhearted and helpful. Even there he had been too good to them. Had helped them . . . yes, there were horrible things there, too . . . "but you couldn't go against the system . . . discipline was the highest value. It was war."

No, but admitting to these horrible things . . . no, never . . . and that scene with Dov, did he remember that? All he answered was, "It makes you want to puke . . ."

•

The pharmacist Prokop: "When I worked in this dispensary, I often observed Victor Capesius going into a room in the cellar of this block with Josef Klehr. Out of curiosity I kept a sharp eye out, and one day I saw that SS Oberscharführer Jurasek went into the room accompanied by Josef Klehr. Jurasek was a

Kurt Jurasek prior to 1945

technical assistant in the dispensary. Through the open door I could see a built-in closet. From their conversation I heard that the key to this closet was kept in the dispensary. When Jurasek went and got the key and opened the closet, I saw him give Josef Klehr a great many canisters. While he did this I heard him say something like: 'It will probably be a larger operation.' Klehr agreed. I immediately realized that Jurasek was handing out the canisters of Zyklon B on orders from Capesius. This suspicion was confirmed later, because on that day approximately 32,000 Hungarian Jews were gassed. [Marginal comment from Capesius, who always had access to the trial documents, even in his cell: *Theoretically sixty cans, that's five boxes. All lies! The record was nine thousand on June 29, 1944!*] It was only later that I heard it had been such a large operation that, owing to lack of space in the incineration ovens, the bodies of the gassed victims were burned in trenches and on pyres. The burning of so many bodies in the open air caused an unpleasant sweetish smell to fill the whole area. So they tried to find a means to neutralize this smell. Jurasek, himself a pharmacist, was assigned to work on this problem. I suspect that he did it on Capesius's order. [Marginal note from Capesius: *Perhaps on orders from Dr. C. since he as a pharmacist would not know such a thing?*] Jurasek asked me, since I was a pharmacist, what naphthalene was used for. I explained to him that it was a substance that could neutralize unpleasant odors indoors and outdoors. After that Jurasek left.

"A few days later he came to my office, with greetings from my friends at the 'Concordia' company in Kattowitz. He brought a truck from there, loaded with naphthalene. [Marginal note from Dr. C.: *Ash doesn't smell!*]

"In the Auschwitz dispensary, the Zyklon B used to be kept by the yellow cupboard. But Capesius once told the inmate pharmacist that he wanted nothing to do with it. And so then the Zyklon was kept down in the cellar along with the phenol that was used to kill prisoners by injection directly into the heart. Stacks of canisters were kept there like harmless canned preserves. And more of them in the old crematorium, too. And in the so-called theater building."

Letter from Victor Capesius to his former colleague, SS pharmacist Gerber [date of letter: ca. June 1960]:

Dear Herr Gerber! I am happy to have found you healthy at last and back with your family. And it's also a very good thing that French laws will protect you from any further persecution, which would have been an injustice in any case . . . Now I am happy to hear that despite all the perils you have come through everything all right. Are you now forty or forty-two years old? I am fifty-three . . .

They are trying to set this up as an Auschwitz show trial, and so they are trying to find 950 people according to the list. If anyone is suspected of having done anything, they will be brought to Frankfurt. Till now they have found twenty-six people in two years; so it appears the investigations may take a very long time. I am the only arrested officer of the rank of Führer from Auschwitz; the other arrestees are of lower rank. Unterscharführer Perry Broad, who back then was in charge of interrogations, is the only arrestee here sending you his greetings, since you were acquainted with him.

The Auschwitz doctors still living, but with unknown addresses, are: Dr. Josef Mengele, Dr. Fischer, Dr. Rohde, and Dr. Weber. Dr. Münch from the hygiene department is living near Munich, and, having been acquitted, is free to practice. The dentists are also all at liberty. I have spoken with Dr. Schatz and Dr. Frank. Forty people were hanged in Auschwitz: doctors, commandants, and Oberscharführers.

Juraszek [correctly: Jurasek] is the only Oberscharführer of our group whose address I know and who is free, although he is being accused of the same things as you and I (Zyklon B and selections). I have testified that only Führers, and not Oberscharführers, and then only doctors, performed the selections.

Walter Berliner, Strauch, and Reichel are dead. Dr. Wirz [correctly: Wirths] hanged himself. Standartenführer Dr. Lolling took poison, Blumenreuther is still living, but will not testify in our favor because of "lack of knowledge."

Unteroffizier Frymann and Rottenführer Dobjansky [correctly: Dobrzanski] have not been found. What I have said about you and me is that when we were off duty we spent time at the home of Armin Rump, the town druggist of Auschwitz, the one who moved from the Bucovina, from Dorna Watra. And that I also had spent weekends with Dr. Schatz visiting the Stoffel Csechischowa farm; the family now lives in Munich.

Prosecuting Attorney Kügler reproaches me, saying it is pointless for me to keep presenting myself as a helpful and decent human being, like when I say that I helped the inmates in every possible way—he says that is not the question here and it won't do me any good. But I am also defending myself because the prosecution has said that I am under suspicion of having killed people of my own free will, that I killed for pleasure, and other base motivations.

Kügler thought I should just concern myself with the specific points of the accusation. I said that I did

Zu Zyklon-B.   - 4 -

KLEHR Josef Chef Desinfektorkommando:

B R E I T W I E S E R Arthur, Johann SS-Rottf. geb 31.7.1906 in
nicht Kleiderkammer   Lemberg, wohnhaft Bad Godesberg, Wörthstr.56 .
                            Gegen 10000 DM frei. War in Polen bis 1959 in
                            Haft. War dort verurteilt u. begnadigt .
solche Aussage nach   Jetzt von Petzold, Schlupper u. dem Apotheker
AU Bemühung   Henry Storch, direkt u. indirekt belastet .
erwiesen   "   "   bestätigt auch dass das Zyklon-B
                            Gas zu keiner Zeit in der Apotheke gelagert wurde.
                      ? Soll als ausgebildeter Desinfektor bei der ersten
                            Vergasung das Gas eingeworfen haben . 3.10.1941

F R A N K E Willi   SS-Uscha Desinfektor bis (Anfang 1943) etwa.
                       16.8.1942. Krankenlager nach Birkenau verlegt, u. dort
                       verh (SDG)

† K O C H Hans   SS-Uscha u. (SDG) Desinfektor u. Kammerjäger .
Peter...AU-Proz.   geb:13.8.1912 in Tangerhütte. Vor dem Krieg
...HW   Hamburg 19. Henriettenstr.19 . Hat mit Theuer
such.und Akte   von Anbeginn teilgenommen . Wurde zu Lebenslang
8256-8349 in Akte   in Krakau verurteilt 22.12.47 . In der Haft gestor...
470 447/53 Urteil
die Urteile Nr 8257-8513

R I E G E N H A G E N Erdmann SS-Rottf. u. Desinfektor bei Verg.
                       belastet. SDG. In Polen laut Golik zu 3-4 Jahren
                       verurteilt, ob noch lebt ? geb:7.1.1901

S C H M U C K E R   SS-Rottf. u. Desinfektor aus
~~S C H M U N T K E R~~ Teplitz-Schönau/O.S. 2388/15 .

† T H E U E R Adolf SS-Uscha. SDG. Desinfektor u. Kammerjäger .
Ortsv-SDG   War 1940-10.1941 im RKB Stammlager u. hat dann
                      mit Koch beide als (Gasmeister) bis 2.November 1944
        (24.)   Vergasungen durchgeführt . geb 20.9.1920 Troppau
                      Sudetenland . Ist tot . (Suicid) in Troppau ...
                      ...

W O S N I T Z K A Georg SS-Rottf. Desinfektor. SDG. ab 1942 bis
                   Ende 2.Nov.44 dabei . geb: 30.8.1911 in (Kattowitz)
                   2388/15 u. 3805/23 belastet. Nicht gefunden .

not feel guilty on any of the points. In fact, if Strauch had not said what he said about Zyklon B in the trial of the doctors, then nothing would have happened.*
In today's questioning Prosecutor Kügler stated that it had been learned I had visited the dentists Dr. Schatz and Dr. Frank even after the war, and that I had not mentioned this in my interrogation. He probably suspects I am hiding something, perhaps that we had divided up the gold from the teeth among us. Dr. Frank did visit me once in Göppingen, but I had never visited him in Auschwitz, although he had lived there with his wife and children in a house, as so many SS comrades did, but I had not socialized with him. The dentist Dr. Willy Schatz, on the other hand, had a good hunting dog, and he was with me several weekends at the Stoffels' place in the Beskidy mountains, fourteen kilometers from Auschwitz, to do some hunting. And in the fall, after September 1, we went on larger shoots with beaters.

Dr. Lolling committed suicide on October 20, 1945, death from poison. And Glücks killed himself the same way on May 5, 1945. I also mentioned him in my cross-examination. I don't know if the court recorder noted these dates down, I couldn't see as she was sitting behind me. In any case, there were no protocols of the testimony distributed. It can be assumed that Ontl did not check with Hermann Langbein, or else he would not have said some things the way he did, he would have been firmer on his chronology.

---

*The inmate pharmacist Strauch, a "friend" of Capesius, had maintained in the Degussa Trial that Zyklon B had been administered by Capesius in the SS dispensary!

Herr Ontl didn't know the name of the inmate pharmacist either, although he had been in Auschwitz since 1942 . . .

Prosecutor Kügler was very displeased with me, not only because I would not acknowledge having taken part in the selections that were ordered . . . Prosecutor Kügler said that they had hoped, if I had admitted that to them, that they would not need to call in the Jewish woman doctor* from Romania. Now they will have to see about getting her to come here, to which I replied nothing. I had disputed many of the charges that they made, and then Prosecutor Vogel got very excited and said I couldn't expect him to take what I said to be the truth. That would mean that the others would just be lying. I said that my witnesses will refute that statement easily; so then Kügler said, So just give us their names now. I said that my attorney thought that could wait until after charges had been brought against me. Kügler then said: But I am not charging you with anything. No, I said, you are just conducting a legal investigation, but to most people that's the same thing, and in all my fifty-three years I had never had the luck to be in court before, which is why I am the layman here. Then Kügler says: Yes, I already know Mr. Eisler is trying to find exculpatory witnesses for you, to which I said: Is that forbidden? No . . .

Point II accuses us of having stored Zyklon B without the proper safety warning elements, and of having dispensed the chemicals each time. The incriminating evidence is based on Strauch's statement in the trial against Sturmbannführer Pflaum, who was

*He was referring to Dr. Gisela Böhm.

the squad leader of the disinfestation and insecticide unit. In this trial, Pflaum was bribed to commit perjury as a favor to Minister Auerbach (who was once Pflaum's prisoner), and said that the dispensary had been using Zyklon B without safety warning elements. (In the trial our names were not mentioned at the time, but three years later, after Strauch's death, it came back to haunt me.)

Pflaum and the camp administration must have had Zyklon B, and they must have been in charge of all the disinfection teams, who would delouse and disinfect the barracks, etc., with Zyklon B, and likewise Unterscharführer Klähr [sic] would have been part of that group. According to Höß's book, the camp administration had gotten the Zyklon B from Dessau. I have stated that Zyklon B was not stored in the dispensary, nor was it administered or handed out by us. Nor were any of us ever in Dessau to get Zyklon B. Pharmacist Szikorzky [correctly: Sikorski] and his acolyte Tadec were here as witnesses for the prosecution, but at least in that regard they acted honorably. Of course, they did state that once in 1941 a can opener for Zyklon B was received in the dispensary, and then picked up at a time when Szikorzky [sic] was the only pharmacist in the Auschwitz camp. Moreover, they said, Jurazek [sic] had a key to the theater building, which I disputed, since nothing we had was ever stored there. I ask you also to answer to this point.

During my first interrogation I stated right at the outset that you, Herr Gerber, only came much later [to the camp] (without any date) and were specifically assigned to the SS dispensary, which was built on the other side of Birkenau, and that you had done a lot of

work on it, when it was bombed out in November
shortly before it was to be put into operation. The only
incriminating thing here is the time period July 1 to
October 15, 1944, the period of the Hungarian
transports, as Hermann Langbein says he saw a table
of duty assignments, in which we are supposedly listed.

Langbein, an Austrian, and Gohlick [correctly:
Golick], a Pole, the two clerks who worked for Dr.
Wirz [correctly: Wirths], in that narrow room by the
dental station, drew up lists of people to be killed by
injection in the infirmaries: Strauch told me this, too,
after the war. According to him, these two old-line
Communists had taken their own people off the list,
and replaced them with Jews who were in the
infirmary, since their numbers had to jibe. So in this
way these two men were sitting in judgment over who
would get exterminated, or be in line for
extermination. If you know anything about this, a
short incriminating statement would be important,
nothing much can happen to them, since
manslaughter has been under the statute of limitations
since June 20, 1960—still, in Frankfurt they would
have less credibility as incriminating witnesses.

> With best wishes,
> Yours,
> Dr. Victor Capesius.

9

From his cell, Capesius gives his wife and his lawyer general directives. And even this rather concrete directive: "Klehr should
be asked by Laternser during the trial: 'In the years when you
were in the disinfection unit, who gave you the various experi-

mental preparations for disinfestation and pest control? Pharmacist Krömer or Dr. Wirths?' Klehr says now, that he got all his orders from Dr. Wirths only, and never from Krömer, says he really never had anything to do with him. So Krömer had nothing to do with Zyklon B either. Only Wirths, or his stooge Ontl, ever had the authority to give orders about the gas! But Langbein would like to cover for Ontl and his boss Dr. Wirths, because he is a friend of the Wirths family, even today."

So it's all about tactics, about the pretense of innocence, not about Auschwitz and his conscience. For Capesius feels absolutely no guilt; his conscience never bothers him. And Adam even believes that about him, he says it is nothing other than *the inability to feel guilt, almost as bad as the crime itself, because it was precisely this inability that made Auschwitz possible in the first place!*

Capesius wrote to his brother-in-law Hellmut, his wife's brother in Vienna, from whom he had received a letter, in which he [Hellmut] said that he, "Vic," was probably guilty in the eyes of men, but innocent before God. Capesius knew exactly what he was referring to, for he roundly cursed the age into which he had been born, thus:

All best wishes, if tardily, for your birthday, and for your anniversary. May it be granted you in your life on earth not to experience a third world war.

With your thoughtful and eloquent words, which moved me to tears, you have brought me great joy here in my cell, but the content was not good for my "censors," since they could infer from it, even if they cannot make any comments, that my nearest relatives have doubts about my innocence in the eyes of men, whereas one's innocence before God is totally irrelevant to the courts. So I beg you, as I also wrote to L . . . , write letters as gushy or as sober as you like,

Handwritten letter from Capesius to his brother-in-law Hellmut about Zyklon B

but no letters about me or my family. I have expressed
this wish often before . . .

Point II of the prosecution case is now finally
negated, as Klehr has turned up here in the prison,
and voluntarily assumed all guilt; thus any accusations
against me involving the administering or dispensing
of Zyklon B for all the transports are void. *Because my
innocence has been proved,* as it has finally come out, I
no longer have anything to do with it. But please keep
even this information strictly to yourself, please don't
tell anyone else, because there is always the risk that I
would then get a letter, and after all I don't know
anything yet officially. Your *Spunemult.**

From Capesius's notes and letters during his incarceration:
Further directives of Dr. Capesius. Capesius often wrote in the
third person, as though he were providing his friends their
witness testimony and their written statements. Here, a letter
to the Stoffels, the couple he often visited on weekends to go
hunting in the Beskidy mountains:

Dr. C. who loved hunting, too, and who took his
German hunting license exam in Oppeln from the
ranger there in early June [June 5?], was a frequent
weekend guest in our home, where apart from hunting
we also spent Sundays enjoying one another's
company and that of friends from neighboring estates.
Particularly after Dr. C. returned from his trip to
Romania, the last week of September [Saturday,
September 23, 1944], we would be hunting every
week, either at our estate, or we would drive to the
neighbors' place and hunt there . . .

*Romanian for "talkalot."

Sometimes Dr. Willy Schatz, a dentist from Hannover, would also come, with his excellent dog, Treff.

Dr. Capesius always stressed how the whole atmosphere of Auschwitz depressed him, as he would sometimes glimpse an arriving train when he went down to the so-called ramp to pick up doctors' valises, and he would make occasional despondent comments about this.

On May 24 there was a particularly devastating air raid on Berlin. That weekend [May 28–30] Victor was with his compatriot, the pharmacist SS Hauptsturmführer Josef Becker, known as Pepi, in the Central Military Hospital in Berlin, and he was able to see the devastation firsthand. On this particular weekend he was talking about it so much that we asked him to keep quiet about it, as we had guests—Frau Rump, three sisters, and my sister-in-law as well—who had all just arrived. Everyone was still in a festive mood, even dancing, despite the rain coming down in sheets; on Monday we all had to leave early with the coach, since making the trip by bicycle was too much to expect even of Victor. It was only for the fall hunt that he came back driving a DKW 100 ccm motorcycle, which had many problems, but still was faster than the bicycle for covering the fourteen-kilometer distance to our place.

We often visited Dr. Capesius in the SS dispensary and we also knew the pharmacist Strauch, his blond assistant, Éva, and Berliner, the bookkeeper. Our dental work was done for us and our Polish employees by Dr. Schatz, and now and then we had prescriptions filled either here or in town. We knew Strauch and

Éva, and the pharmacist Sikorsky [correctly: Sikorski] across the corridor as well, and we often chatted together with them. We always got the impression that they were all happy with their boss. Strauch in particular would sing his praises; he also had access to Victor's correspondence, and his photographs, which he took out of the desk drawer without hesitation and showed to us. We also often brought little packages with us, since, due to his feud with Dr. Wirths, Capesius would only have dinner with Strauch, and we would make sure that Strauch and Éva could also eat with us. A woman known as "The Bible Bee," who was a farmer's wife about fifty years old, would also bring lunch from the Casino.

Herr Lill, who had brought his wife, Lotte, as a nurse with him in the division, had to keep her welfare in mind. At first, everyone said that the Russians behaved normally, and that proved to be true.

In the end Herr Lill sent his wife to Vienna with Dr. Capesius, where she remained until the war ended, that is, till Easter, and then before the Russians arrived she rejoined her husband in the division.

But now it was autumn [1944] and we often took sacks of vegetables, potatoes, and poultry or game with us, some of which Strauch would cook for us, and some of which Dr. C. would send on to Becker in the Central Infirmary, because he thought that would help him get special deliveries of medicines.

Occasionally I would peek into the cook pot at Strauch's, for he could really cook well, especially chicken with rice pilaf. Éva was a friendly creature with blond hair three centimeters long, which later grew into a ponytail, something normally forbidden in the concentration camp: but the others, too, for example the pharmacist Sikorsky, had hair two centimeters long; only Strauch and Berliner were naturally bald.

Everyone gave the impression of being well nourished, everybody was always treated kindly, as his earlier colleagues or my own observations will confirm. About Auschwitz, I would add that we were running the farm property from 1941 on, and beginning in 1942, from the pharmacist Rump's balcony at night, you could see the light of a huge fire burning about four kilometers away, and everyone knew that human beings were being burned here, you could smell it, too, when the wind was blowing in the wrong direction. And we also sometimes heard about people being exterminated.

But it would be quite wrong to say that knowing this situation meant taking part in it, or being able to stop it, for everyone was very careful about what they said out loud, because everything was dangerous.

My aged mother, Armin, generally known as Omi, had conversations with the Polish workers, too, about the resistance movement, etc., and that's how she learned that the officer who came visiting us was in Auschwitz, but that he was good to the prisoners and therefore had nothing to fear from anyone, even when he was alone in the woods.

At the Harvest Festival on October 1, 1944, he danced the obligatory round with all the village beauties, which only underscored his gregarious nature. And he quite liked our Polish manager's daughter.

We also knew the pharmacist Gerhard Gerber, who was a frequent guest at the home of Rump's sister-in-law Adde; at the beginning Dr. C. and Gerber were friends, but this friendship soon cooled. Gerber was raised as a National Socialist, and often could not understand Dr. Capesius or accept everything that he thought was normal; he especially disapproved of Capesius's camaraderie and his lack of distance from the prisoners.

It may be the case that Strauch and Dr. C. got on better because they were closer in age, and so trusted each other more than Dr. C. did Gerber and Jurasek (the SS druggist). The latter we always thought nice and always ready with some amusing observation or other.

We owe Dr. C. a debt of gratitude as well, for in January '45 he constantly urged us to relocate to Bavaria, at least us women. So we prepared ourselves as well as possible, and, on January 15, 1945, in bitter, freezing weather, with two horse-drawn carriages and two Polish drivers, we left the estate and drove westward. At the German-Czech border we sent one of the carriages and both drivers back, and continued with the other carriage to Bad Tölz, where we are still living today. Later my husband turned up here safe and sound as well.

In 1946 [July] Dr. Capesius visited us in Bad Tölz—he had been released by the English earlier. He had been recognized in the Munich railroad station by a barber from Auschwitz and reported to the military police. After seven weeks in prison Dr. C. was sent to Dachau. His photograph was posted everywhere with the words: "Who knows the SS pharmacist Dr. Victor Capesius of Auschwitz, born in Romania, and who can testify about him?" Since there were no incriminating statements made by anyone, in December '46 he was transferred to the camp in Ludwigsburg and released . . .

The letter breaks off here—and it is only a draft; the original was probably sent to the Stoffel family.

This letter is again an attempt to manufacture false documents, tell lies, and come up with false dates for things to exonerate him.

In doing so, Capesius provided quite precise information. He must have gone through mountains of documents; he had long years of confinement in which he could acquire tactical knowledge for his defense in the trial, and then later to ease his own conscience. His pedantic bureaucratic language with its emphasis on numbers only shows how little he had grasped the horror of it all; or, as Adam thinks, he uses these cold facts simply to distance himself from it. The deaths, horror, and suffering all dissolved into nothing but dates, data, numbers, and sums, no longer were they living individuals of flesh and blood, skin, bones and hair, nerves and a heart, no human beings, no destinies, no faces, no suffering. No memories. This is how he talks: "Paula Rosenberg, a sixteen-year-old, arrived at Auschwitz in October '44. She maintains that I, Dr. C., 'selected' her. She had been mistreated in Dr. Clauberg's unit, used for medical experiments. At the trial she had given a memorized recitation in party jargon. There was general agreement not to use her testimony. She didn't even have a prisoner tattoo number!"

INTERROGATION OF WITNESS KARLHEINZ SCHULERY

Witness Karlheinz Schulery: "I myself was a pastor in Romania and graduated from the same school as Victor Capesius. I was several classes after him. I know the Capesius family from Sighişoara, where their family's pharmacy is located. My father-in-law, who became suffragan bishop after the fall of Romania, was the town pastor in Sighişoara. And I myself was very often there, and once in a while had contact with the Capesius family in the pharmacy. I knew Capesius as well, for I spent the last years as an army chaplain, a Lutheran chaplain in the Romanian armed forces, and met him occasionally, in his capacity as a pharmacist in the Romanian army."

Presiding judge: "And what was his rank?"

Witness Karlheinz Schulery: "It was customary in the Romanian army for all pharmacists to be promoted to the rank of captain after their training was complete. Just as it was with us chaplains to be given the rank of captain."

Presiding judge: "Yes. And do you know what became of Dr. Capesius after Romania was occupied by German troops?"

Witness Karlheinz Schulery: "Yes. I do know this much about it, first of all, since the treaty between Romania and Germany under the Antonescu government more or less forced us ethnic Germans to join the German army and leave the Romanian army. We were transferred, as it were. At that time, at the request of several officers, ethnic German officers—if I remember rightly, Capesius was one of them, but I cannot remember all their names—I sent to my corps general to ask if it was possible for us officers at least to remain in the Romanian army, since we were not happy about having to go through training again—I had already incurred a war injury. But it was not possible. I was told that we all had to accommodate ourselves, the Romanian state had to yield to the German state. And so we were all called up to German posts and shipped out. I can even remember the exact day, because the next day my son was born. And I couldn't even get the German duty officers to grant me a few days' leave to be present for the birth. We shipped out on, I think, July 28, 1943.

"In Hermannstadt [present-day Sibiu]. Yes. And I can still remember Capesius there. Because all of us officers got together there discussing the fact that we couldn't stay in the Romanian army. And then we went to Vienna, and were put under guard there, I think in the so-called Arsenal, that's what the place was called, and we were not allowed to leave.

"So then we tried to negotiate with them to put us in the Wehrmacht and not the SS, especially us pastors. But this request was refused, for pastors as well as for other officers. We did manage to achieve one thing, a directive in writing, from the SS higher-ups, which I once held in my hands, that none of us Transylvanians—who were all very attached to our church—could be urged or forced to leave the church. That was the only thing we could get, back in 1943.

"Sometime later I ran into Capesius again, and I can remember him saying he had an assignment that he really wanted to get out of, but that he would not be able to. I can't say anything more specific about it."

Presiding judge: "Do you know anything about the conduct of the defendant Dr. Capesius prior to this time, that is, before he was brought to Vienna? What he had done in his civilian profession?"

Witness Karlheinz Schulery: "You know, this is how it was in Transylvania: back there, the ethnic Germans were a minority. May I perhaps explain things a bit more, to aid in understanding the situation?

"We were a minority, and all the minorities lived as much as possible in their own communities, insulating themselves from everything else. We were, actually, although we're not supposed to say it, an oppressed minority, even as Germans. For instance, my family had had a large country estate, and the Romanian state simply expropriated it after we were ceded from Hungary to Romania, and gave us worthless state currency for it. We were under a lot of pressure; no German could buy a new pharmacy or expand an old one. In many places we were increasingly discriminated against. But that was true for all minorities. It is well known that in Romania, out of seventeen million people, several million were minorities.

"A kind of ethnic national organization was set up by the ethnic German Auxiliary. But Capesius was definitely not part of it. I never saw an article by him in their publications—but I didn't follow them so regularly. I was on the same side as Bishop Glondys, and we were constantly treated with hostility by these people. They wanted to take our church schools away, and eventually they succeeded. I really can't remember, but I can say with the best conscience that I never knew Capesius to be anti-Semitic in anything he wrote or said. In our schools, and even in my own classroom, there were two Jews, and we were friends. But of course later the Jews were bullied around a bit in Romania, I think around '42 or '43, I can't quite remember. And we did not cut off our connections with these families.

"So, I can't imagine him participating in anything anti-Semitic."

10

In Göppingen, many years later, I saw Capesius again, I heard him again. He spoke in a heavy, tedious voice. "Selecting" all those people for death, sending them to their deaths? He had not wanted that, could not understand why all these women and children, babies, even, and so many old people, who all came from Transylvania and spoke Hungarian, and some of whom he knew himself, why they all had to die so horribly! But orders are orders.

Capesius: "Because you have to do everything that you are ordered to do, without protest, just like back home . . . that's what Wirths said to me. He was the highest-ranking of the doctors, the garrison doctor, and he threatened me: In this camp I have special executive authority, he said, I can have anyone shot instantly . . . he could have *me* shot."

Frau Fritzi Capesius: "Yes, because you resisted doing 'selections.'"

Capesius: "Right."

Capesius (comments on this in his notes): "On the first Thursday of the month, at a meeting on the first floor, Dr. Wirz [Wirths] declared that in the future I would also have to take part in ramp duty. I let everyone else leave the room first, and then at the door I said to Dr. Wirz that I couldn't do that, that I was not a doctor, and for that reason I asked to be relieved of that duty. Dr. Wirz's answer was: 'You know, I can have you shot immediately, without a court, for refusing to obey an order. In this concentration camp I have special executive authority!' I went down to the pharmacy in a state of shock, and as I walked in I said to Szikorsky [Sikorski] and Tadec and the rest: 'Now these bastards have even assigned me to duty on the ramp.' It was twelve noon and I went to my barrack, and then right to my compatriot Dr. Fritz Klein, Obersturmführer, who was then fifty-five years old. I told him my problem, he had often talked with me before, when we were alone, about the awful situation here, and then he would sort of groan in the way the farmers back home do, saying *'Vai, vai,'* or *'Off, Off,* Vic, when the Germans are paid back for all the things they are doing here, it will be a dreadful catastrophe.' He knew, not precisely but sort of vaguely that all was not quite right with my family tree, so when he saw my desperation, and when I offered him my *Marketenderware* [troops' supplies, roughly equivalent to PX goods in the American military], he said he was prepared to take over the ramp duty for me, and to try and resolve this with Dr. Wirz, which he then did. He then told me after consulting with Wirz: 'It's not your problem anymore; I will do it for you.' But right around the time this conversation took place, the ramp had become quiet. The Hungarian action was over . . ."

And Capesius showed me a document: it was the testimony from Jurasek, the Oberscharführer, who also worked in the SS dispensary:

"The first Thursday of June 1944, the normal monthly meeting of the doctors in Wirths's office, Dr. C. was also given the order (this was the only time that Dr. C. attended). Just before noon, when the doctors were all streaming out of Dr. Wirths's room (around a dozen), I slipped into the room next door, to avoid having to chat with all of them, and I heard through the partly open door, and amplified by the stovepipe overhead, what Dr. C. said: He could not possibly do ramp duty, he asked to be relieved of that. Dr. Wirths's voice got louder and more excited than usual and then he said, loudly: 'This is insubordination. You know, I could have you shot for that right now . . .' and so from that day on, he and Dr. Wirths were on hostile terms. He was a strange officer in many ways, he had no military training, I often had to explain to him about reporting, saluting, etc., and he would take note of only the most important things. He also told us how in Berlin the SS generals, like Blumenreuther in the Central Military Infirmary, would always wave away salutes, and simply ask, in civilian fashion, how things were going.

"After his contretemps with Dr. Wirths, Dr. C. always had Strauch cook his meals for him. Often Berliner and sometimes Éva ate with him, since they worked in the same office as Strauch. Often during this time—it was the noon break—the door would be locked. Dr. C. brought food from the Csechischowa estate, from his hunting buddy Stoffel. Or sometimes "the Bible Bee" brought his meal from the officers' mess, since Dr. C. had sworn never to set foot there again, since that confrontation with Wirths, and never to attend any official evening functions. And from July on I didn't even get his *Marketenderware* anymore, because Dr. C. had given his coupons to Dr. Klein, his fellow countryman. Back then I did not know how it all hung together, because he never gave me the whole story. Dr. C. probably discussed things more with Strauch and Berliner, because he was more open with prisoners than with members of the SS, and I was after all in the SS. And we SS people never got any of his hunting booty either, while Strauch often would prepare a wild duck or a pheasant or a hare or a goose in a casserole for Dr. C. and two or three prisoners in his room. And it was the same with the SS pharmacist Gerber. He went hunting with Dr. Schatz, the dentist; they would travel to the Beskidy mountains and visit the Stoffels, who sometimes would turn up in the dispensary on a quick visit, mostly to try to schedule a dental appointment with Dr. Schatz."

Capesius: "Yes, this wretched business with Wirths. After my confrontation with him I went right to the telephone and called Pepi Becker . . ."

"He's from Sibiu?"

Capesius: "No, from the Banat. He was an Obersturmbann-führer in Berlin, that is, a lieutenant colonel. And he spoke immediately with the Group Leaders who worked for the head man, the highest-ranking officer in the medical section, who was a big man physically . . .

"I know his name, but I just can't think of it now. Well, he certainly read the riot act to Standartenführer Lolling, the ranking doctor over all the camps. What the heck are you people doing, here comes a pharmacist with experience, he wants to help, to work with you, and you put him in a job that has nothing to do with pharmacology. You get right over there and get the place organized."

"So then he came to Auschwitz . . ."

Frau Fritzi Capesius: "Lolling, or who?"

Capesius: "Yes. And then they summoned me to see Wirths."

Frau Fritzi Capesius: "And Wirths demanded that you do selections, and you resisted, and then he said, 'I can have you shot . . .'"

Capesius: "Yes. And then I didn't have to anymore . . . Klein took over that job for me."

"And Wirths?"

Capesius: "Yes, Dr. Eduard Wirths, thirty-three years old, the garrison doctor, Sturmbannführer, had the real authority in the camp about what the doctors were supposed to do or not do; he lived with Dr. Horst Fischer, who hanged himself later in prison in Kiel; Wirths lived in the 'Villa Haus,' and he drove a new Opel."

•

The witness Josef Glück, a businessman in Haifa, formerly a textile manufacturer in Klausenburg [present-day Cluj, Romania], was deported on May 10, 1944, because he was Jewish, with 2,800 other Jews from Klausenburg. Four hundred of them were selected for work on the ramp by Dr. Victor Capesius, but the others went directly into the gas chamber; the transport had left the rail station in Klausenburg on June 11, going northwest, toward Lemberg [present-day Lviv, Ukraine] and Kattowitz [Katowice, Poland]; in the cattle car, along with Glück, were his wife, his two children, his mother, his sister and her two children, his brother, his mother-in-law, and his sister-in-law.

"You are the only one of all those you have named who survived?" the judge in Frankfurt had asked Josef Glück. "Yes," Josef Glück had answered.

The witness had seen the pharmacist Victor Capesius on the ramp that day at Birkenau, taking part in the selection. The pharmacist just asked whether you wanted to work, yes or no. Whoever said no, he sent to the left, into the gas, the others to the right: they were allowed to live.

In early October 1944 he saw Dr. Capesius again with Dr. Mengele. Mengele had come into Block 11 with three officers, Capesius among them. Jewish boys between sixteen and eighteen years old were housed there. They had all guessed what was in store for them. And attempted to escape. Then the camp leader had them all rounded up with dogs. That was on a Jewish holiday. Two days later the boys were loaded onto a truck and sent to the gas chamber.

"While they were doing it, they were laughing," said Josef Glück. "They probably thought it was funny, seeing the boys cry for their mothers."

The witness is overcome by this memory. Then he reaches into his jacket, pulls a small photograph from his wallet, and stiffly reaching out his arm, hands it to the judge, and exclaims, weeping: "Children slit open their arms and wrote their names in blood on the barracks walls . . . My nephew here, this child, wrote: *Andreas Rapaport—lived sixteen years.*" The boy called out to him still on the truck: "Uncle, I know that I have to die; tell my mother that I was thinking of her till the last moment." "This little boy," said witness Glück from Klausenburg in Transylvania, "this little boy knew that he had to die, but he didn't know that his mother had already been gassed."

Witness Josef Glück then collapsed in the courtroom from exhaustion. Weeping, he sat at his table, in his hand the picture of his nephew Andreas Rapaport—*lived sixteen years.*

"According to the statements given by witness Glück, the defendant Dr. Capesius, together with the SS camp doctor Dr. Mengele, selected around 1,200 Jewish boys from Hungary around the end of August 1944. Among these was a relative of the witness by the name of Andreas Rapaport, who then was about sixteen years old. The children were driven in a truck to the gas chambers." [Das Verfahren: Anklageschrift. *Der 1. Frankfurter Auschwitz-Prozess*, p. 2904.]

Notes of the judge in the Auschwitz Trial—the gassing of children: Josef Glück: "In our section of the camp there were children between sixteen and eighteen in Block 11. They were healthy. I myself was housed in Block 14. At the beginning of October 1944 Dr. Mengele came with the camp head and Dr. Capesius into our section. We were just having roll call. The camp head had two dogs with him. The children from

Block 11 had suspected something, they ran away. The camp head then used the dogs to round the children up. It was on Jewish New Year's. Two days later, then, the trucks came that drove them to the gas chambers."

Presiding judge (to witness Josef Glück): "You have just told us that at this selection first Dr. Mengele was present, and that Dr. Capesius was also there. Now we would be interested to learn a little more. You knew Dr. Capesius from earlier?"

Witness Josef Glück: "Yes."

Presiding judge: "And from Klausenburg?"

Witness Josef Glück: "Yes, I saw him there. Klausenburg was not such a big city that people didn't know each other. And also, he was a sales representative for [unintelligible] IG Farben or for, I don't know, Merck or Hoechst."

Presiding judge: "Yes."

Witness Josef Glück: "And so it wasn't such a big thing to know him."

Presiding judge: "All right then. You saw him there. And did you recognize him then again in person, when you arrived on the ramp?"

Witness Josef Glück: "Yes. Yes. I swear to this. I said to the others: 'This man here is Capesius.' And at first we were happy, because here was a . . ."

Presiding judge: "A man from home."

Witness Josef Glück: "A man from home, someone we knew. But there were some people there who said they did not want to work. He sent those people to the left."

.

Capesius in Göppingen: "Yes, but there were 200,000 or 250,000 who went directly to the gas chamber, they got nothing to eat. And attached to every train there were two cars of foodstuffs that were made available to the camp. This food was not given free to the German population, as someone wanted to put it, here in the trial. Two cars were full of food,

Transportweg :

Karpatho-Ukraine - Kaschau - Presow (Ost-Slovakei) - Muszyna -
- Tarnow - Krakau - Oswiecim .

Transporte aus Siebenbürgen sollten den gleichen Weg nehmen .

Die Züge dürften 3 aus entfernteren Gebieten 4 Tage benötigen .

Seite 113.	23.5.44	Dienstag	, Komitat u. Stadt Munkács gerämt:		
Telegr:212	24.5.	Mittwoch	, bisherige Gesamtzahl		117.082
"	25.5		" "	45 Züge	136.800
Ferenczy	28.5	Sonntag Pfingsten'	2 58. Züge "	60 Züge	184.049
Tele. Veese.	31.5.44	Mittwoch	; (Gend .Marosv.Sachw.2.000.000) R.		204.312
" 226	1.6.	Morgens			217.236
" 232	1.6.	inclusiv	, bisherige Gesamtzahl		236.414
" 238	2.6.	Freitag	"		247.856
" 241	4.6.	Sonntag	"		253.389
" 243	6.6.	Dienstag	, " "		274.949
Ferenczy	7.6.		89 (92) Züge "		275.415
Tele.W.245	8.6	Donnerstag, 94 " Karp.-U.u."Siebenb.abgeschl		289.357	
		Differ.Honvd-Arbeit.auf 310.000,			
	16.6.	Freitag , Zone 1. 2. u. 3 Totalew.			340.162
	6.7.	Donnerstag " 4. mit 41.499			381.661
Ferenczy 14.5. 28.6		28.6. " 129 Züge			380.000
Geh.Ber.306	8.7.	Samstag Zeitp.Horthy-Stop			422.911
Tele. 309	9.7.44				429.028
Ferenczy	9.7.	147 Züge			434.351
Tel. 1927	11.7.44	Zone 1 -5 total gerämt,6 nur Periph.			437.402
Tel.289	30.6.	Beabsichtigte Aktion Budapest unterblieb u.			
		so blieben Familien insgesamt Personen			300.000
		Ausserdem jüngere Männer Honved-Arbeitsd.60- 80.000			

1941 geschätzt 850.000

the Hungarian government was responsible for that, they must have been stuffed full: one car with sides of bacon (Transylvanian *Speck*). Yes, they all came from Transylvania. And smoked split pork. And then beans and peas in sacks, as well, the cars filled to the brim."

"And so they got all that, the prisoners?"

Capesius: "Yes, yes."

Frau Fritzi Capesius: "But that was too little!"

Capesius: "No, for those who worked, it was not too little, because they got two thousand calories, and could get more food on their own. For whenever they found something on the ground or at their work that they could sell, then they sold it to someone on the outside. And the baker, the white-bread baker, he would give them bread and more bread, for gold and diamonds."

"A real black market."

Capesius: "It certainly was."

Excerpt of a letter from Josef Glück to Hermann Langbein in Vienna:

Before the deportation I was living in Klausenburg (Kolozsvár) and I was arrested there in early April 1944 by the Hungarian police. In early May 1944 I was deported to Birkenau, where I was housed in the Gypsy camp (F-Lager). I was trying to work in the womens' camp BII, after my wife was placed in the infirmary there, because she was expecting. After it became known she was expecting twins, there were attempts made to induce an early birth, and so she was placed under observation.

On October 13, 1944, Dr. Mengele and some officers (among them a pharmacist, Dr. Capesius from Segesvár [Schäßburg, Sighişoara]) made an appearance in the womens' camp BII, where these men made a selection. Eighty-five women were sent to the gas chamber. On this occasion, my wife, among others, was sent to the gas chamber.

Notes of an attending judge on the seventy-ninth day of the proceedings (August 20, 1964):

b) Selection of women. Statement of Josef Glück:

"One day, when I was in the infirmary—it was October 13, 1944—to talk with my wife, I heard someone call: 'Dr. Mengele is coming!' Right off I jumped out the window of the barracks, someone shot at me from behind, and I ran away. I returned to my work commando.

"After some time I saw women coming from the infirmary, clad only in a long shirt—there were eighty-five of them. I knew that that meant death, by gas. There were four or five SS men present at this selection: Dr. Mengele, Dr. Capesius, and two or three others. Dr. Capesius did not make the selection, but he was a member of the commission. I saw Dr. Mengele together with Dr. Capesius.

"Signed: Josef Glück."

•

Capesius made notes in his cell during the trial. There is a whole file of his annotations (he showed me the file when I visited him, and gave me some to make copies of). One of them says something like: "Herr Steinacker* should look over what I handed to him on the day after the interrogation of witness Langbein. Notations, which, since they're in my handwriting, could serve as instant proof!" And it goes on repeatedly about this one key date, Pentecost, May 29 and 30, 1944, and then June 1944, when the Hungarian transports arrived

---

*His second defense attorney.

from Transylvania, which represented the lamentable and tragic peak of the extermination program in Auschwitz. Most of the witnesses accuse him of doing ramp duty on these dates. It was then, because of the sheer mass of doomed humanity arriving from Transylvania, that all the doctors, including pharmacists and dentists, and even SS officers had to "perform" duty on the ramp, when the Sonderkommando in the crematoriums was increased from two hundred to eight hundred men, when ten to fifteen thousand human beings were arriving daily, and often far more than nine thousand victims a day were gassed (some Sonderkommando workers even speak of over twenty thousand a day)—at that point, Capesius, too, participated in selections on the ramp.

In his cell, Capesius made tactical annotations on the trial: "As to [the testimony of] Wilhelm Schul and Albert Ehrenfels [Ehrenfeld?], Fräulein Popp and Fritzi should ask, probably at Roysa Royal Cluj if there were any other deportees from that time, like Flechsig and Kloy. If Fräulein Popp could find out, it would be important to know whether they came here [Auschwitz] in May or June, before dawn, and the date, since the prosecution witness Glück changed [the month mentioned in his testimony] from May to June.

"Material on Dr. Klein. There is possibly a book on Bergen-Belsen that pictures Dr. Klein, for Bergen-Belsen is the most photographed concentration camp by Britons and Americans . . . Also, eventually arrange for a visit to Bergen-Belsen.

"September 6, 1960, 11:00 to 1:00, presentation to the court by detective Iring . . . opposite me was Hauptscharführer Ontl, the master sergeant of the infirmary, who reported directly to Dr. Wirtz [Wirths]. Maintains he had little to do with us from '44 on, mainly in order to take over the construction of the SS hospital and to get the Block 1 operational. Gerhard Gerber, SS Obersturmführer and pharmacist, also was involved in this. Ontl maintains the hospital was full at the beginning of

September and bombed (annihilated) at Christmas. Then Ontl testified that there was a list of names in the orderly room across from Dr. Wirtz's room on the first floor, and had always been one. According to Ontl, I had been more or less on probation since 1943 (Kügler was horrified by his witness) and then in 1944 I had been detailed with the two dentists Dr. Frank and Dr. Schatz and the pharmacist Gerber to do ramp duty. In any case, he said, from that date when we were supposed to do it, in summer (the first Thursday of July, he didn't have the date), our four names were certainly listed regularly and we would have been assigned to the duty when the orderly office called. When questioned, though, he could not state that he personally had ever called, or seen me on the ramp, since he had never been there himself. About Obersturmführer Dr. Klein, he at first maintained that he had arrived after me, although I know that I was assigned him because I was his first fellow country-man. Nor did he know that Obersturmführer Dr. Klein had taken over my [ramp] duty. I explained about the *Marketender-ware* and that I had given him all my coupons. Prosecutor Kü-gler then asked: Were you a nonsmoker then, too? To which I replied yes, I had not smoked since the age of fourteen. I had sent Dr. Klein to Dr. Wirtz and they had agreed! Kügler wanted to know how Dr. Klein as my substitute was notified each time. That I didn't know, I said, in any case not by me. To the ques-tion, how did I think that Dr. Klein really had so much time to stand in for me, I stated that in 1944 there were so many doc-tors and professors there for the prisoners, that his assignment as camp doctor was more a formal designation, because he could leave the therapy to be done by a person of the appropri-ate nationality. (No objections were raised to that.) Then they wanted to know further, what rules we were given in those doctors' meetings in Wirtz's room; I knew nothing about it, or whether there were ever discussions about that, and I ex-plained, as Dr. Klein had explained it to me, how he had the

Hungarians on the ramp already sorted out even before they had reached him, by calling out to them in Hungarian: he had the boys over fourteen with their fathers, and girls over fourteen with their mothers, and the younger children with their grandmothers. I didn't say anything about the pregnant women. Kügler said, If that were correct, you could have been done with three thousand people in a half hour, which, after what had been heard, I denied.

"Then they showed around two hundred photo enlargements, about 10 x 15 centimeters, or passport photos, but there were apparently only four taken of the ramp, and with the help of these photos I explained where my bags would have been sitting, and that on the ramp, when people happened to be standing near my bags, I would ask for doctors. I knew, after all, around six thousand of them from Romania; then Kügler said, A lot of your doctors were gassed, to which I said: Not a single one, and no health workers either, if they were wearing an armband."

Capesius suggested to the defense that they adopt this tactic for the trial: He had constantly been confused with Dr. Klein, who had ostensibly taken over his ramp duties for him, and so he forced the court over and over again to refute C.'s thesis. And so, during the trial he lied to back up this sudden inspiration.

Capesius: "I didn't mention Dr. Klein in my first interrogation, because I was afraid of incriminating his daughters in Romania. I only brought Dr. Klein back into play after I was told that it would not matter if I named him."

In private letters he even admits that when he was first arrested in Göppingen he had been in a cell with three "foreigners" and he had "had talks" with them. "The older one knew all the ins and outs of the penal code and always committed only those thefts that got him the least time in jail." Perhaps this man "had even bragged a little bit," it continues, in his slovenly, sometimes barely understandable language, and had permitted these gangsters to talk to him only, "because I wanted to prove my innocence with a witness, that I could walk away free.

"During the time I was imprisoned in the POW camp, camp 2375, until April 17, 1946, some ethnic German prisoners arrived in February or March, Saxons from Transylvania ["Siebenbürger Sachsen"], country boys, who had done duty as guards in Auschwitz and in Bergen-Belsen. They asked everywhere whether anyone knew the druggist of Auschwitz, or if he was perhaps here in the camp. When this group was brought to me, they told me that Obersturmführer Dr. Fritz Klein had been with them in Bergen-Belsen. They had been charged jointly in the Bergen-Belsen trial. Only through his [Klein's] frank and honest statement that in 1944 only doctors had the power of deciding on the ramp, while the other SS men were just used as guards, had he prevented worse things from happening to them. They would be sent to England for two or three years to work on farms. Dr. Klein had given them one assignment: they were to look for Dr. Capesius, the druggist of Auschwitz, his compatriot from Reußmarkt, wherever they went. They were supposed to tell him that he is facing his death calmly, and he is just happy that he, Klein, by his intercession in Auschwitz, was able to shield him, Dr. Capesius, from guilt. Further, they were to inform him that he had run across the pharmacist Éva Citron Bard [who was probably Capesius's mistress] again in Bergen-Belsen. Éva had had typhoid fever, and he had helped her and personally obtained food, medicine, and vitamins for her and so helped her through; in this way, Éva came through the war all right.

"This he had done as a last kindness for Dr. Capesius, because he knew that he surely would have wanted it that way.

"Éva, the former inmate pharmacist, could now testify for Capesius as a witness: he, Dr. Klein, had no more need of witnesses. Éva could now say who Capesius really was.

"Dr. Klein along with Mengele had selected Éva—both parties knew that—since she had been assigned as a new pharmacist straightaway, and a short five weeks after her arrival she was allowed to work in the SS dispensary. A month after that Frau Dr. Böhm and her daughter came to the SS dispensary to pick up medications. And they, too, were helped by Dr. Capesius. Pastor Schulery and the pharmacist Konnerth* can attest to this."

Statements of the witness Dr. Lingens in the Auschwitz Trial concerning the defendant Dr. Capesius: "All I know about Dr. Capesius is that he ran the camp pharmacy. Dr. Klein was then the same age as Dr. Capesius is today. Their faces bear absolutely no resemblance to each other. At that time I saw Dr. Klein often. I can confirm that they are similar in stature. But their facial features are different. Dr. Klein spoke accent-free High German. I did not know that he was from Romania. The language of the two was not similar. Dr. Klein spoke more without accent; Dr. Klein spoke like someone whose mother spoke German. He may even have spoken a little Swabian dialect— he spoke Transylvanian the same way I speak Viennese. But for me, Dr. Capesius sounds like someone who had one parent that spoke Romanian. Dr. Capesius speaks German like a Romanian, more like a foreigner."

•

Capesius tries again to clear himself with tricks: This is what he wrote in his letters to his defense lawyer and to his wife: "Jurasek (the sergeant first class in the dispensary!) should state whether he drove in the medical van with us to Berlin, or has he testified otherwise? Karl Konnerth should try sometime to make a list of the places he was between September 1, '43, and April 1, '44, no signature, just as an aid to my memory.

"The CIBA representative (Fräulein Bostel has his address) should write me a plan for the same period, too, so that I can see how the separate phases of my life fit together. I spent time

*His pharmacist colleague from Transylvania.

with both, with Konnerth and Bostel, at the beginning of my time in the SS, in the Hotel Zentral while our uniforms were being made in Berlin. At the end of October '43 and the first days of November (coming from Dachau: Dr. Stamm!) I was having my last visit with Fritzi, eight days in Sighişoara, I drove out from Dachau and went back there after. But when exactly were we in Warsaw, in the central hospital there (Was it the Uprising!)? I remember the ghetto was shot up so much that not a stone was left standing. The name of the Hauptsturm-führer from Graz that we were with (we were supposed to learn obedience there!) is in the red address book. (Possibly ask Hans Post to visit him and ask him a few questions! That way I would find out more precisely on what date I returned to Dachau for the second time, while Dr. Stamm was off at the front. But please make no mention of the medical experiments there!) It would be good, too, to find out the death date for the pharmacist Krömer, my predecessor in Auschwitz, because everyone gives a different date, and some put his death as early as fall of 1943. Were we one month in Warsaw or six weeks? Where were we for Christmas 1943? But please, only write what people really know exactly!

"Further: In the minutes of the proceedings for the doc-tors' trial, what is said there about Zyklon B and Dr. Brandt?"

Statement of the witness Marianne Adam (November 16, 1964) relating to the defendant Dr. Capesius: "My name is Mari-anne Adam, née Willner, I am forty-one years old, married. Profession: X-ray technologist. I live in Oradea, Transylvania, Romania.

"At the selection there was a broad-shouldered SS officer with a strong face who spoke flawless Hungarian. He was ex-ceptionally friendly, nice, and jovial. He explained to us in Hungarian that whoever felt tired should go over to the other side. There they would find a rest camp. And they would also be able to meet up with the other members of their family whom they had lost. Everything there would be nice and comfortable. At that point, a great many went voluntarily over to this other side. Instinctively I did not go over, although we still did not know anything. But I wanted to stay with my friends. I did not know this SS man. I had never seen him before in my life. From our train car, about fifty persons went into the barrack. One hundred from the car just disappeared. There had been only women in the car."

When asked who that officer had been, the witness answered: "At that time I did not know. But in the prisoners' block I lived together with a young medical student named Lilli Blum. She said to me that the officer in question was from Transylvania, that was why he could speak such good Hungarian, he was a druggist and was named Capesius. Lilli knew that because her father was also a druggist."

Then the witness was led to the middle of the room opposite the defendant. The witness recognized Dr. Capesius immediately.

When asked whether she had seen photographs of the defendant after the war, the witness said: "I did see one picture of him. After the liberation I found my husband. He had been transferred to Sighişoara, to the Müller Sanatorium. My husband worked in this sanatorium. So I went to Sighişoara as well. I volunteered in the sanatorium office. In Sighişoara everybody was already talking about Dr. Capesius having been in Auschwitz. In the sanatorium office I found two interesting documents in a drawer: an SS book and a Romanian military booklet with a photograph, and the signature of a Victor Capesius. I looked at the photograph and said to my husband: This man selected me in Auschwitz. I had thought Dr. Capesius had died, and so I turned the documents over to the appropriate authorities. That was the security police, the Romanian state security authorities in Sighişoara."

Dr. Capesius: "I did not select this lady, because I never selected at all. It is odd that this lady will not say definitely the time of her arrival in Auschwitz. Witness, were you sent to the ghetto in the period between June 30 and July 3?"

Marianne Adam: "Much earlier."

Dr. Capesius: "If this date is correct, then your transport occurred in a time when I was in Romania, to visit my family."

•

Statement of the witness Salomon, née Böhm [relating to the Defendant Capesius]: "My first name is Ella. I am forty-four years old, married, a professor by vocation. I live in Odorhei, Romania.

"At the end of May 1944 we arrived at Auschwitz in a train transport, it may have been the thirtieth or the thirty-first of May, perhaps even the twenty-ninth of May 1944. We came from the ghetto near Odorhei.

"I already knew Dr. Capesius before our arrest. My father had called me into his medical office and told me that a kindly pharmacist was there and he wanted to give me a present. I saw Dr. Capesius then again in Auschwitz."

Prosecutor Kügler, on the 162nd day of the proceedings (May 24, 1965), on the case of the defendant Dr. Victor Capesius, said this: "The unique and monstrous part of this situation for Capesius was that it wasn't just about the nameless masses, but that all of a sudden he was confronted with people whom he had earlier known personally or professionally, people who were completely unsuspecting, who saw in meeting him a lucky sign, and trusted him. What kind of a human being must this Dr. Capesius be, who—knowing that those he directed to the left with a wave of his hand had only one or two more hours to live—with a friendly smile and a few calming, reassuring words, sent the families of his old friends and business colleagues, their wives and children, to their deaths?

"How much emotional brutality, what diabolical sadism, what pitiless cynicism must it take to act in the way that this monster acted! And to think it would only have cost him, this Hauptsturmführer of the SS, literally a word, only a gesture, to give these few people their lives, these few who hardly mattered against that great mass of people. Not only did he not do that, but, on the contrary, he also lured these unsuspecting innocents into climbing onto those trucks, which meant death, with false, lying words—this is so incomprehensible that expressions like 'diabolical,' or 'satanic' are much too weak for such deeds. The intensity of will of the perpetrator can be judged from the statements of these three women."

Vera Alexander: "Capesius once visited our block doctor, Frau Dr. Böhm. He said to me, if I felt sick, he could bring me into a rest camp. By then I knew what that meant, and I said I wasn't as sick as that."

Magda Szabó: "On arrival, the officer said that the camp was still far off. The older people, the sick, the weak, and children should ride. He spoke very beautifully, in Hungarian, even. He had a broad face. It was Capesius. You don't forget a face like that easily."

Marianne Adam: "When we arrived in June '44 and were assembled in rows of five, a broad-shouldered, strong SS officer with pronounced cheekbones was standing there, who was friendly and charming. He was cheery, laughed, acted jovial and good-natured. He spoke extraordinarily good Hungarian. Whoever was tired, should go over to the other side. There was a rest camp there. Everything there was nice and comfortable. We could meet our relatives there again. Many friends went. I did not, instinctively. I wanted to stay with my friends on the other side. Around a hundred of the women thus went to their deaths."

The prosecutor closed his plea with these words: "And we live in the Federal Republic of Germany, which no longer allows the death penalty, although a large number of these defendants—I am firmly convinced of this—would have deserved the death penalty. The absolute penalty that the German penal code allows for in the case of murder—lifelong incarceration—should at least be applied to those defendants found guilty of perpetrating these crimes. Perhaps the time in prison will bring about a miracle, and cause the defendants to reflect, to look inside themselves and to shake their consciences, these

Kripo
Ffm
2087
/ 60

consciences of which, up to now, we have seen not a trace. Perhaps then the defendants will come to realize the difference between a state based on law and a state based on crime, and to compare their fate with the fate they prepared for their unlucky victims. One thing they will have to say to themselves: they have no claim to clemency according to the laws of this state, nor should they expect any. For in their case, mercy would be out of place. Prosecutor Grossman began his introductory plea with the words of the President of our Republic [Heinrich Lübke]. May I close my plea with the words of another head of state, the late French

Victor Capesius, Frankfurt am Main, 1960

President Auriol: 'We are willing to forget, if the Germans are willing not to forget.'"

Adam: The unique thing in all of Auschwitz was that Capesius met so many acquaintances on the ramp, not just doctors and pharmaceutical colleagues with their families, for whom, with Klein and Mengele, he was the angel of death, and yet neither in that decisive moment nor afterward was there any awareness that he was committing a crime; there is not a trace of any conflict of conscience.

But Capesius was also Mengele's mouthpiece, he translated and told the victims in Hungarian what to do. It is unbelievable how he tried to turn all that to his advantage in the trial.

•

Capesius maintained in the trial that he was not in the camp on July 3 and 4, 1944, but on the Stoffel estate in the Beskidy mountains. They were old acquaintances from Bucharest, and like a few other ethnic German Romanians, and like the former *Volk* Group Leader (a cavalry captain), Fabritius, they had been allocated an estate in the Beskidy mountains.

Statement of the witness Stoffel (January 7, 1965): "After I was moved out of Romania I was given an estate, in October 1943, fourteen kilometers from Auschwitz. In April 1944 I learned from the pharmacist Rump in Auschwitz that Capesius was here. Shortly after that I met Dr. Capesius in the Rumps' home. About a week before my birthday we arranged for Dr. Capesius to come visit us in the Beskidy mountains for my birthday. My birthday is June 7. The birthday was celebrated on a Saturday after June 7, 1944.

"Dr. Capesius then came often to visit us for the weekend. He almost always spent the night. He came either with the train or on his little motorcycle. He probably spent the night after my birthday party. I don't remember the first time he spent the night.

"I definitely arranged for Dr. Capesius to go back to

Auschwitz in my coach once or twice. But I don't think he ever came from Auschwitz with the coach."

On further questioning the witness said that he had been sought by the defendant Capesius's brother-in-law, a man named Eisler. At first he stated that he had only met Eisler once, in the railway station restaurant. But after his wife's interrogation he then conceded that Eisler had also been in their home, and that he had met him another time hunting in Austria, on land leased by Dr. Capesius. This had slipped his mind earlier. After he had reviewed the events of that time with his wife, for several weeks, he wrote a six-page report about them.

Notation: The witness was sworn in.

Statement of the witness Hildegard Stoffel (January 7, 1965):

Accessory Prosecutor Ormond: "When I asked you earlier, Frau Stoffel, if you had talked about Auschwitz with Capesius, you said, 'Not I.' Who, then?"

Witness Hildegard Stoffel: "Yes, well, I don't know to what extent he talked about that with my husband. You must remember, on a big estate where there is so much to do, and for me it was completely new, I had so much in the kitchen and all the rest to do, that I never had much time to just relax with the many guests that we always had around. Weekends in particular, we had so many guests, fourteen or sixteen people at the table, a housewife just doesn't have time to amuse herself.

"And in any case I am always reluctant to have upsetting conversations like that, since we had already gone through so much that was upsetting—the bombs in Weimar, too, and then all the difficulties with the partisan attacks on the estate— that I was always happy not to have to listen to such upsetting topics."

Accessory Prosecutor Ormond: "Frau Stoffel, you say that you often had fourteen to sixteen guests for the weekend, as I understand."

Witness Hildegard Stoffel: "Yes, Yes."

Accessory Prosecutor Ormond: "Can you remember then with such exactness, if you had such a large number of guests, that Capesius was there regularly, too?"

Witness Hildegard Stoffel: "Yes, absolutely, because mostly he came on Saturday, and in the beginning he was always alone. The others, they never came until Sunday morning."

Accessory Prosecutor Ormond: "And when did he go back again?"

Witness Hildegard Stoffel: "He never left until Sunday evening."

Accessory Prosecutor Ormond: "So it was usually the one night from Saturday to Sunday."

Witness Hildegard Stoffel: "Yes, and then I was particularly happy about him, a compatriot of mine, since, you have to remember, I was the only person for miles around from Transylvania. And when you have someone from home around, someone you can speak a word or two with in the old home dialect, when you are so far from home, you don't forget that."

Accessory Prosecutor Ormond: "Were you yourself ever in the concentration camp at Auschwitz, or near it?"

Witness Hildegard Stoffel: "Yes, I was there several times. In the town next to us we had a little dentist, a Pole. I had my teeth fixed there, too. But since my legs were always swollen and no one knew what the problem was, I said to Dr. Capesius that I thought I should visit the dental office in Auschwitz, you know, that department, or the head dentist, I don't know what he was then, this Dr. Schatz, and have him look at me and make an X-ray of my teeth. So I was in the office several times. I had some teeth pulled and also had a small denture made. The Polish dentist couldn't do any of that for me. And it also seems to have been successful, for my problem with swollen legs stopped, or the problem subsided. So I was there a few times."

Accessory Prosecutor Raabe: "How many times, would you say?"

Witness Hildegard Stoffel: "I can't tell you exactly. Four or five times, or maybe even six times in all, that I was there."

Accessory Prosecutor Raabe: "Frau Stoffel, did you not find what you saw there especially upsetting—the prisoners walking around, the barbed wire?"

Witness Hildegard Stoffel: "No, I must tell you, when I received this summons I tried to remember. And I also saw on television that you had been there. The entrance, where I used to go in . . . that was all very nice. There were flowers planted, there were nice, clean barracks. I can't remember now whether the dental department was a solid building or was it . . ."

Accessory Prosecutor Raabe [interrupting]: "Did you see the barbed wire?"

Witness Hildegard Stoffel: "Yes, I saw it. I had already seen it when I came in with the coach."

Accessory Prosecutor Raabe: "Yes, now, didn't it make an impression on you, those overhanging concrete pillars with these huge tangles of barbed wire, and the high-tension wires—or you could at least see that they were electrified—and the starving prisoners behind them?"

Witness Hildegard Stoffel: "No, I saw no prisoners."

Accessory Prosecutor Raabe: "You saw no prisoners at all?"

Witness Hildegard Stoffel: "No, no, no. I saw none. But in the dispensary where Dr. Capesius worked, I saw many prisoners. There was also Dr. Straub—my husband calls him Strauch, I think his name was Straub. And there was another pharmacist—was he from Berlin, or was his name Berliner, I don't know. And there was a young woman, she came from my country, it was very near to my hometown. Evi she called herself. And there was another young man . . ."

Presiding judge [interrupting]: "So, the entire staff working in the dispensary and in the dentist's office, you saw all of them?"

Witness Hildegard Stoffel: "Yes."

Presiding judge: "And did you want to tell us something more?"

Witness Hildegard Stoffel: "Yes, those people didn't look like prisoners. They were well nourished, well dressed, always very positive and happy. So I didn't see anything bad about their environment, at least in the dentistry office. There were a great many chairs lined up, and there were a lot of prisoners working as dentists or assistants. I don't now remember what their actual professions were. They all looked very good and they all worked well together, on me, too. I was never actually . . ."

Presiding judge [interrupting]: "Like the German dentists . . ."

Witness Hildegard Stoffel [interrupting]: ". . . treated by Dr. Schatz."

Accessory Prosecutor Raabe: "Frau Stoffel, did your husband and your son go hunting with Herr Eisler?"

Witness Hildegard Stoffel: "Yes, they did."

Accessory Prosecutor Raabe: "How often?"

Witness Hildegard Stoffel: "Once. For five days, I think it was, or six. They went with Herr Eisler. Eisler was visiting us, maybe three or four years ago. He was in our home. He brought my husband and my son an invitation to go hunting. Both of them then went to Austria. My husband knew Eisler. In our house nothing was said about Auschwitz. But Eisler did tell us that Dr. Capesius was in prison awaiting trial.

"Eisler said to my husband that it would be good if he would try to remember and get down in writing everything that happened then. So then we tried together—my husband and I—to put something down in writing."

Later Frau Stoffel explained further: "The letter my husband wrote and gave to Eisler had been written before they went hunting. We wrote that letter during the Easter vacation. That was before the time Eisler visited us in our home."

Prosecutor Kügler: "Yes, sure. Fine, I wanted to hear it from you. And who did this hunting preserve belong to?"

Witness Hans Stoffel: "It was leased by Dr. Capesius, people said."

Prosecutor Vogel: "After this account I would like to ask the witness again: Could it be that the story about the hunt and the possibility of going hunting for several days was connected by Herr Eisler with his request for you to write some kind of confirmation for Dr. Capesius?"

Witness Hans Stoffel: "In no way. I would never have let myself in for that. That would have been bribery, really."

Prosecutor Vogel [interrupting]: "So on this point, you think, your memory is quite reliable?"

Witness Hans Stoffel: "One hundred percent."

Prosecutor Vogel: "Good."

Witness Hans Stoffel: "Because personally I have no interest in hunting. In retrospect, after the conversation, it was just my son who was interested in going hunting, not me."

•

The prosecution places the following into the record in the Auschwitz Trial on the 162nd day of the proceedings (May 24, 1965): "If earlier we said that the defendants, while not comprising a sworn conspiracy, were still a secret and mendacious community, then we should not neglect to mention the chief representative of this way of thinking, the defendant Capesius. As the only SS Sturmbannführer he is not just the highest-ranking of the defendants, but he also exercises considerable influence on them, and is essentially himself responsible for the defendants' refusal to incriminate one another. The only one of them to free himself to some extent from this arrangement in the past few months is the defendant Baretzki. On the other hand, defendant Kaduk, for example, with whom the idea of unconditional obedience is particularly deep-seated, has been unable up to the present day to bring himself to break the wall of silence, and to pierce the web of lies of his superior, the accused SS Führer, despite some initial attempts. If one day he comes to the insight that he has thus squandered his only chance for a pardon, by then it will be too late. But back to Capesius, who—and this is what is remarkable—even from his jail cell radiates an evil, demonic influence on those around him—yes, even extending to the outside world in the person of the oft-mentioned Herr Eisler. His powerful position is made even stronger by the large sums of money at his disposal. Where does this money come from, which has enabled Capesius, a 'refugee' driven from his homeland, after working as a pharmacist for only three years starting in 1950, to construct a life for himself, which must be considered remarkable even in *Wirtschafts wunderland* Germany, the land of the economic miracle?"

Why is it that all of a sudden I have sympathy for Capesius, when I now read the letter he wrote from prison to his wife: "To see the doctor in the clinic I was bound hand and foot in heavy chains, orders from above . . . If the itching hadn't been bothering me so much, I would have declined this appointment. Ostensibly they were being so severe because they were afraid I might escape."

And he asked his attorney Laternser to free him from the torture of solitary confinement: "Arrange for me at least to take walks in the prison yard with Hermann Krumey and Naischmacher, so I can have someone to talk to."

The first shock had been his arrest on the street on that December 12, 1959, outside his pharmacy in Göppingen, then "being transferred by express train with two plainclothes detectives." And then "on the very day I arrived in jail, being faced with former prisoners. Etc." Etc.? What did he feel, on seeing his victims again for the first time? (The dead, who had not survived the ramp, he could not see again: there were thousands of them!) But no, he even says, he had communicated better with them (including the dead?) than with the SS officers, and in all its absurdity, this is probably true. Just the fact that he spoke Hungarian with them gave things an aura of hominess and familiarity. Not to mention his pharmacist colleagues and doctors. A sort of friendship had developed with the former pharmacist inmate Dr. Strauch from the Auschwitz dispensary, and even after 1945 the two kept up an active correspondence. But after his "transfer" in December 1959, he had only "solitary confinement, solitary walks in the yard, or with snitches and spies." For four long years at night the ceiling lights, as bright as day, were turned on from outside by a loud switch, since "allegedly he was on suicide watch," and then after falling asleep, waking up in a panic almost every hour—"year after year, that ruins your nerves."

Capesius was incarcerated twice, in 1945/46 as a British POW in Neuengamme concentration camp, and, after being reported by a former prisoner, in the former concentration camp at Dachau. He was known since 1959 to the Zentralstelle Ludwigsburg, the federal agency charged with documenting and investigating claims involving Nazi crimes, and he was brought in several times for questioning about Auschwitz, and by the police. No, he did not go into hiding, not Capesius. He always registered himself under his full name, and lived and worked as an "innocent" man, which he considered himself to be; even his service rank and his camp activities were known to the police.

In Göppingen, Capesius showed me the verdict of the denazification court in Stuttgart, Seestrasse 1, made on October 9, 1947, document ID#37/40644 Pal/Häb, which certifies him as not guilty and not incriminated: "The person in question" has proven "by presenting forms of evidence" that he was "forcibly called up into the Waffen-SS," and thus the court has come to the realization that he cannot be considered a member of a criminal organization. Nor was he suitable for membership in the SS, since he was categorized "racially as a type III" (eastern type). He was even a "council member of the church parish of Reußmarkt." He has also presented definite proof that the ethnic Germans from Romania, as the result of the two-state treaty between the government of the German Reich and the government of the kingdom of Romania, were forcibly drafted.

Moreover, he was "not active in the SS, not in the secret field police or border police," but "only" worked in the "health service," in the "Zentralsanitätslager" (central medic camp) in Berlin. His assignment was "the preparation of medications for the individual troop units: in daytime he oversaw his duties according to regulations, as in a commercial business, and he stopped work at fixed, specified times each day." Even his promotion to Sturmbannführer was only a "consolation prize for leaving his homeland." And, "according to the Information in the Document Center he was never a member of the Nazi party.

"Thus the person in question has refuted the allegation of Article 6 cited against him that he is one of the chief offenders. The court has for this reason come to the conclusion that the person in question has not incriminated himself with respect to the law."

Thus, the secretiveness and periphrastic hedging of the Nazis, for whom Auschwitz never existed at all, was of use to all the perpetrators of the camp. In the military pay book of the "druggist of Auschwitz" was this entry on August 16, 1943: "Now assigned as a replacement troop unit, garrisoned at the Zentralsanitätslager (central medic camp) for the Reich-SS medical staff and the police of Berlin-Lichtenberg."

Victor Capesius had to live alone, without his wife and three children, for the Iron Curtain divided them; he could not go back home, either: a court in Klausenburg had sentenced him to death in absentia. Going home: impossible. Homesickness: unbearable.

As Romanian German families began to find one another again after the war, especially those fathers, brothers, uncles, cousins, and other relatives who had been demobilized from the military or the SS, or returned from captivity, Capesius was by then already in Göppingen, West Germany, where he owned a pharmacy, a showy house, a cosmetic salon in Reutlingen. Where did he get the money from?

In the Auschwitz Trial, the prosecutor accused him of the following:

1. In Göppingen he converted, at considerable expense, a butcher shop into a modern pharmacy, and he received a license to operate the pharmacy, and at the beginning of October 1950 he opened up the "Marktapotheke," an excellently equipped pharmacy.
2. Additionally he operates a large, modern cosmetic salon in Reutlingen.
3. He was able to buy a comfortable condominium apartment.
4. In Styria, Austria, he leased an expensive hunting preserve.
5. He took part in so-called hunting safaris in Africa.
6. The oft-mentioned Herr Eisler traveled through Germany at Capesius's expense and, in a very unusual fashion, at least unusual in Germany, induced or tried to induce former Auschwitz prisoners and SS members as well as others (eight are known to these proceedings alone) to make statements exonerating him. You will recall that the witness Wörl testified in his statement that there was plenty of money available for such purposes, and that the sum of fifty thousand deutschmarks was mentioned in this connection.

7. Capesius was the only defendant in a position to afford a defense lawyer of his choice, and to pay him.

"The statements that I will now cite prove the extent to which Capesius systematically and ruthlessly took advantage of the situation in Auschwitz, will show that he purposefully pursued his own material interests, and will show how he was guilty, not of robbery or of extortion—for the people whose property he appropriated were already dead—but rather how he perpetrated this particularly hideous form of looting the dead.

"These statements will prove that the accused, Capesius, had a highly personal stake in remaining at Auschwitz and in the continuation of the murderous events there, a fact that legally is highly significant, and reveals the true intentions of the accused. At one point in his report, Broad mentioned the very widespread custom in Auschwitz with respect to the valuables confiscated from prisoners on their delivery to the camp: some people would set them aside as a kind of old-age insurance for themselves. But according to what we have heard, none of the accused persons indulged in this practice to such an extent, with such business-like efficiency, and as unscrupulously as did Capesius. Specifically: 'The prosecutor cites the witness Prokop and the matter of the luggage and gold dental prostheses in the attic of the pharmacy. And that he threatened him to say nothing about it: "Prokop, you know why you are here. Sooner or later you will be a candidate for death. If you ever mention a word about this, then that time can arrive before you expect it. I hope you have understood me correctly."' The witness, who sorted the false teeth from the trunks for Dr. Capesius, melted them down in the crematorium, and turned over the result, a lump of gold weighing seven hundred grams, to him, maintains that Capesius 'organized' the gold for himself. And the witness Szewczyk knew that the prisoner Sulikowski sorted the suitcases that Capesius brought back from the ramp, and was forced to give him the

money (dollars and other money in foreign currencies). And the
witness Wörl, who knew that diamonds were hidden in the prisoners' medications, said: 'The valuables were much more important to Capesius than the life of the prisoners.' Strauch said to
Wörl that he couldn't give out any of them, since the medications had been all rummaged through and ruined in the search
for jewels. And finally, Broad: 'Capesius was well known as an
"organizer" and sent packages to his sister in Vienna.' "

By 1956, Capesius had already petitioned the Red Cross to
get his three children out of Romania, and had probably invested quite a lot of money in the "family buyback" program
from the "red" state, which was common then. So in the fall of
1962 his youngest daughter arrived in Göppingen with a legal
passport; in the fall of 1963 his wife and second daughter; and in
October of 1964 his third daughter. But he could not pick them
up at the airport and embrace them in freedom; he had been sitting in a cell in the Hammelgasse, Frankfurt, since 1959.

From Dachau, where he was assigned in November 1943,
prior to Auschwitz, he went on an eight-day leave to pay a last
visit home, as he said himself in Göppingen: "In the Dachau
concentration camp, there was this Hauptsturmführer Stamm,
a sensible man, whom I was supposed to train under. I liked it
there." After he arrived in Berlin in the summer of 1943, things
got even better for him, he said, but this was probably a lie to
confuse people, because in all probability he came to Auschwitz
not in February 1944 but as early as fall 1943: "Because the SS
tailor shop had been bombed, we waited around six weeks for
our uniforms to be finished at the police tailors. A very pleasant
six weeks in civilian clothes, lots of theater and cabaret. And we
lived in the Hotel Zentral with its enclosed garden." Capesius
was there with Pepi Becker, a cunning ethnic German from the
Banat who was good at finagling things, so later he didn't end
up in Auschwitz or at the front, but stayed on in Berlin in a
cushy job in the central infirmary.

Capesius: "After we got our uniforms, we were scattered to the four winds."

How did this unwitting criminal, this seemingly normal Babbitt, father, husband, pharmacist, and SS captain manage his career after that?

Dachau was, in his view, "well run": the men would march off to work with their spades on their shoulders, singing "We Are the Peat-Bog Soldiers."* Of course, eventually, little by little, things changed, and his undoing at Auschwitz inched closer and closer, for Capesius was "useful," and he was "needed"; he had, without noticing it, put his free will "in cold storage," and simply cooperated and went along: "Later I was assigned to the main military infirmary in Warsaw, where I was with twelve other Romanians. They were supposed to give us lectures and demonstrations there, to give us that German polish. And absolute obedience to orders . . . Four to six weeks later we went back to the Waffen-SS infirmary in Berlin, and I was once again detailed to Dachau—to Stamm's department, and was supposed to cover for him while he did his obligatory time at the front. But then I got transferred again out of Dachau, before his return, and had to report to SS Group Leader Blumenreuther: the week prior to that I spent in Vienna with my wife's family. When I reported for duty, I was sent off to Standartenführer Lolling in Oranienburg [actually Sachsenhausen concentration camp]—I was to replace a pharmacist colleague who had become ill. Dr. Lolling gave me my marching orders to Auschwitz, where I was to replace the ailing pharmacist Krömer in the SS dispensary; I thought it would be like an SS infirmary, like in Dachau, where I had been living."

---

*"Wir Sind die Moorsoldaten" was originally composed and sung by early Nazi resisters in camps; it spread to Republican Spain, and has become a protest song in many different countries up to the present day. —trans.

11

Roland belongs in the Innsbruck landscape, the mountain panorama, he fits well with Trenker & Co.,* Tyrolean hats, chalets, and yodelers. It's just that his calm, unhurried voice doesn't quite fit, quiet, charming, gentle, and reassuring though it may be: there is a coldness in those fish eyes of his, and in that knowing laugh he lets out after quoting a Hölderlin poem. There is an awareness of the thin ice we are standing on: that laugh sounds almost obscene after the poem, and yet naïve, and gentle, in a horrible way. On top of that, his verve, his weird enthusiasm, a propensity to get caught up in his own excitement, to drown out everyone else. He sits there in his apartment with its cheap plastic curtains and reproduction furniture, his lips pursed as if to whistle, but with a froglike, lecherous aspect, pink and soft, but full of knowing, deliberate deceit: that grin we know so well, and yet it's so alien, so infinitely strange, as if we had dissected ourselves and were looking at our insides, our very guts: we, too, helpless, mercilessly given over to death. And at the mercy of someone familiar, whom we suddenly see as an unfeeling executioner, providing us the proof that nothing can exist except us, this clot of flesh and blood, our consciousness an ephemeral watery bubble, nothing, to be chopped off with the head.

"But we had to go along"—I hear his voice—"there was no other way. Listen, I enlisted, naturally, I deserted from one army to another . . . In '41 in the second Thousand Man Campaign [after the German-Romanian treaty that co-opted the Romanian armed forces into the German Wehrmacht and the SS] while on break from my Romanian studies I sneaked over the border in disguise and joined the SS; in a camouflaged truck, we joined up

---

*Maker of traditional Alpine folk costumes. —trans.

with the 'Das Reich' division that was returning from the
Serbian campaign. In Temesvar [Timişoara] we even did guard
duty in our civvies for the German Army, guarding a German
prison camp, and with German guns, we were relieving our
German comrades, because they were undermanned. But back
then everything was all mixed up, and we Transylvanians were
kind of a state within a state . . .

"Even as a young man I came upon my grandfather Michael's patriotic poems about Germany, which struck a very
responsive chord in me. We Transylvanians were always *pru-
dentis* [*sic*] *et circumspecti*, you know. You know? That's how
we're known in history. But in an instant, in 1940, it was no
more, we were all caught up in the excitement . . ."

"Yes, even in Auschwitz, it was mostly ethnic Germans," I
interjected.

"Nearly all, yes, nearly all! And the SS was one third ethnic
Germans, anyway, one third was other Europeans. And only one
third were Germans from the Reich, by the end of the war . . ."

"Amazing . . . I didn't know that . . ."

"The guards were a pretty mixed bag. Besides the hard
core of the guards, the old 'barbed-wire fighters,' as they once
jokingly called themselves, an ever-larger number of ethnic
Germans came to Auschwitz (there were around 350 Romanian Germans in Auschwitz). In the final phase, you saw many
uniforms other than SS uniforms.

"When I was with the SS outside Moscow in 1941, my fin-
gertips got shot off, so I couldn't play the piano anymore; since
I was then unfit for front duty, I was transferred to Auschwitz."

I had set the microphone on the table, Roland sat in front
of me, and he started talking in a rushed, hysterical way; I
could hardly get him to slow down; I got the feeling he just
needed to "free" himself through talk. He said, "You know,
that I was THERE? The worst day of the whole time THERE
was May 29, 1944, the first day of Pentecost," he said, without

looking at me: "Pentecost, my men were up there in the tallest watchtower in Birkenau . . . My guard company had to do watch duty very often in those days . . . ramp duty, too . . . walk the people selected to the gas chamber . . . and in the crematoriums. Very tough duty. Since mid-May, trains were constantly arriving, they came day and night. All the trains drove under the main tower of Birkenau. Hmm? All the trains had cars sealed shut, with bars in the windows. Hmm? So, every train drove through an endless tunnel into Birkenau. They didn't know where they were going. Also Frau Dr. Böhm, yes, and her daughter Ella arrived on that day. In one of those cattle cars, and they drove in under that gateway. I couldn't see them. I only looked down on the roofs of the cars as they rolled forward. Yes, it was horrible, I could see everything happening down on the ramp from up in the tower: when one of them after three days on a trip from hell had enough strength to speak, to move, then he would pray, I saw it when I had ramp duty. Tough duty. Many of them were dead in the cars, a fearful stink as the doors were opened, others were still breathing. The children cried, the women whimpered, and the men called out for their families.

"Yes, I remember that day, because afterward we got together with some other comrades in our house and we celebrated Pentecost with Commandant Höß, and a Transylvanian pastor who was there, also a volunteer, gave a little talk.

"But my men, some of them were either from Transylvania or the Banat, stood there till nightfall in the big watchtower over the entrance. Oddly enough it was the gateway for all trains to Birkenau. Whenever a train came through with a loud whistle, right under the watchtower, then the guards had to be extra alert—pay really close attention, I would tell my men, and especially at night, particularly then. A guy from Denndorf [a village near Sighişoara], a big tall guy—Gunnesch was his name—he was manning the machine gun alone that day, pointing down at the mob, as they all unloaded onto the ramp. A 360-degree view from the tower. It's all open, and you have to look really sharp and make sure no one escapes. Yeah, that's how it was then. *Orders are orders.* There was no back talk. High-tension electric barbed wire fences, with white insulators— before anybody got close enough to touch it, you were supposed to shoot him."

Adam: You must keep in mind that both Capesius and his accomplice Klein had to take "professional" glimpses through the peephole in the door of the gas chamber. And sometimes they supervised the awful process when they closed the doors, bolted them shut, and even screwed them tight, as if those poor gassed victims could break down the door! Then an SS man would extinguish the lights in the gas chamber—so the last minutes of their lives the victims were standing jammed together in total darkness, and screaming—it was hell itself. Additionally, in Crematoriums I and II a prisoner would switch on electric ventilators. These ventilators sucked all the air out of the room. It was torture, and even without poison gas, the poor people inside would have slowly suffocated. But it had to happen fast. When the SS doctor gave the command—or the pharmacist Capesius was often there, and Klein, too—then the "Gas Fritzes" did their thing—the SS executioners protected with gas masks—and would shake the Zyklon B canisters into these open pipes coming out of the ground by Crematoriums I and II, and then they would be closed immediately. In Crematoriums III and IV, the executioners would climb up on ladders, open up hinged doors in the outside walls of the gas chambers, and scatter the poison inside. I often saw Dr. Mengele, and the other doctors and pharmacists as well, give the command to pour the poison gas pellets into the chambers.

Defense Attorney Laternser: "Yes. Now one last question: What reputation did the Capesius family have in Sighişoara?"

Witness Karlheinz Schulery: "The Capesius family was considered very religious, and a family that socially did a lot of good. I don't remember if I mentioned it: he and his brother, too, the whole family, were much respected in Sighişoara. Because our Transylvanian churches and our religious schools were not supported by the government, even though we were the biggest taxpayers in Transylvania. No, we had to pay for all that out of our own resources."

•

Innsbruck, May 1978. *Roland:* "Yes, Capesius. He went hunting in the Beskidy mountains. And once in a while he would treat us to a hare. He had friends there, and Dr. Fabritius, the former *Volk* Group Leader, was also in the area.

"Well, he used to complain, our old Group Leader Fabritius, that he never felt particularly happy at his country place. He sort of felt this time in the Beskidy mountains as enforced exile.

"And it was, too. The whole sorry business stemmed from this man Andreas Schmidt, who had presented his father-in-law with all these SS recruits! But not you, no, you actually volunteered for the SS!"

"Yes—the first Thousand Man Campaign! But that was in 1940, after the new *Volk* Group Leader Andreas Schmidt was at the helm . . . and so then they exiled our cavalry captain Fabritius, who had been the Group Leader up to then, to the Beskidys. So they gave him an estate in the Beskidy, too. And we, my wife and I, paid him a visit, in 1940. They didn't let him go back home anymore, since Andreas Schmidt was in control. The political divisions back then, they were shouting, even shooting matters. A caricature. But with Andreas Schmidt it got serious.

"It all started in our area on November 9, 1940. Getting serious, I mean. It was in the hotel Zur Traube in Mediasch. That's when they proclaimed the formation of the new *Volksgruppe* under their Kapo, Andreas Schmidt, with the help of some leaders from the Romanian Gardists. And then all of a sudden there was this earthquake, people said (word of mouth always worked wonders with us!). Everything was shaking. And because everyone had drunk so much, they thought it was they themselves shaking, but it was the earthquake. And when they found out it was an earthquake, that was fine with them, since now there was an external, explainable reason; they knew now that it wasn't their own shaking. But, to be very exact, it all started with a wedding. With the wedding of Christa Berger . . ."

•

Transylvania 1940. And I can hear Uncle Daniel's voice, Roland's father, Daniel, who was deeply unhappy about his son's "career." "Yes, that was the *Schwabenherzog's* [Swabian duke's] daughter, head of the SS Expansion Office, Gottlob Berger, a clever Swabian. He had built up the SS army. Because the Wehrmacht refused to turn over enough draftees to the SS, he had the bright idea of calling up the ethnic Germans, he wanted to get like a million and a half recruits. And we had the honor of being the first. And so the Swabian duke took him as his son-in-law, this little up-and-comer, Andreas Schmidt, a snot-nosed upstart, no one knew him, he was just a student in Berlin. The rumor was that he took up with Berger's daughter just to become the general's son-in-law. And so the wags were saying then: 'Hitler is from Berchtesgaden—Schmidt's in Berger's garden!'

"And in May 1943 there came this agreement between Berlin and Bucharest. This meant that ethnic German Romanians had to serve their military service with the SS. And a lot of them were assigned to the concentration camps."

Witness Willy Osthues in the Auschwitz Trial, former SS judge from the SS and police court of Kraków: "The Waffen-SS inducted a great many ethnic Germans in the last years of the war, especially from Romania, Bulgaria, Yugoslavia, and so on. They were simply stuck into an SS uniform, and from then on they were members of the Waffen-SS. And then, on further examination later, it turned out that they weren't 'kv' (*kriegs-*

verwendungsfähig: fit for combat), indeed, that they weren't even 'gv' (*garnisonsverwendungsfähig:* fit for duty on base).

"And so now they were assigned, for example, to guard duty. I don't know this from my own experience, I only know it from the literature, that when the Dachau camp was liberated, many of the guards had only been assigned to duty eight or ten days previously—shifted from the Waffen-SS via the RSHA, the Reich Main Security Office."

In a dissertation by Paul Georgescu from 2005 on the Romanian Germans in the SS, who were primarily assigned to the concentration camps, the question is asked why "ethnic Germans" had to perform this "dirty work." The answer given there is that Himmler, in spite of or perhaps because of Berger's son-in-law Schmidt, the *Volk* Group Leader, had categorized the Transylvanian Saxons and the Banat Swabians, in fact all "ethnic Germans," as inferior and having less fighting ability and morale. Military prejudices in general were prevalent. Many "ethnic Germans" had less training: they came from the Romanian army. And they were considered "second-class Germans" with inferiority complexes, for which they tried to compensate with an exaggerated sense of obedience.

Roland Albert: " 'That was one nice wedding they held in Christa Berger's parents' home in Stuttgart,' " my father Daniel once said sarcastically to your grandfather Karl, the church trustee. Papa Gottlob lived in style. It was quite fitting: Stuttgart was the original hometown of many ethnic Germans in the east. There wasn't much publicity on this glittery *Reichsdeutsche* German wedding: blood to blood, kiss to kiss, spit to spit. Not much later this became earth to earth, dust to dust, ashes to ashes. Their happiness didn't last long. Barely one or two thousand Saxon SS volunteers had gone to war, and the first already fallen for Führer, Reich, and father-in-law Gottlob, when the young bride died, too—tuberculosis.

"No, it was certainly no church wedding. *So they don't believe in God*, they whispered back home. Your grandfather, the
trustee of the church, didn't know what to say, for he swore by
his *German church*. And it was even worse at the funeral:
maybe the father had known that Christa had final stage TB,
just like the Lady of the Camellias; she died in Kronstadt
[Braşov, Romania]. They gave her a funeral procession the
likes of which had never been seen in Transylvania, escorted
by a troop of uniformed horsemen. The burial rites were not
performed by the bishop but by a certain Herr Kaufmes, a
big wheel in business and the party. And worse than that:
the bishop was there, but wore traditional Transylvanian
costume.

"Yes, I still remember how my father and your grandfather
argued about it," he said, laughing, and continued: " 'What do
you think about how our bishop behaved, Karl?' said my father. My father was enjoying it, pacing around the big dining
room: 'I always said, he is no Christian, my dear boy. It's all
about the *Volks* church, just the church. But the new bishop,
the Nazi bishop Staedl, in the procession in folk costume!
Don't make me laugh!! And the bride, our properly Nazified
lady, Madame, went to her grave in good pagan style.'

"And then your grandfather, amazed: 'So not wearing his
bishop's vestments, I don't understand it. There wasn't even a
cross, as there should have been. That's just not right!'

"So the lady, the poor girl, the young woman from Stuttgart: yes, she spoke Swabian dialect. And her body was low-
ered into the earth of Transylvania, to that beautiful hymn of
Gerhard Tersteegen.

" 'Well, at least they did that much,' grumbled your grandfather.

" 'Yes, yes,' mumbled my father. I see him before me, as if
it were today!

"That German heart was a cold heart. We carried that chaos inside of ourselves, it was not outside!"

•

Roland: "It was horrible enough, for sure! But for me, Hitler was so great, too, that I almost . . . sort of . . . maybe . . . uhhh . . . forgave him, considering the millions of people killed by bombs."

My mother defended Roland: "He is surely no monster, but his thinking is hard to understand, and completely at odds with his true nature, as I know it."

He speaks of orders, as if that were the explanation. It is not an "accident" of German history, for him. "That was the way it had to be, almost, although *without all these unnecessary harsh measures.*"

"And the bombing deaths . . . well, it certainly wasn't the bombing victims that murdered all those millions in the camps . . ."

"Yes, maybe I linked those things together too much, quite possibly, to make myself feel better," said Roland bitterly. "I regretted it so deeply! For me as a Transylvanian German, it was the most horrible thing I could have ever experienced; I would have thought of a totally different solution, but I still thought that everything would eventually turn out for the better. That it all had a purpose!"

"Even those dreadful, unthinkable things that you went through, Roland!?"

"Well . . . [Pause.] I couldn't keep them from happening. I feel in no way responsible for them! I don't feel guilty. Not even slightly. A game, a game, the world is a game, and we have to play along!!! You know? The wheel of the world. Do you know Nietzsche's reply to Goethe's 'All that passes is merely a metaphor'? It's 'The imperishable is merely your image / God the tricky one / just a poet's flim-flam / World-wheel, rolling on /

grazes goal after goal / The grumblers call it fate, the fools call it a game.' With Nietzsche, the fool is the artist, the poet, the highest man: 'World game, tyrannical / mixes 'seem' with 'be' / Eternal foolishness / mixes us right in.' "

12

Dr. Lucas in the Auschwitz Trial: "On the very first day over a glass of schnaps I was told about what was going on in Auschwitz—including the gassings. I said I was a doctor, my job was to save human lives, not destroy them . . . They assigned me to be the medical head of the Gypsy section and the Theresienstadt section of the camp at Birkenau. The Gypsy camp was in dreadful condition. The barracks had no windows, just a hole front and back. There were no beds or cots, just wooden boxes where five or six people had to sleep. The sanitary conditions were a catastrophe. There were no toilets. Even the term 'latrine' was inappropriate to describe the facilities they had to use to relieve themselves. There was almost no water supply. I don't know how many prisoners there were. You couldn't get any numbers. There were maybe six to eight thousand prisoners in the camp. The Gypsy camp was for families. The inmates didn't wear prisoner's clothing. Their hair was not shaved off. Most were undernourished, emaciated skeletons. The prisoners suffered from diseases that to that point were unknown to me. A condition called 'Noma disease' was very widespread. It appears in insufficiently nourished and physically run-down people. First a blister appears on the mucous membrane of the mouth. Then this turns into an ulcer. Eventually this breaks through to the outside of the cheek. Then a hole forms, through which the jaw of the afflicted person can be seen. After consulting with the inmate doctors, I turned in a written request to change conditions in the camp. But I got no answer."

•

Adam: I saw something very disturbing once in the Gypsy camp: Jani and Peter played "selection" with the other children— indeed, there were almost one thousand children there. The children formed two lines, just as they had seen on the ramp. Boys and girls, one line each, and in front stood Jani and Peter, the "officers," with caps on, upon which they had written an "SS" in pencil. Next to them were the "staff prisoners." And then the smaller and weaker ones went to the left, just as Jani pointed them to with a gesture of his arm: then they had to walk slowly toward a pile of rocks, which was in a circle and covered with bright red paper cut into little strips, so that the paper waved in the wind: this was the crematorium. And there, they had to take all their clothes off and lie down, as if dead, on the ground.

The Gypsy camp was directly adjacent to the camp for the sick. It was almost a daily occurrence for the children from this Gypsy camp to "organize" [steal] something or other. From us, they would take something to eat. One day there was a great disturbance in the Gypsy camp. There was crying, some trucks came, and the Gypsies knew what was in store for them. Some of the SS men had lovers among the pretty Gypsies in the camp, and they had certainly told some of them about it. The "news service" in the Gypsy camp was good. When I heard about the commotion, I got scared. I was fast on my feet, and ran to the washroom. Near the washroom I hid in the bushes and watched. Then I saw the Gypsies being beaten. I was a bit late, the clearance operation was just about over. Boger and a few other SS men were still there. I saw them search through the blocks and pull out the children who had hidden. The children they found in the blocks were brought to Boger. Boger grabbed the children by their feet and smashed them into the wall. That was done with six chil-

dren. I felt sick. I ran back to my block. This is all true. I saw it with my own eyes. The children were five or six, maybe seven years old.

I believe the children were dead. It happened out in the open. I didn't see anything else.

13

Capesius in his cell (May 20, 1964): "There are all sorts of privations for someone in solitary confinement. You have no company, no one to talk to. There is no sex with a wife or a girlfriend, and everyone has to deal with this somehow. Over a period of nine months I ate only a portion of the food given to me, you can really take off some weight in this way. After a loss of forty pounds I was practically impotent, and had no desire for intercourse. But you can only keep up this regimen for so long, given the nervous tension you feel all the time. I am eating again, I take vitamins and my nerves are better, but this then leads to sexual torment, or at least need.

"Even in Auschwitz, setting up a bordello for the inmates was just a stopgap measure. But in many of the commando teams, including the dispensary, there was a mixed staff, and for this reason my inmate workers did not suffer sexual deprivations, since in 1944 my inmates were better nourished than many people were back in the Reich, because along with the luggage of the doctors came highly nutritious food, and the Poles would get ten-kilo packages at least once a month. These were often accompanied by gifts from the neighbors back home of the particular person, especially very nutritious foods. Here in the Hammelgasse prison they only allow you one five-kilo package at Christmas if you are in pretrial detention. Sentenced prisoners doing time here, on the other hand, are allowed half a chicken and a cake when their family comes on monthly visits; we in detention are given at most a bottle of Coke from the soda machine here, and that's supposed to keep us from escaping?

"Back at home there are people who need taking care of. My wife was only here for one year after twenty years in Romania, and she had to deal with every conceivable kind of workman here herself. After twenty years of separation, my children still have no father, all three are still in school, because their studies are not accredited here, or only partially. Those are all problems that they could have dealt with differently if they had had a father who was free, instead of a father in prison. What good is it to have a father who will be free in three years, because they haven't got any evidence on him? The children are being punished, too, even though their father has already served two thirds of the sentence imposed by the court.

"The respect of the world is gone, I am branded by the press, and then that little theater piece of Weiß's*, where he quoted me, but it was really Klein: *You'll see each other again in an hour* . . . They were speaking lines on stage . . . books about the trial, and the mention of Auschwitz in every article, even when it has nothing to do with the subject; but in many countries, this witch-hunting promotes sales.

"Wealth and property are gone. Debts are piling up, and along with that, many families are starting to feel alienation, although my family does not show any signs of that. Here, many of the arrestees' marriages are coming apart, which is common with people in prison for the first time.

"Of course, a peaceful conscience is a great comfort, but when you find out how the accusations are exaggerated with lies, you just don't understand the world anymore. The witness can be presented as unreliable, but he still gets featured in

*Peter Weiß's play *Die Ermittlung* (*The Investigation*). —trans.

all the books and in the theater, even if his testimony was rejected in the first verdict: the accusation that you sent 1,200 children to the gas chamber sticks, because '*scripta manent.*'

"Despite everything I have not given up hope of being able to take care of my family. I am hoping, maybe as early as December, for the detention order to be lifted. Will it actually happen? I hope so, despite the seven bitter years I have spent here!"

•

Capesius, who while in prison studied many books on Auschwitz, and even wrote summaries of some of them, including *This Was Oswiecim* by Dr. Filip Friedmann, now knows more about Auschwitz than he ever could have known during his time there. In his cell, where he had years of time, he made many marginal notations in these books in his crabbed scrawl. For instance, in Friedmann: "Borrowed from June 14, 1959, to September 20, 1960: *The Story of a Death Camp*. Translated from the Yiddish into English. 1946." In 1960 there were still very few sources on Auschwitz; *The Informed Heart*, a book by Bruno Bettelheim, the Viennese psychoanalyst, who had also been in the concentration camp, had just come out.

Only now, after it was "all over," could Capesius, like so many others, retrospectively see the dimension of this crime. And it is quite clear that he only slowly came to this realization during the time in his cell. I see Capesius, the prisoner in his cell. I can imagine how shaken he was by Friedmann's report and the others. What was going on inside him? Had he slowly come to accept his punishment? Certainly he had not during the trial. He sits at his little desk. He scribbles little notes about chapter 4 of Friedmann's book: "The description is shocking, of a winter transport arriving from Flossenbürg in Bavaria, on December 18, 1943; 1,200 prisoners left, 948 arrived at Auschwitz alive, and only 393 survived after that. This according to Dr. Bruno Fischer, professor of psychiatry at Prague University, who was also a prisoner at Auschwitz."

Sympathy for Capesius? I read that he had to pay forty thousand deutschmarks in trial costs. That was a lot of money then! He was separated from his daughters and wife from 1943 to 1963. And then the trial in 1965.

PROFESSOR FINSTERER

Capesius in Göppingen: "Yes, when you see those horrible things, it is so depressing, it makes you want to vomit. You feel like you will puke any second. At first. Then you get used to it. But there was one man who didn't get used to it: he did selections for a while."

"Who was that—Dr. Lucas?"

Capesius: "Lucas. You are well informed."

"I read everything that I . . ."

Capesius: "*Omnia.* It wasn't Lucas who said that, it was another guy, a big, tall guy. No, wait: it was the lab assistant; she worked in the lab. In any case, Lucas wasn't the way those seven holy sisters described him in such a positive way. It was the Sisters of the Holy Cross who got him out of that whole thing . . ."

"But he felt that his time there was a humiliation, having to do that, just being there in the first place. His conscience was tormenting him . . . And so then he asked the bishop. And a high justice official, too."

Dr. Lucas in the Auschwitz Trial: "On my home leave I looked up the bishop of Osnabrück, Dr. Berning. I told him about conditions in Auschwitz, and asked for his advice. He told me that one should not obey immoral commands, but one need not risk one's own life. I also spoke with a highly placed lawyer, but he couldn't give me any real advice . . .

"Eventually Dr. Wirths got wind of things and got really vicious. He ordered me to go on the ramp, alone. I was all by myself there, four different times, as the only doctor on the ramp. In these four cases, the people had already been unloaded when I got there. They were lined up in rows of five or six. In front of them was the commandant, the head of the detention camp, and other SS leaders in a group. I then went to Commandant Kramer and explained to him that I was not in a position to perform selections. I said that I was having a gallbladder attack or some kind of intestinal problems. Kramer then did the selection for me, without any problem. I got away from there as soon as I could. How long I was on the ramp each time, I don't remember. In any case, I never did selections myself. I was never at the crematorium either, and I never supervised medics throwing in the gas pellets."

Presiding judge: "After these attempts had failed, the accused, on returning to Auschwitz after home leave, wrote letters to his former boss in Nuremberg, Dr. Bader, who was then the garrison doctor in that city, and described more or less specifically what was going on in Auschwitz, and asked for his help in getting out of Auschwitz. Dr. Bader answered the accused to the effect that it would be impossible for him to use his influence here, and that he—Dr. Lucas—should just himself try to wangle a way to get out of Auschwitz; and, moreover, that the accused should not be writing about such matters in such a frank and open manner, and that he would ask him to be more cautious."

•

Capesius: "Yes, sure, Lucas. But I know someone else who asked the bishop, through her uncle, her uncle was a professor in Vienna, and told Innitzer . . ."

Frau Fritzi Capesius: "The bishop . . . the cardinal . . ."

Capesius: "And told him what was going on there."

"They talked about it in Vienna, on leave?"

Capesius: "Yes."

"To whom?"

Capesius: "To Professor Finsterer, a member of the Thursday Circle . . ."

Frau Fritzi Capesius: "Professor Finsterer is my uncle, and when my husband was in Vienna . . ."

Capesius: "In this Thursday Circle, they always met at Cardinal Innitzer's. It was sort of a *jour fixe.*"

Frau Fritzi Capesius: "So Finsterer told Innitzer . . ."

Capesius: "And then Innitzer said, you can't do anything about it, that's just how it is, we should be happy that we came out of it as well as we did."

Frau Fritzi Capesius: "Austria, in general, came out of it well, after all."

"But there were many Austrians in the camps, prisoners and guards both . . ."

Capesius: "But that hardly matters."

Clearly, it didn't matter what happened there. Not even to the Pope, or the cardinal. And not to the eminent Professor Finsterer, either.

Frau Fritzi Capesius: "The Pope was not interested, but he did know about it."

"Yes, he knew."

Frau Fritzi Capesius: "The Pope knew it, and so did Innitzer."

•

Adam: Among other things, the Vatican received a report from Rudolf Vrba, who was able to escape from Auschwitz. In this report, Vrba described the preparations that were being made in Auschwitz to exterminate the Hungarian Jews. A representative of the Vatican met with Vrba to discuss the report. Still, the report was kept for internal use only. Furthermore, Pope Pius XII was said to be a friend of Germany and of Hitler himself. Four days after his installation as pope, with the help of the German-speaking cardinals Bertram, Schulte, Faulhaber, and Innitzer, Pius wrote a letter to Hitler, in which he addressed him as "Most Highly Honored Adolf Hitler." Researcher Meike Rosenplänter, to whom I have written, investigated this thoroughly, and this story is a typical example of the age-old sophistry of the Vatican: In 1964 Pope Paul VI directed a group of Jesuit scholars to prepare a work for publication containing the most important Vatican documents of the war. The work came out in eleven volumes between 1965 and 1981 under the title Actes et Documents du Saint-Siège Relatifs à la Seconde Guerre Mondiale. *But it turned out that the most important documents were not included, and the Vatican would not release them. The eleven volumes were a cover-up. The Vatican had traditionally been anti-Semitic. The Vatican itself was the prime cause of anti-Semitism. And Hitler had come from the Catholic tradition that the Jews had nailed Christ to the cross. Pius XII himself was an ardent anti-Semite.*

•

Capesius: "But Innitzer realized that this had to be kept secret. And Innitzer was higher up than the bishop of that other guy, Lucas . . . But I never brought up the Innitzer matter in the trial, because of her uncle. And he had probably heard something about me . . ."

Frau Fritzi Capesius: "But by then in 1964 he was already dead, Victor . . ."

Capesius: "Okay, but his wife wasn't dead, or his kids. Still, it's always a shock when people start talking about something like that, it makes the whole family suffer . . ."

Frau Fritzi Capesius: "No, excuse me, Finsterer said . . . I myself told my mother about it, and Finsterer's whole life ended wretchedly; in the end he went insane. This super-intelligent man . . . he did have lucid moments, too, when he would say: I accept this as my punishment. He was extremely religious, a fervent Catholic: I accept this as my punishment, this suffering, because I knew about it but could never find the courage to do anything against it."

Adam: Frau Capesius was half-Jewish, too . . .

"Yes. And she also spoke about the fact that, contrary to what people say, some Jews in Auschwitz did put up a fight, did resist."

Adam: Yes, there were many instances, and of course there was the Kampfgruppe Auschwitz. And our resistance group in the crematorium. There was also religious resistance. I can never forget this scene; one of my companions in suffering has written about it, and it's in my journals, too:

"It was Passover 1944. A transport arrived from Vittel, France. Among them were many very highly respected Jewish personalities, a rabbi from Bayonne, Rabbi Mosze Friedman, God rest his soul, one of the greatest scholarly authorities on Polish Jewish life, that rare figure, a true patriarch. He undressed in front of the gas chambers with all the others. Later, an Obersturmführer came in. The rabbi went up to him, grabbed him by the lapel of his coat, and said to him in German: 'You vile, cruel murderers, do not think you will succeed in exterminating our people. The Jewish people will live forever, they will never disappear from the stage of world history. But you despicable murderers will pay dearly, with ten Germans for every innocent Jew. You will end, not just as a power, but as a people. The day of reckoning will come. The blood that has been shed will cry out for vengeance. Our blood will not be still until the flaming rage of destruction flows over your people and annihilates your bestial blood.' He spoke these words with the fierceness and energy of a lion."*

Capesius: "But anyway, whom could you tell?"

Frau Fritzi Capesius: "Please . . . back then . . ."

Capesius talks excitedly during this.

---

*Cf. "Auschwitz Notebooks," a manuscript of unknown authorship, Sonderheft 1, Oswiecim 1972, p. 122f.

Frau Fritzi Capesius: "Given how things were then . . . because now you can see it from another perspective . . ."

Capesius: "And Innitzer also said, later . . ."

Frau Fritzi Capesius: "I saw it on television, but many years later: there was a film on Innitzer or a memorial program of some kind. And Innitzer said: Today I was given a large donation from my friend Professor Finsterer, as reparation, a financial gift to the Jews to ease their fate, to 'ransom' them—I think you could do that for some of them—in any case it was a special campaign to buy their freedom. And Finsterer donated a significant sum to this campaign . . ."

"Was this uncle a Jew, also . . . since you yourself are half-Jewish?!"

Frau Fritzi Capesius: "No, no, no, Finsterer was absolutely raised Catholic, and he studied, I think, Catholic—was it theology?—no, medicine. Finsterer grew up as a very poor child, the child of poor parents."

THE GERMAN OBSESSION WITH
RACIAL "PURITY" AND
THE GERMAN LANGUAGE AS A CURE

I

I told Adam that I had indeed found more documents. Perhaps without realizing it, Capesius gave me some notes of Professor Finsterer's, or possibly to prove that he had spoken with him about Auschwitz; Fritzi, who was from Vienna, had hinted that "yes, even in Vienna things like that" were done. "Particularly with the children at Spiegelgrund." And the professor had known about it, and brought it up with Innitzer, but not gotten anywhere, and this lay heavily on his conscience. Moreover, Capesius also knew about the psychiatrist from Hermannstadt, Dr. Jekelius, whom he had visited in Vienna. Jekelius was the director of that sanatorium called Spiegelgrund, where sick children were murdered in his euthanasia clinic. Crazily enough, this Jekelius was also married to Hitler's sister Paula, and was really part of the innermost power circle. Admittedly, though, Hitler, afraid that the public would learn about the frequency of mental disease and idiocy in his family, didn't want anything to do with his relatives.

In the papers Dr. Jekelius left behind, there is one "objective" note regarding his wife, Paula: "My wife, Paula Hitler, should remain unknown, according to the wish of her supremely powerful brother. The whole family should remain unknown. Hitler was ashamed of his family background, but this background explains a great deal. Paula herself complained to me, after reading *Mein Kampf*, it must have been in 1957, that Adolf never mentioned her in the book." Hitler's sister Paula wrote to a friend in 1955 on the Soviet practice of *Sip-*

penhaft [arresting an entire family for the crimes of a single member]: "My dear brother would find it quite proper that even we would not be spared this." On Hitler's request, Paula had to renounce her family name: in 1936 he invited her to the Olympic games at Garmisch and required that she "go under the name of Wolf and live strictly incognito." She lived on 500 reichsmarks per month, paid to her by Hitler, and only avoided being arrested by Russian authorities because in April 1945, on orders from Berlin, she had been taken from Lower Austria and brought to Berchtesgaden. And she lived there as "Frau Wolf" until her death in 1960. Documents concerning her contacts with Nazis who fled to Argentina in 1945 are scheduled to be published soon. The maintenance of her grave in Berchtesgaden is paid for by former SS officers—one of them arranged for himself to be buried in the same place. "We were allowed to visit Hitler one single time. The atmosphere was frosty. We were strangers," Jekelius writes in a letter. "But in Hermannstadt I was treated with the greatest respect. And the Volksgruppenführer [*Volk* Group Leader Schmidt] outdid himself with obsequious compliments. And invited us to his home; at that time he was still living with Christa Berger, the Obergruppenführer's daughter, who died of TB shortly after. Schmidt really considered himself the new Nazi nobility."

The psychiatrist Jekelius was reputedly a lady-killer. Psychically damaged as Paula was, like her brother Adolf, she had sought his advice at the Steinhof Clinic in Vienna. They say that she was "taken for a ride" by Jekelius. There was an affair, she wanted to get married, but her brother had dictated: "Paula, you cannot get married till the war is over!" She was living in Berchtesgaden, and her job, together with other relatives and staff, was to see to it that all the presents that Hitler was given after the Anschluss—cups, embroidery, mugs, vases, crystal, etc.—were distributed among Adolf's various country homes, and furthermore, she also took over managing these households. In one of them (not Berchtesgaden) a room was supposed to be furnished in Transylvanian Saxon style, and the Sebastian-Hann Society in Hermannstadt was to take care of this, because the devotion to the "Führer" in Transylvania was pathological: a real subject for a psychiatrist!

Paula and Adolf together had had a dreadful childhood: psychoanalysts even think that this childhood, and the genetic damage rife in this alcoholic and inbred family, could explain the deeds of this greatest criminal of all time. Paula Hitler lived modestly and in seclusion together with her psychiatrist in Vienna, whom she outlived by several years. Her biography is ultimately a tragedy. She believed that she had to defend the honor and the legacy of her brother Adolf, whom she called the "greatest son of our Austrian homeland" (October 12, 1957), who "wanted the best for Germany" (December 28, 1957). But it is important to note that the little doctor from the Steinhof was promoted to the post of director of the hospital, through Paula's intercession. I learned from Dr. Herwig Czech that the Transylvanian Jekelius was responsible for the "child euthanasia program" in Vienna. The actual killings were brought about primarily with medications, and thus could be completely integrated into the normal activities of the various wards. In Vienna there was the euthanasia clinic Am Spiegelgrund. This Viennese "Special Children's Ward," that is, the institution charged with the observation, reporting, and, when required, murder of the children in question, was set up on July 24, 1940, as a part of the Städtische Jugendfürsorgeanstalt Am Spiegelgrund (Municipal Institution for Youth Welfare "Am Spiegelgrund") on the site of the then-named sanatorium and care facility Am Steinhof. The space necessary for this and other installations was made available through the murder of approximately 3,200 Steinhof patients in Hartheim. The director at the time was the husband of Hitler's sister, Dr. Jekelius. These euthanasia killings took place in one of a total of nine pavilions, Pavilion XV. It had been directed since early 1941 by Dr. Heinrich Gross, who thus reported directly to the leader of the clinic Am Spiegelgrund, first Dr. Erwin Jekelius, and later Dr. Ernst Illing.

Hitler also had those of his relatives killed who resembled him too closely and might publicly expose the insanity in the family. On January 23, 1932, Aloisia, Hitler's second cousin, who for years had worked as a chambermaid in the famous old Hotel Höller across from the Exposition Palace in Vienna, was brought to the medical officer of the hotel. The manager of the hotel thought that this always-conscientious employee might be overworked. But the medical officer noted down: "Has been behaving very oddly for about one week. She is fearful of walking through the hotel hallways. She sees ghosts." On February 18, the court came to the decision that Aloisia should be interned in a closed institution. Her fate is evidenced by the number 2155, which she wore on the transport to Hartheim. She was not allowed to see where she was going; the bus's windows were painted over. The systematic murders of people like Aloisia are the only such program of the Nazi regime that bears Hitler's personal signature. On December 6, 1940, Adolf Hitler's second cousin died in the gas chamber at the extermination facility of Hartheim, Upper Austria. On the Führer's personal order. The Transylvanian German Jekelius was the director. He knew he had to carry out the order. Hitler's second cousin, Aloisia, warehoused in his facility, had to die. The madness that was also part of Auschwitz: Hitler had to hide it, because he himself was mad.

Was Hitler's family background in part a reason for the murders at Auschwitz? Was it the dictator's self-hatred that led to Auschwitz? Was he unconsciously wanting to eradicate his family background of retardation and insanity? Aloisia's ashes, just like those of the approximately thirty thousand others who were murdered, were dumped into the Danube or the Traun

River at night. After the war's end, Aloisia's sister Victoria, also categorized as "feebleminded," was a patient at Am Feldhof, a closed institute in Graz. The Hitler and Schicklgruber family came from the tiny Austrian village of Spital. It smelled. It stank. Even the very name stank. Albert Speer wrote in his memoirs that he brought on one of Hitler's most violent fits of rage when he told him of a plaque in honor of the Führer in Spital. Speer: "Hitler completely lost control of himself, shouted for Bormann, who came in, shaken. Hitler screamed at him: he had often said that the name of this place should never ever be mentioned. But this fool of a Gauleiter had put up a plaque there. It was to be removed at once."

Self-hatred? Yes. And today we know that in early 1944, three years after Aloisia's death, when Heinrich Himmler, head of the Gestapo, sought to damage Hitler, he sent some explosive papers to the Chancellory of the Führer. They were classified as "Secret Reich Material" and concerned Hitler personally. Himmler gave top secret information to the Führer's secretary, Martin Bormann, information that called into question the mythological status of the "leader of the healthy German *Volk* community," the supreme Führer of the German people. The secret paper contained rumors about the Führer's relatives, "some of whom," it reported, "were half-idiots or insane." The sources of the rumors were said to be "oppositional figures in Graz St. Peter," specifically the Graz resident and great-aunt of Hitler, a strict Catholic, who was the legal guardian of the orphaned "idiot descendants" of the Schicklgruber line.

Hitler had had to battle rumors about his heredity ever since his first political appearances. In the Jewish cemetery in Vienna there are gravestones of "Hüttlers." Inbreeding, insanity, incest. As only Thomas Bernhard could describe it.

Who Hitler's father's ancestors were is uncertain to this day: Alois Hitler, the father, "switched" the name of Schicklgruber with that of his stepfather Hiedler, long after his own parents were dead. He became "Hitler" because the witnesses for the alleged paternity of Hiedler could not read, and thus did not notice that the notary and the pastor wrote "Hitler" instead of "Hiedler" into the document.

2

Jekelius knew that in Transylvania there was a pronounced and widespread fear of "genetic damage" and of insanity. That was not the least of the reasons he had studied psychiatry. And why he had ordered "mercy killings" in the sanatorium Am Steinhof with a clear conscience.

If you want to understand their madness, thought Adam, who had certainly lived long enough in Sighișoara with Edith, a Saxon, to know all about the *nervattigen* (jumpy) Saxons, *you have to be able to empathize with this constant anxiety.*

Yes, I said, that's exactly it . . . We Transylvanian Saxons all have a weak spot in us, that's why it was always the uppermost duty of a Saxon to learn self-control, to check oneself, to hear and obey orders! That was the way our SS man Roland put it, too: "No argument!" But everyone else said that, too, every day. And we had an inferiority complex about the Germans from the Reich, the "real Germans." My father said once, "Certainly we Saxons are not all racially pure, there are many village idiots in our midst. Some of the families are given to screaming fits. And all these weirdos. Oh, and the inbreeding that has been going on for 850 years! Are we perhaps already Jewified?"

And my mother, all naïve and giggly: "Imagine, I run into Birä-Will on Baierstrasse, the guy who's a little off—if you annoyed him, he could spit way up in the air with fantastic skill, and with great elegance and precision it would land right on your ear.

"Now I want to show you how Milli, the town crazy, used to dance to the 'Dragonfly Song.' It happened even in the best families," Mother explained. "I can still see her before me, this Milli, she was a horror to everyone. Her wild strands of hair all knotted together underneath her big dirty beret, and her downcast, weepy eyes, her head hanging down: bad genes! From the general inbreeding: drink, marriages too close within families, even Heinrich Binder, the bishop's grandson, was an idiot, as if struck by God. Aunt B had two sons, both retarded. Once Father wanted to do a good deed, so he invited Heinrich for Christmas. It was awful what happened then. You remember: what good was it, that he could play with blocks so well, could really build amazing things with them—he was sulky, unkempt, and after a while he stopped washing, and instead of going to the bathroom he just sat on the edge of the bed. The medical people came and took him away. His aunts had scolded him, and so one day he wrote them a telegram that said: *I cleaned the toilet, Heinrich.*

"Milli was cute, pretty as a picture, but at sixteen or seventeen she went over the edge, poor Milli did, couldn't hold her head still, couldn't speak properly anymore, just babbled, letting long strings of drool dribble onto the floor, and making everyone sick. She always left a shiny trail of spit behind her. But she could still play the piano, she played fabulously, as if she were directed by a dream, as if someone inside her was playing. Unfortunately, people said she had a Jewish grandfather, or great-grandfather, *iewen de Ballegrieß wor jiddesch!*"*

Roland: "Of course, at home there was also a sort of homogamy, or mating of like with like, that worked against the random mixing of blood. So here the issue is at least marginally arguable, whether we are talking just about the choice of a spouse based on external considerations like property or so-

*"After all, her great-grandmother was Jewish."

cial position, or whether the boundaries that are set in this way should also include certain genetic or blood-based criteria: for it is the dark instincts of the blood in the depths of racial consciousness that brings these couples together in the first place! Then, when we were in our difficult and fateful struggle, something had to be done about inbreeding. And the only possibility for any kind of new blood was the Reich. And that clearly had to be generously promoted, and many people complied with this. And so did the Volksgruppenführer [Schmidt]! The question was important, since a regrettably high percentage of town fools, village idiots, and weaklings of various kinds were polluting our bloodlines. Special measures had to be taken to deal with them.

"The weak spot was within ourselves. Where do all these weirdos, crazy people, and village idiots come from? Even the bishop's grandson was *plem-plem* [cuckoo]. Something had to be done. The filth . . . the sloppiness . . . we all had to pull ourselves together, not just let things keep declining. For the sickness of the body here is the result of a weakening of our moral, social, and racial instincts.

"Criticism in all forms means undermining, desecrating the *Volkskörper*, the body of the people. The Führer Adolf Hitler, exaggerating slightly in his *Mein Kampf*, saw and described those who pollute the *Volkskörper*: tramps and chicken vendors, vermin, the mentally and physically sick, but hand in hand with the intellectual acrobats and ink-slingers, they defile our sound genetic heritage and our race; but we will succeed in destroying these, these parasitic bacilli. To purify the blood in the body of the people, we have our concentration camps. Everything Christian is now just a hindrance to us, so Judaified has it become. This Jewish Bible—nonsense! We will conquer even death! We rule with death, and through it. That was Hitler's view."

3

Adam: Yes, race madness and fear of idiots, the obsession with purity! Everything "alien," everything "foreign" to the species and allegedly "sickly," had to be "burned" from the body of the folk. Fire would purify. Fire. Hitler's insane dream of purifying the Volkskörper *of everything "foreign," this would strengthen the German "musketeer" and thus allow the war to be won; after 1942/43 it led into the madness of mass extermination camps. There I wrote against that "reality." And survived. It's true. But every day, too, I had to see the young rabbi, he was spared, his pyre burned day and night and he only had to make sure that it didn't go out. There was plenty of nourishment for the "nothing" through fire: everything "useless," such as photos, diaries, letters, marriage certificates, diplomas, prayer books, and Torah rolls, too, was burned. Complete life stories, family histories, and even YHWH, God, was burned . . .*

And at the same time, this nakedness, you know, this naked life, you can't comprehend, it is like the taking back of Creation, the obliteration of the world, of God, too, who created man in his nakedness . . . The SS made absolutely sure, not only in the gas chambers, but at the shootings, too, that the people were stripped naked before they were shot. For their clothing was valuable and could not be spoiled by blood or made unusable by bullet holes. They were much more important, these miserable products, than those human beings who were created by God. What was more precious to them were coats, dresses, mens' suits, underwear, children's clothes, baby's diapers, furs, shoes, stockings, hats, gloves. After every gassing or shooting these last possessions of the victims were stacked up in the undressing rooms. Among them lay bundles and rucksacks with medicines, foodstuffs, toys, jewelry, books, photos, along with all the other personal trivia that people care about and that they hold on to for as long as they can. The amount of property that was left behind by so many murdered people was so large that an average of twenty prisoners in the Sonderkommando took more than one hour just to sort roughly through the things and carry them out. In the crematorium yard trucks stood waiting and the inmates loaded the clothing onto them; the trucks were then driven off by the SS for further sorting and storage in the "Canada" warehouses. Useless things (from the SS viewpoint) such as photos, books, and religious articles like phylacteries and prayer shawls were burned in the trash incinerators of the crematoriums. These, too, were witnesses from the death zone.

.

Adam spoke of shame; he often mentioned shame as an all-encompassing feeling after the liberation on January 27, 1945.

Adam did not like to talk about *then*, as opposed to Roland or Victor Capesius, who were happy to have me put a microphone in front of them, as if they could free themselves, as if it were a father confessor who would loosen all the knots within them, as if they were secure with their experiences, as if they still more or less were rooted in some kind of a "normality," made to fit in with wife and children, school, kindergarten and Christmas parties "there." Roland even said, "Otherwise we couldn't have gotten through it." All around, though, the "horrible," the "it made you want to puke," and the stink and the fires that were forever reddening the sky.

It's poetry that can save lives, even in Auschwitz, said Adam. It can even bring the dead very close to us, they actually live inside us, speak in us, sometimes singing, but weeping as well. These unheard voices—like the tinkling of glass in our ear—they are telling us that they see us. And what they see is a terrible image: the material, the body dissolved, the sickness lying deep within, we could not see it, hear it, or feel it. A kind of dimensional limit is reached . . . If you can see THAT, then you no longer are on earth . . . We told those poor people, who then turned into ashes, to go into the showers, to bathe. When they went, they started to cry. Women, children, men. They held tight to one another. Mothers brought their babies with them, at their breast . . . I did not look them in the eye. I was always careful not to look them in the eye. The heavy oak door was closed. Then the gas from above. What you heard was a humming, a weeping. Sometimes screams. After half an hour, the door was opened. On the chamber floor you saw something that reminded you of small pebbles, green, like little dice—the remains of the gas pellets, and masses of bodies, a meter high, one fallen on top of the other. While the bodies were still warm, they were easier to pull apart, but after ten, twelve hours they got as cold as ice, as heavy as stone. And it often happened that the warmth of the gas made the skin dissolve. They lay on top of one another. Like a heap of trash. A huge dense mass all clawed and tangled together.

•

I had spoken to Adam about the Slovenian painter Zoran Mušič. He had seen this horrifying sight of stacked-up bodies in Buchenwald; and he, too, saved himself through writing, through his journal. He wrote down everything in it; it was like casting a lead weight off his soul: "Toward evening the dying, and those already thought to be dead, were laid together like pieces of firewood, in a stack like a funeral pyre as tall as a tower. A hallucinatory tower, which moved, and groaned. And this groan was probably their last utterance." I have a painting by Zoran Mušič hanging in my house, the cry of a dying human being: "Even today, the eyes of the dead accompany me, hundreds of gazing eyes . . ."

I do believe that all these murdered victims, the more than fifty million dead from the Second World War, have exerted and will continue to exert an enormous force in the world. I am reminded, too, of a watercolor by Ernest Gaillard, Adam said, *a perspective that shows the last view onto the camp from the entrance gate, which is right in the center of the painting: a chim-*

ney rises brick-red into the sky, dominating the low, gray barracks, out of which great masses of smoke are roiling . . . Four hanged bodies. Two "Mussulmen" in coffins. Mountains of corpses.

"Is it possible to turn all that into beauty? Is it possible?"

Yes, said Adam, that's exactly what I wanted to do, because I was convinced that the dead cannot just disappear like that, that there is a gateway, just as in the Hasidic idea that this grave of smoke as a bridge to God actually exists; in his poem "Death Fugue," Celan has wonderfully transformed this mass murder into an escape, so that these criminals, without wanting or knowing it, have caused an enormous historical caesura, a millennial rupture in the perceptible world, such that this escape—from them, from history, and from a hell on earth—also points to a kind of salvation, and reveals the criminals' nullity, their void as a historical instrument, like the devil in Faust.

"People ask over and over, 'Where was God when this happened?' Do you mean He knew about it, even permitted it, in order to bring about a radical change of direction . . . ?"

Yes. I prefer to call God the All-One, a force that is forever young, and which willed it—without this One nothing at all can happen, and whenever we talk about this in our human language and our shortsightedness, we are always inadequate to the task . . . It goes so far beyond our understanding. I have heard of people who survived their own deaths, THERE in the camp, and who passed through that "grave in the air," and through that infinite bright light beyond body and beyond bloody history, like the many people we hear of today who have returned from near-death experiences, and also from those on the battlefield, even from those in Hiroshima. From all these a fantastic, beautiful message, barely comprehensible to us, that death is merely a transition, a being set free for a world of light, filled with love, just as was set down in ancient texts and handed down to us—for instance in the tenth book of Plato's Republic, *or the various Books of the Dead—and these messages from the victims were only possible because they had come back from the condition of death and then were able to tell us about it! Yes, and that is what gives me hope that their suffering was not in vain, that the millions did not die in vain . . . and this, just THIS is beautiful! This is what is unimaginable, incomparable, beyond language; even in its negativity—precisely that crime of the Nazis, who savaged the poor human body with such ruthless "banality," as if it were "proven" that man is a void, just pure materiality, all those millions, material just to be scrapped, annihilated, and reduced to mountains of bone, hills of hair—and finally, to be "processed" into ash: death itself annihilable, man a number, just a fateless construct, and beyond that, nothing. Nothing? The concentration camp has proved just the opposite, has brought it about, has set it in motion: after all, in Hebrew, God is NOTHING. And hope? Is it not absurd to imagine that hope gains ground through this paradoxical radicality, that the unknowable that is death now is made general, is made history? No, for it is precisely the unsayable, or the absurdity of trying to say IT, that is the truth!*

And the language?

Language is illuminated by a reflection of that light. Especially THERE in the death camp, language opened up more than is otherwise sayable, for all those in that special condition so close to death.

Mušič, the painter,* did not just paint; he also kept journals, as if only language could really be redemptive: "I was in a feverish state and felt the irresistible need to draw, to keep this grandiose and tragic beauty from escaping me. 'I lived only for the day. Tomorrow would be too late. Life, and death—they all hung from these pages of paper.' "

Adam: You cannot imagine what a frenzy overcame me

---

*Cf. Schulze.

when I felt I could finally let loose with what I had gone through, could write about it; before that I thought, How can you talk about things that are impossible, which absolutely SHOULD NOT exist, which are not to be understood and not to be believed? Nightmares that were LIVED! Filth, stink, rottenness, mountains of bones . . . And even everyday life as crude as a dung heap, as foul as a latrine trench . . . raw power, raw meat . . . and beauty in death?

I see it: a little girl in a pigtail, all alone, hears what I heard, too . . . her dress Bordeaux red, her hands at her side like a soldier.

She looks down and wipes the dust from her little shoes. Then all quiet again. Boger comes. Takes the child by the hand. She walks with him obediently to the Black Wall. He stands her there with her face to the wall. She turns around again, and looks at him. Big brown eyes. Boger turns her head to the wall again. Takes two steps backward, takes his carbine, points it at the back of the girl's head, takes two steps forward. Shoots. The smell of powder and blood. The girl falls into a heap. Without a sound. Action. Time. Betrayal. The words "pigtail," "little girl," "looks at him." Betrayal. Everything. And. Nothing. No word was spoken. Nothing but the shot; tripping feet, boots, the clicking of the gun lock. Reverberation. Chickens. Dogs barking. Trails of blood. Flies, fat, bottle-green, shiny. Concrete.

German, I say. And I am already certain that it is the only language that can get to the center of this . . . and not simply because it is my mother tongue, or that it could restore to us the lost ability to speak of God, for since Auschwitz God has departed the realm of human experience. And a return would have to come from the idiom of death itself . . . But given the gas chamber, no articles of faith or consolation are valid anymore, to say nothing of literature. Something was revealed THERE by the dead, which has no equal in anything else that existed on this earth. In the gas chamber, they learned something that we can only wonder about, and for which they paid with their life.

But how could you possibly have ever written German there?

Adam: It's still my mother tongue! And even there I defended it. I didn't hate it in the camp like my Polish, Russian, and French comrades, and I wrote German. Silence was not good, to remain mute would have been giving up, and ultimately even a kind of agreement, acquiescence with the unimaginable horror of it all. For everything that had anything to do with emotions, with friendship, solidarity, sympathy, conscience, and love—was resistance, was halfway to rebellion. I even felt it in the "standing bunker" [a cell so narrow the prisoner could only stand — trans.].

You know, in the camp I often thought about Dante's Ugolino, even in the bunker—Ugolino, who had to suffer death by starvation, in the Hunger Tower, with his sons; when I came into the bunker, I also thought about Father Kolbe, who chose this death voluntarily to save another, a man with a family. I personally knew two men, Kurt Paschale and Herbert Michael—both were sentenced to death by starvation in the "standing bunker" by the Political Department (Boger). Given only water, they held out more than forty days.

Hunger as torture, yes. As a death sentence. The camp was full of hunger ghosts: full of "Mussulmen." They were the starving undead. But all of us, every day, were nothing but random survivors, yet guilty, too, for doing nothing, for betraying all those abandoned to the agonies of the gas chamber, the bunker, the whipping bench, the hanging post, execution at the Black Wall, hanging . . . We lived our daily lives. The SS theirs. And the sacrifice of Father Kolbe broke through that, into that other Realm of Light . . .

Everywhere in the camp it was clear what primitive types of men came to predominate things, the dreadful ways they used their single chance to "get ahead," to get power and become part of the "elite." This was quite evident in Auschwitz, and Auschwitz only worked that way: with the proles, the underclass, the formerly disadvantaged, and, among the inmates, it was the criminals in particular who made up the Kapos. It was a rule of stupidity and anticulture, naked brutality. For a while I was a "runner" and brought reports to the camp Gestapo. I still remember it perfectly: in the office of the leader of the dreaded Division II (the Political Department) all the specialists and clerks were gathered together. The boss, SS Untersturmführer Max Grabner, a man of medium height, gave a briefing, holding forth self-importantly from behind his desk. His disorganized syntax and faulty grammar made it obvious that, despite his silver epaulets, you were standing in front of a completely uneducated man. The initiated knew that in civilian life he had been a cowherd on some Alpine pasture. Now he proudly wore the uniform of the SD (Sicherheitsdienst, the security police), with the rank of Kriminalsekretär, or master sergeant, in the Gestapo.

These monsters, these animals who only looked like men in uniforms, felt nothing beyond "duty," carrying out a supposedly "historic" assignment.

The Black Wall stood in front of the one stone wall in the yard of Block 11. There the unlucky were shot, naked, sequentially, with a small-caliber handgun. I was required to look on. And I was overcome by a deep shame.

I almost had a guilty conscience, for I was relatively well-off in "Canada," where I was at first, before they reassigned me to the Sonderkommando, probably as a punishment, I don't know— but maybe it was because the Kampfgruppe needed me as their contact there.

Yes, I belonged to the Kampfgruppe Auschwitz, and had the opportunity of working as a contact in various different commandos; that was how I got to work in the "Canada" warehouse along with Dr. Berner, and then in the women's camp at Birkenau, which was right next to it. Kielar had taken me along as

*part of the "installation team," and we could move about at will
there; then I was a "body carrier," was in the HKB [Häftling-
skrankenbau,* or prisoners' infirmary], *but finally was assigned to
the Sonderkommando in Crematorium I; it was amazing, you
know, the Austrians accepted me as an "old boy"* König-und-
Kaiser *Austrian—I had lived a few years in Vienna, and even
had a slight Viennese accent. You should know, Austrians and
Poles carried our organization. And I was particularly fond of
Burger, the enthusiastic leader of the Kampfgruppe; he was a
little younger than I, one of the youngest of all, and had the whole
thing firmly in hand—everyone respected him. He was an authority figure. Most of all we feared the camp Gestapo spies, with
their interrogations, tortures, and bunkers.*

4

Roland, who usually preferred not to talk about "horrible"
things, then proceeded to talk about his experiences: "The
Gestapo chief of the camp, Grabner, used to devote each weekend to 'cleaning out the bunker,' as he would, uh, cynically
put it. Once I was forced to see all that too, since Grabner was
constantly putting me off, he didn't have time now, I should
go with him someplace, there is a staff meeting happening.
Jakob, the 'block senior' [*Blockälteste*] of Block 11, who knew
just about everything, and then one of the female Gestapo
interpreters, well, they confirmed that it was like this every
time: after the briefing the entire department was required to
go into the camp . . . And then they would wait for the camp
Führer, SS Hauptsturmführer Aumeier, to show up in the
business office in Block 11 . . . followed by his eager marshal,
SS Unterscharführer Stiewitz. Then an SS doctor would turn
up as well, and quite often it was our countryman Dr. Fritz

Klein . . . interesting, you know? The overseer of the cell block
and several block leaders would complete the commission,
which then would move into the cellar, to begin with the
'cleanout' operation. A duty supervisor with a giant bunch of
keys opens the first cell door. He has to push back two iron
bolts as well. This prison is inside the perimeter of high-tension
electrical fences surrounding the camp: escape is not possible.
A nauseating stink spills out of the narrow, overcrowded cell.
A prisoner yells, '*Achtung!*,' you know? and then these hag-
gard, emaciated figures in their dirty blue-and-white rags line
up in a row in the cell, their faces expressionless. You can see
that some of them are only able to stand up with great effort.
With the composure of men whose will to live is already broken, they let the following process simply take its course, a
process that perhaps they have successfully gotten through a
few times before, one that decides between life and death. At
the door Aumeier holds out a list of all those detainees whose
fate he and Grabner are here to decide. The first gives his name
and how long he has been in the cell. The camp Führer asks
the marshal quickly the reason for his detention. Cases where
the prisoner was detained by Department II (the Political Department), which would include attempted escapes, were Gra-
ber's responsibility. So the two camp bigwigs then decide:
penal category 1 or 2. The prisoners categorized in these two
ways leave the cell and have to line up in two groups in the
hallway. The others are kept in 'pretrial detention.' The 'offenders,' those prisoners given penal category 1, are lucky
enough to get off with a beating or are assigned to particularly
hard labor for a time. Not so for the unlucky ones whose fate
has been determined by the coded word 'penal category 2.' In
clear sight of everyone, Aumeier pencils a thick blue cross beside the name in question, carefully marking the corners with
little hash marks. The meaning of 'penal category 2' was a

mystery to no one now. The group of less severe offenders, who were granted their lives this time, were brought into the camp for the appropriate punishment to be carried out. The large common cells on the ground floor and second floor of the block, which often contained over a hundred people crowded together in a single room, were emptied out, at least those that had a view of the yard, and the inmates, men separate from women, were brought into cells on the other side. The candidates for death were brought into a washroom on the ground floor. Inmates of Block 11 working as cleaners and clerks cover the window with a blanket, and help their unlucky comrades undress. Then they take an indelible pencil and in large strokes they write the inmate's prisoner number on his or her upper body, to enable them to register the bodies in the morgue or the crematorium: these men and women have visibly finished with living, and know, perhaps with some relief, that in a few minutes they will be freed from their tormenters and released from all the sufferings they have endured.

"Prisoner executions were originally held in the gravel pit. But the noise of the shots was disturbing. One day, Marshal Palitzsch got a small-caliber pistol from the slaughterhouse in Kattowitz. Silencers were made in the camp metalwork shop. Since then the executions of thousands were carried out conveyor-belt style, in silence, at the Black Wall in the yard of Block 11. Palitzsch, and then the camp Gestapo people, Dylewsky, Stark, Lachmann, would shoot the prisoners in the base of the skull. And Hans-Andreas Draser, from Hermannstadt was there, too, of course! The body-carriers Obojski and Teofil were always present at the executions. Sometimes I was part of the commando team, loading the bodies onto the trolley and taking them to the crematorium."

5

Adam had written about his detention in the bunker on his little paper rolls; he also wrote a lot about it later, from memory. *In the block, August 1944. The next day: The cell is full. The commission comes again. The same procedure. Only three are left in the cell. Suddenly it's dark. They have hung a blanket over the air shaft.*

Steps, a shot, over, and over, and over.

Today there are a lot of them.

They walk faster, before the muffled noise of the shot rings out.

They have to strip naked in the washroom, then, one after the other, Jakob or the nice Polish guy takes them out to the Black Wall.

Steps, a shot. Not a word, not a cry.

It is weird in this darkened cell. As if the blanket over the window had taken all the air away. A quarter hour ago there were nine of us here together.

All the blood. It flows in rivers across the cement floor.

One day, it is somehow bearable with three in the standing cell, but it gets bad the next day: they shove in someone new. And then someone else. Soon, there are ten in this hole. You can hardly breathe the air. Feels like we will suffocate. Muffled. The brain is stupefied. The tiny window. The bucket uncovered. Yet we talk, how many spies are here, maybe this bruiser here, a thug. I say nothing. No reason to. No reason. Supposedly he was a drunkard and a hooligan in Birkenau. Blessed are they who believe.

"Straighten things up, the commission's coming," Jakob says. He is the block senior warden here. We clean the cement floor with paper and cardboard.

Then they arrive. We live through our ears. We form one row, facing the door. The key shrieks in the lock. I feel my heart in my throat. Grabner, leader of the Political Department, in front,

then as adjutant, Draser, the Transylvanian Unterscharführer,
Hofmann, SS Obersturmführer, second camp Führer, then Mar-
shal Lachmann. And Jakob, too. I salute.

They put me to one side. "He's going to interrogation!" Jakob
pulls me out. "Nothing's gonna happen to you," he whispers, and
slaps me. Lachmann follows behind me on his bike. Flowers out-
side the SS barracks. And then the Political Department build-
ing, the camp Gestapo. I have to sit in an anteroom and wait, for
hours. Then, finally, the interrogation starts. But then it gets
interrupted by a phone call. A Sturmmann [storm trooper]
takes me back to the cell. In front of the gate leading into the yard
there's a truck with a tarpaulin cover. Jakob takes me into the
cell. It is empty. Are all of them, stiff, pale, and bloody, lying
underneath the tarp; and the German thug, too? The Polish boy
who was crying early this morning, calling for his mother?

•

Defendant Boger in the trial: "That is correct: at Auschwitz,
executions of inmates and other persons . . . took place often.
Without exception these shootings were carried out, as far as I
know, at the so-called Black Wall between Block 10 and 11. I do
not know whether shootings were also performed in gravel pits
outside the inner sentry perimeter. I can neither support nor
deny this claim. I only heard that before my arrival in Auschwitz
a lot of Russian commissars were shot outside. I don't know
where these executions happened, nor who carried them out.

"Executions were carried out as a rule because a court-
martial had pronounced the death sentence, or there were at
least orders from higher up. I know of no case in which a
member of the Political Department or some other SS member shot an inmate on his own initiative. Excluded from these
are of course those cases where inmates were fleeing from the
sentries. I personally never had a reason to use a weapon in
Auschwitz, and never shot a single person. There were two
small-caliber Mauser pistols kept in Block 11, for use in the

executions. These were quite ordinary weapons, but of course they had insertable magazines of from ten to twelve shots."

Adam's suffering colleague in the Sonderkommando, Filip Müller, said at the trial: "However, in the extermination facilities they did not kill with Zyklon B only. The SS considered it unnecessary to operate the gas chambers for groups of under two hundred victims. They did executions by shooting in Crematoriums I and II. Men, women, and children had to undress in the washroom next to the hall with the incinerating ovens, then line up with their faces to the wall in groups of five. We were forced to be present at these executions, and hold the victims still by their ears, while SS men stood behind them with small-caliber weapons and held the barrel at the back of their heads; the shots rang out over and over, countless times, and the women, children, sometimes very young children, and men, sometimes really old men, sank down into the blood on the cement floor. Many would pray and sing, countless times.

"Sometimes, despite the use of overwhelming force, the SS was unable to squeeze all of those doomed to die from the transport into the gas chambers. So then a number of men, women, and children from these transports were 'left over,' and they would end up at this wall, the last thing they ever saw. The gun barrels ran hot, shot after shot."

•

Capesius: "But there were cases of even the SS men losing their nerve. Several of them had to be removed from their posts, because they had nervous breakdowns, and one even voluntarily stayed behind in the gas chamber and died with those poor naked people."

•

Adam: Naked, standing there at the wall, many were quiet, but many screamed and cried, especially the children. Often they would hold one another's hands, a whole family: father, mother, and children.

Adam's diary: David Nencel, one of my fellow sufferers in the commando, was tormented by the memory of an execution. It was the only time that the SS forced him to hold the victims during an execution. With the passage of time Nencel had been granted certain privileges, since he was a skilled watchmaker. The SS men "organized" valuable watches from the property of victims murdered in the crematoriums. Nencel was given the appropriate tools to repair them, as well as a workbench in the room of the Kapo in charge of Crematorium I. It was while working there that an SS man ordered him to "assist" in an execution. This was a traumatic experience for David Nencel, which he could talk about only with the greatest effort, struggling to find words:

David Nencel: "Sometimes individuals would have hidden with their children, and were found out later. The SS didn't let these people wait for the next gassing—they killed them with a sport rifle. At that time I was in my workroom working on a pocket watch, when they brought in a woman with a child holding her by the hand. They needed someone to help them. The woman had to undress, then they took her to another room—I don't remember where. They took a completely ordinary rifle—the kind used for sport shooting, I think—and placed the weapon at the back of her head and the bullet came out of her brain. I remember now, they shot the child first. Can anyone in this world describe the pain of this woman— what torture this woman went through? That's what they did when they found individual Jews someplace."

6

Roland: "Yes, Poland, France, the Anschluss, the occupation of half of Europe. Then came the Eastern Campaign. And the terror of the bombings."

Is this really possible: to compare not just the bombings,

but even the treks of the refugees, with Auschwitz? Here is how the outrage in his voice sounds in my ear:

"Yes, don't you know how many German women and children, how many old people in East Prussia, in Poland, and in Yugoslavia were killed? Millions. The refugee treks and then the bombing terror. The persecution of the Jews was maybe more horrible than the murders of Germans, but it was more precisely organized, so that it only involved a few." (And it sounds as if he, who had been part of those few, could take the guilt from off the shoulders of the German people.) "But this mass annihilation of Germans, you know, which is a well-guarded secret in archives, you know, and which nobody talks about, well, for me, that is murder, that is genocide, and the other thing, well . . . I wouldn't like to travel to Poland or Czechoslovakia now . . ."

"And yet, there was anti-Semitism in our country as well . . ."

"The persecution of Jews by Transylvanian Saxons was unthinkable, it really shocked us Transylvanians!"

"And yet they were still assigned to do it."

"Yes, that, too, on top of everything else! They had to kill their own compatriots, namely, the Transylvanian Jews. There were many Transylvanian Jews in Auschwitz. And Gypsies, the lowest in the hierarchy! But the Jews, Capesius tried to save them, for the most part."

"My God, there were 400,000 in the 'Hungarian Transports.' How could he ever have saved them all!"

"But he tried, at least."

"Yes, sure, but how many could he save?"

"On the other hand, today now, I kind of have second thoughts about considering the Jews a people without regard to any national borders!

"Still, I would like again to stress: those people who were involved directly with the extermination of the Jews, you can count them on your fingers. There were very few . . . To saddle all eighty million German people with the guilt for these things, I think that is the height of nonsense . . ."

Roland exuded gentleness, but also uneasiness. There was something irritating about his facial expression, something felt by others, without their quite knowing what it was.

"So you want to write a book," Roland inquired. "What are you interested in?"

"The reasons for our disappearance."

"Aha. I see. You are a compulsive critic! Nietzsche has a good phrase: Human virtues—goodness, helpfulness, noble-mindedness—they are nothing but a kind of luxury item that we can't always afford. I found that somewhere in Nietzsche, and I agree with it."

"Aren't those the uppermost, highest values?"

"I would say there are no highest values. Philosophy is always determined by biology: I want to live, and to survive."

Roland's face was indistinct, a big, blurred egg.

"But I also think," he continued, suddenly very quiet, "freedom of conscience is the highest value."

"Then why didn't you run away from Auschwitz as others did? Was such an act a capital offense?"

Roland looked at me with his fish eyes, in some amusement: "Of course it was a capital offense. Desertion. But, no, that wasn't it. I didn't lack the courage. But I was for order, for unconditional discipline. And where could I have gone, anyway? After all, those were *my* people running things, who needed me . . ."

Then he quoted a poem of his grandfather Michael's: " 'Be faithful to / your language and your customs, / be true to your dear departed ones! / Stay close to the center of your people / whatever its fate may be!' "

And then he said something that bothered me greatly, confused me, something that combined the aesthetic with the horrific: "You know, when I was there, I thought it was all a dream, that it wasn't me, but another person, a ghost who was there. That I had simply dreamed it all . . .

"The rest," he stammered, "those other things, they are ju-ju-just . . ."—and he sank back into inarticulate sounds, perhaps going back beyond his memories—"j-j-j-j-j-just terrible as an actual event, but the German people are not murderers . . . they have been diabolical, right? but . . ."

"For instance, their love of orderliness," I hear myself say.

But Roland is struggling again for words, producing only low, inarticulate syllables, not sighs, nor words, just hesitant sounds:

"I didn't have the guts to desert from Auschwitz, like some of them did. It was because of my love of order . . . that I . . . that I . . . that I stayed there.

"And after that, I became a religion teacher."

IT WAS JUST LOVE OF ORDER
AND SENSE OF DUTY

I

Capesius in Göppingen: "I was often told during the trial, 'Well, you could simply have volunteered for duty at the front!'

"I could not volunteer for the front, I was too old. Because there were young doctors at the front, who were lieutenants, who were Obersturmführers, they didn't want a pharmacist who was a Sturmbannführer or even a Hauptsturmführer, who would then outrank them in the SS hierarchy."

"Did you ever try . . ."

Capesius: "No, they said we couldn't do that, that we were not needed there, that we could only be used behind the lines."

"So what happened with Roland—because he did volunteer for duty on the front, I believe, and then he was transferred there . . ."

Capesius: "When the whole thing was over . . . that's what we heard, certainly . . . when he was reassigned in November '44, by then everything was all over. At that point, they transferred everybody that they wanted to get rid of . . . so people wouldn't notice too much. November '44. By then everything in the camp was all over, because the Hungarians came in May, June, July, and then a few more people in August arrived, and then that was it with the exterminations . . . But the requirement of absolute obedience was in effect, always."

From Accessory Prosecutor Henry Ormond's plea in the Auschwitz Trial on May 24, 1965: "This leads me to make a few additional remarks about another myth—the myth of *Befehlsnotstand,* or the requirement of compulsory obedience to orders from a superior, which over the past few years has become an outright falsification of history. When the Zentrale Stelle der Landesjustizverwaltungen [Central Office for the Investigation of Nazi Crimes] was set up in Ludwigsburg in 1958—late, but not too late—it began to investigate this matter more thoroughly, and to take a closer look at those witnesses who were handed on from one proceeding to another, and to check their statements somewhat more intensively. And note: it turned out that not a single instance could be substantiated—I repeat, not a single instance—where someone could have been brought before an SS or police court, let alone—as they liked to portray it—been summarily shot, hanged, or gassed; that is, someone who declared his inability to participate in criminal killings could expect not to be punished!"

"But most of the incriminating evidence against you was in connection with the transport from Klausenburg . . ."

Capesius: "Yes, sure . . . that all happened in the week of Pentecost."

"Nice Pentecost . . ."

•

Karl Wilhelm Keul, known as Ali, my mother's youngest brother, was twenty-six when he signed up . . . Squad leader (Scharführer) in the barracks, and in 1942 he went to the concentration camp at Neuengamme. "So tell me, do you know anything about Ali?" I asked Roland.

"The last time I saw him was in 1942 in Stralsund. We were in the same barrack. He was a recruit there. He had enlisted. He had interrupted his studies, and later he joined an SS military geology unit. But in Stralsund he was doing his recruitment training time. It really didn't agree with him. It was really no fun. No fun at all."

[Roland here sings the "Westerwald Lied," a famous Nazi marching song.]

Heute wollen wir marschieren,
Einen neuen Marsch probieren,
Übern schönen Westerwald
Ja da pfeift der Wind so kalt . . .
Oh, du schöööner . . . Weeesterwald tiriititititi . . .

And Roland's voice went on and on. "Your mother's favorite brother was not assigned to the death march to Dachau in 1945, because he was an engineer with the military geology unit. He was supposed to stand guard at the tunnels in the Nordhausen labor camp at Dora II, which had been damaged by heavy Allied air raids, then do some blasting underneath the Kyffhäuser Tunnel to make a storage place for secret Reich documents, to be kept there for a thousand years."

2

Ali sat in his station house or in the SS barracks and wrote a letter home; he didn't like writing, but it eased his homesickness, the ache of *Heimweh*. He could see them all in his mind's eye: they were seated in a circle in the big smoking room as Mama read his letter aloud. Mama could only with difficulty make out his large, clumsy handwriting, and everyone was flush with excitement when finally his letter came *from up there*: "AO [Undisclosed Location], August 2. My dear ones, I got your family letter about Uncle Hans's fiftieth birthday and the five issues of the *Großkokler Bote*. They made me very happy and in my quiet way I am missing the orchard, the family, and all the treats served at these parties. My work here is very interesting, and I like it very much; the only thing is I have to do a lot of guard duty, somewhat similar to Roland's, and that is really one of the most exhausting duties here. As a result I have a high level of sleep deprivation, so much so, at any rate, that you shouldn't complain about my not writing enough! Roland wrote me recently with a question. He wants to take a leave so he can go back to his studies, and wants me to find out about that here, since no one where he is seems to know about it. So I got the exact requirements here from a leading officer of the Battery, which he can refer to, and based on these regulations, he, as a wounded veteran, is absolutely entitled to do so. Hopefully that will all work out, so he can finally get out of Auschwitz . . ."

Soldaten sind Soldaten in Worten und in Taten, und kennen keine Lumperei, Valleri, vallera juchheißass, Rosemarie! ("Soldiers are soldiers, in words and in deeds, and they never do anything mean, valleri, etc. Rosemarie!")

So they were all sitting around in the big smoking room in the Baiergasse house or the Holzmarkt house, and Mama read the letter aloud to them.

When I showed my parents and Friederike these letters, in which the word "Auschwitz" is mentioned so often, Father said, "Look, Eri, it's right, see, here it is in writing, and I thought we never knew anything about Auschwitz . . ."

But Mother then said right off, without thinking: "But, Kurt, that was *a different* Auschwitz back then!"

"Yes," said my grandfather, "we heard of Auschwitz, sure, we were there, too, the grand duchy of Kraków and the duchies of Auschwitz and Zator. Oh, Galicia in 1915. The flesh wounds, the burnt villages after the battle, the whinnying of the horses and the cries of the wounded!" But Ali, whose real name was Karl Wilhelm, didn't know anything about all that; he was a war child, poor thing, and susceptible, and he wrote home from the Neuengamme concentration camp:

"AO, August 5. I am finally getting around to finishing my letter. In this mail I am also forwarding those issues of the

Großkokler Bote on to Hermann. Alas, it has turned out that all our hopes for the weather were in vain, because on the very next day the usual crummy weather returned, and today is uncomfortably chilly. Summer can hardly have lasted one hour here. I did get a cold from the weather, but the new medicine worked, and my nose is almost back to normal, and that awful cold is finally gone, though I can't breathe quite as well as I would like through my nose. Has Roland really become an Untersturmführer? That's a break. Oh, and Tommy was here, too, a couple of times. Things aren't nearly so bad here as you imagine. Mama really shouldn't worry needlessly about little old me. We are in no danger here, and we have a good air-raid cellar as well. Be sure to give my best to all the uncles, aunts, cousins, nieces, and nephews who signed the letter. Many fond greetings from Your Ali."

Kommt ein Vogel geflogen, setzt sich nieder auf mein' Fuß. Hat ein Brieflein im Schnabel, von der Mutter einen Gruß. [German folk song about a bird bringing a letter from a mother to her child —trans.].

Sighişoara: During my visit "home" in Adam's house, we came to speak of Roland and Victor Capesius, and when I said I knew Capesius well, that I knew him back from childhood, and that my mother even went out with him, Adam laughed and said, *You Transylvanian Saxons, you all know one another, as if you were all relatives.* My mother knew him from his student and *Kränzchen* [a fraternity-like student organization] days—I found photographs of her and him in Sighişoara, taken in the yard of their friends the Milds, you remember, in the Gartengasse, not far from what was then the hospital for diphtheria patients . . . *Yes, sure, I remember, the former district judge* . . . Yes, and the three girls kneeling in the grass, with Capesius (whom they just called Vic), a hulking presence behind them, making some kind of "blessing" gesture over their heads; Mother said that Vic had something "brutal" about him, cold and objective. But he always like to sing: "I'm dancing with you into heaven, the seventh heaven of love."

". . . and he courted me," she told us, "but I gave him the brush-off, he was too big for me. He always seemed so beefy and heavy, and with that face, too, I thought, he's got Gypsy blood in him, somebody there crossed the line back when. But he could dance; we waltzed together very well. And he visited us in the garden, too. He would bring his female friends from the *Kränzchen*, the Mild sisters, and even Paula to our parties. These were mostly Sundays: then garden paths were all nicely swept and raked. The blue polka-dotted cloth was on the veranda table, and we had placed a bouquet of wildflowers in an earthenware jug on Ami's (my mother's) blue 'glass box.' On one occasion, Ami had just made huge portions of *gefüllte Ardei* [stuffed peppers] and sent Marischka, the Hungarian maid, down to the cellar with the vanilla cream cake. Harry, our German shepherd dog, was dozing at the veranda door. Suddenly his ears pricked up, and from the other side of the brook we could hear Aunt Cäcilie's voice calling out melodically, 'Hopp hopp,' the family greeting. That led to a loud and demonstrative scene of welcome. Yes, it's our beloved Aunt Cäcilie, dressed as always in her white dress and wide-brimmed straw hat with black silk ribbon, greeting everyone with her characteristic torrent of words. And beside her, quiet, softspoken Uncle Daniel with his kind blue eyes. Then her two sons Roland and Reinhard. Roland always had a thing for the Brown Shirts, the 'renewal movement' as it was known around there. This time Vic was there, too, but he had not a clue about politics. Roland had joined up early. And I recall, once he even wore a soldier's cap or an SA cap to one of these gatherings. I can still see him gently fondling the death's-head emblem, as if he had some deep-seated longing he couldn't shake, and he would just go on and on . . .

"After greeting one another in the garden we would get our swimming things and go down to the Schaaser Brook and swim. Down below the weir, we would cool off at a little waterfall. Vic was kind of an unlovely, big-boned hulk. He was heavy, and hairy, too. He talked about Vienna, where he had just come from; I think he was very materialistic, doing deals, and clearly interested in acquiring valuable objects and money. His eyes would gleam as he talked about it, and he didn't really have any other interests; he was not as cultivated as Roland or Reinhard, and certainly not like Aunt Cäcilie or Uncle Daniel. I don't think he felt comfortable around us. He constantly talked about his girlfriend in Vienna, a 'high-class *Wienerin*,' trying to make me jealous, which I thought was tasteless. And he always walked beside me, once he put his arm around me. I didn't know your father yet. I first met him on a hiking trip in the Hargitha Mountains. Vic was along on that trip too. There's a photograph of our group celebrating New Year's Eve in the dining room, it shows the big table and the Christmas tree—all our friends were there, and in the picture Vic is looking at me, he's holding a glass of wine—I am seated, he is standing—he looks like a big black mountain leaning down over me. We are all in costumes for New Year's, he's a chimney sweep, in top hat and blackface. He gave me the creeps, even out of costume there was something weird about him, some lurking violent streak in him. And sometimes he seemed absent, staring off into space. Anyway, at that particular party in the orchard, after we swam, we ate raspberries in the vegetable garden and shook the acorns from the oak trees. We had set the long family table up on the terrace beneath the old oak trees. Everybody took a seat, my father greeted all the guests, and Aunt Cäcilie recited a poem: she always was ready with a Goethe quotation. Everybody was touched by this gesture, but soon we all turned to more epicurean pleasures, as the peppers were served.

"Moved, and touched. So beautiful. But then the 'shiva-ree' starts. Everyone talks at once, Aunt Cäcilie the fastest and most eloquent. My father grumbles, he 'can't hear himself talk.'"

A bad family trait. Why are they always yelling? Out of control. No one listens to anyone else. It's like a nimbus that takes in the whole family, pulling it in, this atmosphere of closeness at the richly set table on the oak-shaded terrace—you could cut this atmosphere with a knife, grasp it; there is security in these surroundings, in the cool shade, in this element of happy intimates: everything is so simply and beautifully arranged, like the dishes on the table. So why are they all shouting at one another? As if they were in danger, as if they were drowning or had to assert themselves against something. It's as if there were really more to them, as if they should have had more self-confidence than they actually had, more than they could use here, in any case. Or is it a kind of trance, this togetherness, where they could forget their ever increasing dread, this silent fear of whatever was coming?

"The men are quieter," said Mother, "as if they had long since accepted the inevitability of something coming; it is such a nice refuge here, yet it's as if this were all not quite real anymore: the oak trees, the terrace, the view out over the familiar outline of the fortress, the Buna Mountains, the surrounding area; the spruces, the coltsfoot growing between the rocks—it's all like it's in the distant past, frozen in time, on this little island. My father takes a big sip of local Nadesch wine, and then says to Roland's father, Daniel the organist, sitting beside him and gazing intently at him through his round granny glasses: 'Since the lost war in '18 and the collapse of the monarchy, nothing is like it used to be. Even the ground sways beneath our feet: nothing but uncertainty since we became part of Wallachia.'

"Suddenly dark clouds fill the sky, it is oppressively humid, but still no rain. Finally, dark shadows scud soundlessly over the ground. The air smells of ozone, of freshness. The first big raindrops start to come down. We quickly bring the chairs inside. And when we are all seated cozy and dry on the summerhouse veranda, it's like a dream. The lightning strikes nearby, the thunder crashes. 'Oh, Jesus, great-grandmother, grandmother, mother, and child,' Ami cries out in fright, as if the words could protect her like a spell. Harry howls in terror. Roland says, 'Yes, there are distant homelands within us, streaks of clouds, we think constantly that something bad could happen at any minute.' Roland is sitting with Vic at the window, looking over at the silhouette of the fortress, still visible between the low-hanging clouds and the streaming rain: it's pouring, in buckets: already a river of yellow clay-colored water is shooting down the gorge, the pathways are all little brooks. 'Too bad,' Vic says, 'now we can't go up to the dance floor, I was so keen on it, I brought the gramophone for nothing.' 'What do you mean, come on, we'll go up to the attic, not much room for dancing, but enough for two couples—you could play your dance records—have you got anything classical, Schubert or Beethoven?' 'No, I'd rather hear the Charleston or Strauss waltzes,' Vic responds. 'Philistine,' Roland mutters.

"And then the old folks, sitting and talking on the veranda, hear this: *Oh, Donna Clara, I saw you dancing there* . . . and *Oh, maiden, come back, come back, come back to my green side, I like you so much, so much, so much.* And of course: *I'm dancing with you into heaven, the seventh heaven of love* . . . or *Cornflower blue is the color of women's eyes in love* . . . and *Where the North Sea waves break upon the shore* . . .

"And then Ami sings right along: *We belong together / just like the wind and the sea / to be parted from you / I just could*

never do . . . And Vic's awful singing, you could hear it above
all the others, the loudest . . . But Roland says: 'It's these very
songs of ours that reveal the essential difference between us
and the Jews. Can you imagine that they really understand
and feel our songs? . . . All that jazz, that American 'asphalt
music' they're poisoning the world with . . . in Berlin or New
York. Paris, too . . . this negrified . . . this nigger music.' "

Roland, the ever-sensitive aesthete, sitting before me in
Innsbruck, at a round table, scrutinizes me with his pale bluish purple eyes, as I say:

"And so you inquired at the administration office . . ."

"At the SS administration office, yes, I made an inquiry
about how I could get released from Auschwitz to pursue my
studies. Yes—well, I submitted the request, but it was never
approved. I did try. But the best medicine for me then was
getting married. My wife came with me. And my son was born
in Auschwitz, as you know. As a sideline I was a religion teacher,
when my guard duties allowed. My wife taught music in the
main school, the German school they had there. It was life like
anywhere else. We planted a vegetable garden, kept bees, planted
flowers, went hunting and fishing, there were afternoon coffee
parties, birthdays, Christmas parties with Commandant Höß.
Kling Glöckchen, klingelingeling, Kling Glöckchen kling. And
the kids would recite their Christmas poems: *Von draus vom
Walde komm ich her . . .*"

*From the plea of Accessory Prosecutor Henry Ormond in the
Auschwitz Trial on May 24, 1965:* "It turned out that those
individuals who were not willing to participate in *Einsatzgrup-
pen* executions or concentration camp murders were punished,
at most, by being sent to duty at the front.

"With this I come to the fable of those requesting duty at
the front being turned down, a myth which was offered up to
us in many different variations by nearly all the defendants.

"To judge from the defendants' statements, they longed for

nothing more eagerly than to be able to turn their backs on the concentration camps and be sent to the front. So it is remarkable that we find no such requests for front duty in any of the personnel documents of the defendants that have been preserved. These documents contain all sorts of things, but not this."

So Roland never did leave Auschwitz voluntarily, and perhaps never even wanted to. But he stayed alive, and his story continued. Ali never returned home from the war.

3

Innsbruck, May 1978. "So your barracks were located more or less outside the perimeter? That's what I have heard about the guards, anyway," I asked Roland. He just growled, "Yes, yes . . ."

But today I know better. Capesius had made a list of the guard troops with descriptions: "1940 SS Death's-Head Sturm-bann, till the end of 1942 four companies. In 1944, fourteen companies of the Waffen-SS were in charge of Auschwitz I, II, and III. There was a guard dog unit with 150 dogs." And Roland appears as an SS Untersturmführer. They were the *esesmani* (SS-men) of the camp, and they were not just doing guard duty in the towers or along the large outer and smaller inner sentry perimeters, as I thought earlier, and as Roland led me to believe.

Documentation from Auschwitz proved that SS Guard Company Four was in place as early as July 1940. The leaders of this company were, among others: SS Obersturmführer Josef Kollmer (May '41–December '42), SS Obersturmführer Franz Halbleib (December '42), and SS Untersturmführer Roland Albert (September '43).

Unterscharführer (sergeant) Richard Böck, a member of Company Four, tells of a gassing. And also of an execution:

"One day when I was still in Guard Company Four, the leader of the company, Kollmer, asked for volunteers for an execution. There were enough volunteers so that I did not have to participate. But then I did observe the execution. Kollmer was in command. Before the shooting, they read something in Polish. The prisoners—Poles—were lined up in a gravel trench and shot. Any one of them who was not yet dead received a pistol shot in the back of the head from a young blond man who later became Untersturmführer."

And that beastly Kaduk, the most feared man in all of Auschwitz, was in Company Four.

There is a list compiled by Hermann Langbein with many members of the SS guard troops who were sentenced in Poland, some of whom were also executed. For instance, Alexander Bülow, fifteen years; Johann Gaisberger, life; Paul Götz, death sentence, carried out December 22, 1947; Gerhard Haubold (guard dog unit), twenty years; Kurt Kirchner, Johann Klaar, and Hans Mössner, death sentence carried out; Erich Mehrbach, leader of the guard dog unit, executed January 1, 1949; and many others.

Roland had removed himself from Auschwitz. He fled with his family, first to the mountains, where his children used skis to get to school. Then his wife got sick and died. Using his grifter's skills he got somebody in Vienna in the appropriate bureaucracy to destroy his records. "Yes, in Vienna people are still human beings!" he said.

Capesius: "His cousin or somebody from Innsbruck threw out the case . . . He was a lawyer there, or something like that, in Innsbruck. Or a close acquaintance. Ask him, he'll tell you. And he got rid of all his papers. No more papers existed, so no more incriminating evidence could be presented, and the people who could have made such an accusation were in part already dead."

Roland: "To calm our nerves, *there* at the end . . . The best thing about it was when our son was born there. But we had to keep that a secret. We falsified the documents. He was . . ."

"Why did that have to be kept secret?"

"It was never supposed to be mentioned! For my personal safety as well. The fact that I had been in Auschwitz wasn't known until 1963. You know, the trial. [Long pause.] Hmmmm . . . Officially, that is. It was brought up officially by the other side. That whole thing with Capesius, that was never public. You know."

"But your name is in Langbein's Auschwitz book."

"Did you see my name there? That's very interesting. But only my name?"

"Name and rank: Untersturmführer. That's it."

"It's like a miracle that I got through the whole thing. I

Wilhelm Friedrich Boger (first row), Victor Capesius (second row), Oswald Kaduk (third row), Emil Hantl (fourth row). Opening day of the trial in the plenary chamber of the Frankfurt City Hall (Römer), Frankfurt am Main, December 20, 1963

survived two war crime trials that never really got off the ground, because the witnesses' testimony was so contradictory, in my case as well. For me Auschwitz was small potatoes anyway. My main guilt lies elsewhere, in Flossenbürg, where I had complete responsibility. I had the whole troop under me when we evacuated Flossenbürg. That was where things were worst, you know. That I ever got out of there was pure luck. But I would like to tell you a few things about being in an American prisoner-of-war camp. So here. I was in an American prison near Freiburg. So this Jew from Hannover, Jakobson, was hanging around there. An emigrant to America, get the picture? And picked out the SS people. And so some, who had been incautious enough not to throw away their pay books, among them a half dozen Transylvanian Saxon compatriots from Alish, just ordinary enlisted men that you couldn't pin anything on, well, this Jew forced them to stand at attention at the camp entrance. Behind them stood a couple of Negroes, you know, who stabbed them with their bayonets in the legs . . . until they fell over and then were shot. After three days they were all dead. That was the daily deal. Hundreds, thousands of innocent men died. And I had to keep sucking up to this Jakobson guy, stay on good terms with him, you know, I was camp adjutant. I could take that liberty, because I was working together with the American camp leaders. Organizing the camp. I could easily go to them and speak with them . . ."

"They didn't know you were an SS officer?"

"Well, our uniforms were all the same. I just took off the collar tab. I had just one goal: to get home. I had to see my family. I dreamed up the most incredible schemes, and they worked. Have you heard?"

"Well, Hermann [a brother of Ali] also got free, in the most amazing way."

"Yes, Hermann took part in some incredible things, too.

In Freiburg, I had two 'offices.'* *Two.* An American one and an 'official' one. And I could issue discharge papers. And hope that I didn't get caught issuing papers with the wrong blood types."

"So you had one?"†

"Yes, sure, I had one."

"Hermann didn't have one."‡

"Well, then he was lucky. And I had a kind of private office in which I forged pay books and helped people get their freedom. Wehrmacht pay books. Forged. And I had the official American stamp. That was top secret, and it was used to stamp onto discharge papers. And so I could actually issue discharge papers.§ And I had made out one for myself in case my own discharge didn't come through. I had to make a deal with Jakobson, you know? After everything I saw, everything I went through, it's a miracle that I am sitting in front of you now. But my wife did not survive it, because she was so afraid for me."

"Was it just fear, or was it a guilty conscience?"

"It was simply fear," Roland said gently. "It was just fear, pure and simple," he whispered.

"But you say yourself, you were psychologically very resistant."

"Yes, interestingly, I was very resistant."

Roland exhibits more clearly than any of the other SS

---

*Roland uses the word *Kanzlei*, or office. According to the author, Roland's story is a mixture of fantasy and reality. He refers to an American prisoner-of-war camp near Freiburg in which he traded in false documents. —trans.

†This refers to the blood-type arm tattoo that all members of the SS were required to have. —trans.

‡As a physician, Hermann did not need to have the tattoo. Thinking in advance of eventual American captivity, he purposely avoided getting one. Roland, on the other hand, was afraid of his being discovered, as that was a clear sign of having been in the SS; while regular German army soldiers could be released, the SS were not. —trans.

§For German prisoners of war in American captivity. —trans.

members I know the true extent of his inner, emotional devastation. I told him about my teaching career, that at eighteen I was already a "Herr Rektor," and how proud I was, feeling like a big shot when all the local farmers would stand up respectfully as I walked through the lanes of the village. Roland responded, "Right, I know, that's the way it was *there*, the young people on guard duty, these twenty-year-old guys, felt exactly the same: when they got a stripe or two, they felt like they *were* somebody, they stood up extra-straight, started feeling they were special, and bossing people around. That's all they knew: giving orders and taking orders. So they would use groups of prisoners to help maintain order. Ordering, and obeying, they had brought that with them from home. And for them, as you well know, there was *no back talk!*"

4

Was it all just a dream? And Vic—a dead man? Just like so many of the victims, is he living the life of a dead person now, and doesn't even know it? Did it seem to his wife, the Frau Doktor, who treats him so nicely, so caringly, as though he wasn't the one who sent her relatives to the gas chamber . . . ?

As if I could find the answer to this puzzle in Göppingen . . . with Dr. Capesius and his wife, sitting in a little anteroom in their drugstore, but I could see the shelves, the counter, and thought I was hallucinating—everything was just as it had been back home at the Crown Pharmacy, even down to the sharp, clean smell of medicines.

And even he sometimes forgot for a second, staring off into space, as if he were back there, too: "Your Honor . . . Oh, excuse me, Herr Schlesak, it's you, of course, I know, my dear friend Eri's son."

And Fritzi Capesius defends him again in her cultivated

voice: "You must understand, Victor has often been confused since then, just as he was back during the trial; four years in solitary confinement, and then all those people and lights, he was befuddled and distracted, and his lack of concentration really had an effect on most of his responses in the trial. They even say that once, during the testimony of those horrible stories of killing children with carbolic acid injections, he was smiling absentmindedly . . .

"Nor should we forget, Victor has been severely depressed since then. He has even made written notations about it.

"But really he has only pure phenol in the dispensary to make, say, eardrops with," she added.

"You could also say 'carbolic acid,'" her husband interjected.

So what does the druggist feel now when he "thinks back"? I kept asking, and got no answer. And Frau Capesius said that it could be he had just dreamed everything that happened "there!"

Frau Fritzi Capesius: "All this horror, Victor has sometimes said, it was all just a bad dream. Not dreamed by him, but by somebody else."

"And the trial, sitting there on the defendant's bench, that was also just a dream?"

Capesius: "Yes, in the trial, everything was different from the way things were in Auschwitz."

"What was different?"

Capesius: "Well, what my inmate pharmacy assistant Sikorski talked about . . . And he knew so much more than I did . . . After all, he got to Auschwitz before I did."

"But you also knew a lot of the people who came to Auschwitz in those horrific transports . . . You had known some of the Jewish prisoners . . ."

Fritzi Capesius: "Yes, the Jewish doctors . . ."

Capesius: "But only a portion of them stayed at Auschwitz, those people that were selected out for labor went on to Germany in the next transport."

We spoke of the witness Josef Glück from Haifa, originally from Transylvania. He lied at the trial, said Capesius. "The Jews were happy to come to Germany, gratis, to come to Frankfurt for the big trial in the sixties."

He, Capesius, did not meet the witness Glück for the first time at Frankfurt, but earlier, namely, "there."

•

Roland: "I was a teacher *there*, I taught in the main school *there*. The German school. It was a pleasure. Teaching back then. I will never forget those kids. The pupils, you know?"

"Were those the children of . . ."

"The guards and officers and so forth."

"So you all had a more or less civilian life there."

"Yes, that, too. We had music. We had . . ."

"Including Christmas parties and such?"

"Yes, you had to have distractions. And my wife taught there, too. Taught music. Also."

Roland's combination of gentleness and edginess has a way of getting on my nerves.

His voice is still in my ear, it stays with me, his unctuous diction drives me crazy, because I know it so well, it's so familiar, as familiar as my own, it's as if I spoke that way myself . . . that's how it feels, and yet it isn't that familiar Transylvanian accent, somewhat broad and harsh, or even the occasional use of dialect that really gets on my nerves so much.

"And you didn't have any pangs of conscience?"

Roland: "No."

In this he is no exception. In the Auschwitz trial, except for Dr. Lucas, there was not a single defendant who felt guilty.

The prosecutor: "The defendants consistently maintained silence before the jury at Frankfurt, they did not choose to remember anything, they found nothing to regret, and so they were sorry about nothing. They never tired of assuring the court that they had always merely done their duty, that they had had no choice but to follow orders. Law is law, and orders are orders. At the trial's conclusion, filled with self-pity, they reaffirmed their feelings of innocence. Defendant Robert Mulka, adjutant to the camp commandant, cited the truly fateful historical circumstances; the medical orderly Josef Klehr, who killed thousands of victims by injecting phenol into their hearts with a hypodermic needle, even insisted that he had felt great pity for the victims; the torturer Wilhelm Boger had really just been carrying out the orders of his superiors—of course, 'without reservation.' And so it was a negative kind of truth, so to speak, when the lone accused prisoner in the Auschwitz trial, Emil Bednarek, in his final summation explained, 'I could not have acted any differently. I feel no guilt before God or mankind.' "

"Where there is no responsibility, there is also no guilt." Thus by pointing out that he had only been obediently carrying out his bounden duty—as had SS Obersturmbannführer Adolf Eichmann, who had been found four years before by Fritz Bauer, and who had believed in all seriousness that the court would acquit him—the druggist of Auschwitz did the same thing:

Capesius: "I was not guilty of anything in Auschwitz, and I ask you to acquit me."

Like Capesius, Roland also said he did not feel in any way culpable. Not in the least! Roland showed me his books, gushed about his pupils. His wife had died from fear, he said, in his quiet and gentle-sounding voice: "She feared for my freedom, you know? Since I had been three years in Auschwitz. And had been arrested repeatedly. By the Germans, the English, the French, the Austrians. I was always having to wangle my way out of something.

"I was always getting calls in the middle of the night, you know? And who was downstairs in the street? A former Kapo, of course, who along with me was supposed to comb through Austria looking for exculpatory witnesses for Dr. Capesius, for our druggist Capesius, who had been unjustly found guilty and sentenced. And he was really a friend of mankind, this guy.

"Do you know the feeling? The war, the camp . . . an unending nightmare."

"And did you also shoot people?"

"Believe me, it was not me who did the shooting. But now I know how it is when someone, someone who is supposedly me, has to fire a bullet into another person—you almost jump, the noise scares you so much, and this other person falls over dead on the spot, but not you, no, you're still alive, you have to live, but not him. But you don't notice this until later. And you don't believe it. You pull the trigger, but you are still there. It's like it is with spoken words, which dissolve the minute they're said. You tell yourself, this is your enemy, someone who will take vengeance or something, but it doesn't help."

Adam said that there is no explanation whatever for the camp, that everything just unrolls, as in a nightmare; morality is just laughable, all that matters is *naked life* and the machinery of the camp, which has its own laws, a totally different planet: in fact, hell itself. And this applies to both victims *and* perpetrators, the distinctions between them blur completely into a gray zone, in which there exists only *the guilty* in our sense, but a sense in which *there* makes *no sense, and which it is completely impossible to understand in normal life.* All outrage, any sense of indignation is just childish, absurd, in fact, a sign that you have not understood a thing.

Roland: "Behaving normally, acting as one might at home or somewhere else, that drew attention, even in our group. You learned that fast. When Dr. Klein arrived at Auschwitz, he inspected the barracks he was assigned to, he chatted with the woman inmate doctor, and with the inmates, just as any doctor would, drank coffee with them, was affable and straightforward; he found the way the prisoners were housed in the infirmary 'impossible,' and promised to put things right. But that was all forgotten by the next day; he had probably been given a reprimand. From then on he maintained the distance appropriate for an SS officer."

Adam: And the situation of the inmates: woe to any of them who thought they had any freedom of choice, if they thought they could be a human being. That was their downfall.

So it's wrong to say Roland is crazy, but he still has the Auschwitz "bacillus" in him. Borowski, Améry, Primo Levi— all committed suicide. Yes, even a whole series of SS officers and Auschwitz doctors killed themselves. Capesius talked about this with Gerber, his colleague in the dispensary. Even his nemesis Dr. Wirths hanged himself!

So is death the only appropriate response to "that situation"?

Roland's girlfriend, Helga, kept pacing out of the room, then coming back in, terribly nervous. He nattered on endlessly, unchecked, irritatingly loud, a stream of words issued from his old-man's baby face.

Roland's wife, a fragile-looking Swabian from the Banat, had died after the war. There is a photograph of her and Aunt Cäcilie in Innsbruck. Her first symptoms were stomach pains, then it went to her heart, and in the end it was cancer. Cancer of the soul.

MORALITY REVERSED

The SS doctor Münch in the Auschwitz Trial: "A human reaction in Auschwitz was only possible in the first few hours. After you were there just a short while, it was impossible to react normally. Because of the duty roster, everyone had some kind of skeleton in his closet. You were trapped, you had to go along."

Eyewitness SS soldier Ruprecht: "In Birkenau I knew Blockführer Weiß. He was fond of drink. Once when he was drunk, he said: 'Mother, if you knew that your son has become a murderer.'"

Presiding judge: "You heard that?"

Ruprecht: "Yes, I heard it myself."

Very odd circumstances were partly the result of the effects of the war's events, but also through being together in the murder machine. On my visit to Innsbruck, Roland mentioned that someday he wanted to write about "how beautifully humanity had blossomed there."

Holluj, a former inmate, said during the trial: "On September 13, 1944, English or American planes bombarded the garment workshops. About one hundred people were killed in this attack, prisoners and SS men, and about the same number were wounded. Volunteers swiftly brought stretchers from the hospital—I was one of them. We carried the wounded, including SS men, into the hospital, so that their wounds could be dressed and surgical procedures performed. The next day the camp administration sent potted cyclamens and chocolate from the Red Cross to the victims. We took this as a gesture of appreciation, since we had given aid to the SS victims as well. But later all the seriously injured prisoners were gassed."

Another Polish witness corroborated this report. Kowalczyk: "In September 1944 many inmates and SS members were wounded in a bombing attack. Some of the SS were brought to us in the operating room; they were bandaged up and some operated on. After the operation they kissed our hands."

Adam: Humanitarianism was forbidden in Auschwitz. Everything that happened happened completely backward, against all morality, but also opposed to all normal expectations. Whoever didn't grasp this was doomed. And of course anyone who openly opposed it was also doomed. Resistance was possible only through tactics and lies; you always had to appear slavishly obedient to every order, even the most absurd. It was a gigantic system of lies and secrecy. In fact everything was criminal and menda-

cious, including what the SS did. You only survived if you lied and stole and betrayed, if you worked against everything that was allowed there, which was practically nothing. The most extreme example of resistance in the face of death was our group, the Kampfgruppe. But the SS, too, concealed and hushed up everything. There was no gassing, for instance, but just "Sonderbehandlung" (special treatment); the cause of death was always falsified. Even the most minor SS official clearly realized that all of this should not be happening; all the perpetrators knew intuitively that they were taking part in a horrendous crime. But woe to anyone who let the secret out, who told anyone outside what was really happening. The SS Unterscharführer (sergeant) from the Political Department, Perry Broad, told the Frankfurt jury in his famous report that Auschwitz had always been secret, but that by 1944 this secrecy had slowly started to unravel, that it had to come out:

Broad: "At night the red sky over Auschwitz was visible for miles. Without those giant wooden pyres it would have been impossible to get rid of the huge number of bodies of those who had died in the camps, or the corpses from the gas chambers. The chimneys of the crematoriums in Auschwitz had become overheated and developed dangerous cracks. Even though talkative sentries were punished with draconian measures, and blamed for breaking the veil of secrecy, still the penetrating, sweetish odor and the flames at night betrayed the secret of what was happening in Auschwitz at least to the immediate neighborhood. Railroad workers told the civilian population that thousands of prisoners were being transported daily to Auschwitz, but that the camp was not being enlarged accordingly. The police escorting the transports confirmed these statements. The result of this was that an official party spokesman [Gauredner] in the town of Auschwitz, while addressing a largely hostile audience, was forced to throw in the towel and leave the rostrum. The indignation in the German press about

Katyń [massacres of Poles by the Russians], and its comparison of this with the ethics and morality of their own conduct of the war, struck many of the SS in the camp itself as amusing, to say the least. The sentries had gotten too good a view of the extermination activities, which in fact only the Sonderkommando were supposed to know about. The leader of Section VI, SS Oberscharführer Knittel, who was charged with looking after the troops and with their ideological training, was described by the guards because of his theatrical nature as the enlisted man's 'Savior,' and in his lectures he had to focus all his efforts on combating widening demoralization."

LOVE IN THE DEATH CAMP

I

Adam's diary: One day the SS brought in a truckload of sick "Mussulwomen," i.e., starving, emaciated women, who were in fact "undead," no longer really alive. Only one girl was able to hold herself upright and stand on her own feet. She turned to a healthy, well-built young man, whose name was Jankiel, and said to him that she was only eighteen and had never slept with a man. "I want to know what it is like, before I die, will you do that for me?" Jankiel was horrified, turned away, and hid.

He told us about this after she had gone to the gas chamber, and we kind of put him on trial about this. We argued vehemently about it. But Jankiel said to us, "It was totally impossible! Are you out of your minds? She was a naked, stinking Mussulwoman, filthy, covered with excrement from head to toe. And then the idea of dying, of her being taken straight into the gas chamber . . . How can you imagine anybody could think like that . . . No, I couldn't, I never could have, even if it was the last request of a dying person . . ."

DRASER AND THE JEWISH GIRL

Dr. Ella Lingens was the only German (Austrian) prisoner doctor in Auschwitz. She had helped Polish Jews escape to Switzerland and was arrested in 1942, and was sent to Auschwitz without a trial. When she came down with typhus, she was saved by her former fellow student Dr. Rohde: "I can't let you die here in this filth." She lay sick in Block 10 for four weeks, and she thought that all her experiences in Birkenau were just nightmares caused by her fever. Dr. Lingens, the "Aryan" Viennese doctor of the block, knew that Dr. Fritz Klein, the camp doctor from Transylvania, was "a raging anti-Semite," who had often volunteered to work at the "Black Wall" and for the "selections" at the ramp. So she knew that, with him, she could never intercede for a Jewish woman who had been "put on the list," that is, been selected for gassing. There was in fact a case in her block for whom she could have approached Klein, but she refrained. A young Jewish woman, Frau Lejmann, in agonies of "fear and despair," began to weep hysterically when her number was "put on the list," and she begged Dr. Lingens for help. The doctor knew that Lejmann had a "relationship" with a Transylvanian named Draser, in the Political Department, and she tried to help. "I went to the Political Department of the women's camp, had an interview with the Unterscharführer then on duty, and informed him that a female prisoner was listed to be on the transport that very day, and that Unterscharführer Draser, in the general political bureau for the whole camp, was extremely concerned about this prisoner's condition, and had asked me to look into the matter. I said to him that I doubted that allocating this prisoner for transport would accord with Unterscharführer Draser's wishes, and requested that other arrangements be made in this case. His answer both amazed and depressed me. 'It's good you are pointing this out. In fact you would have been committing a punishable offense in not informing us of Unterscharführer Draser's wishes. If the man needs the woman, then of course there is no question of taking such action in her case. Another woman will have to go in her place. Take the matter up with the security officer on duty immediately.' And now I knew: the punishable offense was precisely the opposite of what I had feared to do—of what was in fact moral and normal."

But who was this Hans-Andreas Draser who was involved in an affair with the Jewish girl? I learned from Capesius's documents that he came from the Hermannstadt area and in 1944 was twenty-nine years old. He was a junior squad leader and reported to the much-feared Gestapo chief Grabner, and was also an accomplice of the sadist from Stuttgart Unterscharführer Boger, who had "participated" in actions in the bunker as well as in the executions at the "Black Wall," and who had then invented the notorious Boger swing, or *bogerowka*. Adam explained how once he had had to look on as prisoners set up a rack in the Political Department, under the supervision of Dylewsky and Broad, also members of the camp Gestapo.

You know, another Transylvanian, an Unterscharführer, was there! So the candidate for "intensified interrogation" was placed inside the rack and, like a tumbling toy, put onto the swing: the poor soul had to sit on the floor of the rack, with his knees drawn up and his hands bound over them, and a stick was forced under the backs of his knees and under his arms, thus bending him over into a ball; hanging there in the rack while Broad and Dylewsky beat him with leather cattle prods, so that he whirled around like a top. After two or three hours of this he was taken out and carried off; by then he was no longer recognizable. Most died shortly after this torture.

By the end of 1944 torturing and killing like this had become routine. The witness Dunja Wasserström reported on the man Draser from Hermannstadt, an SS functionary in Boger's Political Department. Her testimony before the Frankfurt jury about an incident in November 1944:

"That day they were bringing Jewish children into Auschwitz. A truck pulled up and stopped for a minute by the Political Department. Then a little boy jumped down. He had an apple in his hand. Draser and Boger were standing in the door of the Political Department. The child was standing by the truck playing with his apple. Then Boger went up to the child, grabbed him, swung him by the feet and smashed his head against the barracks. Then he calmly picked up the child's apple. And Draser told me to wipe up 'that mess' on the wall. About two hours later I was called in as an interpreter for an interrogation of Boger's, and I saw him eating the child's apple, cool as a cucumber."

THE COMMANDANT'S LOVER

Witness Gerhard Wiebeck: "Standartenführer Höß [the commandant of Auschwitz] was a married man—he lived with his wife and children in the 'Villa'—and had begun an affair with a Czech female prisoner named Hodys; she had become pregnant. To keep the matter secret, Höß had his lover placed in Block 11, and into the 'standing' bunker. These were tiny cells about one to one and a half square meters in size. At the bottom edge was a tiny little hole that one had to crawl into, and there the prisoner had to stand for as long as it pleased the camp administration. In the case of Hodys, he [Höß] had directed that no food be given to her, [despite her being] pregnant. She was to starve to death. But even dehumanized as they were, some members of the guard detachment could not carry out this order. One or two of them would occasionally give her something to eat. So she was able to eke out her wretched life a bit longer, and I freed the woman from this martyrdom. [Pause.] I brought her into a clinic in Munich. And then she gave complete testimony, we made written records of it and got her to sign it along with other pieces of evidence. So Standartenführer Höß was relieved of his post at the camp. A more humane commandant, [Arthur] Liebehenschel, replaced him there. Our investigation continued."

THE BROTHEL: PAUL AND LOTTE

Adam: And there even existed a brothel in Auschwitz. There were "coupons" for it, given for good conduct, but they could be bought and traded, too.

Dr. Fritz Klein at the Bergen-Belsen trial shortly before his execution: "In January 1944 brothels were set up for the prisoners in Auschwitz. The girls who entered these brothels did so voluntarily. It was one of my assignments to find girls for this purpose. About thirty-five of them were brought before me and I selected from them the ten best, in my opinion. The girls in the brothels were examined twice a week by a Polish doctor, who was himself a prisoner."

Adam: That was in Block 24. In the end there were eleven German girls and nine Polish ones. A "ticket" cost one mark for a sexual act of twenty minutes. Every prostitute was required to service six customers per evening. There were no racial limitations or prohibitions, since even Jews could take part . . .

And so to be able to see Kapo Paul, Lotte, the Jewish girl from Transylvania, volunteered for this commando. The concert hall and the whorehouse were in the same building where the musicians practiced in the evening. And next to the library of this "culture block" was the Political Department. Torture and art, screwing and screaming, all together. So the brothel was on the second floor, windows half open. And the ladies' heads would appear in them. And on the first floor all the camp big shots were pushing to get in. Even the prisoner doctors. And Paul came regularly, too. He gave away his food, he stole, to get these coupons. So he came through the orderly room to "Madame" and was treated "hygienically" every time. Then he raced down the stairs. The whores were in the hallway, all in various colored nightgowns, mostly pink, with frills, black stockings, elegant lingerie, too, all from the personal effects storage room (Effektenlager). They had everything here. Auschwitz was really the richest place *on earth. And they "earned" good wages, they could have any-thing, they would all try to bewitch the Kapos and the block se-niors (*Blockälteste). *They made arrangements among themselves, and Paul always got Number 10, where Lotte would be waiting for him.*

Lotte, the prostitute: "But Block 10 was the 'experiments' block for women. Sometimes there were 'fun' days. For some, these were wonderful days, going to pick herbs in the woods, taking delight in every little growing plant, and in every spring flower . . . We were lucky to be part of a commando like that. But they only wanted to lull us, before their experiments, we knew that.

"In the camp, everything was withered and dead, but the woods were alive: singing birds, budding twigs. Like a knife to the heart, such contrast. At noon we would return, dead tired. We knew the routine:

"Afternoons, the court-martial. Evenings, the execution. We could hear it all, it was in the square between our block and Block 11. Toward this side all our windows were nailed shut with boards, and the block seniors made sure to check that we didn't peek through the cracks.

"The shootings began at seven. Everyone was very ner-vous. Every shot went through your whole being. Then a pause in between. Wait. Who is falling in these very seconds . . . ?

"It was as if it were you yourself, it was your turn, over and over. You shivered with them. Not a word. The command, then the shot, then the noise of the bodies being dragged away. Over and over again.

"The screams of the victims, again. One who pled for mercy, because she was still so young and wanted so much to live?

"So much blood. Those beautiful women, shot. Naked."

LOVE STORIES

Paul: "There were lovers who used the brothel for their own purposes. Like Lotte and me. Happiness in the Auschwitz whorehouse, when Lotte and I could lie together. Paradise in hell. Sleeping together for one mark. Then we would tell each other about our lives before the camp. Whispers, kisses, embraces, love. We could even cry and moan. To cry out of happiness, and not out of pain—that was so rare there! Yes, even inappropriate.

"The other girls and women—but never Lotte—they would dress up as men and climb out the windows at night for orgies and drinkfests, mostly with the SS.

"But when I couldn't come, couldn't get hold of a coupon, then I sent her my love letters through 'the mail.' A Polish plumber, who has access everywhere, was our trusty postman. He carried the mail in his shoes. And he did it for free, he was a political type with high morals, and this was how he eased his conscience about not having resisted in any other way. These things, love, friendship, and kind words, were in fact the only possible resistance in Auschwitz. And of course helping someone to escape.

"That such 'normal' behavior could go on unpunished was a miracle, for if the plumber had been caught, that would have meant weeks or even years at hard labor, or at least the famous twenty-five strokes with the whip on his backside, which every prisoner had to count aloud."

2

Adam: But besides death, they also used love, sex, and reproduction as a means not just for total control of the individual, but also to carry out their mad ideas of racial control and genocide. Himmler even thought of it as an adjunct to the gas chamber. The unborn as well as the born were to be exterminated before birth. One of the "experts" assigned to this was Dr. Horst Schumann.

Capesius: "Dr. Schumann, he was a sadist, not even an SS man, he went around the camp in an air force uniform; I sometimes ate lunch with him in the officers' canteen, and he would act the big shot and brag about his experiments. I really couldn't listen to it after a while, but kept my mouth shut, since he had his orders, just like Clauberg or Wirths, directly from Reichsführer-SS Himmler. I know, because once we were sitting with Professor Clauberg, and he said he had just reported to the Reichsführer that he had his sterilization method completely perfected."

Adam: I had access to Block 30 and to this experimentation center—I was more or less a go-between for the Kampfgruppe Auschwitz resistance group and I also was in contact with the resistance within the Sonderkommando. It was a miracle that Langbein, who worked in the sick bay and had connections to Dr. Wirths, as did Nyiszli to Mengele, would sometimes get special passes for me, or kept transferring me from one commando to an-other. I will definitely tell you more about this, because it is impor-tant: it's constantly being forgotten that there was this resistance, which kept up our morale and allowed us to survive as human beings. There was this underground of help, not just an under-ground of evil and corruption; or let's say, there was also this "positive corruption" . . . Even your friend Roland gushes about the "humanity that blossomed there," supposedly.

But you know, there I hardly had any perspective for as long as I was a prisoner—on the whole I knew very little, even if I knew a lot more than most, but later on you found out more; I did see this murderer of a doctor in the experimentation bar-racks, this Schumann, but at the time I didn't see through it; he was an "Aryan" type, pretty boy, still young and probably plan-ning his postdoctoral work, if possible working with Professor Clauberg the gynecologist, whom he was often seen with. Clau-

*berg was a misanthrope, temperamental, imperious, and at the
same time a kind of caricature with his hunting clothes. He also
hung around the SS medical clique and was hoping for an academic chair in genetics. Schumann was cold as ice, had no human instincts, even though he wasn't in the SS. He was more of
a "proper" butcher; I heard things about him from Berner, and
from Langbein and the prisoner doctors as well, that made my
hair stand on end.*

*Schumann had gotten the idea from Clauberg to try testing
his mass-sterilization technique "naturally." So they did the experiment, but not in Schumann's X-ray lab with its two huge
X-ray machines; this lab was in Block 30 of the women's hospital,
where poor Greek Jewish women were held. He would observe
these women from his cranny through a little window, made
radiation-proof with a little lead shutter, fixing his cold gaze,
unmoved, on the women who were screaming as their ovaries were
being burned. But not here—no, the experiment, on which he
likely would base his postdoctoral thesis, would be performed in a
cell "luxuriously" fitted out with carpets and other amenities.*

*Dr. Berner had been brought in also as a prisoner doctor,
and I watched him helplessly standing by. He whispered to me
with a bitter smile in Hungarian: "Well, this research knows no
bounds." The subjects for the experiment had been carefully selected: they were the lovers who had previously been subjected to a
sterilization process . . . Paul and Lotte. They had been seen in
the brothel together by the spies, who were everywhere. And Lotte
was subjected to this horrific radiation treatment. She cried and
whimpered, while it was being done, and even more later . . .
Clauberg had given her a "caustic fluid" injection as well. Paul
was also given "treatment." Schumann had picked these two because he assumed, since they had not been allowed to be together
for the past few weeks for "tactical" reasons, that they would simply fall on each other when they could finally meet; so Paul had no
longer been allowed to accompany the plumbers' commando into*

*the women's camp, but could only glimpse his beloved from his
window, and she him. These monstrous doctors were probably
thinking of Pavlov's dogs, salivating and secreting fluid . . . In-
flamed by their forced separation, so went their thinking, the two
lovers would now perform a sexual act as the doctors' guinea
pigs. But these human monsters forgot that love is a gift from
heaven, and that the act of love is a sacred event, unthinkable
without a spark of the divine.*

*So the SS doctors' expectations for their love experiment were
completely thwarted, of course; love cannot be explained by hor-
mones or secretions or electrical impulses in the brain, nor can
the effect of sterilization on love be researched in this horrible
way. The way it turned out was completely at odds with what they
expected, and this, too, I view as an amazing and deeply intimate form of resistance. After two orderlies led the lovers into
their cell, they crouched together in a corner, seemed listless and
looked as if they were sleeping. They did not touch each other, or
even exchange words—they seemed numb, or sick, or even dying.*

One doctor, Dr. Fischer, who was housed with Wirths, voiced
a protest against this "experiment," but he was an oddball.

*The filmmaker Alexander Kluge also reports on this experi-
ment [in his* Lebensläufe*], sensitively combining the testimony of
two eyewitnesses: some of this came from my friend and brother in
suffering, Dr. Berner, but more of it, importantly, is taken from the
journal and letters of Dr. Wirths, one of the doctors who was part
of these experiments. He also uses notes taken by Schumann himself,
and Kluge includes his own empathetic sense of these events.*

[From Kluge's *Lebensläufe*:] *Dr. Schumann:* "This pas-
sivity was particularly unwelcome, since high-ranking
guests had arranged to view the proceedings; in order
to speed up the progress of the experiment, Wirths, the
base doctor and director of the experiment, ordered the
two prisoners to remove their clothing."

"Were the subjects embarrassed?"

Dr. Schumann: "It did not appear that they were embarrassed. They essentially maintained the same positions as before, even without their clothing, and appeared to be sleeping. Let's perk them up a little, said the director of the experiment. Recordings were produced. Through the peephole, it could be seen that they did initially react to the music. But they relapsed into apathy. It was critical for the experiment that the subjects finally begin, so that it could be determined whether their induced infertility would be maintained over a longer period of time. The team participating in the experiment was waiting in the hallway a few meters from the cell door. They were quiet for the most part, having been told to communicate only in whispers. An observer followed the progress of events inside. The two prisoners were to be lulled into the belief that they were now alone.

"Nonetheless, there was no erotic tension in the cell. Those in charge almost thought they should have chosen a smaller cell. The subjects had been chosen with care. According to the documents, the two subjects supposedly shared a strong erotic attraction for each other."

"Who were they?"

Dr. Schumann: "Lotte, daughter of a Transylvanian Jewish lawyer, born in 1917, thirty years old, with an 'Aryan' husband, after Gymnasium studied art history, was known in the small town of Bistritz to be inseparable from the male subject, a certain Paul, born in 1900, no known vocation. Lotte left her husband, who could have saved her, for Paul. In 1944 she followed her lover to Prague, and then to Paris. There they were arrested as Jews. They were sent in a transport from Drancy to

Auschwitz. In the camp they tried to see each other. According to our observations they met several times in the brothel. Lotte had voluntarily chosen to be a prostitute. Thus our disappointment: now that at last they can, they won't."

"Were the subjects not willing?"

Dr. Schumann: "Basically they were obedient. So I would say: yes, they were willing."

"Were the prisoners well nourished?"

Dr. Schumann: "The subjects selected for this experiment had been particularly well nourished for some time before it began. Now they had been lying together in the same room for two days, without any observable attempts at intimacy. We gave them protein jelly made from eggs to drink, and the prisoners consumed it avidly. Oberscharführer Wilhelm had the two prisoners sprayed outdoors with garden hoses, after which they were brought back inside, but even their need for warmth did not lead them to seek each other."

"Were they afraid of the 'libertinage' or 'free thinking' they thought they were being subjected to? Did they think that this was a test in which they had to prove their morality? Was the misery of the camp now building a wall between them? Did they know that if a pregnancy resulted, that both their bodies would be dissected and examined?"

Dr. Schumann: "It is unlikely that the subjects knew that, or even suspected it. Rather, the camp administration had repeatedly given them reassurances that they would survive. I believe that they just didn't want to. To the disappointment of Obergruppenführer (general) A. Zerbst and his entourage, who had specifically come here to see it, the experiment could not be carried out, since every means we employed, including force, did not lead to a positive result. We pressed them skin to skin, then kept them within centimeters of each other, as they slowly warmed up, swabbed them with alcohol, and gave them alcoholic drinks, red wine with protein, meat to eat and champagne to drink, we dimmed the lighting, but nothing led to sexual arousal."

"Did you try every method?"

Dr. Schumann: "I can guarantee you, we tried everything. We had with us an Oberscharführer who knew something about these things. He tried everything eventually—methods that had always worked in other cases. Of course, we couldn't exactly go in ourselves and try our luck, since that would have been race defilement [*Rassenschande*]. None of the methods we tried led to arousal."

"Were the observers aroused?"

Dr. Schumann: "Well, certainly more than those two in the room; at least, it looked that way. On the other hand, that would have been strictly off-limits. Given that, I don't think we were actually aroused. Maybe just upset about the thing not working out.

"It was not possible to force an unambiguous reaction from the subjects, and so the experiment was abandoned. It was tried again later with other subjects."

"What happened to the subjects?"

Dr. Schumann: "The resistive subjects were taken outside and shot with a small-caliber weapon, one after the other. They were standing together, naked, but were not allowed to look at or touch each other."

"Does this mean that, after a certain amount of suffering, love can no longer be brought about by any means?"

MY GOD, SCIENCE!

I

Capesius: "From Dr. Nyiszli, Dr. Münch also got fresh human livers to use as culture mediums for the Hygiene Institute. Moreover, in the 'Canada' complex, there were two large barracks that were run as an institute for anatomy and pathology, not mentioned by Nyiszli or anybody else, but where many specimens of fetuses and abnormalities were kept, according to someone who had been in the know."

Who was this someone—not Capesius himself? And how did he know? Tadeusz, who after all was assigned to "Canada," and Adam Salmen both tell of this.

Adam: Yes, I saw it, too, you can only do these things as a robot, a zombie, not as a sentient human being—that was the Nazis' achievement: a human being really was only a machine made of meat, a higher form of animal, a "breed," nothing but the physical body of a "consanguinity." Only the visible mattered, the outside, the twentieth-century insanity, which they called "civilization." Without revealing what we had to see there, just a single example, a horrific image that haunts me still, these images keep coming, the dead live on. Three hundred bodies on trucks, for burning. A sling around my arm, the other end of the sling around the arm of a corpse, as I drag them over the sand to the truck, stacking them up, making "neat" piles of them, trampling on their exposed bellies.

•

Dr. Lingens: "The Dahlem-Auschwitz axis. Under the leadership of Otmar von Verschuer, the final, fatal consequences of race-based science and research were revealed, to which, under National Socialism, there were no limits.

"Verschuer, publisher of the journal *The Geneticist* (*Der Erbarzt*) since 1934 and since 1936 an expert on biology in the Research Department for the Jewish Question (*Forschungsabteilung Judenfrage*) of the Reich Institute for History of the New Germany, was considered an eminent scientific authority on research involving twins. In 1942 he returned to Berlin and replaced the retired Eugen Fischer as Director of the Kaiser Wilhelm Institute (KWI), after he had led the newly founded Institute for Genetics and Racial Hygiene at the University of Frankfurt am Main from 1935 to 1942. His close contact with his former doctoral student and assistant in Frankfurt, Dr. Mengele, turned out to be extremely beneficial for Verschuer's research, for after Mengele assumed his position in Auschwitz (May 1943), the largest Nazi extermination camp became a 'research laboratory for the KWI for anthropology, human genetics, and eugenics that was unique in the world.' (A former KWI student, Dr. Nyiszli from Transylvania, then became Mengele's assistant in Auschwitz.)

"Verschuer's compulsive obsession with research was massively supported by the German Research Association (Deutsche Forschungsgemeinschaft: DFG). Mengele was a direct participant in some of Verschuer's research projects; being 'on the spot' gave him unlimited access to 'research materials.' Verschuer kept the DFG appraised of these projects in his research reports: 'With the permission of Reichsführer-SS Himmler, anthropological examinations are being performed on the most diverse racial groups of the Auschwitz concentration camp, and the blood tests are sent to my laboratory for processing.' Auschwitz, the 'world's largest genetics laboratory,' became a true paradise for genetic research. The preferred objects of study in this were Jews, Gypsies, 'dwarves, and people with "deformities"—but most especially twins; twin research was the hobbyhorse of both men, teacher (Verschuer) and student (Mengele) alike.'

"My once-revered science teacher Eckhardt Hügel from Sighişoara wanted to be a part of this, as much as Roland wanted to be in the SS. So I read with horror in Eckhardt Hügel's *Race Research and Ethnicity* (*Rassenforschung und Volksgruppe*) (pp. 107–14): 'The question of race is the fulcrum of the historic changes in world events today: Race, today, presents a challenge to men of action. And race has long stood at the center of our worldview as the prime value, the measure of all things.' Hügel was the head of the *Sippenamt*, or Office of Families and Clans, in Hermannstadt. As a teacher he kept an eye on all his pretty female students. Hügel: 'From the viewpoint of racial politics, fertility is of critical significance . . . so it is not a peripheral question as to whether alterations in the composition of the German *Volk* group are being caused by variances in fertility. On the other hand, what is being done about increasing population of inferior peoples? Besides inhibiting their reproduction, to what extent has an *eradication* of inferior genetic stock been undertaken?' "

2

And then in 1944 in Transylvania the watchword was: every German mother should present the Führer with a child. There is the famous question of a peasant woman: "Will Herr Führer come to us, or do we have to go to Herr Führer?"

"The stink of humans in stalls, Aryan breeders' blond pubic hair, all just for us *Volks*," said Uncle Daniel mockingly, "the folkish fecund womb is fertile, that's where it crawls out of . . . and Germany the mother opens her womb for the

Führer's floppy cock; millions of children, millions of sheep for him. Cannon fodder. *Sieg Heil.* Eradicate everybody that's sick, ungrounded, unblond, or 'wet,' away with the whiners."

"Disorder," said Roland, "is bastardization. Choking vines, phalluses, jungle snakes. Zeus, bringer of light, the ordering will of the state. Breeding, Zeus, and man."

•

No wonder health was so important! Out on the blue veranda, Grandpa mused for the umpteenth time: Deep at the heart, in back of it all: *orders.*

Roland in his SS uniform with the flat-topped cap and death's-head insignia. Roland was repeatedly home on leave, he was home suspiciously often; this time it was a transport of Gypsies that he had escorted, and in the summerhouse up on the Steilau at breakfast he talked of "selection," and that we should be proud of being Transylvanian Saxons.

Roland: "But we can't allow any fragmentation, no, that would be a sin against world order; unity is everything. Sickness must be eradicated, excised from the healthy body. Our ironclad unity, that is everything . . . race struggle, blood, and breeding. And above all, the wonder of biology and race!"

3

Prosecutor Kügler: "Yes. Were any kind of medical experiments carried out in the crematoriums, and where?"

Witness Filip Müller: "Experiments were performed. During the Hungarian transports in 1944, in a room in the crematorium there were two Hungarian doctors, pathologists. One of them, if I remember correctly, was called Dr. Nyiszli, a powerfully built man. They carried out experiments. And they were often joined by Dr. Mengele. These two prisoners (doctors) were then brought into Crematorium IV, where they performed dissections in the room next to the oven—that was the room that led from the locker room to the incineration chamber. There, in that room, another man who was not a doctor worked with these two Hungarian doctors. And he came from Theresienstadt. I personally saw them take somebody, a hunchback, and put him into a barrel. Then they put in various salts and acids, to get at his skeleton. And they removed flesh from the people who had been shot."

Adam survived, as if by a miracle; he had been a member of the Sonderkommando, which was usually liquidated every three months. He knew not only Frau Dr. Böhm, but also Dr. Nyiszli, the Transylvanian doctor from Großwardein: he knew him well and saw him often; Nyiszli had his own bedroom and his own dissection room, and as the slave doctor of Dr. Mengele and Dr. Wirths, the garrison doctor, he "lived" near Crematorium I, where there were enough bodies to dissect. Adam said Nyiszli had had a larger perspective than he had: *Nyiszli could move about the camp freely with his pass from Mengele, and his room was near the ramp; when a transport arrived he first heard the commandos, the SS yelling, then the noise in the heating room of the crematorium, the noise of the electric motors for the fifteen ventilators that brought the fire in the ovens up to 1,800 degrees C.*

Capesius: "From spring of 1942 on, the death trains with Jews rolled into the extermination camp. In that year alone, 166 transports arrived with approximately 180,000 deportees, and in 1943 it was 174 with around 220,000 people, and in 1944 the Reichsbahn brought in about 300,000 victims in 300 trains. In cattle cars."

Dr. Nyiszli: " 'I need to have methodical work here,' said Dr. Mengele, 'because we will forward our proceedings here to the Race Biology and Anthropology Institute in Berlin-Dahlem.'

"That's how I learn that the experiments being done here

were conducted by one of the most renowned scientific institutes in the world.

"I get new twin corpses. Four pairs from the twin section of the Gypsy camp are brought in. They are the bodies of Gypsy children not even ten years old.

"I do the dissection of the first set. I take notes about every phase of the process. I open up the cranial cavity, take out the brain and the attached glands. I inspect everything. Next I open the rib cage, and take out the ribs and breastbone. Next I remove the tongue through an incision below the chin, together with the esophagus, the trachea, and the lungs. So I can see clearly what I am looking at, I clean the organs of blood. The smallest, most insignificant-looking spot or the least discoloration can be an important finding. Now I have taken out the heart. I hold it under running water and wash it off. I turn it in my hand this way and that. On the outer wall of the left chamber I notice a tiny, round, pale red spot, hardly different from the surrounding tissue. It can only be the result of a needle puncture. I can no longer fool myself! It is a puncture, done with a very fine needle. A hypodermic needle, of course. So the child was given an injection into the heart. But why? One only gives injections to the heart in cases of dire emergency, for instance, in a case of cardiac arrest. I will know in a minute. I open up the heart and expose the left chamber. In a normal dissection, the blood in that chamber is taken out with a spoon and weighed. Here that is not possible, because . . ."

•

Frau Dr. Böhm: "So Dr. Dering, too, but especially Dr. Max Samuel, who had been a well-known gynecologist in Cologne, aided the SS doctors with their 'difficult work.' Of course they did not eat with us, but once Wirths said that Samuel worked with such zeal surgically removing parts of the women's cervixes for his cancer research, which caused them all great pain, one

after another, that even he had to ask him to slow down. Samuel
had a pass from Wirths and could even go outside the camp.

"So from this you can see how much even the inmate doctors brought guilt upon themselves. And always just out of
fear? Or because there was this famous ashen gray zone, in
which particularly they and the Kapos were all caught up together in this monstrous yet everyday evil? Because corruption
and 'connections' is really the only chance you have of staying
alive? That's how it was for Samuel, who implicated himself in
crimes. Because Dr. Samuel's daughter was in the camp, and
he thought he could 'protect' her in this way. And then in
1944 they shot him anyway, with a small-caliber weapon, because he knew too much; Muhsfeldt shot him. He was the
commandant of Crematorium I.

"And life went on, and on . . . even in Auschwitz. And it
was simply a fact that nothing ever disturbed the course of
daily life in the least, there never came any eye-opening moment or any psychic transformation, even though the events
were so horrible that normal perception just could not take it
all in. The chimneys belched smoke day and night. Everyone
smelled the omnipresent sweetish odor of burnt human bodies, it penetrated everything, invisibly, like a finely dispersed
corpse inside of everyone."

4

*Adam: There was the gray zone and there was Jewish complicity.
But the most difficult thing of all to comprehend was the complicity of the Jewish leaders and the "Jewish Councils"—without
their cooperation the genocide would never have been possible. So
in Berlin, for example, the responsibility for capturing and ar-
resting the Jews lay exclusively in the hands of the Jewish police.*

And it was always the recognized Jewish local authorities who were members of the Jewish Councils. Even Hannah Arendt, in her book Eichmann in Jerusalem, *wrote that this role of the Jewish leaders in the destruction of their own people was, for Jews, the darkest chapter in the whole dark story.*

Eichmann himself was amazed that there was no resistance, let alone sabotage, on any side from the normal officials and authorities in Germany. Everyone cooperated willingly, and eagerly. And everything worked smoothly, under the cooperation of the Jewish organizations and authorities. As if they were all going somewhere on holiday with their families, and not to their deaths, the Jews obediently followed all the orders and reported as required with their luggage.

Hannah Arendt: "The Jewish Councils were notified by Eichmann or his people about how many Jews were required for the next scheduled transport, and in accordance with that they made up the lists of those to be deported. And the Jews got registered, filled out countless forms, answered endless exhaustive questionnaires about their property, so that when it all got confiscated there would be no complications, and then they would assemble punctually at the collection points and climb into the freight cars. Those few who tried to hide or flee were found by special Jewish police troops.

"Eichmann saw only that no one protested, that everything worked, because everyone was 'cooperating.' "

Adam: It was sheer madness—a bureaucracy forcing this mass reality on its "citizens"! But the worst of it was that the Jewish Councils did it in order to save the most prominent Jews, that is, themselves. And they enjoyed their new power. The Jewish elder of Łódź, Chaim Rumkowski, drove around in a kind of coach, printed money with his own signature and stamps with his picture, while the women and children, babies and old people, were turned to ashes.

5

Adam: There was also the gray zone of the "Exchange," a kind of super flea market. I went there with Kielar and Borowski, and both have described this "excursion."* I was a bit repelled but also curious to go, as one of the Saxon Scharführers had asked me to "get" something for him, he was going "down" to Transylvania on home leave; the Saxon had just popped up in the block seniors' office, and he had called me in. This was the time of the Warsaw Uprising; I had gotten rather sassy and I no longer took off my cap for the SS, nor did I stand at attention for them. There was hate in my eyes now, not fear. The SS man stood there, rather uncertain of himself: "I am going on leave, you will, please, find something for me, the best would be a brooch in a gold setting." ("Please?" Yes.) He reached into the briefcase he had brought and pulled out two fat SS sausages, cigarettes, and two bottles of schnaps. "I will be back tomorrow afternoon." Then he went off.

I went to the Sonderkommando's "Exchange." A commotion of many languages. Babel. Laughing, arguing, shoving, singing, the smell of roasting onions, the fragrance of an orange. But on the stove they were drying clothes; it had rained, the clothes gave off a musty smell, no, they actually stank, it nauseated me. A Kapo paraded by in an elegant getup, wafting a trail of French perfume behind him. In one corner, directly beneath the roof, were two Jews bent over, one unshaven with a yellow growth of beard, using a needle to pick bits of plaster or broken teeth out of gold dental crowns. He just gave me a brief sidelong glance and kept on with his picking. A dead man on holiday, playing with the remains of other dead men. Little pieces of plaster fell to the floor. Some bounced off the pans of a little scale hanging from

*Cf. both Kielar and Borowski.

a nail in the roof beam, gently swinging back and forth, giving off little metallic singing sounds; someone had written JUSTICE *on the arm of the scale. On a sateen-covered down quilt lay a crazy jumble of coins, gold engagement rings, diamond rings, gold teeth, brooches, chains, and watches, whose weight made a depression in the quilt; an incredibly wrinkled, ancient Jewish jeweler from Amsterdam, emaciated practically to a skeleton, stared at me with one eye; the other eye was covered with a glass lens through which he peered at the wares. I was able to communicate with him, half in Yiddish, half in* lagerszpracha. *"So show me what you have." I pointed to the bottles of schnaps. The ancient jeweler (how ever did he pass the selection? He must have supernatural powers! Or gold, maybe, gold even on the ramp?) thrust his hairy paw down into the pile on the quilt, grabbed a handful of gold, and then put into my lap a piece of jawbone with gold teeth and a dental prosthesis. The transports were practically over then.* "Canada, c'est fini," *he said ruefully. Revolted, I threw the teeth and the prosthesis back onto the pile. And then I started bargaining as if it were the marketplace in Czernowitz. For the SS sausages I finally got a platinum watch set with jewels, and for the booze I got the gold brooch the Saxon Scharführer had desired, otherwise nothing but teeth . . . gold teeth, jaws. But little diamonds, too. And for the Scharführer, a new suit . . .*

6

Adam knew a few things about this hypocrisy, this "gray zone" of morality: *Even if the Germans outwardly pretended they were performing "with decency" an assignment in the camps that was "critical" for the war effort, they still knew that what they were doing was criminal, and that's why they took the trouble to disguise it. For example, no one ever talked about "killing"; they always used other expressions, usually abbrevations: (S)pecial (T)reatment, (N)ight and (F)og, (R)eturn (U)ndesirable, etc. For their part, the prisoners camouflaged their reports and messages so artfully that they got past the censors without objection. For instance, the Roma (Gypsies) wrote a (seemingly) completely normal letter, ending with the line: "Special greetings from Baro Nasslepin, Elenta, and Marepin," and these words meant "great sickness, misery, and murder." Jewish inmates wrote their reports in Hebrew letters on music notation paper, so that they looked like sheet music.*

In a secret message to his wife in the women's camp, Dr. Nyiszli wrote: "Everything gets turned upside down here, everything inevitably turns out for the worst, for the most terrible, even what would at first seem to be good for us: there are rumors that this is because of Churchill, who threatened Germany with more reprisals, more bombing attacks, if the gassing of the Jews was not stopped immediately! So now, at least the healthy Jews are being picked out and sent to the camps. But you can see the result of that where you are, you complain that you are overfilled. Now a thousand come into every block instead of the five hundred that did before. And in your women's barracks, it's even as many as two thousand, so that you can only sleep 'in alternation,' as one lies on top of the other. But even the newly arriving men have to sleep in the aisles between the plank beds. And it was like that before, too, in those horrible days around Pentecost. But don't worry, you know? How many selections there were in the camp, almost every morning after roll call. And then there would be hundreds, even thousands pushed naked right into the gas chamber. I can still see them, those screaming, crying, naked women . . . You absolutely must volunteer for the new transports going to work in Germany, you absolutely MUST!"

•

Adam: There was huge corruption from the very beginning in everything to do with this madness, the greatest breakdown of civilization in human history, especially at its height, the "Hungarian Action." Starting as early as March 19, 1944, after Germany had occupied Hungary and Eichmann was living high off the hog in a luxury hotel in Budapest, with his own driver, being courted by the rich Jews. There were two rival groups there, the Judenrat, or Jewish Council, set up by Eichmann himself, and the independent Zionist Rescue and Aid Committee (Zionistische Rettungs und Hilfskomitee), headed by the legendary Joel Brand, who had considerable funds at his disposal. Let's not forget, even though Horthy ran an anti-Semitic state with anti-Jewish laws, he refused to cooperate with the Nazis and did not turn over a single Hungarian Jew, and even sent 130,000 Jewish soldiers in Hungarian uniform as auxiliaries to the front; Hungary had been an isle of the blessed and an asylum of safety for the nearly 900,000 "Magyarized" Jews—as opposed to the Ostjuden, or Eastern Jews. Eichmann himself played a cunning trick on the Judenrat, which was headed up by a high official from Horthy's state council, Samuel Stern, along with eleven members of parliament; Eichmann made it appear that he could be bribed, that anything was possible, and so he convinced the Jews of Hungary of the necessity of such a Judenrat. Corruption, small scale to start with—they demanded lingerie, typewriters, expensive pictures, pianos, and money—eventually became routine for the Nazis. Eichmann visited the Jewish Library and Museum, and around a quarter million dollars was demanded. Rumors were circulated that Himmler was willing to spare the Hungarian Jews and to exterminate only the Polish Jews, for a payment of three million dollars. Joel Brand even brought Himmler's offer to the Allies to free a million Jews for a delivery of 100,000 trucks. Payment after payment was made, but what was done in return was exactly nothing. Brand met every morning with the Nazis planning this genocide, absurdly enough in a coffeehouse, an "idealistic Jew" dealing with "idealistic Germans," what a comedy! The Nazis preferred dealing with them, the Zionists, and with Dr. Kastner, who could travel freely, even to Nazi Germany. They negotiated prices for buying people's freedom, and some Jews actually were allowed to emigrate to Palestine. They closed their eyes to forged baptismal certificates and passports. The Zionists were also supported financially by the American Joint Distribution Committee. Lies and deceit—of almost one million Jews only about 160,000 were still alive.

Capesius listed in exact detail those who took part in the "Hungarian Campaign" and analyzed them in his annotations. He writes about the playboy Dieter Wisliceny, who titled himself a "baron" and did business with the Budapest Jews:

Capesius: "Wisliceny, SS Hauptsturmführer, Eichmann's adjutant and representative. Hanged in Pressburg (Bratislava) in 1947. Expert on the transports. Also helped organize the transport from Klausenburg. He was tall and very fat. A round fat face, like a baby's ass. *Height:* 186 cm. *Weight:* 125 kg."

Adam: He helped a member of the Judenrat from Budapest, a rich "baron," Philipp von Freudiger, escape to Romania somewhere. And collected "installment payments" from the Judenrat. Just to meet with him the Zionist Rescue and Aid Committee paid the fat man twenty thousand dollars. He went riding and hunting, lived in luxury hotels, and enjoyed life. In the end even the Nazis no longer trusted him. It was all just a gigantic network of everyone for himself, protection and corruption; what mattered most were one's connections to wealth and "society," especially in 1944 and at the end. All this while the poorest of the poor, old people, women, and children were being sent to the gas chamber— primarily by their own people in the "Jewish Councils"—all over Europe. Once "Baron" Freudiger calculated that maybe half the victims could have saved themselves, if they had not followed the directions of the Jewish Council, but rather had simply run away! But the highest levels of Jewish leadership continued telling their people the fairy tale of Umsiedlung, *or resettlement, even though they knew exactly where that meant: into the gas. It is the great-*

est disgrace of all for the Jews! Again, here, one can only feel hor-ror and shame.

In the camp itself there were hierarchies and protection rings, and corruption was huge, even in minor ways. Dr. Nyiszli could even visit his wife—as Mengele's slave doctor and assistant he got a pass from him "as thanks"—and other prisoner doctors as well were free to move about in the camp. "The prisoner doctors also incriminated themselves," said Frau Dr. Böhm, indignantly. Frau Dr. Perl also wrote in her report about the corruption of the SS and the women in the SS. Höß, the commandant of the camp, complained about their lack of discipline, and their degenerate behavior, like the SS guard Irma Grese, who had sexual relations with a young prisoner.

7

Capesius wrote on her corrupt behavior: "Irma Grese, a supervising guard apparently considered quite beautiful, became pregnant and had an abortion done for her by Frau Dr. Perl, who was then given a shiny new case complete with instruments . . . Grese threatened her with a weapon if she ever told anyone what she had done. Grese had also promised to give her clothes, but she never came by again. She may have been a perverse bitch, I didn't know her, but all of them in such cases certainly made generous presents, since the SS doctors wouldn't help them, because if they did they were risking their own lives."

COMPLICITY OF THE JEWISH DOCTORS

Dr. Nyiszli from Transylvania writes about his medical slave labor in the service of Dr. Mengele:

Dr. Nyiszli: "The blood had coagulated into a hard lump. I cut it up with my tweezers and smelled it. There was the typical sharp odor of chloroform. So the child had been given a chloroform injection to the heart! And this, for no other reason than to cause a blood clot and instant death through cardiac arrest!

"My knees were shaking with fear. I have uncovered the darkest medical secret of the Third Reich. Here people are being murdered, not just with gas, but with chloroform injections to the heart. My brow was covered with sweat. Luckily I was alone. It would have been hard to hide my shock from others. I finished the dissection, made notes of any findings varying from the norm, and described them in detail. But I did not mention in my notes either the smell of chloroform or the coagulated blood in the left heart chamber or the needle puncture in the heart wall. This precautionary measure may well have saved my life.

"Dr. Mengele's documents on these twins lay before me. They too contained all the important findings of the examination, X-ray photographs as well as the previously mentioned sketches, but the circumstances of death, the cause of death, are not entered. And so I do not fill out this paragraph of the dissection report. It is not good to go beyond the permitted bounds in this place, and to talk to anyone about what I have seen! I am no coward. My nerves are strong. But still . . .

"I have investigated many death cases in my life. I have examined more than a few murder victims, people who were killed out of jealousy or revenge, or for material advantage. I have done autopsies on suicides and pinpointed the exact cause of death in people who died of illness. I am accustomed to solving the often obscure riddle of death. I have often encountered breathtaking surprises. But now, a shudder of horror ran up and down my spine. If Dr. Mengele had any idea that I knew the secret of his injections, then ten SS doctors, in the name of the Political Department, would have been on the spot to certify my own death from 'cardiac arrest.'

"After the dissection, I am to turn over the cadavers to the incineration commandos for immediate cremation. The interesting body parts are to be retained for Dr. Mengele to look at. And I have to preserve whatever else might be of interest to the Dahlem Institute. This ends up being put in a package and getting sent, and to get it there faster, it gets stamped 'Express: War-related critical material.' During my duty in the crematorium I expedite countless numbers of such packages to Berlin-Dahlem, which mostly receive lengthy responses from the people there with scientific opinions or instructions. I set up a special, separate dossier to file this correspondence in. The institute almost always expresses its deepest appreciation to Dr. Mengele for the unusual and rare materials that he sends them.

"I also perform dissections on three other sets of twins. I evaluate the abnormalities that they present. The cause of death with them is the same: an injection of chloroform to the heart.

"In this process I make an interesting discovery: three of the four sets of twins have eyes of different color: one eye is blue, the other brown. This can also be found in non-twins, but here it was the case in three of four pairs of twins. It is an extraordinary coincidence to find this high a frequency. Medically it is known as heterochromy, or 'different colors.' I remove the eyes and lay them singly in formaldehyde, and label everything exactly, so they don't get mixed up. With all four pairs of twins I also find something else. As I remove the neck skin on both sides, there is a round, walnut-sized nodule of tissue beneath the upper end of the sternum. When pressed with tweezers it gives off a viscous, puslike substance. Scientifically a very rare, but not unknown, finding. It is known as a Dubois abscess, a symptom of congenital syphilis. It is present with all eight twins. I remove the nodules along with the surrounding healthy tissue and place them in vials filled with formalin. I make careful notes. The only paragraph I don't fill out is 'cause of death.'

"Dr. Mengele makes his rounds in the afternoon hours. I report on the work I have performed. I give him my notes on the eight twins. He sits down and reads them attentively. He is very interested in the heterochromy of the eyes, and even more interested in the Dubois abscesses. He immediately directs that all the material together with my notes be readied for mailing, but I am also to give the cause of death. He leaves it up to me to write; the only thing is that the causes of death must be various. Almost apologetically he says that these children, as I can plainly see for myself, were suffering from syphilis or tuberculosis and were not in any case viable . . . He says no more than that. But, with that, everything is clear. He has justified the forcible, violent death of eight children. I refrain from making any comment and merely note to myself that, in this medical environment, pulmonary tuberculosis is not treated by immobilizing the affected portion of the lung, and syphilis is not treated with neosalvarsan, but with injections to the heart. My hair is standing on end with horror, when I think of all the things I have learned in my short time here, and how much more I will find out before death eventually strikes me. I knew it before I got here, but now, in possession of so many secrets, there is no longer any doubt: I am certain that I will be killed. Is it thinkable that Dr. Mengele or the Dahlem Institute would permit me to go on living?

"It is evening now. Mengele leaves. I stay behind, alone with my oppressive thoughts. Mechanically, I put the dissection instruments back in their place, wash my hands, and walk over to the workroom. I light up a cigarette and sit down, to calm myself a bit. And then I hear a piercing scream, it goes straight to my brain. Then a loud bang and the sound of a falling body. I sit, paralyzed, watching, waiting for what will happen in the next few minutes . . ."

8

Roland: "It was supposed to be a very special event. Mengele's midgets, and all the officers, including our wives and children, had been invited to a concert by the girls' orchestra—including their cellist. But is this even imaginable? Fifty midgets, interesting, right? All decked out in the most colorful and absurd masks and costumes, performing as Mengele's audience and court? Some are done up like circus acrobats, you know, half naked. Others in animal costumes, on all fours. Many with gold jewelery from the 'Canada' group, festooned with gold watches, diamond earrings, and so on. And in the middle of it all, Mengele seated on a decorated throne. A cigarette holder, or was it a Havana cigar in his mouth? The French entertainer Fénelon wrote about this in her book, that same Fénelon who played the violin and became famous through the film *Das Mädchenorchester* (The Girls' Orchestra)! Remember?

"The orchestra played for two hours, mostly light things like *Zar und Zimmermann* or things from *Die Fledermaus*, and folksongs and popular hits. The midgets acted crazy, they danced like circus acrobats, they did somersaults, were applauded, climbed up on a tightrope, more somersaults, and one way up at the ceiling, a *salto mortale*, without a net, curiously enough. And Mengele, all spruced up—his boots gleaming in the stage lights—said, turning ironically to the orchestra: "You have such an enthusiastic, appreciative audience here— and so, this is your last performance for them, your music to heaven." And then he led the entire column of fools on foot, with his four favorites in his slowly moving car, to the gas chamber. For he was convinced of his 'patriotic duty,' the extermination of the Jews, and there could be no exceptions."

•

Capesius: "Whatever Mengele said, or did, well, Klein knew it all better. But Frau Dr. Gisela Perl from Sighet, she was a gynecologist there, she was definitely involved, as was Anna Rosenfeld, another gynecologist; I knew her, too. And they were no longer sending pregnant women directly to the gas chamber. Mengele needed embryos for Berlin-Dahlem, Professor Verschuer's world-famous institute. So Perl did a lot of abortions, until they could get a living, viable embryo. And Mengele was supposedly really happy when he came visiting the office with a glass in his hand. He was polite and forthcoming, and always ready for a joke, but like all of them he could also be the opposite: once he threw Perl down on the floor and kicked her in the back with his boot—she was laid up for months—because she had cooked potatoes on the sterilizing oven.

"But I knew Miklós Nyiszli from back home better. He came with a transport from Transylvania on May 30, 1944, along with his wife, Margareta, and very young daughter Zsuzsa, who was crying. The doctor, yes, I knew him, I often called on him as Bayer's traveling sales rep, he was a forensic doctor, discovered by Dr. Mengele, and he had it good, really good, of course, he could even visit his wife and daughter in the women's camp. But he cut up the bodies, dissected them, for Mengele. Later a lot of people wanted to be big shots and profit from the fame of the world-renowned Mengele. He was one of those. Nuts and braggarts thrived even in Auschwitz. Oh, yes. Mengele often did selections at the ramp and he was there on May 30, not on the twenty-ninth, Miklós is lying about that. And he yells: 'Doctors, fall out!' And fifty of them volunteer, including Nyiszli; it was Pentecost, and that was when I was with Pepi Becker in Berlin, so I couldn't have been there on the ramp then. Dr. Klein told me, he was almost always there, walking right behind Mengele on the ramp.

"And Nyiszli, the doctor from Großwardein, Transylvania, had studied at the Kaiser Wilhelm Institute for Forensic Medicine, as he boasts in his book, saying that Mengele invited him right off to get into his car, and they drove off together, and Nyiszli supposedly was allowed to wear civilian clothes, and his wife and daughter weren't sent to the gas chamber, and he was given a dissection lab in the crematoriums, all beautifully equipped, said Miklós, even though it was just a crummy barrack. And even the part about driving around in the car was a lie, too. Nyiszli was in Monowitz first, and not till the end of June was he in Birkenau at the prisoners' hospital, and then in the Sonderkommando in Crematorium II. I knew him quite well . . . and I ran into him when I got there . . . He was the one who did autopsies and was Mengele's assistant at dissections. He was under a lot of psychological pressure, even though he was well fed at the SS kitchen."

Adam: So not just the murderers and torturers, but also the doctors in Auschwitz were actively complicit. And not just on the ramp. They are and remain the chief criminals. Auschwitz was thus an exception in the human zoo—yes, yes, they just had to use it, who knows how long, as a giant laboratory for their human experimentation.

•

Dr. Nyiszli (describing a dissection of "deformed" victims): "We soaked the bodies of the abnormal people in a caustic bath of bleaching powder, collected the clean bones into packets, and sent them to the Anthropological Institute in Berlin-Dahlem. In this manner the KWI in Dahlem acquired great quantities of 'material' useful for their work in genetic pathology: skeletons, severed heads (of children), aborted fetuses, testicles, pairs of eyes, and countless blood and plasma samples. This was how progess was made in research for the science today known as human genetics."

Adam: How noble, how grand.

Dr. Nyiszli: "Eugen Fischer died in 1967. Otmar von Verschuer's academic career only began after 1945: in 1951 he became a professor of genetics in Münster and later dean of the medical school. From 1952 on he was chairman of the German Society of Anthropology; in 1954 Verschuer was elected to the advisory board of the German Society for Population Policy. But Mengele, whose doctor title was revoked, emigrated to South America and probably died there in a *swimming accident.*"

MUSSULMEN, THE UNDEAD OF AUSCHWITZ, AND THE SUSPENSION OF TIME

I

From Professor Kremer's diary: "September 6, 1942: Excellent lunch today: tomato soup, a half chicken with potatoes and red cabbage (20 grams of fat), dessert, and wonderful vanilla ice cream . . . September 9: Present as physician at the beatings of eight prisoners and at an execution with small-caliber weapon. Got soapflakes and two pieces of soap . . . Present at a *Sonderaktion* (special action) (fourth time). October 3: Today [got] spanking fresh material from a human liver and spleen, and a pancreas as well to put in fixing solution, and fixed lice from typhus victims in pure alcohol. October 31: For the last fourteen days gorgeous fall weather, which motivates the Waffen-SS to take sunbaths day in, day out."

Kremer was a special professor of anatomy at the University of Münster, and titled his postdoctoral thesis "The Changes in Muscle Tissue Caused by Hunger." In August 1942 he came to Auschwitz to continue his "research on hunger." For this work he chose the so-called Mussulmen, men and women who were suffering from extreme hunger and had become greatly weakened both physically and psychologically.

Professor Kremer spoke about this in 1946 when he was in Polish captivity: "If a person in a state of advanced starvation came to my attention, I would instruct the medic to set that person aside for me and to inform me of the date on which that person would be put to death by injection. At this point, those people whom I had selected would be brought to the block and laid out on the dissecting table while they were still alive. I walked up to the table and asked the sick inmate about any details that might have been of interest for my research: for example, their weight before arrest, how much weight they had lost in confinement, whether they had taken any medications, and similar things. After I had received this information, the medic would come up and kill the patient with an injection into the region of the heart. I myself never administered any fatal injections."

"You know," said Roland in a sympathetic voice, "I always went out of my way to avoid them, I just couldn't look on at these things, as if all this which is real, and yet should not be, would happen to me as well. Just like you avoid a ghost, you are afraid of it. You know? Because there is a 'Beyond' out there, which reveals something we want to forget, namely, death, and that the human body is a transient thing. You know? The Mussulman was no longer the master of his own body. He had edema and ulcers, he was filthy and stank. A nonperson, just like in a nightmare, and yet real. Yes, really something which should not be."

That's Roland with his philosophizing twaddle. He just can't stop doing it, I thought. Any minute we'll hear a poem as his "evidence"; he always needs to lose touch with reality and escape into his paradise of "ideas," to keep himself "pure." I always had the feeling that for Roland Auschwitz was just a nightmare, a dream of hell: that he dreamed his own character, as if it were someone else, always in some other world "Beyond," surrounded by ghosts, and he was one himself. And we have that in our family, too. "The mercy of being born late," and thus not guilty, but not guilty for that reason alone—because I was eight years younger than the youngest draftees. But they went through it: the Mussulman was the only truly visible reality there, everything else was unreal and not believable.

Adam knew these companions in suffering from the camp hospital very well, and firsthand:

Adam: Once diarrhea set in, the decline of the starving pris-
oners was accelerated. Their gestures became agitated and unco-
ordinated. When sitting, their upper bodies swayed to and fro.
They made mechanical motions without any apparent reason.
When walking, they could no longer pick up their legs. One day I
saw the following scene in the yard: one of these undead suddenly
started tottering toward us, heading directly for an SS Rotten-
führer who was standing there, but only able to drag himself for-
ward very slowly, and then he stopped. We watched the whole thing
with horror. The poor man, swaying and in apparent agony,
dragged himself involuntarily forward, weakly, like a ghost, a
shadow, pulling his wooden clogs behind him, which clattered
when they struck a stone, which made him fall straight into the SS
officer's arms. The SS man yelled something at him; since the poor
man was not wearing his cap, the SS ogre struck him on the head
with a billy club. The Mussulman stopped briefly, and without
regaining consciousness, even after the Rottenführer gave him
a second and third blow on the head. You could see the poor
man's body still reacting in fear; he must have had dysentery or
typhoid fever, for a thick black stinking liquid was dripping from
his filthy ragged uniform down onto his wooden shoes. This en-
raged the SS man, who kicked the Mussulman in the stomach with
his boot, and as he lay on the ground, trampled on his chest until
he finally breathed his last and lay there in peace. And the SS
swine wiped his club on the grass and walked off, completely
indifferent.

In the trial the Mussulman was described as follows: "Extremely emaciated, dull gaze, an indifferent, sad expression,
deep-set, clouded eyes, pale, gray, thin skin, with a fragile,
papery look, and peeling. Hair tangled, dull, and brittle. Head
long and thin, prominent cheekbones and eye sockets. Mental
and psychological competence also showed radical decline.
The prisoner lost his memory and his ability to concentrate.
His awareness was fixed on one thing—food. Fantasies of eat-

ing dulled the torment of starvation. He only saw what was held directly in front of him, and only heard when shouted at. He accepted blows unresistingly. In the final stages, the prisoner no longer felt any hunger or pain. The Mussulman died in misery when he simply couldn't go on any longer. He was the living symbol of mass death, death from hunger, from the murder of the soul, and from complete abandonment. A dead man, yet still living."

Capesius and Roland described the Mussulmen as people who had been broken, destroyed by camp life, the victims of step-by-step extermination. A prisoner who only got camp rations and no chance to "organize" anything else for himself would die after a few weeks. Chronic hunger would lead to an overall physical weakening, Capesius noted, unmoved, in Göppingen: "Their vital functions were reduced to a minimum. The pulse slowed, blood pressure and temperature went down, they shivered with cold. Their breathing slowed, their voices got quieter, and every movement took great effort."

Adam said with a shudder that Auschwitz was a kind of initiation in human history through extermination and horror.

"Yes, it was truly a 'biopolitical experiment' become visible reality in the Mussulman," was how Roland put it, and it made me shudder; his cynicism completely undid me when he said, "And Goebbels's idea that politics is the art of translating into reality the seemingly impossible—this idea actually took place in Auschwitz, in the Mussulman, who represents the catastrophe of the human subject, his eradication, as a place where everyday life, the present, and contingency can live. That's why we clung so tightly to the everyday. Why, even with the chimneys smoking, we tried to maintain it with all our might. We celebrated Christmas, sang songs, had birthday parties, cozy evenings together . . . Even the prisoners tried to maintain the normalcy of everyday life."

.

Yes, that totally normal, nice, everyday life for the SS in Auschwitz:

Dr. Wirths to his wife: "Auschwitz, September 22, 1944. Michl [Möckl] has returned from Berlin, having placed the remainder of his furniture in safety, and is happy to be here again; he even said he doesn't want to leave here again. Imagine, there actually are people like that!

"For Frau Fischer, who seems to have adapted to things well here, the worst thing is that we all have to work so hard— as if that were any great surprise. So she has quietly reproached me about Horst's appearance—what can I do about it?

"Tonight I was invited out for dinner, but I didn't go. I wanted to write and tell you about all my joys and all my sorrows. We are having company this week; they start to arrive tomorrow. Olga is still sick and has a high fever. Dr. Caesar will be getting married in December . . ."

And here is a prisoner's everyday experience of a completely different order:

Prosecutor Kügler: "Yes—now, sir [to Filip Müller, an eyewitness], I should like to ask you the following. I once was told that in 1944 in particular, the burning of bodies in open pits was being done at such a pace that there was a special commando that had to catch the fat dripping from the burning bodies and shovel it onto new bodies. Is that right? Did you see that yourself?"

Witness Filip Müller: "Yes, that's quite right. It was done in this way: I was in the incineration trenches in Birkenau and also in Crematorium IV, where there were two of these pits in the rear portion of the yard. In Birkenau there were three trenches: one of them later on was leveled or maybe filled in.

"These trenches were about forty meters in length. Six to seven or eight meters across. About two and a half meters deep. In the lower part of the trenches there was a kind of channel or gutter. The melted human fat ran into these little channels. And the prisoners had to pour the human fat on top of the bodies. To make them burn better . . ."

Prosecutor Kügler: "No questions."

·

Adam: Up to that point where the nightmare is the everyday, normal occurrence, turning the subjective self completely inside out, we tried to protect ourselves right up to that point of no return . . . but let's stop this . . . You know, it is true, but so impossibly inappropriate that language fails, it can no longer even be discussed in the fractured form of heretofore traditional philosophy, it's simply inappropriate . . . all of it. Shame is the only way to deal with it. And here, one of the gassed victims, the poet Fondane, got it right: in the gas chamber, in the living death of the barely vegetable Mussulmen, there was no more God, no more consolation, not even prayer, nothing . . . yet it is repeated with every old person vegetating in an intensive care unit, having outlived life itself . . .

·

Adam's diary: There was one of us who was dangerously weakened; we had to protect him from the "selection." And so we hid him from the selekcja *in a bed in the barrack. This was only possible through a network of connections, this so-called* dekowanie, *or cover-up action. We were able to hide comrades from the block seniors or the Kapos, even from the camp Gestapo, since we were already veterans, and thus we were able to hide Boris, and get him transferred to another commando, and another section of camp. So he simply never got found. Of course there are spies all around, a dense network of Kapos, who inform on everyone, they're in every commando.*

Poor Jan is the picture of what a Mussulman looks like; no subdermal layer left, so he looks like a skeleton hung with skin, his weight equals exactly the weight of his bones alone. He stinks horribly, soaked with his own diarrhea, he is literally rotting alive, he sways as he walks, in slow motion, with filthy blankets all over him and an old cement bag on his head. He moves like Jews pray-

ing at the Wailing Wall, back and forth, back and forth. And he looks as if he were actually a Moslem with sunken eyes and a prominent gaze fixed on a distant object, or with eyes nervously looking about, pupils feverish and dilated, a desperate expression, sad and reproachful, his drawn face long and masklike, the contour of the eye sockets and cheekbones clearly distinct, as with corpses. His skin is parchmentlike, scaly, and covered with ulcers, his legs hugely swollen with edema. He is pushed around by everyone like some stinking thing, he arouses aggression particularly from the SS and the Kapos because he stinks revoltingly and no longer responds to anything. Like someone who is already dead, he no longer respects his SS masters, doesn't take off his cap or stand at attention, doesn't salute, treats the SS like thin air, all senses and volition deadened, a sort of undead creature, like something left forgotten here from the Beyond. He is a human being past tense, indifferent to death, no longer afraid of anything. He has left the camp, as much as if he had successfully escaped. Everything which gives them power has no more meaning in the realm of the Mussulman: he has escaped them! He no longer knows his own name, let alone his number. And—nearly 80 percent of all the prisoners are escapees like this, people who are no longer there, Mussulmen or Mussulwomen. And day by day they get sicker, food is all that matters, no matter what rotting, disgusting thing it is, swill from the reeking garbage cans is good enough for them, though it poisons them even further. Nothing matters, not even death, for pain will no longer hurt them in their Beyond. And all the while they rub their hands together, as if they were pleased, had achieved something. They move their arms and shoulders as if delighted with something—but these circus gestures, these clownlike grins, are only made in the attempt to warm themselves. Today I saw a group of them near the whorehouse, there are always a lot of them hanging around there, as if they were looking for the ultimate source of life there. It's eerie, these half-dead creatures, who don't even notice you, who

seem like they just fell out of the sky, rocking back and forth mo-
notonously by their invisible Wailing Wall; they're often almost
naked, even in winter, cloaked only in colored blankets, smeared
rust-colored by the smoke of smoldering garbage, and often they
look like a caravan of Bedouins in the desert. The impression they
make wavers between the comic and the dignity of impending
death in the gas chamber that marks them all. Indeed, they are
already long gone, absent; it is almost a miracle that we can even
still see these ghostly spirits as something earthly.

Today right here by the bordello I notice a group of Greek
Jews, all Mussulmen, waiting for the empty soup cauldron with
its bits of leftover milk soup, which the whores will throw over the
fence. A wild struggle then ensues; each of them tries to scoop up
some of this grease and lick it off his fingers, and then the pot ends
up on top of someone's head, dribbling thick grease all over him,
and the others were licking him up and down like a candy cane,
along with all the filth already on him, then the whole line of
them went to the Unterkapo with this singsong prayer: "Essen
zup," begging for soup. They ate clay, and spruce wood, grass,
rags. And they would cut off a finger, or one of their fellows' fingers, once even one of their noses. They would slit open an arm, to
drink the blood. Cannabalism was common. And they didn't
wait for death to arrive: those who were still dying, only half dead,
were cut open, their blood drunk and their flesh gnawed at. Blood
doesn't coagulate as quickly with the barely living as it does with
the dead. And some of them were forever chewing on saccharin,
which was easier to get. "Mam glod, mam glod,"* they would
mumble. And view each other as edible objects. Some were afraid
to fall asleep. The Greeks were particularly vulnerable; the murderous cold did them in. They were burning with fever. Bloody
diarrhea (caused by starvation) was eating away at them. At the
end, they did not excrete stools, just blood. By then their bodies

---

*"Mother, hunger" in *lagerszpracha*.

were nothing but bones, a dying mass of nothing. And to save gas, they were thrown alive onto the flames. I saw it. They didn't scream, they didn't make a sound, as if even this horror were a salvation. And whenever the chimneys only gave off black smoke and no flames, then everyone knew that just these wasted Mussulmen were being burned. It was only with fresh recruits that they flared up "healthily."

Not even in their deaths were these undead like the others.

The worst thing after the standing cells was the hunger bunker. That was where Father Kolbe died.

Yes, food was enormously important, it was survival itself. For that reason there was a huge number of terms for everything having to do with it: In the morning, for example they would come with the cart or the trolley, the food bringers with the ersatz coffee; at noon, the much longed for lagerzupa, *mostly beet greens, rutabagas, stinking stuff, of a revolting pasty consistency, doled out in single portion pots, seconds, another ladle, for those who could get it, or those arrivals doing the hardest labor. When transports were arriving, the leftover foodstuffs from those who were already killed were shoveled into a* cugankowka zupa *(new recruit soup). This reeking* lagerzupa *of rutabagas was also called* plyty gramofonowe *(gramophone records),* avozupa *was made by the fish- and bone-meal suppliers, or, best of all, the* melzupa *(flour soup), and the famous* brotzupa *(bread soup); all the food items that the gassed victims had brought with them, especially moldy bread, were to be found in it. Evenings at supper, with extra portions of rutabaga or a tiny piece of margarine, there would also be smelly sour milk cheese:* bauernfusz *(farmer's foot) and* kwargla *(cheese).* Wurszt, blutwurszt *(sausage and blood sausage) made from vegetables. And, rarely, that delicacy, potatoes.*

The tortures were endless. But the Mussulmen don't feel anything. And even they were subjected to the daily public beatings, an execution performed in front of all, where even shame was exterminated, where men's and women's buttocks were exposed, then beaten to a pulp, while being forced to count their blows and thank their tormenters, in between their bellows and screams of agony. And the snapping crack of the whip. Dupa nie szklanka, *your ass isn't glass, they wisecrack in their brutal way when administering twenty-five lashes to the buttocks, the* sztrafa *or the beating on the trestle.*

June 26, 1944. "The workshops of the German armaments factories delivered to the administration of the Auschwitz Camp Crematoriums four sieves ordered on June 7 to be used for sifting through human ashes. The sieves are to be used for sifting out incompletely cremated human bones retrieved from the incineration trenches next to the crematoriums, so that they can be crushed in special mortars. The price of the four sieves was 232 reichsmarks."

I asked Adam if, while on the Sonderkommando duty in the gas chambers, he sometimes would find acquaintances or even relatives.

Yes, he said, it is the worst shock to see the lifeless bodies of friends, completely without warning. Thank God, I only learned of my wife's death from a friend. But look here, read what I wrote about one moment there in the crematorium:

One day two people I knew, Mussulmen by then, were brought into the crematorium, they were doomed, and they knew it. I said to them: So why you, why now? And they said, calmly, soon to be released from suffering: That is our lot in life, our fate, you can't escape it.

So we ate together and smoked until it was time. A German came and said: So, now we have to finish with them. And I said to them, Come, my dear friends, I have something to tell you. And I brought them into the gas chamber, to the spot where the gas comes in. Just sit here, you will not have to suffer a second. It is the best place to die!

But even that wasn't enough: among the victims gassed that

*day there were also ten friends and family members. Their white
bodies lying in rows before us. And when we were finished burning the bodies of 390 strangers, we burned each of our ten friends
and acquaintances separately, took the ashes of each one and put
them in a box, wrote their names on them, with their birthday
and death day. Then we buried them and even said Kaddish, so
that each of them separately had his own death.*

*And who will say Kaddish for us? we asked ourselves. When
the Russians came and freed the camp, I heard they found the
boxes. That was a good ending.*

*But when I think back to the beginning: the first day of my "job"
in the Sonderkommando, a transport from Transylvania arrived
in the afternoon. The whole transport went right into the fire, without exception. In mid July of 1944 at three o'clock in the morning
a transport arrived from Transylvania with over 1,500 Jews, men,
women, and children. These were the Jews that Eichmann, despite
Horthy's order of July 2 forbidding it, had smuggled out to be annihilated. We were waiting for them in the undressing room. First
were the women, girls, and children. And there was a beautiful
Hungarian woman with two children, and she said to us: How can
I undress in front of you, how shameful! We said to her, We were
already quite used to that, and before we could say anything more,
the German camp leader came up and said to the woman: Put your
clothes here, and your children's, too, and remember the number on
the hanger so you can find your clothes again.*

*She went with her children directly to the gas chamber. In
August 1944 they brought 250 Polish Mussulmen from some of
the Auschwitz subcamps. They couldn't even walk anymore. The
commandant of the crematorium, SS Hauptscharführer Moll,
came right away and said, "No gas for them." He wanted to kill
them himself, in person. At first he beat some of them to death
with the iron rod that we used to crush leftover bones. Then he
went over and got a rifle and bullets from a soldier. He started
shooting. After he had shot four or five, one of the Mussulmen*

*called out to him: "Commandant!" And Moll, who really was a
sadist, answered: "Yes."*

"I have a request."

"What do you want?"

*"While you are shooting my friends, I would like to sing 'The
Blue Danube' waltz."*

*"By all means, so much the better. Shooting with musical ac-
companiment is even better," said Moll. And he sang "La-la-la-
la-la" and Moll shot them all, until it was the singer's turn. The
last bullet hit him. End of story.*

*I remember, too, that forty children were brought in, thirteen-
and fourteen-year-old boys who could work. I saw one boy who
was still not dead after five shots. And that's how they killed all
forty.*

*Two weeks after that, twenty partisans came, among them
four women, good-looking women. They knew that they had to
die. We expected them to resist, to put up a fight with their fists—
after all, they were partisans—but nothing like that happened.
They were as docile as lambs. We ordered them to undress; only
one refused. Kapo Kaminski hit her. They were all silent and
went into the gas chamber like little lambs.*

*I recall an instance where there were 140 to 150 girls who had
come over to us. They were sitting around and started playing
and laughing. They probably thought they had come to Birkenau
to have a jolly good time. We wondered about that: What was
going on here? A half hour, two hours had already passed, and
they had still not been burned? Then suddenly there was an order
to bring them back. A truck came and brought them to some
room next to the "sauna." And when they all came out of the
crematorium again, all in one piece, we said to them: Light a
candle, because you have gotten out of there.*

*So when they were in this room, they were forced to write post-
cards: We have arrived in the camp. The Germans have given us*

*a friendly reception. We have been given good food and are in
good health. Two days later, they were brought back to the crematorium, and this time they went completely berserk. Now they
knew that they were brought there to die. They killed them all.*

*One time they brought a Hungarian girl with a two-day-old
baby, really a newborn. She knew they were going to die. That
night, we had nothing to do, we sat around, gave her a chair, too,
and sat around eating and smoking cigarettes. She started to tell
us she was a singer. And so she talked with us for a quarter or a
half an hour. We were sitting right next to the ovens. A Dutch SS
officer was sitting with us, quite nice, a good guy. He listened,
too. At the end of her story, he stood up and said, Okay, we can't
just keep sitting around here, now, it's death's turn. We asked her
what she preferred—should we kill the baby first, or her? She said,
Kill me first, I don't want to see my baby dead. So then the Dutch
guy got up, grabbed his gun, shot her, and threw her into the
oven. After that he took the baby, boom boom, and that was it. We
were the only ones who saw the tragedy of the Jews with our own
eyes. That man, the Dutch SS guy, had been in the camp for a
year and a half, and had seen everything, but he just didn't take
in the human tragedy, the tragedy of the Jewish people. We saw it,
experienced it ourselves. At first the work was terribly hard, but
gradually we got to live with it. A human being, like a dog, can
get used to anything!*

KALENDARIUM, JULY 11, 1944

"The appointed Reich Ambassador Veesenmayer informed the
Foreign Office in a telegram that the concentration and deportation of the Jews in Zone V (the suburbs of Budapest west
of the Danube) had been completed on schedule on July 9,
with a total of 55,741. The grand total of Jews deported from
Hungarian zones I through V had now reached 437,401." [Zur

Geschichte des Lagers: *Der 1. Frankfurter Auschwitz-Prozess*,
p. 780.]

•

*Adam: Already by July 2, 1944, there were no more Hungarian
transports arriving. We members of the Kampfgruppe had heard
a broadcast on the radio that we had hidden in the crematorium,
and also had information in July from the partisans that the world
public had protested. The "Zionists" in Budapest had seen to that.
Even the Vatican had raised vehement protest. Neutral countries
like Sweden, primarily, and Switzerland, and then even the fascist
countries Spain and Portugal were handing out passports to the
Jews. And around 35,000 Jews were living in specially protected
houses in Budapest. And a severe air-raid attack on July 2 did the
rest. Churchill had threatened Horthy that Hungary's fate would
be unlike that of "any other civilized nation" if the deportations
did not cease immediately. Horthy acceded, and stopped them. But
Eichmann intervened, and on July 6 ordered another 1,500 Jews
deported from Hungary to Auschwitz.*

*The Red Army's major offensive was already in motion. It is
a little-known fact that the battle on the Romanian frontiers
was even more destructive than Stalingrad.*

2

Roland came home on leave from Auschwitz for the last time
in 1943, home to Mom in Transylvania, home to plum dump-
lings and bean soup, smelling "manly" and reeking of strong
cigarettes, "a handsome man," said my mother of her favorite
cousin, while he banged away with his stubby fingers on the
piano in our dining room. And sang, too. Even today I can
hear his fake-smooth, ever so gentle, yet somehow nervous
voice . . . *"Ich träumt' in seinem Schatten so manchen sü-üßen
Traum . . ."*

And now, from August 23, 1944, on, German Transylvania no longer existed. Over. *Fini.* And Roland Albert was partly to blame. Roland would have vehemently rejected such a statement: "On the contrary," he would have said, "I put my own life at risk to defend my country against the Bolsheviks, even in the concentration camp."

From August 1944 . . . in that summer since May, on the ramps, when our Jewish compatriots were being driven into the gas chambers by the hundreds of thousands by "our" SS men, Roland, Dr. Fritz Klein, Capesius, Draser were all part of it . . . at that time I was ten years old. The brilliant morning sun shining through the oak branches. The fragrance of morning. Everything as ordinary as the taste of an apple, as the wind, the rain, the snow, the sun: like the damp earth, warmed by the sun. August. A swing under the apple tree, and behind that an open bedroom window. The apples falling from the branches with a soft thud to the ground. This was childhood, was paradise, the last seconds of it before it ended. Mother standing under the apple tree in her flowered morning coat. A bell ringing in the distance. The milkman, tall as a tree, with his milk cans clanging. And then he is standing right beside us, saying: "Don't you know, ma'am? The Russians are coming!" Kuurt! cried Mama in horror, the Russians are coming. Papa came running out; he didn't have his pajama top on, his chest was bare, his skin all rosy and white. The milkman said: "It was on the radio!" Beneath his beard, I could see his red lips moving . . . That evening, on the radio, the king . . . his address: To my people.

And then the grown-ups spoke in whispers, all day long. Their faces were pale and worried, as they went into my grandparents' bedroom to talk things over. Radio. The king. Milkman. Russians. *A reversal.* They thought they were dreaming. Is this really possible? A high-pitched audible hum could be heard in the brain, it felt as if time had stopped . . . as if all of a sudden, eternity had caught up with them. Everyone's plans were turned upside down. Everything was floating in uncertainty, even though, outwardly, everything was just as before. Then, in September, small Russian tanks came rumbling in across the river. But the bridges weren't the same anymore, and even the river was no longer the same river. Still, our druggist at the Crown Pharmacy, SS Sturmbannführer and Auschwitz druggist Dr. Victor Capesius, had bravely and valiantly attempted to fight his way back to us here at home: at least, according to the grapevine. He had come as a "liberator." Yes, wonderful: hats off. But he didn't make it. The Asiatic hordes stood between us, huge masses of human matériel. But it all seemed so strange, so uncanny, as if we had fallen out of the world, and were encased in silence: as if the clamorous tolling of a great bell had suddenly broken off amid the strident onrush of time. Heartbeats racing—and then nothing. Nothing. Something unnameable was illuminating us, as if our eyes were mysterious windows . . . and all the burials happening back then . . . especially in Corneşti* . . . women wailing, black head scarves . . . candles . . . incense . . . A cleric sang, in a vestment embroidered with silver, but the dead man was looking straight up at him.† *Doamne miluieşte, milu-e-eşte, la căsuţa ta cea nouă, nu te ninge, nu te plouă.* (Oh Lord, be merciful, be merciful, in your new little home no snow will fall on you, nor rain.) They're so foreign to me, said Mother. And even the languages, our Saxon and German, and their soft, almost mystical language, and even their lamentations, were so different! And yet that death that comes to all had the same fate in store for us. But "normal" death had died, too. In the

---

*A town in Moldava, Romania.
†Funerals here used open caskets and kept the head of the dead propped up on a cushion. —trans.

Jewish cemetery, they buried a bar of green soap stamped with the letters RJF.*

SEPTEMBER 1944: DR. CAPESIUS'S LAST JOURNEY HOME

"They sang 'The Internationale' and the Russian national anthem in our town market square," said Mother. "Imagine— 'The Internationale!' And there was a Russian flak unit in the Villa Franca. And in the train station, long rows of the wounded, with Mongol faces."

Uncle Daniel said it was surely a lack of hospitality to throw our peace-loving boys out of Russia that way, and then force their way into our homeland uninvited as they were; normally the Russians are such a friendly, welcoming people!

Earlier our druggist had tried to arrange an exchange for his family with Frau Dr. Böhm, who had worked in *his* camp in the Generalgouvernement [Poland —trans.]. This had been managed by Frau Zieliński, people said, the wife of the best baker in the village of Sighişoara.

Roland: "On September 21, Capesius had attempted to at least get his family 'out of there.' (Amazing, all that went on! Even the Volksgruppenführer Schmidt had heroically parachuted down behind Russian lines, to help start up a partisan movement . . .) Capesius came back to us in the camp on September 22, 1944; he had been back home, to see what had happened there after August 23, when the Romanians betrayed us and went over to the Russian side. That beautiful fall, the Russians had taken control in Transylvania; they marched

*RJF: *Rein jüdisches Fett*, or pure Jewish fat: this is a reference to the widely believed, but false, rumor that the Nazis made soap from their victims. This has been refuted by prominent Israeli scholars as well as Holocaust deniers. The initials were actually RIF, which stood for the Reichsstelle für industrielle Fettversorgung (Reich Center for Industrial Fat Provisioning). —trans.

into Schäßburg. We were absolutely crushed, you know? And Friederike, that refined Viennese lady, our Capesius's wife, was still living with her three daughters in Schäßburg, working every day in the Crown Pharmacy selling medicines. But the front separated her from her husband, who was on duty up north; the Hungarian-Romanian border was located eighteen kilometers from Schäßburg after the arbitration in Vienna: Romania was now enemy territory, Russian territory. Vic had to go back to Auschwitz; there was an order to gas many of the outside commandos after a Sonderkommando uprising had taken place; since he was in charge of the Zyklon B, he had to report for duty."

Decades later, in my interview in Göppingen with him, I had the impression that Capesius seriously thought that he was fighting this "flood tide" even in Auschwitz, doing something to stop it ("finishing off" subhumans?). But still this was carried out, and had to be, in strictest secrecy . . . "obviously!" You know?

Capesius: "It was always that way, right from the first days: your closest friend, if he was a Sturmbannführer or an Obersturmbannfüher, would tell you, 'Don't talk about this to anyone!' Could you run away? No! No desertion! You would have been caught right away! You would have been hung from the nearest pole."

"I would have had thoughts of suicide, I don't know."

Capesius: "The individual could do nothing to resist . . . and we could only save our fatherland if we could keep the Russians from coming in . . . and we could have prevented that, if we hadn't been betrayed . . ."

"You mean, you could have kept the Russians from coming?"

Capesius: "Yeah, sure . . . we knew what would happen when Stalin came in. And we had to stop that. To keep that from happening, you had to swallow all kinds of things."

•

It is difficult to reconstruct the druggist's last trip to Transylvania from his notes. The notes were made later, when he was in pretrial detention, and during the trial, and they are less a description of the trip than they are instructions to his family and to his attorney; they contain statements such as "Please keep strictly to the diary for the year 1944, which has me traveling on August 25 from Vienna to Târgu Mureş and back to Vienna."

The dates, the entire diary, the reality, were to be "reworked" for the trial. Of course, Capesius clearly didn't go to Sighişoara, which was already "under the Russians." His notes say only, "I got back to Auschwitz again with Lotte on September 21 around three to four p.m."

The "heroism" of Capesius's attempt to "get his family out of there" of course looked quite different in reality!

This is what Capesius writes about Stefan Lill and his wife, Lotte (Stefan, an officer in the SS "Florian Geyer" Division, a Swabian (ethnic German) from the Banat, and his wife, Lotte, a nurse from Berlin):

"The report on my trip to Marosvásárhely (Târgu Mureş) to find my family shows that I first got to know both of them in the 'Florian Geyer' Divison, and that I tried to get to Schäßburg to get information and make contact with my wife.

"But after all attempts failed, and the Russians had marched into Schäßburg with their tanks, Romanian Messerschmidt Bf 109 fighter planes began firing on columns of fleeing refugees (in wagons pulled by buffalos) in the vicinity of the Marosvásárhely railroad station, which I myself saw, during which around fifty peasants' carts were being shot to pieces, and the wild reactions of the panic-stricken buffalos put the survivors in even greater danger.

"At Herr Lill's request (which I at first resisted) I was charged with taking Frau Lill, a nurse in her husband's unit, back to Vienna with me, as a forced retreat was imminent; I was to set her up in temporary lodging there with Dr. Melitta Bauer, my sister-in-law. So the two of us traveled around two days to Budapest, where we spent the night of the seventeenth in two separate hotels. As an officer, I was billeted in the Hotel Majestic, and Frau Lill was put in the hotel for enlisted men and nurses.

"On the eighteenth we continued on our way to Vienna, where I had to report back and turn in the Finnish automatic weapon that I had been obliged to take with me for areas of unrest. Then on the twenty-first I went back to Auschwitz and by four in the afternoon I was back in the dispensary. The pharamacists, and Éva, were waiting for me in desperation, for they had heard from reliable sources that they were planning to liquidate all the office commandos, because they knew too much.

"On that very evening I served my good Hungarian apricot schnaps in the barracks and prevailed upon Dr. Fischer, Dr. Klein, and Dr. Mengele, who were in better standing with Dr. Wirths, to do something to thwart this plan to kill our colleagues; and so they were able to prevent it.

"Strauch was always grateful to me for that.

"The whole operation was much slower now, and even luggage arrived only rarely now, since the Hungarian transports with their masses of humanity had stopped, and the gassing details were almost over; occasionally we still received left-behind luggage from the 'Canada' warehouses.

"Frau Lill had often visited me when I was being held in Ludwigsburg, bringing me food and reading me grateful letters from Strauch, who was in Ebensee, Austria, working for the CIC, and later in a pharmacy."

Capesius continued to write about himself in the third person, as if his identity were gradually being dissolved into "Dr. C.," the SS officer, rather than himself.

"Dr. C. left Auschwitz on the twenty-fifth of August, first traveling to Berlin on matters concerning his leave. He was to escort Frau Dr. Mary Euler as far as the Hungarian-Romanian border, and to do this he had arrange a leave for himself through the head SS office for the southeast front, dealing with an SS general she knew.

"Lotte should make a good report from this; after all, she once wrote reports regularly."

Further directives: "Please remember: I was back home for four weeks, not merely eight days. In any event, I was back in Auschwitz on September 22."

SCHÄßBURG

And my father's captain was there, too; the Romanians were now marching toward the Germans, moving westward, including him, the little captain with his company. He wanted to do something good for Father, and said: *Te îmbraci în uniformă romă nă şi vii cu noi.* You're putting on a Romanian uniform and coming with us. It's better now to fight against the Germans, better for all the foreseeable future. You'll get on the other side of the front. But Father shrank from it as if from something forbidden. No, no, thanks, he said. Now I am going to stay with my family, they need me.

It felt like something awful, like the end of the world.

The overriding emotion was fear. Never shame, never guilt. Not even when people slowly realized what had happened. Their armor of self-defense and self-justification was like iron. Were they now supposed to listen to the enemy? To believe them? To obey them? Conscience: Did this matter with enemies? After all, the battle against the enemy was still going on. Everyone who fought with the Wehrmacht, with the SS, was still at the front. For the Führer and for the Reich. Even though here in Schäßburg there was a strange peace. Under the Russians.

THE SONDERKOMMANDO UPRISING

Kalendarium of the Events of October 1944–January 1945

Chronicle of October 7, 1944. "This Saturday, the resistance organization in the Auschwitz concentration camp informed the leader of the Kampfgruppe in the Sonderkommando that their intelligence had received a report saying that the camp leadership was intending to liquidate the still-surviving members of the Sonderkommando in the immediate future. Also, probably through the same channels, word got out that a 'reduction' of the commandos in Crematoriums IV and V by about three hundred specifically named prisoners was also imminent. The prisoners designated for 'transport' said that they would not meekly go to the slaughter, but would defend themselves. At 1:25 p.m. a group of the affected prisoners mounted an attack on the SS guards who were to take them away, using hammers, axes, and stones. After Crematorium IV had been set on fire, some of the prisoners in Commando 59-B were able to fight their way into the nearby woods. At the same time, the prisoners of Commando 57-B assigned to Crematorium II began their revolt. (The prisoners in Commandos 58-B and 60-B had not been informed of the revolt, and did nothing.) Two hundred fifty prisoners died in the attack, including the organizers of the uprising, Salmen Gradowski from Suwalki; Josef Warzawski (real name: Josef Dorebus) from Warsaw, who had been deported from Drancy to Auschwitz; Józef Deresiński from Luna near Grodnot; Ajzyk Kalniak from Łomża; Lejb Langfus from Warsaw, who had been deported to Auschwitz

from Maków Mazowiecki; and Lejb Panusz (Herszko) from
Łomża.

"That evening all the slain prisoners were brought into the
yard of Crematorium IV, and the rest of the prisoners of the
Sonderkommando were rounded up, and the two hundred reb-
els still alive were shot in the yard. It was a bloodbath. Then the
representative of the camp commandant gave a speech and an-
nounced that if such an event occurred again, that all of the
prisoners in the camp would be shot. After that, normal work
continued again in Crematoriums II, III, and V.

"During the uprising the prisoners killed three members
of the SS: the Unterscharführers Rudolf Erler, Willi Freese,
and Josef Purke."

October 10, 1944. "Three Jewish women employed in the
Union-Werke munitions factory, Ala Gertner, Estera Wajchblum
[other sources give the name as Wajcblum-hora], and Regina
Szafirsztajn [other sources give the name as Szafirsztajn-hora]
were arrested and brought to the women's camp in Auschwitz I.
They were accused of having smuggled explosives from the
magazine in the Union-Werke, and giving them to the prisoners of the Sonderkommando, who were able to make primitive
hand grenades with them for use in the uprising."

*Adam: Fourteen prisoners of the Sonderkommando, among
them Jankiel Handelsman from Radom (one of the organizers of
the uprising), the Polish Jew Wróbel, who had received the explosives from the Jewish women, and five Soviet prisoners of war who
had been assigned to the Sonderkommando in April 1944 were
arrested and brought into the bunker in Block 11. After these
fourteen prisoners were arrested and placed in Block 11, the
Sonderkommando comprised 198 prisoners, who were divided
into three commandos of sixty-six men apiece and assigned to
Crematoriums II, III, and V. The commandos continued working
in two shifts, a day shift and a night shift. Each shift consisted of
thirty-three prisoners. After the destruction of Crematorium IV*

during the uprising, it was not listed again in the daily reports on the prisoners' work teams in Auschwitz II.

In the women's camp of Auschwitz II, two more Jewish women were arrested and charged with having had contact with the Sonderkommando and of having delivered explosives into the camp. One of the women arrested, the Polish Jew Róza Robota, had been working in the property warehouse BIIg, which was adjacent to Crematorium IV. Róza had accepted the explosives that Ala Gertner had smuggled out of the Union-Werke with the help of other female go-betweens, and passed them on to prisoner Wróbel of the Sonderkommando.

The girls were arrested after they were betrayed by Koch, the spy. This time the SS had evidence. Ala Gertner, the young Belgian, and the two other girls were brought into the bunker and tortured in the most horrible way, because the Political Department wanted to obtain details about the illegal movement and the uprising. We were aware of the danger of our situation. Two days later, as the commando marched in, we learned that Róza Robota, too, had been brought into the bunker. It was obvious to us that the girls had not been able to withstand the torture.

We had to deal with the fact that the SS would be on our trail in the next few hours or days.

Those were difficult days. Róza knew all our names and what we did. She was twenty-three years old, a member of a Zionist socialist youth movement, Haschomer Hazair. We all had complete confidence in her. But we also knew how the SS could torture people. None of us could say that they would be able to resist such torture. Who could accuse anyone who weakened under the horrific agony of being beaten, burned with cigarettes, having fingers broken or hair torn out? Can a human being made of flesh and blood stand torture such as this day and night, in the camp all alone, and totally at the torturers' mercy?

For days we thought we would be arrested at any moment. We thought every SS man who went by where we were working was

the one sent to arrest us. It is a horrible feeling to know you are
in such danger, and not be able to do anything about it. We prepared our defense for when we were brought before the Political
Department. Privately, in our hearts, we considered suicide. And,
no, we actually did not fear death. Over the years we had become
used to the idea that we would have to die. By then death seemed
an old friend. What we feared was torture, and particularly
what we, as Jewish prisoners, feared most was bringing down the
whole resistance movement inside Auschwitz.

Several days passed. Every morning they brought Róza out of
the bunker and into the Political Department, and every evening they brought her back. Her clothing was ripped, she was
bloodied, you could hardly recognize her face. We would stand on
the main street of the camp, and try to get her to look our way.
That's how we would have shown her how much we cared, how
much we were with her. But she recognized no one. She was being
dragged along by two guards who held her up. Her strength was
ebbing visibly day by day.

Something happened about then that seems completely incredible now. Jakob, the Kapo in the bunker, turned to us and said he
was willing to sneak Noach into the bunker at night, so that he
could have a talk with Róza. At first we hesitated, since we were
afraid it was a trap by the SS. But in the end, the chance of a talk
with Róza seemed so important that we just ignored the risks.
Noach went inside for his meeting at night.

Jakob got the SS overseer drunk, and got Noach inside the
death house. He opened the heavy iron door. Noach walked into
the cell and found Róza lying on the cold cement floor. At first
she didn't recognize him. These two childhood friends were then
together for an entire hour before Róza even regained consciousness. But slowly she came to her senses enough for her to explain
the events of the past few days to Noach. She said that she had
named no names, but rather had put all the blame onto someone
who was already dead. She reassured us that we had nothing to

*fear. She knew that she herself had to die. But she would remain
steadfast to the end.*

*Noach brought us a note from Róza—a last farewell. She
wrote us, saying how hard it was to leave life, but we had no reason to be afraid, she would not betray anyone. She had only one
request: if any one of us should ever be free one day, that man
should avenge her death. The note was signed with the motto of
the Haschomer Hazair:* Chasak we'emaz *(be strong and brave).**

•

October 14, 1944. The Sonderkommando began the process of
pulling down the walls of Crematorium IV, which had been
destroyed in the uprising.

*Adam: But horrible things happened again in the middle of
October, when the Nazis toppled Horthy, that "old fool," as Eichmann called him, and the fanatic "Arrow Cross" Party member
and anti-Semite Ferenc Szálasi became the head of state. The
extermination facilities in Auschwitz had been dismantled. But
the Reich, now bled dry, needed to resupply its labor force, so the
unspeakable "Reichsplenipotentiary" Veesenmayer set up a plan
with Szálasi to put 50,000 Jews "at his disposal." The railroads
were no longer in operation, and so the result was the insanity of
the November death marches. No one was exempted from these
marches, regardless of age, paperwork, or security pass. Just as
bad as that was the scandalous behavior of the Hungarians
themselves, who still organized many pogroms and murdered
tens of thousands of victims, in the provinces, too, until the country was liberated by the Red Army on February 13, 1945. At
least the major Hungarian culprits—László Endre, state secretary for Jewish Affairs, László Baky, also a state secretary of the
Ministry of the Interior, and the police officer Lieutenant Colonel Ferenczy, who was directly in charge of the deportations—
were executed. They were Eichmann's accomplices—these three*

---

*See also Adler, Langbein, and Lingens-Reiner.

pathological criminals and the Hungarian gendarmerie were all he needed for the organization and deportation of half a million victims!

October 27, 1944. A group of prisoners escaping from the concentration camp at Auschwitz I (this group included the Austrian Ernst Burger and the Poles Bernard Świerczyna, Czesław Duzel, Zbigniew Raynoch, and Piotr Piąty, who belonged to the Kampfgruppe Auschwitz and the camp's military council, as well as the SS officer Frank, the contact man of the organization) was betrayed by the driver SS Rottenführer Johann Roth from Hermannstadt, Transylvania. When the prisoners became aware of the gravity of their situation, they took poison in the car they had intended to escape from the camp in; Zbigniew Raynoch and Czesław Duzel died, but the others were "saved." Two other Austrian prisoners, Rudolf Friemel and Ludwig Vesely, who had been organizers of the escape, were apprehended and delivered to the bunker of Block 11. SS officer Frank, who had done the negotiating with the driver, SS Rottenführer Johann Roth, and who had trusted him, was also arrested.

Adam: If you want to know about your Transylvanian compatriots in the camp, well, besides the notorious Hans-Andreas Draser of the Political Department, there was another Hermannstadt native, a certain Johann Roth, an SS Rottenführer in the drivers' pool, who played an evil role. He had often driven Capesius to the gas chamber. The escape had been planned in meticulous detail for October 27 by eight men, I think, from the leadership of the Kampfgruppe, who were later supposed to free the camp with groups of Polish partisans. Johann Roth, the SS driver, was to obtain German uniforms and then drive Ernst Burger and two of his comrades out of the camp. Roth turned traitor and exposed the plot. This betrayal had devastating consequences: the group could not escape. The partisans waiting for them nearby

*were attacked by the SS, and many of them died in this attack,
among them Kostek Jagiełło, who had escaped from Auschwitz
earlier to set things up. On the night of their planned escape, the
group were brought into the Political Department, and Boger
and Draser tortured them on the Boger swing, to get more information from them: they were not silent. (Draser, by the way, ended
up in a madhouse after the war.) The victims could not hold out
against the dreadful tortures. But at least the whole network was
not betrayed, since Burger was the only one who knew it all, but he
did let out some names, and the other four did as well. The Kampfgruppe was sufficiently weakened by this blow that there were no
more attempts at an uprising.*

October 31, 1944. In Block 11 in Auschwitz I, the Katowice
Gestapo garrison convened a court-martial and sentenced fifty-
nine Polish men and ten Polish women to death. The sentences were carried out in the crematorium of Auschwitz II on
November 1. The prisoners of the Sonderkommando clapped
their hands over the ears of the doomed prisoners to keep
them standing upright, but the victims, brave and steadfast,
did not move, and could have stood freely on their own.

November 2, 1944. This was probably the day the killings in
the gas chambers of Auschwitz II with Zyklon B were stopped.
After that point, the prisoners selected for killing were shot,
either in the gas chamber or outside Crematorium V.

THE LAST TESTAMENTS OF THE SONDERKOMMANDO

November 25, 1944. The process of dismantling the technical
equipment in Crematorium II was begun. First the motor that
pumped the air out of the gas chamber was removed; it was to
be transferred to the camp at Mauthausen. Then the pipes were
dismantled, to be transported to the camp at Gross-Rosen.

November 26, 1944. A "selection" was made from the members of the Sonderkommando previously assigned to the crematoriums at Birkenau, which still numbered two hundred prisoners: thirty of them would be used to operate Crematorium V; the remaining 170 were told they would be taken into the "sauna" to shower.

Adam: A friend of mine, Dr. Berner, a doctor from Klausenburg with whom I had long worked together in the "effects" warehouse, saved my life: he bribed two Oberscharführers who were on guard duty in the crematoriums with diamonds. Prisoners like Berner, who worked in the sorting rooms where they heaped up the booty taken from the gassed victims, were the "richest" and most powerful people in the camp. Time was short, and the schedule was tight, since Himmler had given the order to cease the gassings on November 2, 1944. But already by the fourteenth of October they had started to demolish the walls of Crematorium III, and on the twentieth two medic vans and a prison truck arrived filled with prisoners' documents, files, death certificates, and written indictments from the "registry office." These documents were now to be burned in Crematorium I, as the wretched inmates had been before them. On November 25, another medic van pulled up with documents; two Oberscharführers ordered me to help unload them. Then they took me with them; I was supposed to help them put files in order, once again in the so-called "registry office." Before leaving I could see that my prisoner colleagues had already started ripping down and demolishing Crematorium I with explosives.

We all knew we had just days to live. Evenings and nights, in the company of the last corpses in the cellar, several colleagues had each begun writing down their last will and testament by candlelight, and burying them. Many of them were unsigned, anonymous, as this one is. However, I knew the man who wrote it, for together we had dragged bodies to the crematorium. Here is his testament:

"I ask that all the descriptions and notes signed 'I.A.R.A.'

which I have buried be assembled and published under the title 'In the Abyss of Crime.' They are to be found in various boxes and glass jars in the yard of Crematorium II. As well as two longer reports, one titled 'Resettlement,' in a grave with bones in Crematorium I, and the other, called 'Auschwitz,' in a pile of bones on the southwest side of the same courtyard. Then I made another copy of it, completed it, and buried it in another place beneath the ashes in Crematorium II.

"Now we, the remaining 170 surviving men, are going to be reunited with our wives. We are certain that they are sending us to our deaths: today, the twenty-sixth of November, 1944."

Adam: In November 1944 the SS tried to erase all traces of their monstrous crime: to completely eradicate not only the crematoriums and the documents, but also the Sonderkommando prisoners, the eyewitnesses to the gassings. But beneath the dirt, beneath the ashes, the evidence remained, manuscripts buried in Crematorium II and III, burial tokens, not gold, not jewelry, but trash: crude, banal, ugly, stinking. In a German aluminum pot, in a soldier's canteen with a rubber-topped metal plug, a glass pint jar with a tin screw top, or a cracked jelly jar, the testimony of those who had been murdered. The manuscripts were those of Załmen Gradowski, Lejb Langfus, and Załmen Lewenthal. One eyewitness described two unimaginable events: "Di 3000 nakete" (the three thousand naked [prisoners]) and "Di 600 jinglech" (the six hundred boys):

"In broad daylight they brought out six hundred Jewish boys between twelve and eighteen years of age. They were dressed in long, very worn zebra-striped uniforms; they wore ragged shoes or wooden clogs . . . When they were assembled in the square, the commando leader ordered them to undress on the spot. The boys noticed the smoke belching from the chimney, and immediately realized that they were being led to their deaths. They began running around the square, in uncontrolled horror as they tore at their hair, not knowing how to save themselves. Many of them broke into the most dreadful screaming and crying, a great lamentation of utter hopelessness. The commando leader and his assistant beat the defenseless boys mercilessly, forcing them to get undressed . . . The boys stripped off their clothes, and instinctively crowded together in a tight circle, naked and shoeless, to shield themselves from the blows, and not moving from the spot. One courageous youth went up to the commando head standing near us and begged him to spare his life, and he would do the hardest labor, whatever it was. In answer, the SS officer gave him several blows to the head with a heavy blackjack. Many of the boys ran in a frenzy to the Jews in the Sonderkommando, threw their arms around their necks, and pleaded with them to save them. Others, still naked, scattered this way and that about the large yard, thus hoping to escape death. The commando leader called in an Unterscharführer with a rubber truncheon to help him.

"Their high boyish voices got louder and more desperate with every minute, finally giving way to abject weeping. Their cries could be heard all over the camp. We stood there, paralyzed by their wretched screaming. The SS, their faces arrogantly bearing a smirk of satisfaction, and showing not the slightest flicker of sympathy, stayed right there, raining blows on them, driving them into the bunker . . . Some of the boys were still running wildly around the square in search of shelter. The SS men kept after them, beat them, hitting them with their truncheons until they had the situation back in control, and drove the boys, convulsed with fear, into the bunker."

The fourth, Chaim Hermann, ended his letter to posterity with these words: "My letter is coming to its end, my remaining hours as well, so now I bid you all my irrevocable, final farewell . . . I am now with the last team of 204 people, they are about to liquidate Crematorium II, where I am waiting in utmost tension, and people say we will be liquidated in the course of this week. Excuse this chaotic text . . . If only you knew the cirumstances under which I must write this."

November 29, 1944. In the women's camp at Auschwitz-Birkenau, Barbara Dziewur was born. The baby was registered as prisoner number 89325 (women).

December 1, 1944. The demolition commando for Crematorium II was formed, with one hundred female prisoners assigned to it. The commando was employed to tear down the crematorium.

December 3, 1944. A total of 1,120 prisoners (skilled workers) were transferred to Auschwitz from Mauthausen, among them Belgians, Greeks, Yugoslavs, Italians, French, Germans, Hungarians, Norwegians, Lithuanians, Latvians, Slovaks, Czechs, Romanians, Luxemburgers, and Dutch. There was not a single Jew in the transport. The transferred prisoners were registered as numbers 201237 through 202357 (men).

December 4, 1944. Five hundred Polish prisoners (men) were transferred from Auschwitz to Buchenwald. On December 7 they arrived at Buchenwald in very poor physical and emotional condition. Allied air attacks on the railroad lines had forced the train to stop several times at stations on the way. The prisoners were given no food or water on the journey.

Adam: On December 12 I went into the sick bay. At Christmas I was released. While I was there, news came from Berlin of the verdict against Rudolf Friemel and his friends. We heard that all five had been sentenced to death.

December 21, 1944. Three days after an air raid on the IG Farben factory, American air reconnaissance made photographs from the air of the property, to determine the extent of damage. Near the margins of these air shots the concentration camps of Auschwitz and Birkenau could be seen. Enlargements of these pictures show that the perimeter fences and watchtowers of the former building Section BIII ("Mexico") had been demolished, that the roofs covering the gas chamber and the undressing room, which had both been subterranean structures, had been dismantled, and also that the roof and the chimney of Crematorium II had been removed. The fence surrounding Crematorium III was also gone, and the whole area around Crematorium II was strewn with pieces of wreckage. The target of this "tactical reconnaissance" had been the factory of the IG Farbenindustrie and its production.

Adam: Our friends were brought to the bunker by the end of October, and interrogated repeatedly; imagine the torture they had to endure for two months, until the thirtieth of December. I thought of them every day, and could imagine the torture they were enduring; being screamed at in "German," the questions, the interrogation in "German"—at least for Ernst Burger and for Rudolf Friemel!

December 24. Christmas Eve. But for me, "German" was still my beloved German language, a totally different German, as Polish was for the Poles, and for others Russian or French: deep inside us, it was our holiest relic, like a prayer. We felt that language could be a kind of medicine.

On one of my little notes, in microscopically small letters, I had written a poem in German; with Lewenthal's help I had translated it from Polish to German:

"You want us to speak, but what good are mere words? / We'd have to have enormous strength, the powers of a god, / To speak like the blazing sun, like the quavering stars, / With the sound of the storm wind, the autumn winds, / To strike in anger, like lightning."

Zofia Pieńkiewicz-Malanowska, a prisoner in Ravensbrück, wrote this down:

"Speaking, writing, saying it once again—this is too little! / You know—in the bowels of every man / this awful rottenness lies hidden, which kills . . . / With pathos, they say of us: HE suffered for his homeland! / But we feel in our very bones this wretched

stain . . . / In the very entrails of our souls, lice and filth are still concealed / With the awful stench of the blockhouses, where so many perished so horribly."

And music heightened this effect. No, it was not "O Tannenbaum" or the Polish carol "In the Silence of the Night," or other prescribed songs that affected us. No, not those. In the great hall, after Dr. Mengele had his dwarves perform, it was a Mussulman who moved us so much, we had tears in our eyes and a lump in our throat, many were sobbing, there was something so affecting in the simple child's verse:

> *Szedł w szczerym polu Chrystus Pan*
> *A przy Nim orszak bosy.*
> *Dziateczki co na zżęty łan*
> *Szły z miasta zbierać kłosy,*
> *Cisną się . . .*
> (Lord Christ went walking in the far-off field
> A barefoot crowd was with him.
> The little children, who had come from the city
> To gather the sheaves of grain, crowded together . . .)

Yes, snuffling, coughing. Embraces. Christmas wishes. It was Christmas Eve, after all. Love.
Snuffling.

SILENT NIGHT

Capesius turned over to me an organization chart depicting the official channels for matters concerning the camps: the chart also shows the chains of command (underlined) observed in actual practice, with handwritten entries by our druggist, who, being a neat and orderly Saxon, had even supplied the names of all the extermination camps missing in the chart.

I had shown this organizational chart to Roland, who

looked at it with interest, briefly, before putting it aside, and went on about how, to distract himself from the horror, he had celebrated Christmas with Commandant Höß ... Christmas ... He played "Silent Night." *Holy night, all is calm, all is bright.* And, *O du fröhliche, o du selige gnadenbringende Weihnachtszeit.* With Commandant Höß. Played the piano to forget. The Christmas tree, all decked with candles, to forget. That piney smell . . . And Roland took comfort in the thought: Weren't they somehow locked up just like the prisoners? Yes: and the party, and the music, too, was a small measure they could take against the gas. In the same hellish anteroom of the *anus mundi,* and yet separated from each other by an eternity— namely, by death.

Still, how wonderful Christmas used to be, even in 1942. And now we were under the Russians. Grandpa no longer sat by the Blaupunkt radio in the afternoons, where only a year earlier he had heard the Reichsender radio broadcast proclaim: "Christmas is the most solemn of all our holidays, and no other people can celebrate it as we do. Ours alone is the unique and wonderful exchange of gifts on Christmas Eve." And then the beautiful song: *In der Heimat, in der Heimat, da gibt's ein Wiedersehn* . . . ["At home, at home, there's a reunion."] A year ago, Christmas leave in full SS regalia, wearing the death's-head insignia. But at the party, Roland was in civilian clothes, and a necktie. I crawled underneath the tree with him. He in his white shirt. Tree of life, he said. Winter solstice. Evergreen needles on the presents. Fragrance. The candle wax from the tree of life dripped on our good trousers. Fear. The cane. A whipping? But then I forgot about it. At Christmas, there was always a hint of hysteria in the air. Kids, tomorrow something special will happen, tomorrow we will have a great time. Well, now, nothing good will happen. Retribution is not far off.

But it was Christmas, even for the prisoners in the Sonderkommando, for commando members Wiesław Kielar and Hertz from the Bucovina, and for our Adam Salmen, too, who lived to tell about it and write about it on his tiny paper rolls:

Adam's diary: We are sitting in the cellar around a little coke stove, roasting raw potatoes, "organized" for us by Gienek Obojski, who did not survive, according to Kielar, sitting around the little glowing stove, the potatoes sizzling, a pleasant smell, beautiful as life, a wonderful aroma that drove away the disgusting odor of the chlorine sprinkled over all the bodies piled up there. The bodies don't bother us at all anymore, we live with them every day. And Kielar plays Polish Christmas carols, and German ones, too? "Silent Night" on the harmonica. We sing. Oh, du fröhliche, *in Polish, naturally. The bodies seem to enjoy listening, even the Jewish ones who didn't celebrate Christmas. But no one noticed. It was campfire. Camp.*

Hertz from the Bucovina was cooking the brotzupa, *the bread soup, but when he broke apart the* organizirowanny chleb, *the stolen loaves of bread that came from the last transport—from the gassed victims, that is—there was a flash of gold; rings, little brooches with initials on them, and golden engagement rings were sparkling visibly through the holes in the hard, stale bread, and everybody came running to see.* "Goldzupa," *Hertz murmured,* "złota zupa, złota, złota . . ." *the others repeated in chorus . . . He was a Chasid member, and remembered his wedding in Czernowitz, ah, that golden* jojch (soup) *his grandmother made so well, that golden bouillon made golden yellow with carrots; oh, the carrots here, the nice carrots back home, steamed bright yellow and seasoned with saffron . . . Yes, for their wedding reception, they were like the king and queen united as the bride and bridegroom . . . But Ruth, yes, his bride, had flown up to heaven here as a pillar of smoke . . . She lived with him, when there was still a morning, the coming happy morning. Tears were running down*

Hertz's wasted cheeks. Everyone looked at him in amazement. Tears? For here, there are no more tears.

And then, December 30, 1944. On that Saturday, after evening roll call and after the reading of the verdict, the five political prisoners, members of the Kampfgruppe Auschwitz and of the camp military council, the Austrians Ernst Burger, Rudolf Friemel, and Ludwig Vesely, and the Poles Piotr Piąty and Bernard Świerczyna, whose escape attempt had been foiled by the treachery of Johann Roth, the SS Rottenführer from Hermannstadt, or who had been arrested as the organizers of the escape, were publicly hanged.

Adam: December 30, 1944. I will never forget the execution of our comrades on the parade ground of the main camp: besides Ernst Burger there were two other Austrians and two Poles, who looked dreadful when they were brought onto the yard to be hanged.

Just before the lever was pulled, before they died in agony, they cried, "Long live Poland," and "Long live Austria," screaming curses at the SS across the parade ground, not stopping even for "Shut up, scum," not even when they were shot in the arms and legs . . .

Dr. Berner: "When I read reports on the hanged men, I was horrified by how they died. Till my dying day I will never get over this sentence: 'After three minutes, the victim's third vertebra broke, and he died.' The mere sight of the gallows spread fear.

"We were expecting the sentence to be carried out on the following day. A short winter day, which passes like a shadow. We had no idea that the five had already been hanged on the parade ground during roll call. New Year's Eve was approaching. We felt that it was the last time that we would have to spend New Year's in the camp."

"Auschwitz, January 1, 1945," wrote Dr. Wirths to his

"dear wife," "I spent a peaceful and quiet New Year's Day with the Bärs; they hadn't asked anyone else, and so I could spend the time thinking loving thoughts of you. I showed them the pictures of you and the children, and talked about all of you . . . When midnight arrived, after I had drunk my toast to you and was alone with my thoughts, the two of them had tears in their eyes and were truly sad.

"January 2, 1945 . . . In C1 I recognized Mephisto [probably Mengele] and avoided him like the plague. How right you were, darling, in your opinion of him back then!"

And Roland: Where had he spent New Year's Eve, with Capesius and Klein, or even on Fabritius's estate in the Beskidy mountains?

When he was asked by the Stoffels if it was right to murder women and children, he repeated Höß's justification: "We can't allow any descendants who might come back and take their revenge!" Or what Klein said: "The Jews are the enemies of mankind, not just ours!"

Roland in Innsbruck: "Of course I am religious, I was even a religion teacher. But who nailed our Lord to the cross? The Jews!"

"You taught religion? In Auschwitz?"

"Yes, I taught religion at the German school in Auschwitz."

"And were you also present at the shootings at the Black Wall?"

"Yes, sometimes. You had to put up with all kinds of things. And I could."

"But on top of that, you were still a religion teacher?"

"Yes, in the main German school. And I did it with conviction. The Old Testament preaches the Jewish religion: I am the God of Abraham, Isaac, and Jacob, who led you out of Egypt. Right? And the Jewish Torah, that's just it. This tradition has lived on in the Jews for three thousand years and more. And the Jews, in so far as they are of the Mosaic faith, have a religion that's suitable for them. While the Germans have none . . .

"But to create a religion? That takes incredible toughness. And cruelty, too. To do that you have to be intolerant. No religion can be tolerant . . ."

I asked him if with that he meant Nazism, too, whether that too was a religion, which would perhaps fill the void after the death of God.

Roland: "Yes, that was a kind of religion, too!"

And then he talked about Hitler's prophecy of the "catastrophic collapse" of world Jewry. In the beginning he believed that Hitler would create a new religion, a "folkish" one.

Roland: "We never had our own proper religion. We just adopted the Jewish one. And that is our tragedy, that we could never create our own religion. For a people like that can never really survive. We became barbarians, when we lost our own Gothic tribal culture. And when the German people miscegenate as they do today, then it's all over: peoples should not mix with one another. A people is there to fulfill a mission. I don't mean to get emotional, but their divine mission consists to some extent in preserving their own kind.

"Yes, and in this sense, the Old Testament is wonderful proof of this fact, even Nietzsche constantly sang its praises for this . . ."

". . . that extermination was necessary?"

"Yes, just as a religion really can only be a religion of a 'folk.' That every religion, every healthy religion, is basically ancestor worship. An ancestor cult. And the conflict, even with the European peoples, arises mainly from their having adopted an alien religion, one that was native to another people: namely, the Jewish religion, you know?"

"And in Auschwitz, then, Europe, the world, was supposed to be *healed*?"

". . . we have all become Judaicized, Nietzsche pointed that out. Basically we took over the Jewish religion, and that doesn't totally fit us."

"But only the Old Testament," I dare to interject.

"Yes, that's the garment, but the garment doesn't fit us, does it?"

"But even the New Testament doesn't fit, does it?"

"That fits even less, because the New Testament already contains the general concept of humanity . . ."

"What religion would be appropriate for us, then?"

"We have none, that's our tragedy, you know? And we can't make one up for ourselves either. But we still have to live. Because a true religion can only be a cult of ancestor worship . . ."

"So, a belief in the dead, in death? For our ancestors are the dead!"

"Yes, an ancestor cult. The Japanese still have this in Shintoism. I don't know how much it is still practiced. But that's where they got these fantastic guys from, the kamikaze pilots. It's almost eerie, their contempt for their own deaths. The duty to give up one's own life to give life meaning."

"And the Germans, they had, let's say, the Germanic religion?"

"They don't have any religion! We can't create one, either. We really can't."

"Well, Hitler tried it!"

"No, he didn't, he never did that! That's an exaggeration. He wasn't that stupid. You can't say that."

"But they really cultivated it, this Gothic stuff, that crazy Sütterlin handwriting, and including the calendar . . . calling February 'Hornung' . . . They cultivated paganism, we were the new heathens . . . and yet all of that is really alien to us. And how is death seen? As 'the hero's death,' is that the new religion? Fatherland, Reich . . . ?"

"No, no. It's the 'folkish' side of it that would have led to ancestor worship . . . performed with all necessary brutality, yes, that too was a sacrifice, being strong, an absolute must!"

Roland belonged to the Study Group for Research into the Jewish Influence on German Church Life, and had some connection with the Bishop of the (Transylvanian) Saxons. This bishop, Wilhelm Staedel, was the bishop of the German Christian Protestant Church in Romania (1942–1944), and cultivated and propagated anti-Semitism . . .

Roland had participated in the beatings of many prisoners, one even on New Year's Day 1944: "A beating on the 'Prügelbock' [sawhorse] looked like this: The victim's legs were clamped tightly to the crossbar. Two prisoners held the offender by the arms. An SS man or a Kapo would beat the prisoner with a blackjack or a whip, and, interestingly enough, the victim would have to count the beats out loud. And at the end the victim had to thank his torturers, usually breathless and exhausted, by shouting 'Twenty-five, received with thanks.'"

Adam: The horse was built expressly for the purpose; there were grooves in it to hold the victim's legs tight, and a shelf-like extension to expose the victim's buttocks, you know? And there were other indentations for the arms and head. But then, there was also a very simple device, where the victim's feet were simply bound inside a box. There were collective punishments during roll call, and the lagerfirer *would determine the penalty. There were also fifty- and even hundred-blow beatings, which amounted to a death penalty, and were much more cruel than any hanging or shooting, even more horrible than being burned alive in the ovens. One Serbian prisoner famously survived one hundred blows, a* setka, *but then he had to spend four months in the infirmary lying on his stomach. As a kind of prelude to the pronounce-*

ment of sentence, there was the karny meldunek, *or penal notification. Here the poor victim would be forced to stand often for up to a day under the crossbar of the horse, in a bent-knee position. And prisoners were often hanged. The prisoner would stand in shackles beneath the movable gallows. The sentence would be read to him, first in German, then in Polish. Then exact instructions were given to the executioner, another prisoner. The victim would then be made to climb up on a wooden box; the executioner would place the noose around his neck, the cover of the box would drop down into the box at the pull of a lever, and the condemned prisoner would drop down only a few centimeters, ending with a brief jerk. The death agony would thus often be drawn out up to ten minutes. The longest minutes of a life, now ending.*

"During executions at which all the SS officers would be present, the alarm level of the SS guard companies would always be elevated," said Roland, who had commanded a company of guards. "And even on the first of January, there was an execution to mark the beginning of the New Year."

THE END

January 1, 1945. One hundred Polish men and one hundred Polish women who had been sentenced to death by police court-martial were shot in Crematorium V in Birkenau.

January 5, 1945. Six prisoners identified as "secret messengers" were taken from the men's camp BIId at Birkenau and transferred to the Mauthausen concentration camp. There were five Poles assigned to the Sonderkommando: Wacław Lipka (prisoner number 22520), Mieczysław Morawa (prisoner number 5730), Józef Ilczuk (prisoner number 14916), Władysław Biskup (prisoner number 74501), and Jan Agrestowski (prisoner number 74545), as well as a Czech prisoner (number 39340) named Stanislav Slezák, who ran the X-ray equipment used for sterilization experiments performed on men and women in Camp BIa, Birkenau, under the SS doctor Horst Schumann. They were shot on April 3, 1945, in the crematorium building at Mauthausen. Slezák's diary has survived intact. All he could cry out was "Long live . . ." and then eternal silence . . .

On January 6, 1945, the word went out to the "Union" commando that the women members of the squad would have to return to barracks early. As always when such an unusual command was given, this gave rise to all kinds of speculation. Work was usually only stopped earlier for "selections." But this time all the prisoners were called back, while with selections, only the Jewish women were called . . .

On January 6, 1945, in the women's camp at Auschwitz
the four Jewish prisoners Ala Gertner, Róza Robota, Regina
Szafirsztajn, and Estera Wajchblum were hanged.

*Adam's diary: Today, January 6, 1945, the next execution
took place, this time on the womens' camp parade ground. They
were four pretty young girls from the "Union" commando.*

Adam gave me the eyewitness account of Raya Kagan, the
woman from Kharkov who worked in the camp Gestapo commando and the "registry office"; she titled her report "Women
in the Ministry of Hell."

"A few days after New Year's, a gallows was erected in the
women's camp. It was meant for the four girls from the 'Union.'
The sentence was to be carried out at roll call. Our commando,
which worked until seven-thirty, had hoped to avoid this 'spec-
tacle,' but a half an hour before work ended, the SS man on
duty gave us the order to march back to camp immediately.
Our blood froze. Just before that, the air raid alarm had
sounded and the camp was plunged into darkness. But even
these events did not delay the execution of the sentence. As we
marched into camp we were all of us shaking all over. We heard
that two had already been hanged during roll call, and now the
time for the other two had come. We prisoners had to assemble
in the cellar of Block 3. At the signal we were led from there to
the blocks where the 'Union' commando was living, and between which stood the gallows. The commando Kapos cursed
and beat their prisoners to get them lined up next to the gallows. Then we heard the voice of Hößler, the women's camp
commander. The crowd obscured my view of the gallows and
the speaker, and I could only hear the occasional word. 'Thus
will all traitors be destroyed!' Hößler screamed, as he went on
to denounce the presence of 'such elements' in his camp. 'Powder commando up front!' The order echoed, then died away in
the stillness of the camp. This commando, which the heroic
girls had belonged to, had to stand in the front row for the

execution. I stood between Ella and Lola and thought: 'I have to see it all—I will have to remember it all.' So I fought back my fear and glanced briefly up at the gallows, but I could only make out indistinct shadows."

TRANSYLVANIA, JANUARY 1945

January 11–13, 1945. Black Sunday. Our people were deported to Russia. On Black Sunday. And from Schäßburg, too, all the young "Saxons," the ethnic Germans, male and female, had to go to Russia, to the Donetz River basin, to help in the reconstruction. George was the only young man of the family who had stayed home. The Russian commandant of the town had decreed: "Just Germans." So, just as the Germans before had ordered "their" Jews to assemble in the market square, now it was the Saxons' turn.

Friederike, George's wife: "When the announcements from the Russian commandant and the police became public, everyone obeyed, just as they always had, without protest or concern for their own lives—just as always, blindly following the new authorities as we had the old ones. The Baruch family, and Frau Mehler, they laughed at us and said, 'If you were ordered to report to the marketplace tomorrow morning to be shot, you would all show up, right on time. But we, the Jews, had done exactly the same. Maybe we are all too much like each other, maybe that's why this tragedy had to happen between us.' And there was young Roth, the barber's son, he reported like all the others, like my George, too. They all had to report to the girls' school at one in the afternoon. That was the assembly point. They were guarded by the Romanian police, and the Russians, but they really didn't need to be guarded; they would certainly never have run away! And when they didn't call young Roth—they had called all of them, except for him—he raised his hand just like in school and said,

'Excuse me, but I wasn't called.' Or maybe he said it in Romanian?! I can't remember. Anyway, we really were incredibly stupid!"

KALENDARIUM OF EVENTS AT AUSCHWITZ, JANUARY 13 AND 14, 1945

Between 11:17 and 11:30 a.m. the Auschwitz factory of IG Farben was bombed for thirteen minutes. While the ninety-six Liberator bombers used in the bombing were not attacked by German planes, three of them were shot down by antiaircraft fire. Even in this attack, there was no attempt made to destroy the extermination facilities at Birkenau. The squadron of Liberator bombers dropped more than a thousand bombs from a height of 7,500 meters. In this attack portions of Auschwitz I were hit by numerous bombs. About three hundred people were either killed or wounded, including prisoners housed in the bombed barracks. Air photographs were taken of Auschwitz during this attack. For the first time, there were high-quality photographs in which Auschwitz I and II were clearly visible. Thirty-five years after the war, Dino A. Brugioni and Robert G. Poirier inspected these photographs and were able to determine the following: there was a large transport train of eighty-five freight cars on the rail spur in Birkenau; there was a column of about 1,500 people marching on the main road of the camp; the gas chambers and Crematorium IV were in operation; the gate leading into Crematorium IV was open; the goal of this column of marchers was probably this crematorium. The photographs lead one to conclude that the concentration camp at Monowitz was still occupied, that the snow on the barracks roofs was melting, and that the snow on the streets between the barracks had been cleared. Auschwitz I was also still in operation. It was clear that the snow on the roofs of some of the blocks was melting—with the exception of Block 10, the earlier site of Professor Clauberg's experiments; so the blocks were still

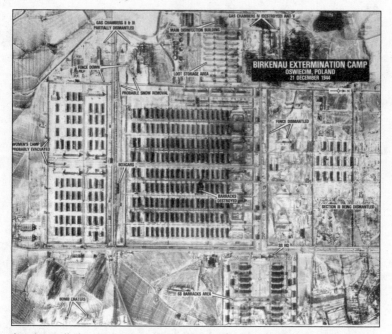

Auschwitz II. American air reconnaissance photograph, December 21, 1944

being used to house prisoners. In Auschwitz II–Birkenau, Section BIII ("Mexico") had already been completely dismantled. The snow covering the barracks roofs in the former women's camp in Camps BIa and BIb indicated that they were empty. Melting snow on roofs in Camp BII showed which ones were still being used at this time. However, the photographs of the gas chambers and Crematoriums II and III show that these facilities were partially dismantled by this time, and that the work of dismantling and destroying them still continued.

Dr. Nyiszli: "Once more, the days pass quietly and uneventfully. As we have heard, Dr. Mengele has left Auschwitz. There is a new doctor in charge of the concentration camp, or rather, 'the work camp Auschwitz,' for since New Year's the concentration camp has been officially dissolved. It has been changed into a work camp. Everything is fermenting, rotting. I got hold of a newspaper on January 10, in which I read of the beginning of the Russian offensive. The distant rumble of heavy artillery rattles the windows in my room. The front is edging ever closer.

"On January 17 I went to bed early, even though I wasn't tired. It might have been midnight when I was shaken awake by a powerful series of explosions, blinding light, and the rat-a-tat of machine guns. I heard doors being slammed, and rapid footsteps walking away down the concrete floors of the hall. I jumped out of bed, needing to know what was going on around me, and opened the door. The lights were burning in the furnace room; the doors to the SS rooms had been left wide open. Clear indications of flight.

"And even the large oak door of the crematorium was open. There was nothing to be seen of the guards. I looked up to the watchtowers, which were also empty . . ."

Capesius: "Josef Mengele fled from Auschwitz shortly before the Red Army's arrival, and took cover with a Wehrmacht unit. This unit was interned by the Americans, but Mengele escaped identification and was released under an assumed name. He somehow made his way to his hometown of Günzburg, and starting in the autumn of 1945, he hid in a remote village in Upper Bavaria, and at Easter 1949 he fled to South America."

Adam: A short time after the camp was evacuated, because of the threatened attack from the "Bolshevik hordes," Capesius arrived at Bergen-Belsen.

Frau Dr. Böhm: "Around early January 1945, the evacuations in Auschwitz began. As a result of these measures I went through three different camps. First I went to Ravensbrück (via sealed freight car), then to Malkow, and finally to Tauchau. Where I saw my daughter for the last time. These different relocations from camp to camp were made partly on foot, and partly using motorized transportation. When we marched we were guarded by heavily armed SS units, and any prisoner who could not make it any further, or who got out of the line, was shot on the spot."

.

Adam: January 18, 1945: In the camp it now seemed to us like the end of the world had come. Shame, together with death and hunger, created a condition of complete confusion. In this chaotic situation, we did not know how close we were to our final extermination, but we had a sense that there was an order to that effect from the very center of this hell, from Adolf Hitler's headquarters, by his personal command: to completely raze the camp to the ground, along with its inmates, but to evacuate anyone who could still work. A powerful air raid and the approach of the Red Army made it impossible to carry out this plan, thank God, and the SS took flight. From Dr. Berner I learned that he had stayed behind with the sick, around eight hundred in number, at the hospital in Buna-Monowitz; that around five hundred of them froze or starved to death during the winter storm that January, and that they took the body of their friend S., who had just died of starvation, to a mass grave in the courtyard, had taken this little pile of skin and bones and dumped it into the snow; the trench was already full to overflowing. They took off their caps and saluted the poor heaped-up bodies lying in the filthy, trampled snow.

FROM THE KALENDARIUM

"January 19, 1945. At one o'clock at night the last large prisoner transport left from the main camp at Auschwitz with 2,500 men. At Rajsko this transport was joined together with the last column of prisoners from Birkenau, 1,000 men.

"In the morning, a division of SS men moved into the men's hospital camp BIIf and selected prisoners capable of doing work. These prisoners had to carry out the bodies that had not been cleared away for the past week, and take them off to Crematorium V. The corpses were stacked up there, and the SS members lit the stacks of corpses on fire. The prisoners also had to search through the effects warehouses and look for valuables that the SS might want. Before the SS members pulled out, they stacked up all the suitcases on the site and lit them on fire."

Adam: Dreadful filth everywhere. The SS had fled from their headquarters in a great hurry. We discovered half-filled plates of frozen soup on the tables, which we devoured, and full mugs of beer, which had frozen into yellow ice.

There were beds in all the barracks that held dead bodies stiff as boards. And no one thought to take them away. The ground was frozen too hard to dig graves. Many of the bodies were just laid on top of one another in gravel trenches, but even after just a few days the pile rose up above the edge of the trench, a ghastly sight from our window.

Primo Levi wrote about January 25 and 26*: "The number of ravens had increased, and everyone knew why. The noise of artillery was only heard at very long intervals. We all told each other that the Russians would be arriving soon, even in the next hour; everyone proclaimed this, everyone was sure of it, but no one could clearly grasp it. For in the camps, you forget how to hope, or to have any faith in your own future . . .

"Just as you can become tired of pleasure, of fear, and even of pain, so it is with expectation: you get tired of waiting. Now, on January 25, when the connection to that horrible world—but still a world, nonetheless—had been broken off for eight days, most of us were so exhausted we couldn't even wait anymore.

"We were in a world of the dead, of masks. The last traces of civilization around us and inside of us had disappeared. The

*Cf. Levi, If This Is a Man.

job of bestialization, of turning humans into animals, started by the triumphant Germans, was completed by the defeated Germans."

FROM THE KALENDARIUM

Liberation,* January 27, 1945. At about nine a.m. the first Soviet soldier, a member of a reconnaissance unit attached to the Hundredth Infantry Division, walked into the site of the prisoner hospital in the auxiliary camp of Monowitz. On the same day, a military doctor with the rank of captain arrived at Monowitz and started the first relief actions. During the afternoon the Soviet troops advanced on the main camp at Auschwitz and encountered resistance from the retreating German troops. In the battles pursuant to the liberation of Monowitz, the concentration camp Auschwitz-Birkenau, the town of Oswiecim itself, and the whole surrounding district, 231 Soviet soldiers were killed; two of these Soviet soldiers fell directly in front of the gate of the main camp of Auschwitz.

"At three p.m. the first Soviet reconnaissance teams entered the Birkenau camp and the main camp of Auschwitz, where they were jubilantly welcomed by the liberated inmates. After the area around the camp was swept for mines, soldiers from the Sixtieth Army of the First Ukrainian Front entered the camp and liberated the surviving prisoners. On the site of the main camp there were forty-eight bodies, and in Birkenau six hundred bodies of men and women who had been shot in the last days of Auschwitz. As the soldiers of the Red Army moved into the Auschwitz, Birkenau, and Monowitz camps, there were still more than seven thousand sick and exhausted

*An exhaustive examination of this subject is found in Andrzej Strzelecki's *The Evacuation, Dismantling, and Liberation of KL Auschwitz* (Auschwitz-Birkenau State Museum, 2001).

prisoners. Dr. Otto Wolken, who had remained on the camp-site and acted as an aide to organize relief for the prisoners, and also was involved in securing the documentation detailing the crimes committed by the SS, estimated that there were 1,200 surviving sick prisoners in Auschwitz, 5,800 in Birkenau, and 600 in Monowitz."

•

Adam's diary: January 27. Four cavalrymen appear on the scene; young Red Army soldiers, overly cautious, their raised machine-gun barrels pointed defensively at the camp. Arriving at the barbed-wire barrier—a few timid words, furtive looks at the heaps of bodies, as they walk toward us. Heavy fur caps, healthy, rustic youths' faces beneath. For us, in our hollow-cheeked non-world, with death our only fixed reference point, they are joyous figures calling us back to life. For their part, though, they cannot say hello, their faces are frozen. (Awaken, now?) Expressionless, self-conscious. But it wasn't pity, no, for the moment the cause of their shyness was unclear.

Roland: "I was there in January '45, in the snow and ice, on the evacuation march from Auschwitz to Bergen-Belsen, and from there to Flossenbürg, where I was briefly the commandant of the guard detachment. I chose not to look when my guards would shoot the prisoners who had collapsed and leave them lying there. ('I was sorry, but it had to be!') I always had books in my satchel with me (for instance, Hölderlin: 'So that the world will run its course without interruption and that the memory of the gods is not extinguished, revealing itself in that all-forgetting form of faithlessness, for we are best off retaining divine faithlessness. In such a moment man forgets himself and God . . .')."*

Adam: Did Roland know, before the court's verdict came, when he was hiding out in a shepherd's hut near Kufstein with

---

*German citation from Hölderlin's "Notes on Oedipus." —trans.

*his wife and two children, that hell is right here, and retribution,
too? Did he know that his wife would perish from it . . . ostensibly
from cancer . . . She grew gaunter day by day; he survived . . .
He, too, a survivor? But without any feeling of guilt, or shame?
No, just fear, fear for his own freedom. The word was that his
wife died, just from fear for his freedom . . . just that . . .*

•

Ali, Mother's favorite brother, was in Buchenwald . . .

On April 13, 1945, Ali, an SS officer, was killed by inmates
during the Buchenwald prisoner uprising near Hottelstedt. He
and his whole story lie buried there beneath a simple wooden
cross.

•

Marianne Adam: "The wretched prisoners, finally having escaped from the hell of the concentration camps, flooded all
the roads of Europe. They were trying to go home. They had
no more families; their parents had been killed. They could no
longer find their children, wives, or husbands. Even back in
their own home countries, people looked at them cross-eyed.
Alas, Hungary was no exception in that regard. People simply
couldn't bear seeing a witness to their own inhumanity come
back. They just couldn't handle it. And even less when some
miserable wretch, totally alone in the world, having finally
made it back home after the greatest effort, when this person
wanted to move back into his own home, to have a roof over
his head. A completely different family had long since been
living in his house, after the Arrow Cross (Hungarian Nazis)
had confiscated and handed over Jewish property to the Hungarian Christians. Of course these families didn't like the
thought of having to move out again. When somebody wanted
their little cow or their piece of property back, so they could
do an honest day's work and earn their daily bread, even if
heartbroken and all alone, well, our nice fellow citizens got
quite indignant about that: 'Why have you come back? Look,

there are more of you coming back than ever went away in the first place!' and things like that. So it's no wonder that so many Jews left their homeland; a homeland that they were first beaten out of, and then again, those few who were still alive, driven away by hate and disgust!"

AFTER AUSCHWITZ, CAN YOU GO HOME AGAIN?

Capesius went as far as Oranienburg and Berlin, then headed north to Husum and Flensburg, probably together with Rudolf Höß, where they met Himmler for the last time:

Capesius: "At the end I was very near him . . ."

Rudolf Höß, camp commandant: "On May 3, 1945, I met Himmler for the last time. Following orders, the remaining camp inspection staff followed Himmler to Flensburg. Glücks, Maurer, and I reported to him there. He had just come from a conference with what remained of the Reich government. He seemed fresh and cheerful and in the best spirits. He saluted us and immediately gave the order: Glücks and Höß were to disguise themselves as low-ranking army officers, and under assumed names—as soldiers who had lost contact with their unit—would cross the border into Denmark and go into hiding there. Maurer was to fade into the army as well, along with the remaining members of the camp inspection staff. Standartenführer Hintz, the chief of police in Flensburg, was to take over from there. Himmler gave us a handshake, and we were dismissed."

(For a while Höß worked as a laborer on a farm, until he was arrested and turned over to the Poles. In 1946 he was hanged in "his" Auschwitz.)

•

Dr. Wirths also made for Flensburg. There the "completely innocent" chief of all the Auschwitz doctors wrote to his wife: "H [Husum], May 24, 1945 . . . How much longer will it be before I can be reunited with you and our dear children? Dear, this is such an unspeakably hard time, this continuation of the horrible war, and yet we shall have to be strong and brave through it all, especially since we can stand before God and man with the clearest consciences. But what upsets me the most is that I have to leave you so very alone and in great need and sorrow, far from all my dear ones, this is what I am most sorry about . . . I hope that my work and my struggles have not been for nothing . . . What crime have I committed? I really do not know!

"And please, you must forgive me also, that in the last days we had together I was so unsympathetic and loveless . . . But I was really at the end of my rope.

"Meanwhile we have floated the idea that I can speak with the English . . . but despite the best conscience that will be difficult, since it is hard to image how much understanding the other side will be able to muster for the difficulty of what I was asked to do. Whether they can understand how hard this necessity weighed down upon me."

A short time later garrison doctor Wirths, the chief of the doctor criminals of Auschwitz, hanged himself.

•

Hermann K., a native of Schäßburg and an SS doctor who also ended up in Flensburg and Husum, witnessed with his own eyes the final battle for Berlin, and its downfall: "As of April 28 there was a Soviet city commandant, General Bersarin. When Hitler committed suicide on April 30 with his new bride, Eva, the Red flag was already flying atop the Reichstag. The Führer left his last will and testament; he had branded Göring and Himmler as traitors, and appointed Dönitz as commander. And berated the Germans for their weakness. They deserved their fate. The SS blew up the subway tunnels, and the wounded, women, and children who had sought shelter there drowned. I personally saw to my amazement and horror the

SD [security police] going through the bunkers. They shot
deserters in the back of the head, and 'cowards' were hanged
from the trees. The Weidmannsbrücke bridge was a particularly sinister site in this regard. But also in a sense ideal, in that
it sums up in one image that zone we still live in: ruins inside
and out, when you walk, you pass through a landscape of crag-
ged blocks that had once been buildings, fading light, blood,
and deafening noises, real life as it played out before you was a
reproduction of every nightmare that has ever been dreamed
since the deadly dances of St. Vitus. Only the final edition of
the *Panzerbär von Großberlin* (The Armored Bear of Greater
Berlin: a newspaper urging fanatic resistance to the end) as-
serted that the course of events would reverse, and that the
miraculous terror weapon was in readiness to deliver the final
blow for victory; the destruction was total, rubble was everywhere, and everything the ancient prophecies foretold, from
the Book of Revelations to Nostradamus, was fulfilled." Thus
spoke Uncle Hermann, as if he had already told the story a
hundred times, and even today he can't stop talking about it.
"The battlefields lit up blood-red with flashes of light, a spec-
tacle from hell. But still, the generals get medals, day after day.
The last air raid took place on April 2—it was almost liberat-
ing, because it was so familiar. By then the first Soviet attack
wedge was at Lichtenberg, and our outermost defense line was
at Niederschönhausen and Fronau. By the next day, Berlin was
at the front line.

"That fiend—who knows who sent him?—was dead. Incinerated, with all his plans and predictions, along with his
dog and Eva. Grand Admiral Dönitz was now running what
remained of the government in Flensburg, his responsibilities
now extending only to unconditional surrender. Shortly before it had been the last birthday of the Thousand Year Reich.
And the V2 rocket would continue as before. The final battle
for Berlin, in the Fasanenstraße, Berlin W15. Thank God I

wasn't there for it. One of my buddies who managed to survive it told me about it: the house was in the middle of the stretch between Lietzenburger Straße and the Kurfürstendamm, Fasanenstraße 71, the home of a plumber named Weißhaupt. He heard the whole thing from Weißhaupt, who had seen it all. He told my buddy, who was from Schäßburg, too, that just before the Russians came and took that portion of the street, a Waffen-SS company came in; this unit consisted exclusively of Siebenbürger Saxons who were completely battle-fatigued and were taking what warm food they could find. These men entered the houses to find shelter from the artillery and machine-gun fire that was already sweeping through the streets. But everywhere the people in the air-raid cellars cursed and threatened them and drove them back out into the street, for they knew when the Russians came in, they would endanger the civilians in the house (alas this was true). At that time Weißhaupt lived on the ground floor in the small super's apartment and so he pulled a young Transylvanian SS man from off the street into his hallway. This young soldier ate his soup standing there: he said he just didn't understand things anymore. For them, back in Transylvania, Germany and the German people had always been the greatest thing they could imagine. And they, the Transylvanian Saxons, had always felt German. He and his Transylvanian comrades had never shirked any duty in the war, but had given their utmost, because they believed it was all for Germany. And they were still filled with hope and courage even when they were called upon to go to Berlin, the German capital. So it was about our people," said Hermann. "I felt bad for them, these young guys, mostly from country villages: and the young SS man said that the majority of his buddies had all died in the battle for Berlin, and now they were being yelled at and chased out of the houses by the Germans, the Berliners themselves, because they had fought for Germany. And then the young Transylvanian guy supposedly cried softly: 'How far from home I am here! I feel so bad for my parents and my sisters. They will be so sad. I will never see them again. We will all die here.'

"One guy in those houses, who at least knew where Transylvania was (unlike most Berliners and Germans, I'm sorry to say) and that it had fallen to Romania, even shouted as they threw the Transylvanians out of their houses, 'Why didn't you stay down in the Balkans where you belong? Why are you here in the first place? Serves you all right!' Then suddenly the leader of this SS company gave the signal, and ordered his people onto their vehicles and shouted to them: 'To the Reich Chancellery! We're defending it!' And somehow that actually recharged all those depressed, exhausted soldiers. But one resident of Fasanenstraße 72 tapped his forehead with his finger and shouted: 'Man, are you dumb or what? You think the Führer is still sitting in the chancellery waiting for you? He hit the bricks long ago!' At that, the men were stunned and climbed quietly into their trucks. Meanwhile the Russians were coming in from Halensee, and had advanced far up the Kurfürstendamm. And when the trucks in the Transylvanian SS company turned the corner from the Fasanenstraße onto the Kurfürstendamm, heading toward the Kaiser Wilhelm Memorial Church, some Soviet Katyusha rockets ('Stalin's Pipe Organ') slammed right into them and blew all the vehicles to smithereens; there were only a few moaning, screaming wounded men left alive, and they were mowed down by the advancing Russians.

"It's so horrible that in these doomed men's last hour, their belief in the sense of their suffering and dying was taken from them."

•

Back then, the big bell in the mountain church in Schäßburg rang very often. Many people never came back, and for each person who never returned, the bell tolled.

And I remember Baila, who was living in the Baruchs' house, a distant relative of Ella and Gisela Böhm, and I can't stop thinking about *her* return from the camp:

Baila: "Well, it's a hurt that never stops. And I have it here in my breast, right here, this great big hurt, the feeling that I could go on crying, crying forever, but I can't do that either, all I can do is keep on living . . . and just keep waiting for death . . . So I didn't go into the gas chamber—the dear Lord wanted it that way, that I should live, and come back—but for what? In '46 there were no more Jews around here, our houses all kaput, everything we had, gone. And my children—the girl and the boy, good kids, you know—I never saw them again, not once, and there's nobody can tell me where they went, where they died, those little ones, they cried for their mama for the last time, and Mama wasn't there, she was someplace else, *oy vay*. And when we got home again . . . somehow things went on . . . somehow. But we were kaput. We lived like we were machines: everything happened like it was mechanical, all by itself, we didn't feel anything anymore, because we were kaput, totally kaput. And that nobody can fix, no way, never! But what use is complaining? This is a hurt that will hurt till death. I know, in German you say pain, but I say hurt . . . And when a holiday comes, then the big hurt is right there again; yes, it doesn't go away, 'cause there's no people left from my people. So we just sit around in the room and think, how it was, and how it is today."

THE MOST SIGNIFICANT FIGURES

Roland Albert, SS Untersturmführer (second lieutenant). Born April 21, 1916, in Segesvár/Schäßburg, Austria-Hungary.

Roland Albert, a student in Klausenburg, interrupted his studies and as of December 1940 was a member of the NSDAP (Nazi Party) and a member of the Waffen-SS (SS# 467018). Albert was part of the SS garrison at Auschwitz as of January 28, 1942, and was employed in the guard unit. In his own words: after a brief training period he was sent to the Russian front, was wounded on August 12, 1941. After a short hospital stay he was declared no longer fit for combat, and was transferred to a unit for recovering wounded, and from there in January '42 to a guard unit at Auschwitz. He did not know what awaited him there, and had thought it was a prisoner-of-war camp. After his promotion to SS Untersturmführer in May 1943, he was assigned to several SS guard companies, including the Third and Fourth Guard Companies, as company leader. After Auschwitz Albert went into the Second SS Tank Division, "Das Reich." According to his own account, he was the commandant of the guard units at Flossenbürg in April and May 1945.

APMO: D-Au I-1, Sturmbannbefehl Nr. 87/43 v. 28.5.1943, Nr. 119/43 v. 5.8.1943, D-Au I-4/5, acc. pay book; AGK: SOKr-431, Documents in the Criminal Case against Adolf Becker et al. Bl. 76a, 87, BDC: Personal Files of Roland Albert, Personal Questionnaire.

[Zur Geschichte des Lagers: Soziologische und demographische Fragen der SS-Besatzung des Konzentrations- und Vernichtungslagers Auschwitz— Eine Analyse ausgewählter Merkmale. *Der 1. Frankfurter Auschwitz-Prozess,* p. 545.]

•

Witness Dr. Mauritius Berner. Born December 19, 1902, in Mikeszásza, Austria-Hungary (today Micăsasa in Romania); according to other sources Dr. Berner was born in Mikelaka, Austria-Hungary (today Micălaca, incorporated into Arad, Romania).

Persecuted as a Jew; deported from Hungary; in the KZ Auschwitz from May 29 to October 1944; work commando: changing room; prisoner no. A-16058. At the time of the trial Dr. Berner was sixty-two and lived as a physician in Israel. A witness for the prosecution, testimony on Capesius.

Spouse was Ida Berner. Children: Helga Berner, Nora Berner, Susi Berner (all murdered in Auschwitz!).

•

Witness Gisela Böhm, née Mendel. Born: May 30, 1897, in Segesvár/ Schäßburg, Austria-Hungary (today Sighişoara/Schäßburg in Romania).

Persecuted as a Jew; deported from Hungary; in the KZ Auschwitz from May 29, 1944, until its evacuation; prisoner physician; prisoner no. A-25382. At the time of the trial Gisela Böhm was sixty-seven and lived in Romania as a pediatrician. Witness for the prosecution, testimony on Capesius.

•

Defendant Wilhelm Boger. Born December 19, 1906, in Stuttgart, Germany. Died April 3, 1977 in Bietigheim, West Germany.

CV: Son of a merchant; Mittlere Reife (high school diploma) 1922. Entered the NS-Jugend (later Hitler-Jugend). Commercial apprenticeship 1922–25; from summer 1925 employed by the Deutsch-National Handlungs–gehilfenverband; joined the Artamanen-Bund (voluntary work service); from spring of 1932 unemployed; after 1945 arrested by the U.S. military police; after fleeing while being extradited to Poland Boger worked as a laborer on farms until 1949. Employed in 1950 at the Heinkel Co. in Zuffenhausen.

Boger was the leader of the Department of Interrogation from December 23, 1943, until evacuation. Member of the SS unit in KZ Auschwitz from December 1, 1942, until evacuation: last military grade was SS Hauptsturmführer (captain). At the time of the trial Boger was fifty-seven and married.

He had been in detention awaiting trial since October 1958. Boger was sentenced for murder in at least five cases and for being an accomplice to murder in at least 109 cases to life in prison and five years hard labor.

•

Defendant Dr. Victor Capesius. Born February 2, 1907, in Szerdahely/ Reußmarkt, Austria-Hungary (today Miercurea Sibiului/Reußmarkt in Romania). Died March 20, 1985, in Göppingen, West Germany.

CV: Son of a doctor and druggist; elementary school and gymnasium in Reußmarkt until graduation in 1925; studied pharmacology in Cluj/ Klausenburg; Romanian military service 1931; continuation of study in Vienna until graduation in Vienna 1933; subsequently a drug sales representative for Bayer in Leverkusen; released from British prisoner camp in 1946; Capesius then studied electronics in Stuttgart; in July 1946 he was spotted by a former prisoner in Munich, and arrested by the American military police; after release Capesius continued work as a druggist.

Jobs during the Nazi regime: 1941/42 a druggist in the Romanian army; after the treaty agreement between Germany and Romania Capesius was drafted into the Wehrmacht; trained by the Waffen-SS; at KZ Auschwitz he was the leader of the SS pharmacy from fall of 1943 until evacuation of the camp; member of the SS garrison from September 1943 until evacuation, by his own account only from February 12, 1944; final rank: SS Sturmbannführer (major). At the time of the trial Capesius was fifty-six, married with three children. In detention since December 1959. Victor Capesius was sentenced to nine years in prison for being an accomplice to murder. Defense attorneys: Hans Laternser and Fritz Steinacker.

•

Hans-Andreas Draser. Born February 13, 1915, in Szerdahely/Reußmarkt, Austria-Hungary (today Miercurea Sibiului, Romania).

Political Department (Department II): SS-Unterscharführer (sergeant). Documents. Named in the interrogation of the witness Willibald Pajak (Day 99 of the trial, October 9, 1964).

•

Professor Hans Finsterer, M.D. Surgical chief of the clinic at the Alser Hospital, Vienna IX, Garisongasse 9. After the war he was received by President Truman and decorated with the highest order of the International College of Surgeons and given the title Master of Surgery. His wife is the sister of Hermine Bauer, née Fuchs, the mother of Frau Friederike Capesius, wife of the defendant Dr. Victor Capesius.

•

Gerhard Gerber. Born August 5, 1915, in Strasbourg, France.

Department: Garrison Doctor (Department V); SS druggist; member of the SS garrison in Auschwitz from mid 1944 until evacuation of the camp. Rank: SS Obersturmführer (first lieutenant).

•

Witness Josef Glück. Persecuted as a Jew; deported from Hungary; in KZ Auschwitz from June 11 till October 1944. At the time of the trial Josef Glück was sixty-six and lived as a merchant in Israel. Witness for the prosecution, testimony on Capesius.

•

Maximilian Grabner. Born October 2, 1905, in Vienna, Austria-Hungary. Died January 24, 1948, in Kraków, Poland.

Political Department (Department II); leader of the Political Department from June 1940 until his arrest on December 1, 1943, by an investigatory commission (Kommission zur Untersuchung von Übergriffen in den Konzentrationslagern), for the murder of prisoners and the theft of prisoners' property: SS Untersturmführer (second lieutenant); member of the NSDAP since August 8, 1932; member of the SS since September 1, 1938. Sentenced to death by the Supreme Court of the People's Republic of Poland on December 22, 1947, and executed.

•

Irma Grese. Born October 7, 1923, in Wrechen, Germany. Camp marshal Irma Grese, former sales clerk, was known for her cruelty. In July 1942 she became an SS guard in the womens' concentration camp at Ravensbrück, and was transferred from there to Birkenau in March 1943. The twenty-two-year-old Grese was arrested in Bergen-Belsen on December 13, 1945, the same day as Dr. Fritz Klein, and was hanged in Hameln.

•

Kurt Jurasek. Born July 12, 1922, in Vienna, Austria. In KZ Auschwitz from spring of 1943 to September 1944; department: Garrison Doctor (Department V), SS pharmacy; SS Oberscharführer (sergeant first class); member of the Waffen-SS since 1939. Jurasek was forty-one at the time of the trial and lived as a druggist in West Germany. Witness for the prosecution, gave testimony on Capesius and Klehr.

•

Defendant Oswald Kaduk. Born August 26, 1906, in Königshütte, Germany (now Chorzów, Poland). Died May 31, 1997, in Langelsheim-Lautenhal, Germany. Career: son of a blacksmith; one of seven siblings; attended primary school in Königshütte; trained to be a butcher; worked in this vocation, and later as a fireman; in 1946 recognized by a former prisoner of KZ Auschwitz and one year later was sentenced to twenty-five years in a work camp by a Soviet military tribunal; he was pardoned in 1956 and released from the Bautzen Penitentiary and went to West Germany; worked as a nurse in West Berlin until his arrest on July 21, 1959.

Positions during the Nazi regime: Member of the General SS since late 1939; later joined the Waffen-SS; transferred from the Fifteenth Totenkopf-standarte (SS Death's-Head Unit) in Oranienburg for basic military training; in the KZ at Auschwitz first as a member of the SS guard unit and as of December 1941 as a first marshal; member of the SS garrison from July 1941 until evacuation of the camp. Subsequently transferred to the camp at Mauthausen; final rank: SS Oberscharführer (sergeant first class). Age at the time of the trial: fifty-seven, married, one son. Pretrial detention from July 1959. Oswald Kaduk was sentenced to life in prison for murder in ten instances and joint murder in at least two cases. Released from prison in 1989.

•

Dr. Fritz Klein. Born November 24, 1888, in Feketehalom/Zeiden, Austria-Hungary (now Codlea/Zeiden, Romania). Died December 13, 1945, in Hameln.

Klein studied medicine in Austria-Hungary and did his military service there. He completed his studies in Budapest after the First World War. He became a very early member of the NSDAP. He lived as a general practitioner in Transylvania. From 1940 he served in the Romanian army. In 1943 he decided to take German citizenship. In May he joined the Waffen-SS and was assigned to serve in a unit in Yugoslavia. SS rank: Obersturmführer (first lieutenant).

On December 15, 1943, he came to Auschwitz, where he initially was the camp doctor in the women's camp at Birkenau. After that he took over the post of camp doctor in the "Gypsy Camp." He took part in numerous selections on the ramp. For a time he was a doctor in the main camp at Auschwitz, and in 1944 he was transferred to the KZ at Neuengamme. From here he went to the camp at Bergen-Belsen in 1945. In Auschwitz he became known as the "correct murderer"; he seldom raised his voice, and he could just as easily and coldly select victims for the gas chamber as he could protect others from it.

After the liberation of Bergen-Belsen on April 15, 1945, he was arrested by the British. He came to trial in the court at Lüneburg and during the trial he confessed his participation in the selections at Auschwitz. He was sentenced to death and hanged on December 13, 1945.

•

Witness Adrienne Eva Krausz, née Mátyás. Persecuted as a Jew, in Auschwitz in 1944. Work commando: latrine cleaning. At the time of the trial Adrienne Eva Krausz was forty-one and worked in the United States as a doctor. Witness for the prosecution, gave testimony on Capesius.

•

Dr. Johann Paul Kremer. Born December 6, 1883, in Stolberg near Cologne, Germany. Died January 8, 1965, in Münster, West Germany. Member of the General SS since 1935/36. Member of the Waffen-SS since 1940. In the KZ Auschwitz from August 1942 to November 1942. Department: Garrison Doctor (Department V); SS doctor; Rank: SS Obersturmführer (first lieutenant). Sentenced to death by the Supreme Court of the People's Republic of Poland on December 22, 1947, in the Kraków Trial against Liebehenschel and other defendants. His sentence was commuted to life imprisonment; he was pardoned in 1958 and released. At the time of the trial Kremer was eighty years old and living as a pensioner in West Germany. Witness for the prosecution, testimony on Klehr.

•

Witness Hermann Langbein. Born May 18, 1912, in Vienna, Austria-Hungary. Died October 24, 1995, in Vienna, Austria. Persecuted for political reasons; in KZ Dachau from May 1, 1941, until August 1942; in KZ Auschwitz from August 20, 1942, until August 25, 1944; prisoner clerk at the garrison doctor's office; prisoner no. 60355; one of the founders of the Kampfgruppe Auschwitz, in May 1943; after August 25, 1944, in various external camps and in the main camp at KZ Neuengamme; after 1945 a member and later general secretary of the International Auschwitz Committee. At the time of the trial Langbein was fifty-one, living as a writer in Austria. Witness for the prosecution, gave testimony on Boger, Klehr, and Scherpe.

•

Witness Ella Lingens. Born November 18, 1908, in Vienna, Austria-Hungary. Died December 2002 in Vienna, Austria. Persecuted for political reasons; in KZ Auschwitz from February 20, 1943, until December 1, 1944; prisoner doctor in BIa (women's camp); prisoner no. 36088; subsequently in KZ Dachau until the end of the war; after 1945 a member of the International Auschwitz Committee. At the time of the trial Ella Lingens was fifty-five and was working as an expert consultant at the Austrian Federal Ministry of Social Administration in Vienna. Witness for the prosecution, gave testimony on Boger, Capesius, Kaduk, and Lucas.

•

Dr. Franz Lucas. Born September 15, 1911, in Osnabrück, Germany. Died December 7, 1995, in Elmshorn, Germany.

SS Obersturmführer (first lieutenant). KZ doctor. Passive resistance and refusal to participate in the murder of prisoners resulted in his being punitively transferred several times. At the beginning of 1945 he was threatened with court-martial in Sachsenhausen. He was accused of having performed selections and of having supervised the insertion of Zyklon B gas pellets into the gas chambers.

•

Dr. Josef Mengele. Born March 16, 1911, in Günzburg, Germany. Died February 6, 1979, in São Paolo, Brazil. Member of the NSDAP from April 1, 1937; member of the SS from May 1938; SS Hauptsturmführer (captain); in KZ Auschwitz from May 30, 1943, until January 1945; department: Garrison Doctor (Department V), first the head doctor in BIIe ("Gypsy Camp"); at the behest of the Institute for Genetic Study of the Kaiser Wilhelm Institute in Berlin he also ran an experimental laboratory in BIIe ("Gypsy Camp"); after its dissolution in August 1944 camp doctor in BIb (women's camp).

•

Otto Moll. Born March 4, 1915, in Hohenschönberg, Germany. Died May 28, 1946, in Landsberg am Lech, Germany.

Member of the SS from May 1, 1935; SS Hauptscharführer (master sergeant); in KZ Auschwitz from May 1941 until January 1945; in charge of the crematoriums in Auschwitz-Birkenau in 1943 and also from May to end of July 1944; assigned to the Department of Protective Custody (Schutzhaftlagerführung) (Department III), camp Führer of Subcamps Fürstengrube and Gleiwitz I, Kommandoführer of the work commando for gardening; Department of Labor Deployment (Abteilung Arbeitseinsatz) (Abt. IIIa), labor service leader in BIId (men's camp); sentenced to death by an American military tribunal in the Dachau trial, and executed. Work site: Crematorium.

•

Witness Filip Müller. Born January 3, 1922, in Sered, Czechoslovakia (now in Slovakia). Persecuted as a Jew; in KZ Auschwitz from April 13, 1942, until evacuation of the camp; Sonderkommando; prisoner no. 29236. At the time of the trial Filip Müller was forty-two and was living as a civil servant in Czechoslovakia.

•

Dr. Hans Wilhelm Münch. Born May 14, 1911, in Freiburg, Germany. Died 2001, Allgäu region. Member of the NSDAP since 1937; member of the Waffen-SS since spring 1943. SS doctor; SS Untersturmführer (second lieutenant); in KZ Auschwitz from the end of 1943 until 1945; deputy chief of the SS Hygiene Institute in Rajsko. Acquitted by the Supreme Court of the People's Republic of Poland on December 22, 1947, in the Kraków Trial against Liebehenschel and other defendants. At the time of the trial Dr. Münch was fifty-two and was living as a physician in West Germany. Witness for the prosecution, gave testimony on Boger and Capesius.

•

Miklós Nyiszli. Born June 17, 1901, in Szilágysomlyó, Austria-Hungary (now Şimleu Silvaniei in Romania); according to other sources he was born in Nagyvárod/Großwardein, Austria-Hungary (now Oradea, Romania). Persecuted as a Jew; prisoner doctor; prisoner no. A-8450. He was a dissection assistant to Dr. Mengele.

Documentation. Fortsetzung der Vernehmung des Zeugen Filip Müller (continuation of the interrogation of the witness Filip Müller) (ninety-eighth day of the trial, October 8, 1964).

•

Witness Friedrich Ontl. Born August 25, 1908, in Zwittau, Austria-Hungary (now Svitavy, Czech Republic). Member of the NSDAP since 1939; Feldwebel (sergeant first class); SS Hauptscharführer (master sergeant); in KZ Auschwitz from September 19, 1942, until evacuation; department: Garrison Doctor (Department V). At the time of the trial Ontl was fifty-five and living as a dental technician in West Germany. Witness for the prosecution and for the defense, gave testimony on Capesius.

•

Witness Dov Paisikovic. Born April 1, 1924, in Vel'ky Rakovec, Czechoslovakia (now Velikij Rakovec, Ukraine). Persecuted as a Jew; in KZ Auschwitz from May 21, 1944, until evacuation; Sonderkommando; prisoner no. A-3076. At the time of the trial Dov Paisikovic was forty and living in Israel as a butcher.

•

Witness Wilhelm Prokop. Born 1897 in Raciborz, Poland; died 1969 in Wodzisław, Poland. Persecuted for political reasons; in KZ Auschwitz from July 6, 1943, until October 1944; work commando: SS pharmacy; prisoner no. 127846. At the time of the trial Mr. Prokop was sixty-seven and lived in Poland as a druggist.

•

Witness Jan Sikorski. Born January 12, 1917, in St. Petersburg, Russia. Persecuted for political reasons; deported from Radom, Poland; in KZ Auschwitz from July 30, 1941, until evacuation; work commando: SS pharmacy; prisoner no. 19086. At the time of the trial Jan Sikorski was forty-seven and living in Poland as a druggist.

•

Witness Ella Salomon, née Böhm. Born August 1, 1920, in Odorhei, Romania (now officially known as Odorheiu Secuiesc). Persecuted as a Jew; deported from Hungary; in KZ Auschwitz from May 29, 1944, until evacuation; work commando: prisoners' pharmacy in BIa (women's camp); prisoner no. A-25383. At the time of the trial Ella Salomon was forty-four and living in Romania as a professor. Witness for the prosecution, gave testimony on Capesius.

•

Witness Karlheinz Schulery. An acquaintance of the defendant Capesius; military chaplain in the Romanian army. At the time of the trial Karlheinz Schulery was fifty-three and living in West Germany as a pastor. Witness for the defense, gave testimony on Capesius.

•

Witness Hildegard Stoffel, née Müller. An acquaintance of the defendant Capesius. At the time of the trial Frau Stoffel was fifty-two years old and living in West Germany as a homemaker. Witness for the defense, gave testimony on Capesius.

•

Witness Hans Stoffel. An acquaintance of the defendant Capesius. At the time of the trial Hans Stoffel was fifty-six years old and living in West Germany as an engineer. Witness for the defense, gave testimony on Capesius.

•

Fritz Strauch. Prisoner; work commando: SS pharmacy.
Documentation. Mentioned in: Vernehmung des Zeugen Wilhelm Prokop (interrogation of the witness Wilhelm Prokop, fifty-sixth day of the proceedings, June 18, 1964).

•

Witness Magda Szabó, née Guttmann. Born January 16, 1919, in Eger, Austria-Hungary (now in Hungary). Persecuted as a Jew; deported from Hungary; in KZ Auschwitz from June 2, 1944, until January 2, 1945; work commando: camp kitchen; prisoner no. A-11937. At the time of the trial Magda Szabó was forty-five and living in Romania as a teacher. Witness for the prosecution, gave testimony on Capesius.

•

Gerhard Wiebeck. SS Untersturmführer (second lieutenant); member of the Commission to Investigate Embezzlements, Enrichment by Property

Theft, and Breaches of Authority in the Concentration Camps. (Ninety-fifth day of the proceedings, October 1, 1964.)

•

Eduard Wirths. Born September 4, 1909, in Geroldshausen bei Würzburg, Germany. Died September 20, 1945, in Staumühle bei Paderborn, Germany.

SS Sturmbannführer (major); department: Garrison Doctor (Department V); SS garrison doctor in KZ Auschwitz from September 1, 1942, until January 1945. Committed suicide in September 1945 while under British custody.

•

Dr. Otto Wolken. Born April 27, 1903, in Vienna, Austria-Hungary. Persecuted as a Jew; in KZ Auschwitz from July 9, 1943, until evacuation. Prisoner doctor in BIIa (quarantine camp); prisoner no. 128828. At the time of the trial Dr. Wolken was sixty and living in Austria as a physician.

LIST OF MILITARY RANKS
DURING WORLD WAR II

U.S. ARMY	BRITISH ARMY	GERMAN ARMY	GERMAN SS
Private	Private	Grenadier	SS Schütze
Private First Class	(no equivalent)	Obergrenadier	SS-Oberschütze
Sergeant	Sergeant	Unteroffizier	Unterscharführer
Staff Sergeant	P. Sgt. Major	Unterfeldwebel	Scharführer
Sgt. 1st Class	C. Sgt. Major	Feldwebel	Oberscharführer
Master Sergeant	B. Sgt. Major	Oberfeldwebel	Hauptscharführer
Sgt. Major	Reg. Sgt. Major	Stabsfeldwebel	Sturmscharführer
Second Lieutenant	Second Lieutenant	Leutnant	Untersturmführer
First Lieutenant	Lieutenant	Oberleutnant	Obersturmführer
Captain	Captain	Hauptmann	Hauptsturmführer
Major	Major	Major	Strumbannführer
Lieutenant Colonel	Lieutenant Colonel	Oberstleutnant	Obersturmbannführer
Colonel	Colonel	Oberst	Standartenführer
General of the Army	Field Marshall	General-Feldmarschall	(no equivalent)

WORKS CONSULTED AND CITED

BOOKS

Aaron, Soazig. *Klaras Nein, Tagebuch-Erzählung.* Translated from the French by Grete Osterwald, with a foreword by Jorge Semprún. Berlin: Friedenauer Presse, 2003.

Adam, Marianne, and Ella Salomon. *Was wird der Morgen bringen? Zwei Jüdinnen überleben Auschwitz und finden zum Glauben an Jesus Christus.* Translated from the Hungarian by Moshe Fogel. Stuttgart: Edition Anker, 1995; Göttingen: Edition Ruprecht, 2001.

Adler, H. G., Hermann Langbein, and Ella Lingens-Reiner, eds. *Auschwitz. Zeugnisse und Berichte.* Frankfurt am Main: Europäische Verlagsanstalt, 1962.

Agamben, Giorgio. *Quel che resta di Auschwitz. L'archivio e il testimone (Homo sacer III).* Torino: Bollati Boringhieri, 1998. Published in English as *Remnants of Auschwitz: The Witness and the Archive.* Translated by Daniel Heller-Roazen. New York: Zone Books, 2002.

Arendt, Hannah. *Eichmann in Jerusalem: A Report on the Banality of Evil.* New York: Viking, 1963.

Berner, Dr. Mauritius. *Memoiren.* Translated and with comments by Victor Capesius. Unpublished manuscript.

Böhm, Johann. *Die Gleichschaltung der deutschen Volksgruppe in Rumänien und das "Dritte Reich" 1941–1944.* Frankfurt am Main, Berlin, Bern, Bruxelles, New York, Oxford, Wien: Peter Lang, 2003.

Borowski, Tadeusz. *Bei uns in Auschwitz. Erzählungen.* Translated from the Polish by Vera Cerny. Munich: Piper Verlag, 1963. Reissue translated by Friedrich Griese. Frankfurt am Main: Schöffling & Co. Verlagsbuchhandlung GmbH, 2006. Published in English as *This Way for the Gas, Ladies and Gentlemen.* Selected and translated by Barbara Vedder. New York: Penguin, 1992. Reissued as *Here in Auschwitz and Other Stories.* Translated by Madeline G. Levine. New Haven, CT: Yale University Press, 2010.

Broszat, Martin, ed. *Kommandant in Auschwitz. Autobiographische Aufzeichnungen des Rudolf Höß.* Munich: dtv dokumente, 1978; 2002.

Czech, Danuta. *Kalendarium der Ereignisse im Konzentrationslager Auschwitz-Birkenau 1939–1945.* Reinbek bei Hamburg: Rowohlt Verlag, 1989. Published in English as *Auschwitz Chronicle 1939–1945.* New York: Owl Books, 1997.

Demant, Ebbo, ed. *Auschwitz—"Direkt von der Rampe weg . . .": Kaduk, Erber, Klehr: drei Täter geben zu Protokoll.* Reinbek bei Hamburg: rororo aktuell, 1979.

Friedler, Eric, Barbara Siebert, and Andreas Kilian. *Zeugen aus der Todeszone. Das jüdische Sonderkommando in Auschwitz.* Springe am Deister: zu Klampen! Verlag, 2002.

Fritz Bauer Institute and the State Museum of Auschwitz-Birkenau, ed. *Der Auschwitzprozess (The Auschwitz Trial). Tonbandmitschnitte, Protokolle und Dokumente.* (Live tape recordings, protocols and documents). DVD. Berlin: Directmedia Verlag, 2004 (= Digitale Bibliothek 101).

Greif, Gideon. *Wir weinten tränenlos. Augenzeugenberichte des jüdischen "Sonderkommando" in Auschwitz.* Translated from the Hebrew by Matthias Schmidt. Frankfurt am Main: Fischer Taschenbuch Verlag, 1999. Published in English as *We Wept Without Tears.* Yale University Press, 2005.

Gutman, Israel, and Bella Guttermann, eds. *Das Auschwitz Album. Die Geschichte eines Transports.* Translated from the Hebrew by Alma Lessing. Göttingen: Wallstein Verlag, 2005.

Kertész, Imre. *Roman eines Schicksallosen.* Translated from the Hungarian by Christina Viragh. Berlin: Rowohlt, 1999. Published in English as *Fatelessness.* Translated from the Hungarian by Tim Wilkinson. New York: Vintage, 2004.

Kielar, Wiesław. *Anus mundi: Fünf Jahre Auschwitz.* Translated from the Polish by Wera Kapkajew. Frankfurt am Main: S. Fischer Verlag, 1979; 1982. Published in English as *Anus Mundi: 1,500 Days in Auschwitz.* Translated by Susanne Flataner. New York: Times, 1980.

Klee, Ernst: *Auschwitz, die NS-Medizin und ihre Opfer.* Frankfurt am Main: S. Fischer Verlag, 1997.

———. *"Euthanasie" im NS-Staat. Die "Vernichtung lebensunwerten Lebens."* Frankfurt am Main: Fischer Taschenbuch Verlag, 1985.

Kluge, Alexander. *Lebensläufe.* Stuttgart: Henry Goverts Verlag, 1962.

Levi, Primo. *Der Letzte (The Last Man).* Levi's memoirs appeared in German as *Ist das ein Mensch?,* translated from the Italian by Heinz Riedt. Frankfurt am Main: Fischer Verlag, 1961 (Fischer Bücherei 421). Levi's work appears in English as *If This Is a Man.* Translated by Stuart Woolf. Abacus, 1988.

Lifton, Robert Jay. *The Nazi Doctors: Medical Killing and the Psychology of Genocide.* New York: Basic Books, 1986. The complete English language text can be found on the Internet at the website of the Mazal Library: A Holocaust Resource, www.mazal.org.

Lustig, Oliver. *Dicţionar de lagăr.* Bucureşti: Editura Cartea Românească, 1982. English version online at Concentration Camp Dictionary, http://isurvived.org/Lustig_Oliver-Dictionary.

Nyiszli, Miklós. *Im Jenseits der Menschlichkeit. Ein Gerichtsmediziner im Auschwitz.* Edited by Friedrich Herber and Andreas Kilian. Translated from the Hungarian by Angelika Bihari. Berlin: Karl Dietz Verlag, 2005.

Perl, Gisella. *I Was a Doctor in Auschwitz.* New York: International Universities Press, 1948.

Popa, Klaus, ed. *Akten um die deutsche Volksgruppe in Rumänien 1937–1945. Eine Auswahl.* Frankfurt am Main, Berlin, Bern, Bruxelles, New York, Oxford, Wien: Peter Lang, 2005.

Schlesak, Dieter. *Vaterlandstage und die Kunst des Verschwindens.* Zürich: Benziger Verlag, 1986.

Schulze, Sabine, ed. *Zoran Mušič.* Ostfildern: Hatje Cantz Verlag, 1997.

Stephani, Claus. *War einer Hersch, Fuhrmann. Leben und Leiden der Juden in Oberwischau.* Frankfurt am Main: Athenäum Verlag, 1991.

Szűcs, Ladislaus. *Zählappel. Als Arzt im Konzentrationslager.* Edited and with a foreword by Ernst-Jürgen Dreyer. Frankfurt am Main: Fischer Taschenbuch Verlag, 2000.

Wesołowska, Danuta. *Worte aus der Hölle. Die "lagerszpracha" der Häftlinge von Auschwitz.* Translated from the Polish by Jochen August. Kraków: "Impuls" Verlag, 1998.

Wiesel, Elie. *Gesang der Toten. Erinnerungen und Zeugnis.* Freiburg im Breisgau: Herder Verlag, 1989.

RADIO BROADCASTS

Kindheitsmuseum. Südfunk 2, December 25, 1983, and SDR/NDR, May 16, 1984.

Der Tod ist ein Meister aus Deutschland. Was habe ich mit Auschwitz zu tun? Hessischer Rundfunk, May 8, 1981.

Vaterlandstage. Deutsches Leben. SDR/NDR/WDR, March 1, 1980.

These materials are located in my archive, my depository at the Deutsches Literaturarchiv in Marbach, and in the Fritz Bauer Institute in Frankfurt.

INTERVIEWS AND ARCHIVAL MATERIAL

Interview with Victor and Fritzi Capesius in Göppingen, 1978. Tape recording.

Letters, notes, books, and copies of books: miscellaneous documents from the personal belongings of Victor Capesius, which when I interviewed Capesius I was able to borrow and make copies of.

Interview with Roland Albert in Innsbruck, 1978. Tape recording. A large portion of the conversation was recorded. Beyond that, there are notes of conversations, documents and notes on his childhood memories in my archive, and of other family meetings as well.

Notes of Dr. Berner, copies that I obtained from Capesius, "Tape Recordings and Journal Entries from Hell": All these materials were the original inspiration for this book. The conversations and documents preserved are the root material. Also tape recordings made with my family over the years in Aalen, Germany; my own journals; and family letters.

A new study of Transylvania during the Nazi Era: "In nationalsozialistische Verbrechen verstrickt. Anmerkungen zu einer Forschungslücke." In *Zeitschrift für siebenbürgische Landeskunde* 19 (1996), Heft 1.

CPSIA information can be obtained
at www.ICGtesting.com
Printed in the USA
LVHW01s1835050618
5796601LV00011B/1006/P

Nikki Nicole
THE PEN GODDESS

NIKKI NICOLE CATALOG
JOURNEE & JUELZ 1-3
CUFFED BY A TRAP GOD 1-3
GISELLE & DRO STAND-ALONE
FOR MY SAVAGE I WILL RIDE OR DIE
HE'S MY SAVAGE I'M HIS RID'AH
BABY I PLAY FOR KEEPS 1-3

Coming Tomorrow

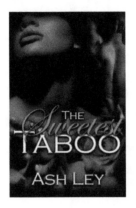

Complete Series Available

"I now pronounce you husband and wife again. You may now kiss the bride."

Thank you for taking this journey with us. It wasn't easy, but anything worth having requires you to put in work. You've witnessed our beginning, and now you have our ending. We're gone for now, but I'm sure we'll see you guys soon. This is the end of the Cuffed by a Trap God Series. You'll see Layla and Shon in their spin-off soon. It's a standalone. Leah and Vell have something in the works also.

The End ...

"I asked Lateef the same thing. It took him a minute to get his words together. He came correct too when he spoke about his wife. He spoke life, and he wants his wife to know how feels also. Go ahead Lateef you can speak.

"Malone Sophia Adams. If loving, you is wrong then I don't want to be right. The first time I laid eyes on you I was mesmerized. Your eyes spoke to my soul and ever since you had a hold on me. You had me in trance. I was destined to have you.

We crossed paths for a reason. It's not a man alive that could stop me from getting at you. Not even your brother Shon. I love you, and I love everything about you. God made you for me. You're the air I breathe. I gave you my heart, and I don't ever want it back. You're my wife, and you're everything to me. I thank God every day you allowed the Trap God to cuff you." Malone was crying. I had to wipe her tears. I meant everything I said.

"Lateef, do you take Malone Adams to be your wife?"

"I do."

"Malone, do you take Lateef Baptiste to be your husband?"

"I do."

To know them is to love them I asked Malone when she's thinking of Lateef what comes to mind, she said Cuffed by a Trap God. I've married a lot of people. When Malone spoke about Lateef I could feel it; her words held so much confidence and power. She meant everything she stated about him. I wanted to know what Cuffed by a Trap God meant? Malone tell us what Cuffed by a Trap God means to you.

"The first day I laid eyes on Sphinx I was going through something. I dated a man for six almost seven years, and he cheated on me and created a whole new family. I hate to even say this because my kids are here. I met Sphinx the same day after all of this happened. Who knew our first encounter would lead to marriage and children? Sphinx cuffed me when he first met me. He never gave up on me. He fought for me when I wasn't deserving of his love. Our road to get here wasn't easy, but it was worth it. I know God placed him in my life for reason. It's our season. Prior to meeting Sphinx, I haven't been to the Trap in months. The one day I decided to go to the Trap. I was cuffed by him."

"Sphinx, it's time." I dapped my OG'S up. They stood in position as I made my way to the altar. The wedding came together nice. Everything looked good and like royalty. My kids looked amazing. Our mothers were holding Laylin and Lateef. I didn't want Laylin to see me she was spoiled and would act up immediately.

"You're good Sphinx she's not going to run off and leave you." I punched Shon in the shoulder he got me fucked up. The bridesmaids and my groomsmen were coming down the aisle. Last and not least. My wife came strutting down the aisle. My face always lit up looking at Malone. She stood in front of me with the biggest smile on her face she placed her hands in between mine. Jah and Latwoin stood next to me. They both were the ring barriers. Samaya and Kennedy were the prettiest flower girls I ever saw. I have rings for them too. The preacher started preaching.

"We're gathered here today to witness the union of Lateef Baptiste and Malone Adams. I'm old school, but these new age weddings they have themes, and meanings. Before I decided to marry Malone and Lateef I had to get to know them. I refuse to marry anyone without knowing their background.

I don't even move the same. I don't do single shit anymore. I don't even fuck off in the Trap anymore."

"Yeah, she's definitely the one if you're falling back from the Trap. You don't have to trap no more leave that shit to the young niggas trying to get it. Invest in stock and bonds real estate and some other business ventures."

"I am." Dro and I finished chopping it up. Giselle came downstairs I assumed Malone was ready. I never known for her to take less than an hour to get ready. It's a first time for everything. Giselle & Dro let themselves out. My wife walked down the staircase. Damn, she was beautiful. Our colors were white and gold. My tux was white, and her dress was gold dripping in diamonds. She had the matching head piece it was dripping in diamonds also.

"I'm ready, are you?"

"I was born ready."

***

Malone and I made it to the church we were the last to arrive because I was trying to get a quickie in and she wouldn't let me. We went our separate ways to get this wedding started.

Giselle doing her hair and makeup would slow up the process. They would be talking about shit they didn't need to talk about. It was cool though because I could chop it up with my nigga Dro for a few minutes while Giselle got Malone right. I walked downstairs to chop it up with my nigga. He dapped me up instantly.

"Giselle you can go upstairs she's ready for you."

"Okay, congratulations." Giselle headed upstairs. Dro lit up a cigar and passed it to me. I puffed it a few times.

"Man, your bachelor party was wild last night. I saw those hoes on Snapchat. Vell was trying to set a nigga up last night. I'm glad I didn't go. I saw Alonzo up in there. I can't fuck around with that shit."

"You, me especially with my track record. Vell and Alonzo stay on that bullshit. My wife is crazy she wouldn't hesitate to kill my ass if she suspected I was up to no good. I didn't even feel right being there last night. Nothing felt right about that shit all. I called my wife to pick me up."

"You're growing up, and when you find the right one, it's not worth the risk."

"She is the one. I only wanted to get married one time, and she's it for me. I put in so much to get her and nothing I do is in vain.

Sphinx

"Malone wake up it's time."

"I'm sleepy is it too late to run?" She yawned.

"Stop playing before I put something long, thick and chocolate in your mouth."

"I love dick for breakfast." Morning came quick. Malone was still asleep. I had to wake her up with breakfast in bed of course. Malone and I were already married, but I wanted to do it the right way and give her the wedding of our dreams in front of our family. We didn't have any friends we had family. We were already running behind schedule because we slept a little later than we should. I started to get dress early because I know Malone would take forever.

"Baby this breakfast is amazing."

"Eat as much as you can because it's 9:00 a.m. and our wedding starts at 11:00 a.m. I don't want to be late to our wedding. Giselle is already down stairs waiting to do your hair and the makeup you don't need."

"Okay baby I am." I knew we were going to be late for our wedding because Malone takes forever to get dressed.

I stroked his beard and kissed his lips. I ran my hands across his eye brows. My nails stroked his scalp. He was something to look at. He had the richest chocolate skin. His dreads were freshly twisted. His beard was trimmed to perfection. His lips and the bottom grill in his mouth blinded me. He had a tight grip on my ass, and he was biting his bottom lip.

"I'm glad you know, don't let your mouth get you in trouble."

"Don't let your hands and mouth get you in trouble."

"I'm always looking for trouble when it comes to you." Sphinx and I sat up for a few more minutes before we both went to sleep. We had a long day ahead of us.

"I did, you wanted it too." We dried off. I ran to the bed, and he was right behind me. I curled up under the covers and prayed he was tired as I was. He snuggled up behind me and started sucking on my neck and fondling my breasts.

"Wake up I'm not finished with you yet. I'm trying to get you pregnant again."

"I'm already pregnant again."

"How you know?"

"I just do, because you can't stay off me. You don't pull out. As soon as you leave I be missing you having with draws and shit."

"I want two more from you, and I'm good."

"Sphinx, that's a lot of kids."

"I can take care of them and you." I didn't even answer him. Whenever I ignored him. He always picked me up and laid me on his chest tonight wasn't any different. I wasn't mad at him. I was just thinking about somethings, and he was too. I noticed his breathing pattern was different. I raised up and looked at him.

"Sphinx, I'm not mad so don't even think that. Whatever happen it just happens. I know you got us and you have since day one."

"I'm not." We barely made it in the house. As soon as we pulled in the garage. Sphinx snatched me up out the car and sat me on the trunk of the car. He put a dent in the hood immediately. I could barely breathe my breasts were bouncing up and down. If Sphinx kept it the back windshield was going to break. He wouldn't ease up. Thank God our garage you couldn't see inside. I was so wet my juices were coating the trunk.

"Can we take it in the house please?" He gave me a devilish grin and ignored me. I could feel the dent in the trunk. Sweat was dripping down his forehead and covering his abs.

"Nope, I want you right here and right now. Get up here and ride your dick."

"Please Sphinx I'm tired, and you've wore me out I don't want to miss our wedding fucking with you."

"You asked for it. You know how I get when the kids aren't home. Sphinx carried me upstairs to our bedroom. He sat me on the bench and cut the shower on. I could barely stand up in the shower, he made a soapy towel and washed me up.

"I'm tired; you wore me out."

"I'm not you asked for it."

"You shouldn't even be here Shon bring your ass on now."

"Vell invited me to this shit. I tried to leave, but he was calling me a pussy whipped nigga."

"You ain't got to prove shit to Vell. That's why he's single now trying to prove something to the next motherfucka." Shon got up and did as he was told. He threw his shirt in the trash. He dapped Sphinx up and followed behind Layla. Leah just shook her head. Vell was eying her the whole time.

"I'm leaving Leah are you leaving too?"

"Yeah, I'm leaving." We headed toward the door and Vell ran up on Leah. Sphinx had to push back in the room. Now was not the time to show your ass. Sphinx mad sure Leah got as far away from the room and in her car before we left. Sphinx carried me to the car. I unfastened my trench coat and sat my legs on the dash board. I reclined my seat, so he could get a good look at me and have easy access.

"What are you trying to do?"

"Get me home, and you'll see." Sphinx started doing 100 mph through traffic. I slid my panties off and threw them at him. I unfastened my bra and threw it at him.

"Don't say shit if you end up pregnant again."

I put on the sexiest lace lingerie I could find. My trench coat was lying on my bed. I grabbed my trench coat and threw it on. I couldn't wait to see my husband and ruin this bachelor party.

***

It took me about an hour to make it to The W. Leah, and Layla were in lobby waiting on me. I could tell Leah and Layla were both pissed. Not more than me.

"Let's go freak." We headed up stairs to the bachelor party. The whole ride up I was nervous on the elevator because there's no telling what we might see. I knocked on the door, and a bitch opened the door. I pushed her out of my way. Layla was looking for Shon. Leah made herself she acted as if she was unbothered. I knew it bothered her to see Vell with a shit load of women. Sphinx was sitting on the couch, and two chicks were sitting next him. I sashayed over to the couch and jumped on him.

"Damn baby you finally came let's go." Sphinx grabbed my ass and started tonguing me down. He grabbed my hand led me to the door.

"Shon what the fuck are you doing." I looked over my shoulder Layla was about to confront some chick dancing on Shon. He punched the bitch so hard off him; she fell on the floor. You could see the blood on the floor.

"Hey, Malone, what's up?"

"Hold on, let me conference Layla in," I called Layla she answered on the first ring too.

"Hey, Malone, what's up you're ready for tomorrow?"

"Yes, so I called you guys because OG Vell decided to throw my husband a bachelor party without his consent. Sphinx called me to pick him up."

"Let's ride because Shon ain't home or answering his phone."

"What about you Leah?"

"I'm not even about to entertain Vell I don't have the energy."

"He's been acting a fool since you left him."

"Layla, if he wants me back being around hoes, ain't the way to do it, but I'll meet y'all up there."

"Okay, they're at The W on Peachtree Street." I hated that Leah and Vell we're going through there little bullshit. Vell wanted to drag everybody in it because he was single. Leah wasn't taking him back at all." It was the middle of the winter.

Malone

I've been calling Sphinx's phone for the last three hours, and it's going straight to voicemail. I have a bad feeling he always answer when I call. This is the night before our actual wedding. All the kids were gone I wanted to lay next to my husband and relax. Leah and Layla wanted to go out. I'm homebody I just wanted to lay on Sphinx and ride on his dick until he taps out. My phone rung and it was from an unknown number. I answered it on the first ring.

"Hello."

"Baby, come and get me from The W Vell threw me a bachelor party I'm not feeling this shit. I don't want to look at these hoes I want my wife."

"Vell wants me to kill his ass. Give me an hour I'm on my way."

"Alright, we're in room 789."

"Okay." I can't stand Vell's ass. I bet Leah didn't know what that nigga was up too. I grabbed my phone to call Leah and Layla, so we could do a pop up. Leah answered on the first on the ring.

"I hear you she gone come back. It's funny how the tables have turned."

"She ain't if you don't get your shit together." I understood what Vell was trying to do, but I just wanted to love on my wife that's it. These bitches didn't even deserve to be in the presence of a nigga like me. I know hoes, and these hoes won't get the chance to get me caught up.

"Nah lil baby I'm cool."

"Are you sure? We can do something else a little more intimate."

"I'm more than sure. I'm married, and I don't cheat on my wife. I don't give a fuck how good you look and how fine you are. You can't cuff or trap a nigga like me. Find you another prey because I'm the wrong nigga to prey on. My wife she's crazy and she don't give a fuck about killing a bitch behind this monster in between my legs." I don't know why this chick was sitting here. I'm not beat. Theses bitches can't do shit for me. I don't need temptation. My wife is the only temptation I need.

"Sphinx, man ease up a little it's your bachelors party. Let these hoes make the money I already paid them."

"Vell I'm already married. I don't care about this bachelor party. It's plenty of single niggas in here that wouldn't mind fucking any of these bitches tonight. I'm not one of them I know what the fuck I got at home, and I refuse to get drunk and fucked up and fuck one of these hoes and lose my wife behind it. Nothing in here is worth me losing my wife and my family. I worked too hard to get it, so I'm good. You need to be trying to get Leah back these hoes ain't worth it trust me."

"Let me see your phone Sphinx." I gave Vell my phone he stuffed it in his pocket.

"What the fuck are you doing?"

"I'm throwing you a small bachelor party. Stop acting like a pussy whipped nigga and look at this pussy I got you for a few hours."

"Vell I don't want to look at these bitches. My wife is it for me I don't give a fuck about these hoes, and I'm not tipping."

"I've already paid them very well. Follow me and enjoy yourself." I followed Vell like a dummy I couldn't wait to use somebody's phone I needed my wife to pick me up asap. Vell opened the room up it was setup like a casino, but it was bitches walking around nude. All my niggas were in attendance.

I looked to my left Shon had a bitch throwing her ass on him like she was ready to fuck. Dino had two bitches on him. Judah had a bitch in his face. Don't get me wrong a couple of months ago I would be all for this shit, but I'm a different nigga now a married nigga. Hoes didn't excite me I knew I could fuck em, duck em or whatever I wanted too. My dick only gets hard for one woman, and she's not here. I'm not a free man I'm married I wanted my wife.

"Can I dance for the Trap God?"

Sphinx

Malone and I were scheduled to get married tomorrow. I kept telling Vell, Shon, and Dino. I didn't want a bachelor party. I haven't been out in months, but I didn't care to do so either. Vell and I had some business to do this afternoon. We had a shipment that came in early it wasn't supposed to come in until next week.

We ran into a slight problem with our ports in Haiti, so that's the reason for the early shipment. Vell picked me up this morning. We've been gone all day, and Malone has been blowing up my phone. I told her I was on my way at least ten times.

I looked at my watch it was almost seven I never go all day without seeing my wife. My phone was dead too. Vell pulled up to The W hotel I'm looking at this nigga like he was crazy because he knew I wanted to go home.

"Come on and get out for a minute."

"Vell I got to get home."

"Damn I have to get something from here. Have drink while you wait."

"Make this shit quick." Vell threw the valet attendant his keys.

"Malone look at me." I turned around to face him. He was smiling trying to read me, but I was dead serious. I'll check Denise and whoever else.

"I love you because you care. I'm in love with you because you care about my feelings and you pick up on things you shouldn't, but you do."

"I love you too that's what I'm supposed to do. If you have a problem than I have one too." Sphinx was tired. I stroked his beard a few times and placed soft kisses on his lips. All his baby mothers had a problem with me because I made sure Sphinx was taking care of his kid's only.

They needed jobs and too stop depending on his money. Y'all hoes need to work for a check not sit back on your ass waiting on his. Sphinx had a shit load of money, but I was the only bitch going to spend it. I don't give a fuck who like it. He's the Trap God, and I'm his Trap Queen.

"I don't know Malone. Denise has been tripping since I married you."

"I'll never tell you to walk away from your son. Why would she have a problem with me?"

"I know you wouldn't." Sphinx and I have known each other for eight months a lot of people had a problem with it. We love each other, and nobody was going to change that. If she had an issue because he married me join the club. If he's been raising your son for ten years and he's been with a slew of women, you decided to cause your son and my husband pain because you're in your feelings, oh well you can be miserable by yourself. I understand why Sphinx wanted to name our son Lateef. If the bitch wanted to be petty my husband can be too by naming our son Lateef.

"Do you want me to speak with her?"

"And say what?"

"What needs to be said. I don't like her making you feel some type of way because of me. You're a real standup guy because the next man wouldn't do it, that's what put you above the rest. You can easily walk away and not give a fuck." Sphinx tapped me on shoulder.

Malone

Our family stayed and played with the babies until visitation was over. I was in a little pain, but it was bearable. Sphinx put the twins asleep and the cribs that were right beside my bed. I knew something was going on with him and for some reason he didn't care to speak on it. I couldn't even sleep because whatever was bothering him had him in deep thought.

He's laid behind me with his arms wrapped around my waist. I could tell his eyes were wide open and he was awake for the longest. I wanted to get some sleep before the twins woke up.

"Do you want to talk about it or you're going to keep it to yourself?"

"Lateef isn't mine, and he knows about it?" I turned around to face him. I could always tell when Sphinx was in a bad mood his eyes were always dark and his veins would be visibly in his hand and forearm."

"What are you saying?"

"What I just said."

"He's not yours? So, what are you going to do? He's been yours for ten years what changed?"

"My babies, hush and let them clean you up." The nurses finished cleaning Malone and the babies up. The nurse was finished with Malone and brought my son to her. She was grabbing for him before they could get close. The nurse placed Lateef in her hands she couldn't stop looking at him. He couldn't stop looking at her.

"He's so handsome he looks just like you. Look his dimples and jet-black curl foils that adorn his head and his bushy eyebrows."

"Daddy did all the work." I laughed. Malone punched me in my arm. The nurse brought my daughter out next. I grabbed my son from Malone. The nursed placed my daughter in Malone's arm. Between, Samaya, Kennedy, and Laylin I already knew I was going to jail for beating somebody's son's ass.

"She's beautiful, and she looks exactly you. She has my lips and eyes and nose. Laylin and Lateese."

"Laylin and Lateef." Malone looked at me. I gave her a stern look. She knew I meant business and now isn't the time to debate me on this. I know she wanted to object because she didn't want to step on anybody's toes and she wasn't. Things happen for a reason.

"You're not a good liar."

"I'll tell you after you have my babies. Promise me you want say shit either." She looked at me and rolled her eyes. The nurse came in to check and see if Malone has dilated some more.

"Mrs. Baptiste you're at nine centimeters. Let's get you prepped for delivery so you can meet your babies." Thank God I couldn't wait to meet my two. Malone looked nervous I don't know why. I grabbed a cold towel to wipe her face.

"Mrs. Baptiste on the count of three push for me. 1,2,3." Malone started to push the nurse instructed her to push again. The nurse yelled she sees hair. Malone had to push one more time. I tried to tell her my kids are a different breed.

My young nigga came out first running shit like his OG like I knew he would. Seven pounds and eight ounces. My daughter came out right behind him screaming as loud as she could. A hell raiser just like her mother she was seven pounds and six ounces. She looked just like me too. Malone wasn't going to like that at all. I cut the umbilical cords. Malone was jealous because I was hogging my babies.

"Give me my babies."

I've known for years Lateef Jr wasn't mine, but I raised him ass my own. Denise agreed to let me be his father. Lately, he's been causing problems and acting out. He's ten years old his teacher called me because he got in trouble.

I heard him say in the back ground why did you call him he's not my daddy. It's takes a lot to get to me, but that got to me. I know Denise told him that, he doesn't even look at me the same. He's my young nigga no matter what I've been trying to pick him up like I normally do but Denise keeps giving me the run around.

I haven't even told Malone all of this. It's been weighing heavy on mind. I don't want to cut a kid off because of their mother. I know it's her because Miles didn't have any family he was raised in the system. Nobody knew that he wasn't my son but my family. My wife doesn't even know that's the only reason why I want to name my son after me. He's the real junior.

"Baby what's wrong?" My wife stroked my beard. I could tell she was in pain by her facial expression. She was worried about me.

"I'm good are you in pain?"

"I am, but you're the only drug I need."

"I can't wait to give you some."

Sphinx

Man, I'll be so glad when Malone gives birth and deliver my babies. Since we've gotten married, she's been acting wild as fuck. I couldn't believe she pulled the nurses hoe card. I felt that bitch watching me, but I didn't want to say shit because I knew Malone would've popped off. I wanted to name my son after me.

It's crazy how I haven't even met him, but I could already feel our bond while his mother is carrying him. Lateef Jr. my oldest son he's not really my son, but I've raised him as he was my own since birth. I'm the only father that he knows. Denise was fucking with my nigga Miles way back when we first started fucking around.

I never knew she was fucking with Miles until I caught them on a trip coming back from Dubai. I came home early, and I caught Miles in Denise in my bed fucking. Of course, I killed that nigga I don't give a fuck how cool we were but if you could fuck my bitch and smile in my face. You'll rat me out.

So, to avoid making a long story, Denise has been causing me problems since I married Malone. Everybody bitch I used to fuck with had problem. She was the one, and I've known that from day one.

"Samaya, you'll meet them in a few hours." I loved Samaya she's the sweetest and smartest little girl. I loved having her around every day. She was my daughter she's been connected at the hip with me as soon as we met.

"I know you're not, but I'm giving you something do. I watched you stand outside of my door and watch my husband for over twenty minutes, but when I ask you to check and see how many centimeters am I? You refused to do your job." She looked at me like I was crazy.

"Shalita you can go home for today. You can't refuse to help a patient, that's grounds for termination." The nurse assigned to me told the little bitch that was watching Sphinx. I busted out laughing. My nurse checked to see how many centimeters I was.

"Seven centimeters." Music to my ears, the twins would be here in no time I couldn't wait to meet them. Sphinx was stroking the side of my face looking at me.

"You know you showed your ass."

"Yep, it ain't my fault you rubbed off on me. I'm still going to beat her ass when I drop."

"Whatever you been crazy. I just brought it out of you." Our family started to flood our room everybody was waiting on the Baptiste twins to arrive, not more than me. I couldn't wait to see what we created. Samaya and Kennedy couldn't wait to meet Laylin. Layla was so mad I came up with that name. Of course, I wasn't going to tell her, and she had a girl too.

"Daddy, I'm ready to meet my sister and brother."

He swore somebody was trying to steal my panties. The nurses came in and started hooking the IV's up to me. Checking my blood pressure and my iron. The nurse that I caught eye fucking Sphinx she was standing in the door starring at him. I tapped the nurse on her shoulder.

"Excuse me could you tell that nurse to come here." I pointed to her in the hallway she tried to walk off.

"Malone, what are you doing?"

"I want to know why she's looking at my husband and his wife is right here. I hate a disrespectful ass bitch."

"Let that shit go and bring my babies in the world." He grabbed my face, and he started tonguing me down.

"Excuse me, Mrs. Baptiste, I brought the nurse in here for you."

"Okay Thank you. Hi, I'm Malone Baptiste, and this is my husband. I notice every time were here you watch him like a hawk. He's very attractive do you know him?"

"No Mrs. Baptiste I don't. He's attractive right?"

"Yes."

"I need you to do your job. I want you to check and see how many centimeters I am?"

"I'm not the nursed assigned to you."

"I can't wait to get my wife pregnant again." He laughed. I wasn't even about answer him. We already have eight kids together. We don't need any more kids eight is enough.

"Malone do you hear me?"

"I do, but I'm not answering you." His fertile ass can't wait to get me pregnant again. This has been the best pregnancy ever, but I don't want to be pregnant again no way time soon. I love Sphinx smothering me.

***

We finally made it to the hospital. Everybody was waiting on us. I wasn't in a rush to get here. I wasn't looking forward to staying here two days after I had my babies. Sphinx grabbed my hand and kissed me on my forehead.

"Mrs. Baptiste are you ready?"

"I'm ready Mr. Baptiste." The nurses escorted us to our room, so they could prep for delivery. Sphinx helped me undress. I refuse to wear a hospital gown he brought me my own. I pulled the gown over my head, and Sphinx pulled my panties down and grabbed them and stuffed them in his pants.

"Because you're hard headed and you're perfect just the way you are. You know I don't want nobody looking at my wife."

"I know but what's wrong with your wife wanting to look good for her husband? I don't want nobody else but you."

"Nothing but I don't want nobody looking at my wife. I'm a selfish ass nigga, and my wife is something to look at."

"I'm selfish too, and I don't want nobody looking at my husband. I caught those nurses looking at you. You better tell them, bitches, I'm crazy, and I won't to hesitate to kill them. Wait until I drop it's on."

"Calm down you know I'm not checking for nobody but my wife. You're the only woman I want. You're the only woman I ever proposed too. You're the only woman to carry my last name besides my daughters." He laughed.

"I better be." It's funny now when I catch bitches still lusting after him he wants to laugh about it. I love him all of him.

I placed a little Vaseline in the palm of my hand and applied to my face. I wasn't going to go overboard with the make up because he would go ape shit. He hated when I wore make up. I grabbed my lipstick attempting to coat my lips. He snatched it from me.

"Malone you don't need all of that shit, and you're about to give birth to my kids. You're putting my kids in danger by taking your time. Who in the fuck are you trying to impress?"

"I just want to look presentable for my delivery."

"You look presentable. I love you curves and all." Sphinx sure knows how to fuck up shit. I threw my lipstick in my bra. I'll put it on in the car. I had my outfit already laid out. It was black sweater dress with some thigh high black boots.

"Malone, where do you think you're going with that shit on? You're not wearing that. Here put this Ivy Park black jump suit on." I can't stand him. He put the jogging suit on me and carried me to the car. Thank God the jogging suit was black. He pulled off into traffic. I pulled my black matte lipstick out of my purse, and it applied to my lips. I could feel Sphinx staring at me. I refuse to look at him. I knew he would say some smart shit.

"Why are you looking at me like that?"

I jumped in the shower and handled my hygiene the fluids from my sack where gushing down my legs. I can bet you any amount of money Lateese was the one who broke my sack. We've been going to the doctor every week, and he's been the more dominate one. His dick is always showing, and he pushes little Ms. Laylin to the back. Sphinx thought that was the funniest shit. I didn't find that funny at all because he was going to be a replica of his father. I wasn't raising my son to be a whore. I couldn't wait to meet him the 3D image didn't do him any justice. I couldn't wait to hold him.

"Malone, what's taking you so long? I have the car packed, and everybody's waiting on us at the hospital."

"I'm coming," I yelled I wasn't in a rush. I was in labor with Jah and Kennedy for three hours. So, I figured the longer I took to get there by the time I make it I would have to push at least three or four times.

I couldn't compare these twins to Jah and Kennedy because they have a mind of their own. I cut the shower off and stepped out the shower. Sphinx was sitting on the toilet with a towel waiting for me. He was so attentive to me it's crazy. He insisted on drying me off with a towel, and I'm capable of doing it myself. He grabbed the Cocoa butter and rubbed my body down.

Epilogue

Malone- Six Months Later

"Sphinx, I think it's time."

"Time for what Malone?"

"My water just broke."

"Okay let me clean you up, and I'll grab your stuff." Oh, my God, I can't believe it. I've been on bed rest for the past few months. I knew the twins were going to come early but not a whole two weeks early. My due date wasn't until November 19th and its November 5th. Sphinx and I still haven't decided on a name yet. I wanted my daughters name to be Laylin after My mother, her auntie Layla, and her grandmother Shaolin.

I wanted to name my son Lateese. Sphinx already had a Jr., but he insisted on naming our son Lateef. I didn't want to step on anybody's toes, but he wants what he wants. I'm ready to give birth and meet my newest creations who took over and controlled my body. I wanted to be as cute as possible on my delivery. Something told me to get my faux locs done last week I'm glad I did.

You know I'm not a traditional ass nigga but what I'm trying to say is will you marry me? Can I cuff you for life Malone? I'm ready for you to be Mrs. Baptiste." She was crying I had to wipe her tears.

"Yes, Sphinx I'll marry you." I slid the ring on her finger and picked her up and carried her to our bedroom. Malone stripped out of her clothes pushed me on the bed and mounted me. She started stroking my dick with her tiny hands.

"Stop playing and get up there and handle your business. I don't like being teased."

"Shh be quiet I'm making the rules tonight, I cuffed the Trap God."

"You did more than Cuffed the Trap God. You put voodoo on me." Malone ran her tongue across my lips. I grabbed her breasts. I wanted her to stop playing with me before I take her down threw there. She still wanted play until I pinned her down and baptized her with this Baptiste dick.

"Do we have too Sphinx? I don't want to argue with you about it."

"We don't have to argue, but I want you to listen to me. I'm riding with you right or wrong. As your man allow to me to correct you if you're wrong. I want you to do the same. There's a time and place for everything. Anytime you feel the need to kill a female give me the heads up, so I can have people in place to clean up your mess. You have to move accordingly."

"I'm sorry."

"Don't be. Malone." It was now, or never I've been wanting to propose to Malone for a few weeks for now, but shit kept coming up. Tonight, was the night. It was just the two of us no interruptions. I positioned myself between her legs and knelt on one knee.

"I love you more than anything in this world."

"I love you too."

"Shh, I'm doing the talking tonight. I know in the past things were shaky but these past few months we've grown. I love waking up to you every morning, and I love coming home to you every night. I Thank God that you allowed me to write my wrongs.

I pulled in the garage, and before I could kill the engine, she was jumping out.

I don't know why she was mad at me because I didn't do anything. I'll let her cool off for a while before we decided to talk. She needed to calm down, and I did too before we both say some shit we don't mean. I don't want to go to bed with any tension between us. I sat at the bar in my man cave and took two shots of Hennessy. I made it upstairs to our room, and she was laid across the bed reading a book on her Kindle. I grabbed her Kindle from her. She started to pout and mumble some shit under her breath.

"Sphinx did you really have to take that from me."

"Yes, because I wanted to talk to you. It feels good outside let's sit on the balcony."

"Okay let me change." I had a few candles outside on our balcony I lit eight of them. I took a seat on the bench on the balcony. I heard the door open, and it was Malone. I motioned with my hands for her to have a seat next to me. She took a seat next to me and laid her head on my chest.

"It's so beautiful out here."

"It is. I wanted to talk to you about what happened earlier."

Chapter 20

Sphinx

"You know you're wrong for doing that."

"What did I do wrong? So, what, I checked her once I wasn't checking a bitch twice without any results. She tried me she knew we were together. Tell that bitch to try again from her grave."

"You can't do that, and you're pregnant."

"I can do whatever I want."

"No, you can't, and we'll talk about it as soon as we get home."

Malone showed her ass at Layla's baby shower I wasn't even doing anything. I curved that bitch every time. I can't believe she did that. She wanted to be in her feelings and sit in the back of the car instead of sitting up front with me.

I wasn't even going to argue with her while I was driving. I was saving it for when we got home. I was watching her through the rear-view mirror.

I knew she could tell I was looking at her she refused to look at me.

I wanted to feel him touch that back of my throat. I started humming and running my tongue at the tip of his dick. I could taste the pre-cum. Shon grabbed my neck. I knew he was about to cum. I didn't ease up until I could feel his knees buckle. Tonight was going to be a good night.

"Okay, sis be careful. Call me when you make it. He loves her too much to do that." Everybody was leaving after Malone electrocuted her ass. Leilani and my mother were cleaning up. I'm tired I want a nice hot bath and Shon's chest. He walked up behind me and placed his hands on my stomach and started kissing on my neck.

"Are you ready to lay it down?"

"Yes." Shon told our mother's they could leave, and he'll clean up in the morning." Shon locked up grabbed us two water bottles and some fruit. Shon carried me upstairs to our room. He tossed me on the bed and pulled my dress over my head. Shon hoovered over me and unfastened my bra and slid my panties down.

"You know I owe you from, earlier right?"

"Yes, and I told you I'll make the wait worth it."

"I'm ready." Shon placed his hands behind his head and gave me a cocky grin. I pulled his slacks off and slid his boxers down. I licked the tip of his dick. I coughed up some spit and spat on his dick. A little spit slid down my chin. I applied so much pressure to Shon's dick. I could feel the veins appear on the side. I knew I was getting the best of him because he started scooting back. I wasn't through with him yet.

"It's a little too late for that." Malone was walking fast toward Sphinx. Leah and I were dead on her heels. Sphinx has rubbed off on Malone. She used to be the sweetest girl.

Now she's mean as a pit bull. Malone stopped by the bar and grabbed a bottle water and opened it. She tapped Whitney on the shoulder. Whitney turned around and had a smug look on her face.

"Can I help you?" Whitney asked Malone with an attitude, now is not the time and you know you're being sneaky with her man.

"Of course, you can," Malone argued and threw the water on Whitney. Oh, my God, she pulled out the taser from her purse and electrocuted Whitney's stupid ass. Sphinx jumped up and grabbed Malone and carried her out. My stomach hurts so bad from laughing. Thank God everybody that wasn't family left already. You could hear Sphinx hollering at Malone. I'm sure they would be arguing all night. Leah looked at me, and we busted out laughing again. I knew Malone was going to do something, but I didn't know what.

"Layla, I'm about to head home. I'll call you when I make it. Pray Sphinx doesn't kill Malone."

"Ok, we're about to find out. Layla, you look a little hungry let's cut the cake." I cut the cake and the inside read it's a girl.

"It's a girl." I was so happy. I wrapped my arms around Shon. I couldn't wait to thank him later for helping me create my princess. We had three tables filled with gifts. I opened a few. I couldn't wait to shop for my princess. Malone and Leah wanted me to open the gifts they brought for me. Leah brought me a Pink Polo diaper bag.

Vell walked up with Sade behind him. He counted out $3000.00 he always does the most. He was trying so hard to get Leah's attention, and she wasn't giving him any. Malone brought a Chanel baby gift set. It was so cute. Malone kept saying it was girl maybe she knew a little something. I nudged Malone because I noticed Whitney was touching on Sphinx and he was moving her hands.

"Okay Layla, I already warned you if I kill this bitch in your house don't say shit. I see now I'm going to have to start making examples out of bitches. I refuse to let a hoe slide."

"Oh, Lord."

She knew she wanted her ex-husband back." We finished talking it was almost 7:00 p.m. and time for the Gender Reveal Party to start. A few of our guest have already arrived.

***

Leilani and my mother had our Gender Reveal Party decorated nice. Tati and Trecie flown up from Miami. Thank God because if they missed this party, I was catching a flight to Miami and egging their house and putting all their cars on flat. I'm real childish. I had to keep my eyes trained on Leah and Malone. My mother and Leilani started a few games for the guest I didn't feel too good because Shon got me hot and bothered and I wasn't able to bust a nut. It was right there on the verge of coming out, and I had to stop.

"Thank you, guys, for coming out tonight to celebrate the Gender Reveal for Layla and Shon. We're going to go ahead and get started. Layla, what do you think it is?" Auntie Linda Faye was the host.

"I want a girl. I want a princess so bad."

"Shon, what do you think it is?"

"A boy of course."

I heard a knock at the door. I ignored it hoping they would go away. It was Leilani and my mother they caught Shon's face in the cookie jar. Oops, we're caught. I placed my face in my hands. I was so ashamed.

"Layla and Shon y'all nasty. Y'all could've saved it for later. Shon move and let the girl breathe." Leilani yelled. Shon jumped up quick.

"Why you didn't say nothing Layla?"

"I tried to tell you to wait, but you didn't want too." Shon pulled up his pants and kissed me on the forehead. He eased out the room, not before my mother and his mother popped him in the arm a few times.

"Layla y'all nasty." My mother laughed.

"Whatever momma I'm sure you and Judah are too. Leilani what's up with you and Lorenzo? What's up with Auntie Chanta and Uncle Day?"

"Don't try to change the subject because we caught you giving the pussy up to Shon."

"I'm not this isn't the first time the two of you caught us." I smiled.

"Judah and I are grown we don't have our parents popping up. Leilani she's feeling Lorenzo, but she's keep her guard up. Uncle Day cuffed Auntie Chanta the first day.

"You look beautiful, do you need me to do anything?"

"No, I think our mothers have everything covered." Shon turned me in the vanity chair. He knelt in front of me and massaged my feet. He started messaging my calves and gripping my thighs. He started taking his pants off.

"Shon, we can't do this right now. Our Gender Reveal Party is about to start in less than an hour?"

"What does that have to do with me wanting to make love to you?"

"I don't want to get my hair and make-up ruined."

"Why does it matter I'm going to mess it up anyway. Just slide your dress up bend over and arch your back."

"Shon, the party, is over at 9:00 p.m., please wait. I promise I'll make it worth the wait." I ran my finger across his top lip. He wasn't trying to hear that he wanted what he wanted. He threw my legs over his shoulders and started eating pussy. He raised up and looked at me and gave me a devilish grin.

"I thought you wanted me to wait?" He laughed. I pushed his head right between my legs. I started to ride his face. I so needed this right now.

I checked Whitney once, and she doesn't want me to check her ass for the second time. I'm not checking a hoe twice behind Sphinx don't believe me just watch."

"So now y'all know. I don't care whose ass y'all beat long as y'all don't break my expensive shit in my house. Please don't let Leilani hear about this shit. I swear she's been on go since she beat Yona's ass. I can't even go shopping with her because if a bitch looks at me wrong, she's popping off."

"You know momma don't play that shit. She can't wait to lay a how down about hers."

"Oh, we all know." Giselle finished putting the finishing touches on my hair and make-up it was flawless. Malone and Leah escorted Giselle out. Our colors were rose gold and white. My dress was elegant but cute. Calvin Klein Sheath Cocktail Dress. My open toed Gucci embroidered metallic leather mid-heel sandal matched perfect. I propped my legs up on the vanity mirror to rub baby oil on my legs and feet. I felt some strong soft hands massaging my shoulder. I knew it was Shon. I looked in the mirror he was so sexy and handsome. His touch alone makes me melt. He looked real eatable. His waves alone were making me seasick. His beard was trimmed to perfection.

"Damn y'all nosey everything is going great." She blushed. I knew it about damn time. I was sick of them. I'm glad they worked it out.

"Leah and Malone, I have something to tell y'all. Don't be mad at me."

"I don't like the way you said that Layla."

"Trust me, Leah, I don't like what I'm about to say. Vell invited Whitney Sphinx ex and Sade a bitch he used to fuck with. I'm letting y'all know a head of time before y'all two have a private conversation saying Layla ain't shit. No Vell ain't shit. Y'all my sisters and I fuck with y'all the long way."

"I swear I'm so good on Vell. He needs to leave me alone and stop fucking with me. I don't even bother him. He's quick to flaunt a bitch in my face, but he's the same nigga that kicks my door in If I don't open. Please carry on I'm not with the get back shit. Especially if you don't to let me play the game with you. I'm about to stop coming to these little events."

"I fell you, Leah, you know I went through that same exact thing with Sphinx. Thanks for the heads-up Layla. I'm confident about where I stand in Sphinx's life.

Malone and Leah were hearing helping me with everything. My mom and Leilani were getting everything together because I was stressed to the max and I didn't need to be. My hair stylist backed out the last minute. Malone called her stylist Giselle to do my hair and make-up. I never used her before, but Malone's hair and face always looks nice. I wanted a nude look not too much because Shon claims he hates, make up, and I don't need all that shit.

Malone brought Giselle up to my women's cave to do my hair and make-up. She's pretty.

"Hey Leah and Layla, this is Giselle, my hair stylist. Giselle these are my sisters."

"Hi, ladies it's nice to meet you. Layla what do you want done. I have a few nice short pixies cuts I've done I brought pictures, or you can show me what you want."

"Okay, you can show me what you have. I'll pick. My face I want a nice nude lip. I'm torn between a gold matte lip or red matte lip, but I'll let you know when we get there." I loved the pixie cut style pictures she showed me. I went with the edgiest one. Malone poured me and Leah a glass of wine.

"Malone, how are things going at Chateau Baptiste?"

Chapter 19

Layla

Shon and I Gender Reveal Party was today. I really didn't care to know the sex of the baby. Shon insisted I could understand where he's coming from because it's our first child. I wanted to be surprised. None the less it was another reason to get the family together. Malone, Leah and Leilani and my mom were throwing it for me.

I was running around acting crazy because the event was scheduled to start at 7:00 p.m. and nothing was ready and prepared to start on time. I still had to get my make-up and hair done. The caterer was running late. A few of the decorations I ordered hadn't arrived yet. For some reason, Vell invited Whitney Sphinx ex and a girl he used too fuck with back in the day Sade.

We were cool, but he knew he was pushing because Leah was coming. I fucks with Leah the long way I wanted her and Vell to work out I'm still praying for them. I don't know what he was thinking about. I knew this shit wouldn't end well.

I'll take my food to go, and you can drop Jah and Kennedy off at my mother's house tomorrow."

"I'm sorry Malone, but damn I kind of had hope that we could work this little bull shit out and be a family again. Especially after you came through for me when I needed you."

"Real women do real things remember that. I'll never do you how you did me. We could never be after everything you took me through. We'll always be cordial for the sake of Jah and Kennedy that's it."

"Who's the father if you don't mind me asking?"

"Sphinx, I don't mind." Crim and I finished chopping it up. I gave Jah and Kennedy a hug and left. I know Crim was feeling some type of way but oh well. One thing about Karma she always comes back around. I was in love with Crim, but he didn't feel the same way I felt about him.

"I'm good Crim thanks for asking time hasn't been on our side. We are better than that. I forgive you, but I want forget nor will I hold that against you or bring it up every time we talk."

"Good are you straight do you need anything? You never did tell me how you got out, do you have to go back to court? Why didn't I know that you were fucking with Twin?"

"I'm straight Crim I don't need anything. I got off because I didn't kill him those were false accusations. No, I don't have to go back to court all charges have been and dismissed with prejudice. You didn't know I was fucking with Twin because you were with Dee-Dee." He started sucking his teeth and grilling me. Don't do that now you weren't doing that months ago when I caught you.

"I'm glad you beat it."

"I am too. Crim, I'm pregnant I wanted to tell you first before you heard it from someone else."

"Damn Malone, you couldn't wait to fuck another nigga and get pregnant? We haven't even been broken up that long, and you gave my pussy away."

"Crim I'm not about to do this with you because I didn't have to tell you. I could've kept the shit to myself and let you find out whenever you found out.

"I got you."

"Okay." Jah and the little brother ran off Kennedy and Jayla followed right behind me.

I found us a table to sit at not to far from the playground where I could keep a good eye on them. Kennedy grabber her sister's hand and they went and played.

I grabbed my phone out of my purse I had a group message from Layla and Leah they wanted to link up later, and I was totally fine with that. I had plans to chill over Leah's anyway since I was kid free.

Crim finally came to the table with the food. He yelled for the kids to come and eat they were running to the table. He sat my food in front of me. He started getting the kids food situated. It's funny how tables turn months ago I couldn't get Crim to spend any time with the kids and me. Now he was making all the plans in the world.

"Malone, what's up how you been? You're a hard woman to keep up with. It's good to finally see you with my kids instead of picking them up from your mother. I thought we was better than that? I know I haven't been the best nigga to you, but I'm sorry I swear to God I am."

I unbuckled Jah and Kennedy from their car seats they saw their daddy and their eyes lit up. I would never deny Crim from being in their life no matter who I'm with. They opened the door quick and ran to him.

"Slow down he's not going anywhere."

"Okay, mommy." I could feel Crim starring a whole in me. My stomach was getting bigger, and it was poking just a little. I grabbed my purse out the trunk. Crim was standing right behind me. I tossed my hair over my shoulders.

"Jail does a body good Malone."

"It does, doesn't it." Crim was licking his lips it really made me feel uncomfortable. I grabbed Jah and Kennedy's hand we finally walked inside of Chick Fila. Crim was right behind us with his other two kids. It wasn't that bad for it to be a Saturday and lunch time. Jah and Kennedy were telling me what they wanted to eat.

"Crim you can place the orders I'll find us somewhere to sit and they can go and play."

"Cool you want something?"

"Yeah a grilled chicken salad with two extra chicken strips," he cut me off before I could say anything else.

"A lemonade with sweet tea, right?"

$\mathcal{C}$hapter 18

Malone

It's been awhile since Crim, and I have had an adult conversation with out arguing. He's been trying to get up with me for weeks since I've been released, but I haven't had the time. Today was perfect he was supposed to get Jah and Kennedy for the weekend.

Even though we weren't together, and we weren't at odds. I still didn't want him to know where I laid my head. Some niggas pretend that they're good, but you never no. With Willadene and Dee-Dee both dead you could never be too sure. I would rather play it safe than sorry.

We agreed to meet at Chick Fila that's were Jah and Kennedy wanted to eat. Crim sent me a text stating that he was there already, and we were about five minutes away. The Chick Fila wasn't to far from my house.

We pulled up Crim was waiting outside of his car with his other two kid's reality set in again this nigga really had a whole family up under my nose for years.

"Cheer up you know you want a mini me running around."

"That's what I'm afraid of. Another Sphinx running around terrorizing little children his age."

"Get the fuck out of here. If you want two girl's, we can try again. We have plenty of time. We can start practicing as soon as your six weeks are up."

"I'm good."

"No, you're not."

"I am. I have Samaya, Kennedy, Laylin."

"Laylin?"

"Yeah, I've been think of girl names for a while."

"I like it. You want to take a nap with me before I have to pick up the kids?"

"Sure, long as it's a nap and no sex."

"What about oral?"

"Take a nap by yourself freak."

"I don't have too." Sphinx carried me upstairs to our room and slid my leggings and panties down. He put that hurricane tongue on me. I hated when he made my legs shake. I wanted to run so bad, but I couldn't he had my legs secured on his shoulders.

"Don't ever tell me no."

"Mrs. Baptiste, could you sit on the operating table for me?" I'll place the cold gel on your stomach. Mr. Baptiste I'll let you place this between your wife's legs since your familiar with that area." I busted out laughing this nurse was a trip. Sphinx did as he was told. The nurse was cool it was convenient to have her come to the house. Our babies were looking at each other. They looked totally different from how and Jah and Kennedy looked.

"Everything looks pretty good so far. They're growing good and have a lot of movement. The weight is normal. Would you like to know the sex of the babies?" I looked at Sphinx, and he looked at me. I wanted two girls he didn't need any more boys.

"Sure."

"Baby A here is a boy. Here's his penis. Baby B she's a girl even with her legs being closed when she did open them I was able to tell. Mrs. Baptiste, you don't look so happy."

"I wanted two girls."

"You can always try again." The nurse brought me some prenatal pills and iron pills. Sphinx showed her to the door. She left her portable operating table here. Long as the babies are healthy, I'm good.

"I am." I smiled.

"Okay go ahead and give me a urine sample so I can tell exactly how many weeks you are and I'll setup, so I can give you an ultra sound."

"Okay." I went to the bathroom to provide a urine sample. Sphinx came in right behind me. As I was wiping myself. Oh, he probably thought I was trying to get over on him like Tiffany.

"You had to make sure my piss was real? I would never make you think I was pregnant and wasn't. I don't have to trap no nigga with a baby. If anything, you trapped me."

"Shut up; I didn't ask you to say shit. Don't assume anything I came in here to check on Mrs. Baptiste with her stubborn ass. You always ruining the moment. Bring your ass on so I can see my babies. I trapped you and what are you going to do about it?" I swear he does the most. The nurse was smiling at us like we did something. Nope, it wasn't that type of party. I gave her the urine sample. She confirmed I was seventeen weeks pregnant. She had the portable operating table setup, so she could perform the ultra sound.

Sphinx was always a gentleman until you brought the beast out of him. I jumped in the shower and handled my hygiene. I stood under the shower and washed my hair. I had a million things on my mind and doubting Sphinx wasn't one of them. Anything that could've happened has happened. I knew God wouldn't put anymore on me than I could bare.

***

Sphinx and I ate lunch it was delicious. He made a Cajun salmon salad it was good with feta cheese and purple onions turkey bacon. I was sleepy again I knew I had to stay up because the nurse he hired was on her way. We were laid up in the family room watching TV every time he would place his hands on my stomach.

The babies would move I don't know if it was voice or what, but they would act a fool just like him. It was cute but painful at the same time. The doorbell rang I assume it was the nurse. Sphinx stood up to answer the door. It was the nurse. Sphinx escorted her in.

"Hi, you must be Mrs. Baptiste?" I looked at Sphinx and rolled my eyes he knew damn well we weren't married. He was pushing it now. I smiled anyway and played along I didn't want to bust his bubble or show off in front of company.

He walked up behind me and wrapped his arms around me and bit the crook of my neck.

"I missed you."

"I missed you too."

"Are you mad at me?"

"No, I'm not mad I'm going to let you lead, and I'll follow until I feel like you're steering me wrong."

"I'll never steer you wrong. I have some plans for us. I love you, and I want this to work. I want to give my kids something I never had a two-parent home." I tilted my head back and looked Sphinx in his eyes to see if he was sincere and he was.

"I love you too keep playing your cards right it'll happen." He bit me on neck again.

"I've been playing my cards right. I've been trying to get you on board, but it's not easy when you're trying to fight this thing we have." He turned me around to face him. He placed my hands on his chest. I could feel his heart beat.

"My hearts beat for you. I need you to get your heart in tune with mine."

"I'm trying."

"Try harder. Lunch will be downstairs and ready for you when you finish." He placed a kiss on my lips and left out.

I'm capable of cleaning my own house. I didn't need the extra help. I looked through the closet all the cute shit that was here was now gone. It was replaced with maternity clothes didn't nobody tell him to do that. I'm showing barely I just had a pudge. I heard our room door open, and it was him

"You finally up. I was just about to wake you up, so you could eat. The OBGYN I hired for you she's coming to the house at 2:00 p.m. I'm having your house packed up don't attempt to sneak home."

"Okay, what happened to the clothes that were in here yesterday?"

"Put up until after you have my babies. Don't roll your eyes."

"Where's my car? I wanted to take Samaya and Kennedy to the nail shop later."

"I gave it back to Shon. I'm your man. I don't need him buying anything for you. I'm your provider. You can drive anything in the garage except my Ferrari. If it's a specific car, you want let me know." I didn't have anything to say I'm speechless.

Sphinx was perfect he always has been. What If I wanted to go home just to relax that wasn't up for debate anymore. I stood in the mirror and brushed my teeth.

Chapter 17

Malone

It's been a minute since Sphinx, and I have woke up to each other. It was bittersweet. No arguing and no bull shit brewing between us. It felt good to lay everything on the line. This is the best sleep that I've had in a long time. I guess it was time for things to change between us. Lord knows I was ready for a change.

Like any other relationship, I had to take things one day at a time and always pray for the best. I don't think Sphinx would hurt me I can't dwell on the dreadful things either. I must keep a positive mind always. He's an amazing father. I wanted to take the kids to school this morning by the time I woke up.

He already dropped the kids off. I grabbed my phone, and it was after 12:00 p.m. I don't know why Sphinx let me sleep this long. I had a doctor's appointment at 2:00 p.m. anyway. I pulled the covers back and stood to my feet immediately. I need a pedicure and a full set. I made the bed. Sphinx had maids and cooks.

"No, you always think you're running shit because you can slang good dick to hook a bitch. I can slang pussy just as well. I said I love you and you better not ever fuck a bitch how you fuck me. I'll kill your ass; you think you're the only one that's crazy. I want you to try me." I was scared to look at Malone I just wanted here to release my dick.

"I love you too."

"Look at me when you fucking talking to me Sphinx." She pulled my hair out of my face, she grabbed my face and pulled it to her lips. She started kissing me and grinding her hips even harder I could tell she was on the verge to busting a nut. We came at the same time. I wasn't done yet and I damn sure wasn't ready to tap out. We made love until the sun came up.

My strokes were long with pressure the only sounds you could hear in the room was the wetness of her pussy. It's funny she wanted to pretend like she was sleep but she's throwing her pussy back at me.

"I thought you was tired." She wanted to ignore me and smile. Okay, I made sure my next few strokes were long and hard and intense. It didn't take her long to open her eyes. I smiled because she was my prey. I wasn't easing up until she told me what the fuck I wanted to hear. Sweat was pouring down my face. She grabbed my hair for support to match my rhythm. She kept trying to get me to look at her I refused too. I saw the tear stains on her face. I kept hitting her with the pound game that I knew she loved. The sheets were soaked.

"Sphinx, I love you." She moaned.

"Nah you don't love me. You love this dick buried between your legs." I kept nailing her pussy to the wall. Next thing I know she clamped her pussy muscles down on me. I couldn't move or hit her with another stroke. Her wet ass pussy was drowning my dick. I know how to swim. She is doing some extra shit she has no business doing.

"Malone stop playing and release my dick."

"Malone stop playing with me. You don't have to give me anything. It's mine, so I'll take it. Who was the last nigga you fucked?"

"You already know who it was you just want me to say it."

"Say it because I don't know."

"Lateef."

"I thought so." Malone thought I was playing I sat her on my face. I sucked the soul out of her she was shaking. She grabbed my dreads. I kept going in. I could tell she was about nut. I wanted her to let that shit go.

"Stop." She moaned.

"Let that shit go and let go of my hair. You better not fall either." I smacked her on her ass three times. Her juices rain down on my face. She was still shaking. I don't know why she was playing with me. I raised up to get a towel to wash my face. I hope she didn't think she was through. I wanted her to ride my dick. I climbed back in the bed, and she was snoring.

"Wake up we're not through yet." I turned her over on her back side. I slid my dick in. Damn, she was tight but wet. I wanted to take it easy on her.

Malone turned her back against me. I could hear her sniffling. I knew she was crying. I picked her up and laid her on my chest. My chest was soaked with her tears.

"Malone look at me. I'm sorry I know it's not enough, and I'm tired of saying it because I fucked up. I don't want you crying because of me. I don't want you to upset my kids. Fucking Deja, I don't even have an excuse for that. I fucked Deja because I could, and she wanted me to fuck her. I love you, and I'm in love with you. You got my heart, and I want you keep it. These bitches out here don't mean shit to me. For what it's worth can we give us a try?"

"I'm scared Sphinx." She cried.

"Stop crying I got you. I promise you I do, and I don't want to hurt you."

"We can try."

"Look at me when you're talking, you know I hate that shit."

"We can try you better not make me regret it. I swear I'll kill your ass in this fucking room."

"Shut up and get up there and ride my face."

"Nope because you'll be trying to get some pussy that I'm not trying to give you."

"I don't think you can be faithful. You've had me looking like a fool more than once. I don't want to put myself out there to get hurt."

"Malone, I've been trying to get you to be with me since day one. I swear sometimes I feel like giving up, but something keeps pulling me back in. I'm holding on to that something. I want to be faithful to you. I wouldn't have you out here looking like fool. You deserve more, and I want to give you more. I don't want to hurt you. I want to cuff you and love you."

"Sphinx let me get this out the way, so you can know how I feel. I knew who you were when we first started kicking it. I knew you had a slew, bitches. You were fucking Deja and seeing it that shit hurt me. You broke me. You couldn't care about me. I wasn't even mad about going to jail because I didn't have to see you.

I would never think you would do that knowing her agenda. I love you Lateef, and I've kept it to myself for so long. It's crazy that I'm admitting it. I've never told you that for more reasons than one. I've been hurt before, so I wear my heart on my sleeve. I rather be by myself and love you from a distance than to let a you hurt me." I'm speechless I don't know what to say for the first in a long time I don't what to say.

"Malone, I knew they were mine. My babies want daddy here." She ignored me. I knew she wasn't sleep that fast. I felt two more kicks. I tapped her on her shoulders again she ignored me. I raised up and stood in between her legs. I grabbed her face and made her face me. Tears were pouring in her eyes.

"What's wrong?"

"Nothing, damn can I cry if I want too? I knew they were yours too." She cried.

"Twins I always wanted some. I'm glad you gave them to me. My kids knew me. How come you didn't want me to know?"

"It's not that I didn't want you to know. I wasn't ready to deal with you. I don't want to be another baby momma added to your roster."

"I want you to be more than my baby momma, but you don't want to give me a chance. I want to put a ring on your left hand. I know these past few months haven't been the best. Give me a chance because I'm trying. I swear to God I am."

"It's hard to give you a chance look at everything we've been through."

"I'm sorry it's not about how you start it's about how you finish."

"It's mine so why can't I grab it? Who was the last nigga you fucked so I can murk his ass?"

"Good night Sphinx the bed is big enough for the both of us. Make sure you stay on your fucking side."

"I'll be on whatever side you're on." I continued to wash up and until the water turned cold. I pray by the time I get out; she's sleep. I just wanted to bury my dick inside of her without any back talk. The water turned cold quick. I hopped out and dried off. I walked out to the bed room, and Malone wasn't there.

I swear she wants me to kill her ass. I heard the balcony door open, and it was her. She looked at me and smiled. She dropped her robe it fell to the floor. She was butt ass naked she knew she was teasing me. I stroked my dick just to let her know she's not the only one going to be teasing somebody. Malone climbed inside of the bed. I climbed in right beside her.

"Can you back up, please? There's no reason why you should be touching me."

"I don't want too. Can I hold you? I haven't had any sleep in a few weeks since you've been gone." She didn't even answer me. She ignored me. I noticed she started breathing heavy. I rubbed her back. I placed my hands on her stomach. I felt two kicks. What the fuck?

I stood on our balcony and puffed the blunt a few times. I stepped back in our room I heard the shower still running. I walked in the bathroom and dropped my clothes. I pulled the glass shower door open and stepped in right behind Malone. She looked over her shoulder and frowned.

"Damn I can't take shower? I'm not gone touch you if you don't want me too?" I brushed up against her ass. I reached for the soap and grabbed her breasts. She started sucking her teeth.

"Say something you already know you belong to me." I grabbed her pussy between her legs, so she'll know it's real.

"Can you keep your hands to yourself please? I don't think it was a clever idea for me to come here." She tried to exit the shower.

"I wish you stop running from this shit Malone. You're too old to play games. I swear I don't want to argue with you. It's okay for you to brush your ass up against a nigga you don't know but If I brush up against you it's a problem? I'll leave."

"You don't have to leave I'll leave. The difference between you and the next nigga he's not grabbing my breasts are my pussy."

The house it's big enough, but I told you yesterday I didn't want to lay by myself tonight either, and you don't have a choice but to lay with me."

"Okay, you keep some shit up your sleeve." She started huffing and puffing like she was mad. I sucked on her bottom lip. I felt her tongue gliding across my top lip. She already knew what type of nigga I was. I make the rules, and she needs to follow. I swear shit would be a lot easier. I'll let her run some shit. I grabbed her hand and led her to our room.

"Shh be quiet my kids are sleep." She didn't say anything she smacked me in the back of the head with her free hand. We made it our room; she let my hand go.

"What are you about to do?"

"Take a shower damn can I do that?" I didn't say anything because the next thing that was about to come out my mouth was smart. I needed to smoke I forgot I couldn't smoke around her because she's pregnant. Our house sat on three acres, and our bed room looked out toward the lake. It was a beautiful view. I'm a hood nigga, and I'm not into views and shit. I need square feet and lots of it. I love how the moon lights up the lake.

Sphinx

Malone and I finally made it home. It took about forty-five minutes. I pulled in the garage and killed the engine. She jumped out and made her way toward our room. I was right on her heels to catch all the ass she was throwing. I grabbed her shorts and backed her into the wall. This was the first time Malone looked me in the eyes without me asking her too.

"What Sphinx why are you looking at me like that? I'm trying to go to my room and relax can I do that?"

"You know why, you can't wear these shorts anymore. I'm trying to see why you're running and we're at home that's unless you have some other plans. All your plans are canceled since you're carrying two things that belong to me. We can go to our room."

"Our room? I thought you said this house was big enough where we didn't have to see each other?"

"It is but you can't be left alone with my babies by yourself. Yes, we are going to our room.

My clothes were lying in the bathroom. I went in the bathroom to change. I knew he was going to say something about my dress.

"You went to brunch with that on?" I just ignored him I knew this was going to be along night. I grabbed my purse and phone and my discharge papers.

If I saw the bitch again around him, I'll kill her on sight, and he'll have to clean the bitch up. I'm not playing with Sphinx or Whitney.

"Ms. Adams everything looks good your iron looks really, but it was extremely low. Carrying twins your iron level must be a certain amount. I'll send you a prescription in at your pharmacy for iron and prenatal pills. You need to see your OBGYN immediately. Dad be sure to take care of her."

"I'm trying too she won't let me."

"Ms. Adams let him take care of you please. I know you've been pregnant with twins before and you think you know it all but these two that you're expecting now both are the same weight and they're fighting for your iron that's the reason why you're in here. They're greedy."

"Thank you."

"You heard what the doctor said? I don't want to hear shit about you dying to go home. You know where home is, you better be glad I didn't show my ass because I wanted too. Stop playing games with me." Ugh, any reason to argue or to make me do what he wants. Therefore, I didn't want to say anything because I knew he would act this way. The nurse brought in my discharge papers.

"Sure." Sphinx grilled me as he was walking out. My babies had a mind of their own. I don't even want to see them. I know they're going to look just like his ass. My mother, Leah, and Layla walked in the door.

"Umm somebody is going to be on punishment and living in the house with their baby daddy after all. Sphinx makes the rules, and his babies do too. I thought he was going to kill the preacher. I had the clean-up crew on standby." My mother laughed, and Leah and Layla joined in.

"Y'all are so wrong."

"No, you're wrong you should've told Sphinx about his baby's months ago. If something would've happened to his babies he would've killed, you."

"Oh y'all knew about this? I would've killed her. I don't care how much I love her. She'll be at home with me. I can't even trust her to carry my children for six more months. She's out here having lunch with fake ass pastors. I've never killed a pastor before, but it's a first time for everything."

"Whatever," Layla whispered in my ear to watch out for Whitney she was nothing but trouble she's his ex. I looked at Layla she rolled her eyes.

"Sphinx you can handle your business, but I need your blood for my babies, and you can carry the fuck on. Whitney, I don't know you, but I'm going to need you to raise the fuck up out my room. My children's father and I are discussing family matters. If he told you to stay in the car that's the safest place for you to be. I don't tolerate disrespect at all, and I feel like you're disrespecting me. Anytime a bitch disrespects me I send her back to her creator."

"Are you threatening me?"

"I am."

"You can't stay with me Whitney I'm spoken for. She and I we live together, and we're expecting."

"Fucking around with him is dangerous." He better spoke up. I was two seconds from stomping this bitch out. She stormed out the room. The bitch won't have the chance to get none of my Haitian dick tonight. I could feel Sphinx grilling me I didn't want to look at him. Thank God the nurse came in.

"Ms. Adams is this your children's father?"

"Yes."

"Can you come with us sir, so we can draw some blood?"

"Praying Hands on You? This preacher ain't about to pray for you or prey on you. I stay woke. You don't look like no square ass preacher."

"You don't look like her square ass baby daddy."

"What the fuck did you just say to me?" Sphinx walked up in Horace face.

"Sphinx don't do this here." My mother tried to break it up. She pushed Horace out of the room to avoid any additional confrontation.

"Malone, what I tell you last night?" The girl Shon and Vell escorted out appeared back in my room. I raised up from my bed because he has me fucked up. I approached Sphinx and her.

"Sphinx, how long are you going to be here?"

"Whitney, does it matter? I told you to stay in the car, but you insisted on getting out. I'm going to be here for a minute. You can catch Uber, or you can see if Vell will give you a ride to where ever you're going."

"Vell ain't giving no bitch a ride," Leah spoke up letting it be known.

"I was hoping I could stay with you." She smiled. I knew he was too good to be true. This nigga kept a bitch in the background.

"You saw me last night I'm Horace. Malone isn't married. I don't see a ring on her finger. She passed out, and I made sure she got to the hospital" I wish Horace would just leave and ignore Sphinx and don't answer any more questions. My mother was in the background singing "the upper room." She needs to cut it out I swear.

"Thank you for making sure she's good. I got it from here partner. You called me here Malone what's going on?"

"My iron is low, and the babies don't have my blood they need yours to avoid me going into labor early."

"Babies? You're pregnant with twins, and they're mine? Why in the fuck are you just telling me now that your pregnant by me? I've been asking you since day one. What the fuck is this nigga doing here? Did you fuck him was it a possibility that he was the father? You said he was just speaking last night; you didn't say that you were fucking with him."

"Don't make this about me and what I'm doing. I'm not fucking with him. He's a preacher, and we had lunch."

"Where the fuck does this nigga preach at?"

"Praying Hands on You Baptist Church in Decatur, Georgia."

"Yeah, Horace I'm good for now. They're going to keep me for a few more hours and run a few tests on me. You can leave my mother and family are here."

"Are you sure?"

"She's positive." My mother interrupted before I got the chance to say anything.

"I'm positive." The door swung open, and it was Sphinx. My heart dropped he was looking crazy and starring at Horace. Hold up I know this motherfucka didn't have a female behind him. "What the fuck is this?" I said loud enough so he could hear it. Shon and Vell grabbed the girl and forced her out of my room. I could hear my mother laughing in the corner.

"Malone, what the fuck is going on and who the fuck is this? You're the same nigga I saw last night, right? I'm going to need you to move around my nigga. This is me."

"Sphinx now is not the time. He was just leaving."

"Malone this shit ain't no coincidence I've saw this nigga twice within twenty-four hours. I thought he was just speaking? How does he fucking know you to be up in your hospital room?" Horace cut me off before I could even answer Sphinx.

"Alright, I'm on my way."

"Malone, why didn't you tell him something was wrong with his babies? God don't like ugly. I've been trying to tell Mr. Travis to leave before Sphinx gets here. He insists on staying here to make sure you're good. I told him we got it. If you add this man to Sphinx's hitlist, I'm done with you."

"Momma we just went to lunch, that's it."

"I don't care Malone stop being so friendly; you should've said no. You haven't even been home twenty four hours. You should be at home relaxing with your babies they miss you. You're out on a date smiling up in this niggas face knowing you can't do shit with him because you're pregnant by Sphinx."

"I know momma. I should've been told Sphinx, but damn I had an appointment to see my OBGYN tomorrow. I was going to tell him I wasn't going to wait until after I had my babies like I originally planned to do. My plans were to tell him today, no matter when I told him it was still going to be a problem." Horace walked in my room. My momma rolled her eyes. I swear she was rude. It was best that he left now because I wanted him to be able to preach on Sunday.

"Are you okay?"

The nurse stated my iron was low and my blood pressure was high. It was severe because I was pregnant with twins. This has never happened to me before when I was pregnant with Jah and Kennedy. I had to call Sphinx and tell him about the babies because I need his blood for my babies. The nurse thought I may be going into labor early. I'm only three months pregnant ain't no way. "I don't want to call him I'm scared."

"Now is not the fucking time to be scared. If you would've kept you hard headed ass at home with Sphinx you wouldn't have to worry about this. God is trying to you something. Please listen and stop ignoring the signs. This happening because Sphinx has the right to know about his babies that you're trying to keep a secret. It's not about you it's about the babies you're carrying." My mother was right, but I wasn't even doing anything but eating brunch. I grabbed my phone and called the last person I wanted to call. He didn't answer, so I called him back again. He finally answered.

"Hello."

"Sphinx, I'm at Gwinnett Medical Center I need you to come up here."

"Is everything okay?"

"No, I don't think so."

"Thank you." The paramedics placed me on a stretcher. I grabbed my cell phone to call my mother. She answered on the first ring.

"Good Afternoon Malone, how are you?"

"I'm okay I'm on the way to the hospital. I passed out eating."

"Are you and the babies okay? Where's Sphinx and what hospital are you guys headed too?"

"I'm okay, and I hope they are too. I'm not with Sphinx they're taking me to Gwinnett Medical."

"Who are you with?"

"I'm with Mr. Travis."

"The preacher from jail?" My mother was sucking her teeth. I could tell she was rolling her eyes from her tone alone. I swear she was team Sphinx.

"Yes momma, he just took me to brunch that's it."

"I'll meet you at the hospital." My mother acts as if she cares more about Sphinx than she cares about me."

***

I arrived at Gwinnett Medical Center thirty minutes later. I gave my insurance information to the paramedics and the intake specialist at the hospital she began to take my vitals. My mother made it before the ambulance with the whole family.

"Church is church. Our congregation is growing. I do a lot in the community with our youth. I run into a lot of women in the community a lot of them have been coming to church throwing themselves at me. I'm not looking for an enjoyable time. Any woman that I pursue I want to do more than just court her. I'm not getting any younger I want a wife and a few kids."

"What about you?" Thank God the waiter brought our food out I didn't have to answer that question. The food smelled good, and I was hungry too. My stomach started to hurt suddenly.

"Excuse me, Horace, I need to use the bathroom."

"Are you okay?"

"My stomach feels a little funny." I got up to go the bathroom. I could barely keep my balance. I fell and passed out.

"Someone call the ambulance." A customer yelled. The waiter grabbed a wet towel and applied it to my face. Horace picked me up off the floor.

"I'm sorry."

"Don't be, let's get you to the hospital to make sure you're okay."

Malone

Horace was a great listener. We arrived at the spot for Brunch quick I didn't even realize that we were here all ready. He was such a gentleman it's hard to believe that he was in the streets. He's a breath of fresh air. He kept looking at me making me feel uncomfortable. Our server escorted up to our seats. I've never been here before it's a nice cute little cozy spot.

"Our you guys ready to order? Do you need time to look over the menu?"

"We need time?"

"Have you ever been here before?'

"Yeah, a few times. My aunt loves to come here on Sunday's she turned me on."

"Okay." I looked at the menu. The steak and eggs and French toast caught my eye. The waitress came back and took our order. Horace kept looking at me and smiling.

"Tell me a little bit about your church?" I knew Leah wouldn't tell me a lie. I wanted to see what Horace had to say about it.

"I'm a gentleman, why wouldn't I want to open a door for you?"

"Thank you for being a gentleman." I made us reservations at JR's Log House Restaurant it wasn't too far from her house.

"Malone, so tell me about yourself since we're finally alone. You were avoiding me in the prison. I wasn't going to bite you."

"Whatever what do you want to know?"

"Everything most of all what makes you happy. What I can I do to put a smile on your face?"

"Just continue to be you and if it's meant to be the smile won't turn into a frown." For the first time in thirty days, Malone began to open to me and tell me a few things about her. I'm a great listener, and I pay attention to detail. I was soaking everything in. I wanted to ask her about who the guy was last night. I'll save that for our next date.

Horace

Before I picked Malone up for brunch. I had to stop by and grab her some flowers. I wanted to get her some flowers while she was in prison, but I couldn't. I grabbed her some fresh yellow roses. I couldn't wait to place a rose next to her cheek. It took me about forty minutes to make it her house due to traffic. If this was her home, she had a nice house. I knocked on her door.

"Who is it?" Yes, this is the right one.

"Horace." Malone opened the door damn she looked beautiful.

"Come in." I gave her a hug. This is the first time that I've been able to touch her.

"These are for you."

"Thank you let me put these in some water, and we can get going." Malone put the roses in some water. Her home was nice and well kept. She tapped me on the shoulder.

"Are you ready?"

"Yeah, I am." She locked up her door. I opened the passenger door for her.

"Thank you! You didn't have too."

"He's a grown ass man I didn't see anything. It's a dangerous game playing get back with a fool it's not worth it."

"I'm not doing anything I'm just having breakfast that's it."

"Okay but he likes you."

"He asked me out in the County, but I declined. Bitch, you need to see this preacher. He invited me to his church. We should check it out. Praying Hands on You Baptist Church in Decatur right off Flat Shoals."

"Bitch that's the preacher that everybody's talking about that's fine as hell. All the hoes have been going to that church just to see him. When Mignon and I was cool, she showed me his picture on Instagram."

"Oh, hell no are you serious?" I laughed.

"Yes, bitch the name of the church gave it up. It's a new church it's nice too. He has a lot of stuff for the kids too."

"Oh Lord, he's fine too."

"He is, but he hasn't given any of these hoes the time of day." Leah and I finished talking.

Malone

How did he get my phone number? Running into Horace last night wasn't a coincidence. He called me and invited me to breakfast to top it off. I didn't want this to happen at all. Horace was very attractive I wouldn't mind getting to know him if I wasn't pregnant. What am I going to do? Let me call Leah to see if she has any answers for me.

"What's up Malone what's the move for today? How was your night? Mine was horrible Vell, and I argued all night."

"I have a date with Horace in a few. My night was okay I didn't go home with Sphinx I came back to my house. I hope you and Vell get back to your happy place."

"I doubt that would never happen. Bitch who's Horace?" I gave Leah the rundown of who Horace was she thought that was the funniest shit.

"What's so funny?"

"Malone don't get that preacher killed. Sphinx is crazy, and you know that."

"It's just breakfast that's it. You mean to tell me he wasn't dating anybody while I was gone, or he did an excellent job with hiding it?"

"Horace."

"Hey Horace, how are you? If you don't mind me asking how you got my phone number?"

"I have my ways it was good seeing you last night. I'm glad your free. Can I take you to breakfast, brunch or lunch?"

"It was good seeing you too. You're persistent."

"Brunch couldn't hurt."

"Okay, I'll shoot you the address or would like for me to pick you up?"

"You can pick me up. I'll text you my address."

"Thank you. I'll see you in a few." I'm glad she agreed to let me take her out. I know she's been through a lot and she didn't date because of that. I'm willing to take it as slow as she would like. Her address came through I knew a perfect spot near her house to take her.

Chapter 15

Horace

What are the odds of me running into Malone Adams last night? I had a number on, her but I didn't want to use it last night, but it's a new day. She's not incarcerated anymore, and nothing was going to stop me from trying to get at her.

I noticed she was with someone last night, but she wasn't married, so she was available for me to pursue. I think I knew him from somewhere, but I'm not sure. He kept grilling me like I wasn't supposed to speak to her that tough guy shit didn't scare me.

Put a ring on it, if not I will. I knew she was feeling me because she made sure to stay away from me. Her contact information was on her paperwork. Yeah, I grabbed her number off her paperwork. I grabbed my cell phone out of pocket and placed a call.

"Hello."

"Malone, good morning! How are you?"

"Who is this?"

"I didn't agree to let you do shit. I let you go home, but I was coming to pick your ass up in about an hour. You don't even know how to act. I wasn't even gone that long, and you were in the club shaking my ass. I'm the only nigga you need to bust it open for." Here he goes I knew him letting me go home was too good to be true. To think that I'll have to deal with this for the next eighteen years blows my fucking mind.

"I just want to relax in my own home. Me by myself I have a million things going through my mind. I have a lot of shit to think about, and I can't do that with you breathing down my neck."

"Who said I wanted to breathe down your neck? I wanted to breathe on something else. Tell me anything."

"It's the truth." Sphinx dropped me off at home for the second time. I know he was in feelings, but I was doing this for me and not for him. If it's meant to be, we'll be together. Only time will tell he has to work for me. I'm not taking it easy on him.

"I have I didn't beat his ass. Trust me I wanted too."
Sphinx and I rode through traffic talking. I missed him. I
missed moments like this about him. I wish he would let
my hand go. Leah sent me a text mad because her and Vell
were arguing the whole time he caught her with some nigga
up in her face.

Sphinx was looking at me like I was crazy he
wanted to know who was texting my phone because I was
smiling. I'm sure he thought it was Horace, but it wasn't. I
hope we don't run into each other again because Sphinx
would swear I was fucking with that man and I wasn't.

"Why are you looking at me like that?"

"You know why." I busted out laughing. Sphinx
was crazy he was jealous, and it looked good on him. He
knew I was up to no good. He just had to snatch my phone
to see who I was texting.

"Damn you and Leah don't have to dog out my OG
like that."

"He should've kept his dick in his pants. You
could've asked you didn't have to take my phone."

"I had to be sure it wasn't a nigga I'm not having
that."

"I thought you agreed to let me be."

"I'm single Sphinx remember that okay."

"Is that what you think?"

"Yes."

"Are you coming back to our home or do I have to lay by myself?"

"I'm going home. I'll drop you off." I didn't feel like arguing with Sphinx. I'm just going with the flow. Once I get home, I need some time to myself, and I'll tell him that the babies are his before the week is out. It's too soon to be staying with him. We needed to talk I couldn't agree to go home with him tonight. I wanted to lay in my bed without him. He needed to miss me some more. Him showing up tonight it doesn't change anything. Sphinx pulled off in traffic, he grabbed my hand and stroked my ring finger. We both wanted to say something, but we didn't say anything.

"Malone." I looked at him, and he was smiling. I knew he was about to say some crazy ass shit.

"You wanted to go home so you can sneak out and be fast in the ass. You got me fucked up. I started to kill that nigga just because he shouldn't even be in your space. My fucking space he still might get it though." He laughed.

"Sphinx, I thought you changed." I laughed.

Suddenly, I felt Kase hands off me. I could feel somebody starring me. I looked up, and it was him. My heart skipped a beat. All eyes were on us.

He stepped up in my personal space. I continued to dance on him. He wrapped his arms around me; he was whispering in my ear how he was going to fuck me up. I'm just glad he didn't show his ass and embarrass me.

The song went off Sphinx grabbed my hand. I followed him to the bar. He ordered a shot of Patron, and he gave me a bottle water. Leah and Vell stopped at the bar. Vell told Sphinx he was out, and Leah rolled her eyes.

"Are you ready to go home or you want to stay for a little while."

"I'm good we can leave."

"Give me your keys." I did as I was told for the first time in a long time. Sphinx led the way he placed his hands behind my lower back and ushered me to valet.

"Damn Malone, it's good to see you again."

"Hey, Horace, it's good seeing you too." Damn Horace looked good, shit.

"Who the fuck was that Malone?"

"Does it matter, he just spoke, and that's it."

"He eye fucked you too. I know niggas, and I don't trust him."

"Hey, Lil momma can I get a minute of your time?"
I looked over my shoulder, and it was Kase. I really didn't
feel like I talking I just wanted to kick it with my girls
shake my ass curve a few niggas that's it.

"Sure." Leah was blowing on the hookah rolling her
eyes. Layla was laughing. Shon and Dino shook their head.
I stepped away from our section Kase, and I were talking.
He asked me did I want to dance. Of course, I love to
dance, he grabbed my hand and led me to the dance floor.
The DJ played **Boo'd Up** by **Ella Mai.**

Ooh don't ever get over you until I find something
new
That get me high like you do
Ooh, don't ever get over you until I find something
new
That get me high like you do

I love this song everybody in the club was singing it
even the niggas. I was in my zone. Kase was behind me,
and his hands were on my hips, I was grinding all on this
nigga.

"Aye partner this me right here. I need to cut in." I
knew his voice from anywhere. It sent chills through my
body.

Malone

Man listen, Leah, Layla and I were having a fucking ball. I swear ATL nights are the best. We're both single minus, Layla, it's just like old times. I miss us hanging out like we use too. We decided to go to The Opium it was lit Money Bag Yo and Quavo are in the building.

All the hoes were out tonight. Yona and Rocky's dusty ass were in the building. Mignon was posted by the bar. Leah, Layla, and I were in our own section. I couldn't drink hard liquor or smoke on the hookah, but I had one glass of red wine.

It was perfect I didn't need much I had a natural high. I met this nigga at the bar named Kase it just so happens that his VIP section is right by ours. I wasn't looking for anything serious I'm pregnant by a lunatic, and I didn't need anybody getting touched because of me, but tonight I could flirt a little bit. Leah, Layla, and I snapped up a few pictures we were dripping on these hoes. Shon and Dino were posted up. I didn't fuck with Tory like that she knew not to come near me.

"OG good looking out I'm on my way out." She loves for me to show my ass. I'm sitting at home missing her, and she's out here giving niggas hope, and she's pregnant with my child. Fresh out the County Party. Who came up with this shit? She's about to be fresh out and get a nigga killed too.

My phone rang it was Vell I don't know what the fuck he wanted this time a night. He was lonely just like me.

"Yeah."

"What's up, you trying to get out tonight?"

"Nah I'm in for the night."

"Oh, your baby sitting while Malone and Leah are out shaking their ass?"

"Malone's at home I dropped her off."

"Nah nigga log on Snap right now, they are live at the spot right now."

"Hold on." I logged into Snap Chat on my phone. Malone and Leah were turning the fuck up. Layla was right with them. Hash tag Fresh Out the County Party. She's pregnant with this little bitty ass shit on like she doesn't fucking belong to me.

"Sphinx, you see that shit, my nigga?"

"Yeah OG what you trying to do. I'm putting my clothes on now meet me up there she got me fucked up. Every nigga that's smiling is about to see what's up."

"It's on I'll swoop you I'm outside of your house right now. Leah can ride with me and Malone can ride with you."

Chapter 14

Sphinx

I imagined Malone's first night home totally different, but it is what it is. I refuse to chase her, but at the end of the day, I gave it all I got. I don't know what the fuck to do. The devil is on my back heavy. The hoe in me is telling me to say fuck it and let her be.

I want to change I don't want to fuck a different bitch every day of the week. It's hard when the one you want doesn't want to be with you. I know she needed her space, but I wanted to be in her space. What the fuck am I going to tell Jah and Kennedy when they wake up that their mother isn't here, and they won't be living here with me and Samaya anymore?

Jah was my young nigga, and I enjoyed having him around. Kennedy and Samaya loved living together. I didn't want to break that up because of Malone's in her feelings. I know she thought it was a female texting my phone, but it was her mother.

I slicked down my baby hairs. I applied a little foundation to my face. I painted my lips nude. I needed a pedicure tomorrow I would get that done. I coated my toes with a clear polish just for a little shine. I shot Leah a text and told her I was on my way. I couldn't sit in this house because I would think about Sphinx all night. I missed him already, but he needed to sweat a little bit.

"They're glad to have you back. What's up with you and Sphinx are y'all together or what? He's real animate about keeping my children as if they were his own."

"No, we're not together." I wasn't ready to tell Crim that I was pregnant by Sphinx.

"Oh okay, when can I see you? You know I owe you my life. Can I take you out to lunch?"

"We'll see each other soon; you don't owe me anything. I'm going to hit you back tomorrow I'm tired."

"I love you, Malone."

"Good night Crim."

"You don't love me anymore?"

"I'll always have love for you, but I'm not in love with you. I'm not going to say it just to validate you." I refuse to go back and forth with Crim. I wanted to go out and let my hair down and sip a glass of wine. I wanted to shake my ass since I'm fresh up out the county. It's hot outside too, and I'm barely showing. I'm carrying the twins very well, ass and titties.

I thumbed through my closet I found a cute little white fitted dress. It accentuated my curves very well. I didn't feel like doing anything to my hair. I washed it and decided to wear it curly in its natural state.

"I hope it's two girls I can't deal with another Jah. You need to tell Sphinx you're pregnant with his kids, he has the right to know."

"I am when I have them, but I have the rights to not deal with his ass until I want too."

"Okay, so where are we going?"

"Anywhere I'm coming to your side of town."

"I don't want that crazy motherfucka to come to my house and act a fool."

"Trust me he's not, we have an understanding." Leah and I finished chopping it up fuck Sphinx he was free to do him, and I was free to do me. I know it'll be consequences when I have the babies oh well. I'll deal with that when it comes. I haven't heard from Crim I need to see what's up with him. I dialed his number, and he answered on the first ring.

"Malone what's up, they finally freed my wife?"

"What's up Crim, cut the bull shit how you been?"

"I'm good and you?"

"I'm good glad to be home and back with my babies."

It's a reason why she wasn't there to welcome me home, and I need to know that. I grabbed my phone out of my bra. I dialed Leah's phone number she answered on the first ring.

"I heard you was free. I was waiting on you to call me."

"You heard? I was wondering why you weren't over Sphinx's house when I was released."

"Vell and I aren't together?"

"What happened?"

"Girl he was fucking Mignon and Yona spilled the tea. I tagged that bitch a few times and him too. I couldn't wait to tell you."

"I thought he was different, are you okay? Let's go out. I'm kid free for tonight, and I'm fresh out the county."

"I'm great you know I wear my heart on my sleeve. You live, and you learn I trusted Vell, but I'm not surprised at all. I'm down to turn a corner. I don't have time for your baby daddy and his brother."

"I haven't told Sphinx the babies are his yet."

"Babies, bitch don't tell me you're pregnant with twins again."

"Yes, again."

Malone

Sphinx can be in his feelings all he wants. I'm in mine too. The ride home was silent we didn't say anything to each other his phone kept ringing, and he kept laughing. I'm sure it was a bitch calling he wanted to get up under my skin it wouldn't work this time. I thought about moving out of state but since he's came to his senses about us not being together and he let me leave.

I'll stay right here in Atlanta. Once I have the babies depending on how I feel I might tell him. I might not I pray they don't come out looking like him. I'm sure they will, the moment I laid eyes on him and was in his presence his children knew who he was. I felt them move. We could co-parent he's a wonderful father I couldn't take that away from him.

He maybe a wonderful lover too but I'm not willing to find out. He pulled up at my house I got out the car I entered my number in the keypad. He pulled off he didn't wait to see if I got in the house good. Now that I'm home I had to call Leah.

"I'm trying to hurt your feelings? I'm not even about to do this with you. Everything is my fault now. I'll take the blame if it means that you'll leave. I refuse to go back and forth with you."

"I'm gone Malone, and you can leave just know it's no coming back. I gave you the opportunity to tell me how you feel, but you can't even do that. When you give birth, I want a DNA test. I need proof because I'm not taking your word for anything. I'll see you when I see you. Everything you do in the darks comes to the light. For your sake and not mine the child you're carrying better not be mine.

If it is and you denied me the chance to be around because of your feelings, it'll be some problems. I'm beast in these streets, but I don't play about my family and my children."

"Sphinx, can you take me home now?"

"Yeah, if you're ready to go now. I'll drop Jah and Kennedy off at school tomorrow, and you can pick them up from there. I'll drop their stuff off at your mother's."

She wanted to go home that bad she can leave. I'm done talking I don't have anything else to say to her. It's wrap I refuse to chase someone who can't tell me how she feels.

"There's nothing you can do but leave me alone and stay out of my way. I don't want you to make anything up to me."

"Malone, why are you trying to hurt my feelings? I said I was sorry and I mean it. I'm man enough to admit that I fucked up. I'm man enough to right all my wrongs. The first day I met you I wanted you. I know I'm not your average nigga and I don't do shit like everybody else. I do shit my way.

What more can I do? You know how I feel about you. I love you, and that's all I want to do is love you. You won't even to let me do that. I've put myself out there more than once for you. I can own up to all my shit. I killed a nigga behind you, and I'll do it again because I love you and I'm in love with you. I don't want to see nobody else with you.

Loving you is hard because you won't allow me to do it. I could easily fuck you over, but I don't want to do that. If you don't want this, I'll stop trying because I don't want to keep looking like a fool. I can get back to being me, and I'll find somebody who'll accept me for me flaws and all."

"Sphinx, can you please stop? I don't want you to touch me. I don't want to be anywhere near you. You and I aren't together. I don't give a fuck about you buying this house I don't want it. My kids and I aren't living here. I just want to go home. If this house is so big why are you over here on my side of the house?"

"I wanted to check on you."

"Don't check on me I'm good. I'm letting you know now that I'm leaving here tomorrow rather you like it or not."

"No, you're not."

"I am Sphinx, do you actually think that I want to be around you? I can't sit in your presence and act like everything is okay and it's not. It'll never be, and I have the right to choose rather or not I want to be here, and I don't. Whoever you were fucking and entertaining while I was away you can continue to do so."

"Malone."

"Good bye Sphinx, please leave me alone, there's nothing that you could do or say to get me to change my mind. Nothing."

"I'm sorry Malone! What can I do to make shit right between us? I know I fucked up and I'll spend my life making it up to you. Whatever you want I'll do it."

 Chapter 13

Sphinx

Malone knows how to drive a nigga crazy. I swear she does her stubborn ass didn't even come back to dinner. I was checking the surveillance on my phone to make sure she didn't sneak out. Everybody was already gone, and the kids were asleep. I walked in our room, and she wasn't in the bed. I went in the bathroom, and she was still in the tub. I stuck my hand in the water it was still warm, but it was turning cold. I reached my hand inside the tub and let the water. Malone looked and me, and I looked at her.

"I'm good you didn't have to do that. You can leave." I ignored Malone and continued to do what I was about to do. I knew she wanted to argue I didn't want to argue. Malone stood up, she tried to exit the tub, and I was right on her heels. I grabbed the towel, so I could properly dry her off. I grabbed the Argon oil off my dresser, so I could give her a massage. She sat on the bed and looked at me. I knelt in front of her and grabbed her feet.

Where was Leah and why wasn't she here? I can't believe Crim let Jah and Kennedy stay with Sphinx. My whole life has changed within 30 days. I'll stay here for tonight, but I'm going home tomorrow.

"I could never be mad at you Layla I just don't like being held against my will. Sphinx and I don't have anything to talk about."

"I can relate, Sphinx's he's in love with you Malone. I swear I never seen him do the things that he does for you."

"He doesn't love me if he did he wouldn't do half the shit he does. He doesn't even know what love is and neither do I. I don't want to find out either. I'm good on love and niggas too."

"Don't be like that Malone. Everybody ain't out to hurt you. Sphinx has done a lot of foul shit to you. You can forgive but never forget."

"I hear you, Layla, I'm so happy that you and Shon are back together."

"I am too" Layla, and I finished chopping it up. I stripped naked I don't know if I'll be able to make it back to dinner. I know I'm not going back to dinner I'm in my feelings, and I have every right to be. I ran me a nice hot bubble bath. I wanted to soak and just think about everything that's going on around me.

I lit a few candles and poured a little bubble bath in the tub. The tub was filled, and the water temperature was to my liking. I climbed in just closed my eyes. I had a million and one things on my mind.

"Okay, ma." Since when she has tip toed around anything. Layla and Ms. Shaolin were following us to the kitchen also. We made it to the kitchen. I placed my hands-on hip.

"Malone, Sphinx brought this house for the two of you. This is your home the kids have been living here with him since you've been away. The two of y'all need to sit down and talk and figure out what y'all are going to do."

"I don't care about him buying this house. I didn't tell him to do it. What the fuck do we need to talk about? I want to go home to my house. I want to be in my own space and far away from him." Layla and Ms. Shaolin was looking at me like I was crazy.

"Malone, I know how you feel, trust me I've been there Shon did the same shit to me. I'm a woman before anything, and I'm riding with you regardless. Just hear him out I don't know how I can sneak you out of here. If I could, I would."

"Why do I have to sneak out? You know what show me to my side of the house." My mother and Ms. Shaolin started fixing plates. Layla and I were walking.

"Malone don't be mad at me."

I missed her so much. Tears poured down my face. Shon stood right behind my mother; we haven't been in a good space in a long time since Twin died. He looked me, and I looked at him.

"I'm sorry Shon." I cried.

"Shh, stop crying. Don't apologize you did nothing wrong. I have too, let you grow up eventually. I don't like it, but it is what it is." He pulled me in for a hug I missed my brother so much. I prayed every night that he pulled through and God didn't take him from me. I looked around the room I was looking for Leah and Vell I didn't see them.

"Malone, you want to change clothes?" The room got quiet. My face turned up instantly. Yeah, I want to change clothes at home. I had to choose my words wisely because our kids were in attendance.

"I will when I get home. Ma, can you take me and my kids home?" All eyes were on me. Don't get me wrong everybody here was family, but I know they didn't expect me to stay here with him? What part of the game is this?

"Come here Malone let me speak with you for a minute."

"No, you're making me sick I can't be around you." I haven't thrown up one time while I was pregnant. I'm almost three months, and this is the first time when he's this close to me.

"Come on let me get you in the house, so you can lay down and eat, and I'll be out your way. You don't have to worry about me. I don't want to make you sick. How many weeks are you? Call your baby daddy so I can speak with him and let him know I'll be raising his kids."

"Don't worry about how far along I am. Me and my baby daddy have a date tomorrow."

"Y'all got a date?" I wasn't even about to argue with him. If my babies were inside of this house. I wanted to see them immediately. I picked up my pace and started walking toward the house I could feel Sphinx staring a whole in me. I finally made it toward the door.

"It's open," he yelled. I opened the door.

"Surprise, welcome home Malone." My whole family was in attendance my babies ran up to me. I gave them the biggest hugs. I placed kisses all over their faces. I missed them so much. My momma and Shon were right behind them. I jumped in my mother's arms.

"I made sure Jah and Kennedy was straight. I paid all your bills. Fuck your job I can take care of you. I spoke with your school you can graduate on time long as you make up your assignments."

"I don't want you to take care of me. I can take care of myself. Stay away from my kids okay. Can you take me home?"

"We are home Jah and Kennedy are inside with everybody else."

"We don't live together. I don't know what kind of games you're trying to play, but I'm good on them. Keep being a bachelor I'll catch a cab home."

"Look at me when you're talking to me. This our home. I know you may be feeling some type of way right now but you ain't leaving here unless you're in a body bag. I didn't hurt you on purpose. I'll give you some space. This house is big enough where we don't have to see each other but you ain't leaving."

"I don't want to fucking look at you. Stop forcing shit on me because I can't force anything on you. I want to be in my own house far away from you." I cried. I pushed him in away from me. I hated the way he smelled. I threw up instantly.

"Are you okay?"

"I'm not getting out this car. Sphinx I want to go home to check on my babies that's it. I can't sit here and pretend like you and I are cool, and we're not. We could never be after you and Deja fucked around or whatever y'all were doing it was wrap. I sat behind bars for thirty days behind some bullshit you done.

You make my flesh crawl I need to get checked because you will fuck anything moving. I pray to God I don't have anything. I fucking hate you." Before I could say anything else. He snatched me out the Bentley, and he was all up in my face. My heart was pounding. I just want him to leave me alone.

"I'm sorry Malone, but you need to watch your fucking mouth. I know I fucked up and I hate you got caught up behind my bullshit. I don't have anything when you got locked up they checked you for everything. If you had something, they would've told you."

"Can you take me home, please? You're missing the fucking point. I was away from my kids for thirty days. I'm not going to be able to graduate on time because of you. I lost my job because of you. I've lost a lot because of you."

Malone

Who told him to come and pick me up? He's the last motherfucka I want to see if it wasn't for him I would've never step foot in the County jail. Did he, think it was okay to pick me up? I want my babies that's it.

I need to make an appointment with my OBGYN to check on my new little ones. I hope he don't ask me any questions about the babies I'm carrying. I know it's childish not to tell him I'm carrying his babies, but I can't deal with him. I don't even want him around me. He sealed his fate with me after the whole Deja situation.

I tried so hard to forget that shit while I was locked up, but I couldn't. It fucked with me so bad my chest was hurting. The car came to complete stop. I looked up, and we were in the middle of nowhere. It was a big ass mansion it looked like a castle.

I don't know whose house this is. I don't care to find out. He jumped out the car and pressed a button. The back door to the Bentley opened. I didn't even bother to look at him because this isn't my house and I didn't plan on getting out.

"Malone let's go?"

"Malone let's go." She looked at me and ignored me and continued to play with her phone. My eyes were trained on her. I grabbed her hand, and she snatched it away from me.

"I'm waiting on my ride Sphinx you can leave."

"Your mother isn't coming I asked could I pick you up instead."

"Why would you want to do that for? I don't want to see you or hear you at all."

"I understand that, and the ball is in your court. I don't want to make a scene out here with you. Let me take you home, and I promise to be out your way. I got you these flowers." She took the roses and threw them on the ground.

"Okay." Malone's stubborn ass followed me to my Bentley. Instead of her sitting up front she sat in the back. It was so much tension between us a knife couldn't cut it. I had so much stuff I wanted to say, and I could tell she had some stuff she wanted to say.

"Malone are you hungry?"

"No, if I was hungry I don't want to get shit to eat with you. Take me home and don't say shit else to me. You and I have nothing to talk about." I didn't even say shit to her because I didn't feel like arguing with her.

I guess it was really time for a nigga to grow up and stop acting a fool out here in these streets and stop dogging these hoes out. My mother always told me when you find the one you'll know and decide to change your ways.

I knew Malone was the one, but she wanted to act like she wasn't. I could commit to her I wanted to commit to her and only her. I just wanted her to express how she felt toward me. She was grown, but she didn't want to act like she was grown. All the back and forth shit stops today. I'm sick of it.

Trina, she's one of the officers that were on my payroll, she sent me a text stating that Malone would be walking out the gates any minute now. I grabbed the white roses that I had for her and sat on the bench waiting for her to come out. Trina sent another text stating Malone should be walking out now.

I looked over my shoulders. I saw her shadow standing in the door. I played it cool until she reached me. It was already a lot of people out here heading to traffic court.

I didn't want her to make a scene. I knew she would show her ass because I'm probably the last nigga she wants to see. I stood up and walked toward her; she was playing with her phone not paying attention.

$\mathcal{C}$hapter 12

$\mathbf{S}$phinx

Malone has been locked up for over a month now.
We finally beat the case that was pending against her. Deja
wasn't amongst the living anymore. I know she's pregnant
with my child. I know because I feel it. I know she's
carrying something that belongs to me. The whole time
she's been locked up I haven't been able to see her. I'm
above the law, and I wanted to sneak in prison to see her on
a numerous of occasions to make sure she's good.

My employees I had working for me at the County
jail, told me she advised them if I was to take a step near
her she tell who really killed Twin. I knew she was bluffing
or else she would've told by now.

I respected her privacy, but I miss her, and I wanted
to apologize. She's supposed to be released today. I've
been out side of the jail waiting for her. I had to beg Leilani
to let me pick her up. She wasn't budging at all. We really
needed to talk. I'm out here in these streets going crazy
because I don't know if she's good or not.

I slid Leah's ring back on her finger. Leah continued to ignore me. I started sucking on her neck she started moaning. I grabbed her panties, and she was wet.

"Stop Vell, please don't do this again." She moaned.

"Why not you're mine?"

"I was yours but us having sex only complicates things. It doesn't solve anything. I don't care how good you fuck and suck me. I'm still leaving." I wasn't hearing shit Leah was screaming she wasn't leaving this house at all.

You matter to me I care about you. Don't throw away what we have over one fuck up. I put it on my life, and God can take me right now. I'll never do it again. I don't want to know what it feels like to lose you."

"If you care so much Vell allow me to leave. Allow me to want to come back to you. Don't force me to stay because I don't want too. I'm not walking away because of one fuck up. I know I'm not those other chicks. I'm walking away because I want too, and I know I deserve more. I'll choose myself every time. You need to see what feels like to lose me. Don't keep me here because you're scared that I'm going to go out and fuck the next man."

"I do care that's why I don't want you to leave, and I'm begging you stay. Tell me what I gotta do. I'll be Keith Sweat begging ass if you want me too. I want you to always choose yourself first. I need you to choose to stay so we can work it out. I only want to be with you. You watched me dropped that nigga in broad day light.

I haven't done some hot ass shit like that in a long time. A nigga can't get at you period you're my fiancé, and you can put this ring back on your finger too. It ain't no breaking up. Can we make up I'm sorry?"

Bitch don't mention my name if I'm not the nigga that's fucking you. If she thought Leilani tagged that ass, she wasn't ready for me. I'm the wrong nigga to speak on. Mignon kept blowing up my phone bitch we're done. Leah thought she was about to leave me I wasn't having that. She came home with me, and she started packing her shit up. I don't know what she was packing her shit up for because she wasn't leaving. I walked upstairs to our room Leah had two suit cases full of shit.

"Come here, Leah." She looked over her shoulder and continued to pack. I walked up on her and grabbed the stuff out of her hands. I tossed Leah on the bed forcing her to look at me.

"What?"

"I love you, and I want you to stay. I'm not letting you leave our house."

"I don't want to stay."

"Leah, I cheated on you. I hate to even say the shit out loud because I fucked up. I made a mistake. In my thirty-five years of living, I've cheated on plenty of females. I never cared about getting caught because they didn't mean shit to me. I know they weren't going anywhere they accepted anything that I was offering.

Chapter 11

Vell

I'm not a dog ass nigga. I love Leah she got my heart. What we had was real none of it was fake. I never wanted to embarrass her in front of everybody. I dogged plenty of hoes, but I didn't want to dog Leah. I was wrong but all it took was for her to catch me one time and I'll never do it again.

If I got caught doing anything I shouldn't be doing it. Mignon wasn't worth it. I should've sent that bitch home when I saw her posted up. She talks to much it blew me Yona knew the spot we were fucking at.

She could've set me up with a nigga or anything. Yona had to go a bitch can't blow my spot up and live to tell about it. I don't give a fuck about what her and Shon had going on she shouldn't have put me in that shit for that reason alone she was going to die. You have an issue with my sister more the reason I need to kill your hoe ass.

"I don't give a fuck about none of that shit Vell. You haven't learned your lesson because I haven't taught you one yet. Nothing you're saying matters right now. Can you please move so I can leave?"

"You ain't leaving without me because we came together."

"I'm leaving without you. Do you think I want to sit around here in front all these people looking stupid after you've been exposed to cheating? I'm not that type of bitch Vell I'm not built like that. I play niggas how they play me. I'm always on some get back shit. The only difference now is you're not my nigga. I don't have to get you back. I can do me without any consequences."

"It's always consequences fucking with a nigga like me. You belong to me remember that." He wasn't feeling anything I said. He snatched my skirt off and ripped my shirt. He threw my legs over his waist. He dropped his shorts, he pulled his dick out and shoved it inside of me. He started pounding me. His dick felt so good. Normally I would match his rhythm stroke for stroke. Any other time I would've rode this big motherfucka like my life depended on it but not today. It was over for us, and he needed to accept it.

You stopped me from fucking him today, but tomorrow you might not be that lucky." I laughed.

"We ain't over it ain't no breaking up. I kill you before I'll let you leave me."

"Go ahead and kill me because I'm leaving and you're already dead to me." He pulled out his gun and cocked it back.

"Can't we just talk about this shit Leah? You really want me to kill you because I won't let you run off and fuck another nigga?"

"Let me do me Vell. I swear you don't have to worry about me. Relationships ain't for everybody, and I told you that shit wasn't for me. I tried, and I'm not trying no more. I don't have to accept shit you're offering. Why do we have to talk about it now?" I pushed Vell out my way I was leaving him rather he accepted it or not. I don't give niggas passes.

"I fucked up one-time Leah. One fucking time yes, I was fucking her before I met you and I didn't stop fucking her. I don't want her, and I don't want to marry her. She doesn't mean shit to me. I learned my lesson, and I'm sorry."

"I told you to leave, but you didn't want to do that. This shit me, and Leah got going on is dangerous. That's my fiancé no matter what she says. It's murking season for any nigga she attempts to bring to the table." Vell shot him five times in the head. I ain't never seen anything like it before this shit was not normal. I started shaking this nigga is real live crazy.

"Did anybody see anything?" Mrs. Leilani yelled.

"No."

"Good because if I hear anything other than that, you motherfuckas going out the same way. Vell, you know the routine." Vell and his niggas dragged Cohen to the back yard.

"Give me the keys I'm out." I snatched them out of his pocket. He picked me up and pushed me toward the back of the house. I kept pushing him off me.

"You see what the fuck you made me do? You were really trying to go fuck that nigga?" I refuse to even look at him. He grabbed my face roughly forcing me to look at him. He started choking me. I punched his stupid ass in his chest and eyes.

"Let me go please it's a wrap. We're here because of you, not me. If I want to go fuck another nigga that's my business. I'm single, and so are you.

"Vell back the fuck up, you had a whole bitch out here and didn't say shit. Now ain't the time you were doing you let me do me."

"Leah I'm not trying to make a scene at Leilani's, but I will."

"You don't have too."

"Leah if you get in that car I swear you and that nigga won't live pass the stop sign. I will have my niggas at the corner to light his car up, and you'll die right along with that nigga. Try me I beg you too."

"Why do you want to do all of this Vell? You got caught, but you never had to creep to fuck any bitch. You can continue to fuck her. If I want to fuck him for a few hours what's the problem? You can have this ring back we ain't shit." I took my ring off my finger and threw it at his ass.

"Leah are you good?"

"Yeah, she good Cohen, you can pull off. I don't want you to get caught up in our shit it's dangerous."

"I asked Leah, she can speak for herself she called me up here." Before I could speak up.

Cohen's passenger door was snatched open. Vell ran to the driver side and pulled Cohen out his car.

"Come in." It was Layla and Leilani. I continued to beat my face I had a date tonight, and Vell wasn't the nigga courting me.

"I'm sorry Leah my brother ain't shit. I smacked the fuck out his ass for you. Leah, what are you about to do?"

"Layla don't apologize for him. Fuck him; he said fuck me. He hasn't tried to apologize or anything, but I'm not looking for an apology he can keep it. What I will say is I have zero fucks to give, and he forgot how I gave it up."

"Don't scoop down to his level your better than that. It's not worth it."

"Oh, but I am. I don't get mad I get even. My date just pulled up. Watch me work."

"Don't do it, Layla."

"It's too late." I grabbed my purse and told Leilani to trash my clothes. I made my way down the steps, and as soon I exited the front door. My nigga Cohen was posted up in the Maserati all eyes were on me. I could feel Vell starring a whole in me. I put an extra pep in my step, he wasn't sure if I was walking to that a car or not, but he knew I was. He walked up behind me and grabbed my neck. I pushed him off me. He grabbed my hair.

Leah

Vell out of all the niggas I chose to be exclusive with. He was the one to fuck me over. Mignon, how could you sit in my face and continue to fuck my fiancé? I don't even know why I was surprised because that's just the type of bitch she was, and I had no business keeping company with her.

Yona came all the way over here to spill the tea and got her ass handed to her also. Vell didn't even break the shit up. Leilani had to get me up off this bitch I damn near killed her ass. I needed a ride home I refuse to ride home Vell. If he still wanted to be on some hoe shit, I could too. I could show a nigga better than I could tell him.

I kept a few niggas in rotation. I went to Malone's old room to shower. I found me a cute outfit to put on. I sent a text to one of my throw backs he was about to pull up in about ten minutes. I knew Vell was still outside. Ask me, do I give a fuck? No, if he was still fucking Mignon after he proposed it meant nothing to him. He just wanted to lock me down. He has life fucked he can do him, and I'll continue to do me. I heard a knock at Malone's door.

"Leah this was before your time."

"Mignon I don't give a fuck about shit that was before your time. Are you fucking him now?" Mignon was quiet. I stood to my feet, so I could let Leah here the recording.

"Listen Leah I got proof." Something told me to record this bitch earlier I'm glad I did. Leah pounced on Mignon like a fucking tiger. I didn't mind leaving, but I was leaving after I watched Mignon get her ass whooped. Vell was grilling me I don't know what for he should've kept his dick in his pants. Stop fucking a bitch that talks too much.

This was just a warning don't let this shit happen again because the next time I'll kill you. Do you fucking understand me?"

"Yes."

"Good, Mignon get this bitch away from my house, and you can take your hoe ass on too. I see everything going and coming on MCafee and Candler Road. I'm the Governor on this block. I saw that little shit you just pulled a few minutes ago. Leah watch the company you keep."

"She didn't come with me, Mrs. Leilani."

"Mignon, you can't help me?"

"No Yona I can't, nobody told you to come down here to fuck with Shon he doesn't want you. How many times does he have to tell you? He's happily in love with Layla move around. You always fucking up shit." I can't believe this bitch she's the one that called me.

"Mignon you have a lot of nerve. I'm the wrong bitch to cross.

Tell Leah about you fucking Vell twice a week at the Marriott in Decatur, but you smile up in her face Monday through Sunday and sip wine on Tuesday. I don't hear you hoe speak up." I laughed. Leah approached Mignon and Vell was grilling Mignon.

"Mignon is this true."

I won't tell you a second time. See bitches got the game wrong this is my house and a bitch can't disrespect me in my shit.

 I'm sorry Shon, but it's Lay Day, and I'm about to Lay this bitch."

"I'm pregnant Shon you need to tell your mother to chill."

"Yona cut the bull shit. I've never fucked you raw, and anytime I busted a nut. I made sure I busted on your face. It's only one woman that's had the pleasure to feel this 100% beef it's not you."

"Shon you don't have to explain shit to this bitch. If she's pregnant, I'll give her free abortion." Mrs. Leilani walked up on me. I wasn't about to just stand there and let her hit me. I swung and ducked. She ducked and upper cut me in my jaw. My shit was leaking she started tagging me real fast. I could barely keep my balance due to the pill. My chest was hurting she was tagging me in my chest. My knees buckled, and I fell to the ground holding my chest. I felt my hair being yanked from my scalp. She drugged me to the tree and rammed my face in the stoop.

"I told you to leave my house, but no you wanted to pop off. Leave my son the fuck alone he's a married man, and he's not checking for you.

"Whatever you say?" As soon as we made it to Leilani's, everybody was looking at us. Shon had his back turned I recognized his tattoos from anywhere. The waves that sat on his head I couldn't wait until he turned around. I started to walk up on him, and that's what I was about to do until Leilani walked passed me and looked.

"Excuse me Yona but what are you doing at my house? You know you've never been welcome to come here. Layla is my daughter in law, and she will not be disrespected you can leave."

"Mrs. Leilani, I wanted to check on Shon I had to make sure he's okay. We were really good friends."

"He's okay but you heard my mother in law you need to roll." I looked over my shoulder and put a mug on my face. It was Layla standing behind me with her arms folded and Leah was right behind her.

"Shon has a mouth of his own he can tell me he's okay with his own mouth then I'll leave." Layla approached me like she was about to jump bad. Shon appeared in the flesh and grabbed her. Damn, he was fine.

"Sit pretty Layla like you been doing. Your mother in law got this. I told the hoe once to leave my house.

"Okay." I saw Mignon headed in my direction. She looked real cute half dressed. Leah must not be out here if Vell is in her face. I'll ask her about that later. I came here for one nigga, and that nigga was Shon. Mignon finally dragged her feet. after she bended over and bounced her ass few times pretending like she dropped something. I know her hoe ass was doing that because of Vell.

"Bout time you made it. You look cute. I grabbed you a Lime-a-Rita. Here's a pill. Do you want to pop one?"

"Yep." I took the pill and washed it down with the Lime-a Rita. I could feel the Ecstasy taking over me instantly.

"Shon was posted outside with his niggas."

"Oh really, hold this drink, so I can make sure my lip stick is popping. Leah must not be here if you and Vell are doing all that flirting out in public."

"Oh, she's down there, she's in the house. He's mad because I'm out here and all his niggas are looking. Last I heard he put a ring on it so why is he worried about little ole me, that's unless he still wants to get this pussy during the week. What Leah don't know won't hurt her. It's all about the bag for me. Vell had it, and he can keep me on payroll. If you want to be technical about it. I was fucking him first we just never stopped."

Mignon called me and told me everybody was posted on the block at Leilani's she threw Shon a cookout. I knew Layla was there, but I didn't give a fuck just because Shon was your man or fiancé doesn't mean that I would stop trying to fuck with him.

I wanted to be by his side so bad when he was in the hospital, but Layla was there morning noon and night. I just needed to get him by himself. I know we could still be something. Shon's cookout had to be something serious because traffic was jammed from Mcafee to Candler Road. I parked at the flea market and walked down to Leilani's.

All the niggas were posted up I made sure I was extra cute just in case Shon had second thoughts or I could come up on a new nigga in the process. I was dead broke too and just started a new job at the call center I wasn't feeling it $11.00 an hour wasn't going to cut it. I could only afford to buy a PINK or Forever21 outfit with this little bitty ass check. I needed a come up quick. I finally made it to Leilani's it was thick I felt a little uncomfortable walking passed all these niggas by myself. I called Mignon she answered on the first ring.

"Hello, where you at Yona?"

"I'm walking toward the house meet me halfway."

Chapter 10

Yona

Be careful who you cross and who you shit on. Every bitch in the hood was my friend and cool with me because I was fucking with Shon. The moment Shon and I stopped fucking around, and he embarrassed me on the block in front of everybody.

All my so-called friends disappeared and stop fucking with me. I was the one they called when they needed something. When I needed a shoulder to cry on nobody was around. To make matters worse, Shon took his Audi A8 from me, so I was back to driving my Honda Accord. I was your go to girl everybody wanted to treat me like an outcast since I was fucking with Shon especially Mignon. I wanted to see Shon I heard he got hit up bad and he was out the hospital.

I was surprised to see Day with them; he didn't take any time snatching Chanta up. Judah knew Day they've done some business together in the past. Sphinx threw a few cocktail bombs. We watched the hall explode.

"Shaolin If I don't see you later you know I'm at home already. Thank you for your hospitality and call me when you touch down."

"Leilani you're leaving so soon?"

"Yes, and I'm taking these four with me." She pointed at our sons and Dino. Before I could say anything, Lorenzo walked up to Leilani and said a few words. I watched Shon like a hawk I could tell he had an issue. He was worse than Sphinx. He couldn't wait to approach Leilani and Lorenzo to see what's going on. I'll ask her about that later. I wanted to lay up on the beach with my fiancé for a few days.

Chanta pulled a sawed off shot gun from behind her back. Bodies were dropping left and right. I made sure we had the upper hand because we had silencers. We were dropping the mob like flies. I was ducking and dodging bullets.

"Shaolin what the fuck is this?" Zeke asked.

"What the fuck does it look like? I can't do business with you. This is Big Vell's mob they don't know me, and I don't know them. I'm rebuilding my shit from the ground up. Remember you shot me in Atlanta I looked you dead in your eyes?"

"Momma, is this the nigga that shot you?" I nodded my head yes Sphinx and Vell pulled their masks off, so Zeke turned around and looked. He patted his back pocket for a gun.

"Aye pussy I want you to look me in my eyes. I'm your fucking killer." Sphinx and Vell yelled as they emptied the clip in Zeke. This was the end of the Haitian Mob but the beginning of something new. Judah ran up to me and looked me over to make sure I was okay. He grabbed the gun out of my hand and passed it to Sphinx.

"She won't be needing this anymore." We left the dance hall and started to go our separate ways.

I sat on the stage I had the DJ to cut the music off. Judah sent me a text stating they just arrived and they were coming through the kitchen. Lorenzo and the other ones were coming through the front.

"Let me introduce myself. I'm Shaolin Baptiste, and I'm running the mob. I've always been in the background, but this is my shit. A lot of y'all may know me and some of y'all don't. Frankly, I don't give a fuck. Zeke will still be in charge. Business will continue to run as normal a lot of shit will change, and I'll let you know the changes as I make them. Do you have any questions?"

"I'm not working for a bitch?"

"Excuse me." I stood up and walked closer to this young nigga I wanted him to repeat what the fuck he said.

"You heard what the fuck I said." I emptied the clip right in his head. My sons don't even talk me to crazy. I don't know what Zeke told them, but I was Big Vell's muscle he needed me for protection.

"Do any of you feel the same way? If you do speak now, I don't need anybody doing business with my organization if they have a problem. Speak your peace now so I can CLEAR IT." Everybody was talking at once not paying attention to my sons coming in wetting shit up. Leilani tossed me an AK from behind the stage.

Judah and Lorenzo brought a black industrial van to pick up Sphinx, Vell, Shon, and Dino. They also brought a few of their most trusted men also. I don't think I've been this ready to put in work in a very long time. Anything affiliated with Big Vell had to go. He's been doing a lot of shady business lately that I'll have to clean up. This is the first thing that's going.

***

We made it to the dance hall; it looks like the mob made it before me. I knew Zeke would do this. I'm glad he did because I had this bitch surrounded and I could watch the surveillance from my smart watch. I never trusted Zeke.

"Chanta, Leilani are y'all ready to do this?"

"We were born ready; we got your back." Leilani, Chanta and I we used to run the streets heavy back in the day. I fell back when Big Vell went to jail, and I thought he died. I didn't care to be in them now. I had to take back the mob and pass it to my children. We entered the dance hall. I was in the front Leilani was to my right, and Chanta was to my left.

The mob was sitting around eating and drinking. I notice Zeke by the bar I tapped him on the shoulder. He followed suit.

Shaolin

Sphinx showed his ass last night. I'm not even surprised Vell was more reserved. Judah thought that was the funniest shit. It wasn't funny to me at all; he's a big ass baby. I'm too old to baby him more of the reason he needs to settle down and keep his dick in his pants.

He's trying to fuck up my shit because he's fucked up with Malone after this meeting Sphinx and I needed to have a serious conversation. The meeting was scheduled to happen in one hour. I needed everything to go exactly how I planned it. The boys were dressed and ready to go Chanta and Leilani were still getting dressed.

"I met with Zeke, Big Vell's right hand man last night. Every member affiliated with the mob will be in attendance. Here's the ear pieces when I tell y'all to come in and clear it I mean it. Every member must go.

It's four bullet proof vests in the box and four pieces of head gear. I have this orchestrated to perfection. No fuck ups no faces for future cases." I was ready to get this show on the road. Chanta and Leilani finally came downstairs suited and ready to go.

"I don't get a bad vibe from him either, but the thought of her living in Haiti doesn't sit right with me. I'm her protector I failed her once when she got shot, but I refuse to fail her again."

"You can't think like that Sphinx your mother is very capable of handling herself. Judah he wouldn't let anything happen to her. I witnessed that tonight. You need to get your shit together."

"I hear you. I'm trying to get myself together your daughter acts like she's not feeling me. I can't wait to snatch her ass up when she gets out."

"Give her reason not to." It was good chopping it up with Leilani only time would tell. My mind drifted back to Malone again. I missed her like crazy.

We do need to get to know each other because we're family. You're grown, and you should want your mother happy.

Layla, she's with Shon. Vell you just got engaged with Leah. Sphinx, you're still finding yourself, but your mother wants to be happy don't deny her that." We finished chopping it up. I didn't get a bad vibe from Judah, but I don't want my momma way over here.

I want her to be happy she deserves it but don't throw no shit on me like that again. I could tell she was mad, but she knows me. I see my mother at least three times a week and to not see her at all. I don't care if I'm grown or not.

I wanted to see my momma whenever the fuck I wanted too. Judah ended up staying the night my mother knew I wasn't feeling that shit. I don't want no man fucking my momma under the same roof as me. I heard a knock at my door.

"Come in." It was Leilani standing at the door laughing. I don't know what the fuck she was laughing for, she better not try to pull that shit either.

"Sphinx, what's up? Judah, he's good people. I can read people well. Your mother deserves to be happy allow her that."

"I'm not going anywhere Shaolin." He needed to shut the fuck up and let my mother talk.

"Thank you, Judah. I'm moving back to Haiti. After we have this meeting tomorrow with the Mob everything will be rightfully passed over to you. I'm going to stay out here for a week, and I'll come back home to get everything situated."

"Momma I don't want you moving back over here. I don't know him, and I don't trust him. I need to be able to see you daily. He can move to the states if he wants to be your husband."

"Sphinx, I want to earn your trust. I've been in love with your mother for years. How do you think I feel being away from my fiancé and not being able to see her every day? We have a home in Atlanta she could fly home whenever she likes. I don't want to be away from future wife anymore."

"I hear what you're saying but listen to what I'm saying. You know of me, but I don't know you. I'm not comfortable having my mother in another country, and I'm hours away. I need to get to know you, and then I'll consider letting her move over here. I'm not with it."

"I understand where you're coming from I agree. I was the same way about my mother.

"Let me introduce you. Sphinx this is Judah, my fiancé. I wanted him to meet you and Vell but not like this. Judah, I'm sorry I just got in. I needed to change clothes first before I called you."

"That's why I came over because it's passed an hour. I had to make sure nothing happened to you." I didn't like the way he looked at my momma, and I didn't like the way she looked at him. I'm killing this nigga I don't want him anywhere near my momma.

"What the fuck is going on down here?" Just the nigga I wanted to see OG motherfucking Vell.

"Vell meet Judah, your mother's fiancé?" I laughed. I knew he was about to go slap off. How are you engaged, and we don't know anything about it?

"Momma, what the fuck is Sphinx talking about?" My mother knew she had some explaining to do.

"Vell and Sphinx. I'm still your mother. I need you to watch your mouth and show me some fucking respect. Y'all maybe grown but I'll still put my foot up the both of y'all ass. Judah's my fiancé we've been dating for a few years now. Layla has met him already. I didn't tell the two of you because look how y'all are acting? Y'all are going to run him off."

Leilani was laughing I was talking to her ass too. They snuck upstairs like my word wasn't law. I heard the alarm go off again. I grabbed my gun off the table. It was older nigga walking through the door.

"Yo, who the fuck is you? What the fuck are you doing in my shit?" I had the gun pointed to his head. I'm ready to push a nigga shit, and normally I don't ask questions. I haven't even been here twenty fours, and I'm already about to catch a body.

"I'm Judah, Shaolin's fiancé you must be Sphinx." He laughed. I kept the gun trained on him. I don't trust niggas you could be the ops.

"Shaolin's fiancé? Momma get your ass down here now. It's a nigga here claiming to be your fiancé. I didn't sign off on that shit." This nigga thought this shit was funny. I didn't agree to my mother having a boyfriend. Any man that thought he could date her I was running his ass off and this nigga would be no different. My mother ran down the stairs panicking she knew I was crazy and this nigga could get it.

"Sphinx put the gun down please."

"I'm not. I don't know this nigga, and he doesn't know me." My mother snatched the gun out of my hand and smacked me in the back of my head.

Chapter 9

Sphinx

Sleep refused to find a nigga like me. I haven't sleep in weeks. To make matters worse, I'm in this foreign ass country, and it's after 1:00 a.m. and my mother still isn't home. I don't know what the fuck her and Leilani were up to, but I was about to find out. I've called her phone at least five times, and she refuse to answer. I'm keeper, and I need to be with her always. A nigga got at my mother once there wouldn't be a second time. I wanted to kill these niggas and keep it moving. We could discuss business on US soil. I heard the door open, and it was my mother and Leilani tip toeing in.

"Where the fuck has you two been? It's too late for y'all to be out and y'all not answering y'all phone like y'all God damn grown. Take y'all ass to bed and don't leave this fucking house without me."

"Excuse me I'm grown, and last I checked I was in labor with you eight hours it wasn't the other way around. My father is dead. Take your ass to bed."

They would kill him before he could introduce himself. Sphinx has already called me five times, and Vell sent me a few texts. So, what do you think about Lorenzo?"

"You know Sphinx can't wait to kill somebody. Judah, I like him for you."

"You still didn't answer my question about Lorenzo?"

"Shaolin he's okay I'm open to getting to know him." She smiled.

"I think he may be good for you. He was letting it be known that you we're with him."

"I didn't like that. I instantly thought about Sphinx and Malone. I'm not sure if I want a Haitian God or not."

"Bitch don't do my son, he loves her, and he loves hard. Trust me she's the only one I've ever seen him go ape shit over." Leilani and I finished chopping it up. I noticed Zeke came back with a crew full of niggas. They we're eying me and Leilani like a piece of meat. I already knew they had a problem with me running shit. Too bad after tomorrow I wouldn't even be a problem of theirs.

"You know I got you that'll never change. I had to get at Jacinda since Judah wouldn't let you. I don't trust Zeke or anybody affiliated with Big Vell and the Haitian Mob."

"I don't trust him either. He won't live passed tomorrow to be loyal to me. I called them all here, so I could get a look at every member. I wanted everybody in here so when we have the meeting tomorrow they'll die together. More of the reason why I didn't want our sons here. I don't need anybody to clock my moves. I clock theirs. None the less I could get at the niggas who hit me up and put the hit out on Shon and Layla. You guys could go back home Saturday, and I'll get to spend some with Judah."

"Let's definitely get that done. I love how you checked that bitch in your shit. I heard Judah giving you the business I could tell he was a boss. I noticed you were nervous about him waiting on you at the condo?"

"I knew it was coming only a matter of time. I love the way Judah handles me, yes, he's a boss he used to hustle with a us years ago. Of course, I was nervous about him meeting my sons.

"True, thank you I'll take from here, and I'll call you when I make it home."

"I don't want you to call me when you make it home. I want you to come home with me. I'll be at the condo waiting, and I'll introduce myself to your sons."

"Judah I'll come home to you just give me an hour. I need to be there when you meet my son's."

"Okay, you've got one hour." I wanted Judah in the worst way. I couldn't wait to go home to him. I couldn't let him meet Vell and Sphinx without me being there. The two of them will kill him and ruin my happiness before it starts. Lorenzo and Leilani exchanged a few words. I couldn't wait to ask what that was about. I noticed he kissed her cheek on the way out. Everybody was clearing the mansion out. I was waiting on Zeke to come back with the crew. I had a camera on my dress with facial recognition, so I could see who everybody was.

"Shaolin, what a night. I had fun despite the bullshit. Your fiancé is cool. I wish I would've known you were engaged I'll throw you an engagement party."

"I was going to tell you when I told Sphinx and Vell. Thank you for having my back as always."

"Sure."

"Jacinda was fucking Vell also he's the father of her fourteen-year-old daughter. She was my best friend. I never knew she was fucking him until he died, and her daughter's name was in his will at the bank. Everything is yours it's in the will he left the kids you knew nothing about a few bonds that couldn't be touched until they turn eighteen." I ran after Jacinda and grabbed her long ass weave and rammed her face in the marble floors. God could take me right now and wouldn't be able to keep my off this bitch. No wonder she wasn't answering the phone.

"Bitch don't ever think you could play me and live to tell about it." Judah grabbed me.

"She's not worth it Shaolin." Judah got me up off her, but Leilani tagged that bitch a few times until she tapped out. I knew Leilani killed that bitch because she checked her pulse.

"I want you to hurry up and handle your business. None of this shit is worth it if brings you out of your character." I loved it when Judah raised his voice at me.

"Judah, did I start it? I didn't want to do that, but she came for me, so I had to handle my business."

"I understand that, but you could've done it legally with the courts and police."

"We don't have anything to talk about. I don't have anything to do with your kids that's a personal problem. Hopefully, you have some money saved because any property of mine you had access to your rights have been revoked the day I killed that bastard you call a husband." Valencia attempted to jump bad I pounced on that hoe a few times don't get shit confused.

"Shaolin what do you need me to do?" Zeke asked.

"I need you to get that bitch and her kids up out of here. Round up everybody affiliated with the mob we need to discuss business. I need you to run this shit I'm in the states is that cool with you."

"Of course, you know my loyalty lies with you."

"Good to know Zeke get that bitch out my shit.

"Shaolin what do you need me to do?" My cousin Jacinda asked.

"I need you to get your disloyal ass out my face. You knew this nigga was alive for years and didn't say shit. I'm the reason you're living how your living but after today consider yourself cut off. Find a job because I'm not footing the bill."

"Are you fucking serious?"

"I'm dead ass serious."

"Shaolin, can I say one thing?" Valencia asked.

"Shaolin, do we have fucking problem?" Leilani yelled.

"We might Leilani I'm about to find out."

"Shaolin don't do this here." My cousin Jacinda yelled.

"Jacinda do you know this bitch? Pick a side."

"I'm her first cousin did she tell you that? She doesn't have to pick a side. Your statement alone lets me know what time it is. Blood doesn't make us a family but loyalty does."

"I'm not leaving, this is my home, and I'm running everything in Vell's absence."

"You don't have to go home, but you have to get the fuck out of here. I don't know what Big Vell told you, but I'm the connect. I run the Haitian Mob. It's my fucking mob. My family built this shit from crumbs to bricks. I've always been the overseer. I okay everything nothing moves around here unless I sign off on it."

"Is this true Zeke?" Zeke was Big Vell's right hand man, just the nigga I wanted to see. If he was here every nigga and bitch affiliated with the Mob was here.

"Yes, Valencia it's true."

"Can we talk about this Shaolin me and my kids don't have anywhere to go?"

I was dancing in front of Judah. I wanted this every day. He was whispering sweet nothings in my ear. One thing about Judah he kept a smile on my face. I noticed a few females kept walking by and looking. I didn't say anything, but I noticed it. I knew trouble was coming, but I hope trouble was ready for me. Suddenly three females walked in front of me and stopped. I stopped dancing. I could feel Judah raise up. I started to break free from him because I didn't need anybody in my space. If there was an issue, I came here to solve it.

"Excuse me, but I need you to leave you're not welcome here?" I really didn't want to make a scene, but if a bitch sent for me or came for me, she would get everything that she was asking for.

"Do you know me because I don't know you?"

"We've met you're the same bitch that killed my husband."

"I'm the same bitch that doused coffee in your eyes too. I didn't think you could see. I'm the same bitch that killed my husband? Last I checked he was still married to me and to be technical this is my house, and you can get to fucking stepping because you're not welcome here and your services are no longer needed. This is my shit."

Leilani had a few men surrounding her by the bar asking for her name. Haitian men don't care who you're with, Lorenzo turned around his face was snarled up. You could see the vein appearing on the right side of his face. I knew he was about to say something.

"I need you three to back the fuck up. She's with me; she's not fresh meat. She's my meat." Lorenzo grabbed a handful of Leilani's ass. I knew it was only a matter of time before he said anything. Judah was the more reserved brother but Lorenzo he's a real live Zo, and he's still in the streets heavy he's one of my biggest customers.

"My bad Zo I didn't know, no disrespect." I could tell Leilani was feeling him she didn't say anything, but I knew she could handle her own. Lorenzo and Leilani went in their own direction and Judah, and I went in ours. Judah and I were posted by the bar. The DJ was playing **No Letting Go** by **Wayne Wonder.**

Got somebody she's a beauty
Very special really and truly
Take good care of me like it's her duty
Want you right by my side night and day
No letting go no holding back

"I'm fine handsome I missed you too." Judah grabbed my hand and pulled me in for a hug. I swear I didn't want him to let me go. It's been a minute since I've been wrapped up in his arms. I heard Leilani do a loud cough and laughed. Judah and I looked at each other and smiled.

"I'm sorry it's Leilani correct? I'm Judah Wright, Shaolin's fiancé and this is my brother Lorenzo."

"It's nice to meet Shaolin's fiancé and you too Lorenzo." Lorenzo looked Leilani up and down. I could tell she was uncomfortable. He was perfect for her. That's why I introduced the two of them. Judah and Lorenzo escorted us inside of Big Vell's mansion.

Yeah, I was coming for all of this. I didn't want it, but I damn sure was taking it. If his wife wanted it, she could buy it from me. I recognized a few people I'm sure word would get back to Big Vell's wife that I was in my home. I wanted to see if she could talk shit in person the same way she spoke in the text messages. Judah and Lorenzo escorted us to the bar. Judah knew the only thing I wanted was a few shots of White Hennessey and him.

"Leilani what are you drinking?"

"Patron on the rocks and add salt on my rim."

Shaolin

Leilani and I had an enjoyable conversation I really wanted her to think about what I said. I've raised my children all three of them are grown, and it's time for me to live my life how I see fit. I wanted to be with Judah and the only reason I didn't come here years ago because I knew I would be judged for moving on after Big Vell died.

Nobody judged him he has a whole wife mean while still married to me. Judah and I grew up together. He's a commercial real estate developer he used to sale drugs, but he invested his drug money in a legit business, and he doesn't do that anymore.

He doesn't want me involved with drugs, and I understood that because we both have careers to make an honest living. He only agreed to come to this party, so I could handle my business, and we can start planning our new life.

"Hey beautiful how are you I missed you?"

Big Vell shady ass was living good. I had to check my make-up. I could tell by the cars parked in the drive way we were amongst the elite of Haiti. If a bitch acts sideways, I'll turn this bitch out. Shaolin parked and handed her keys to valet. I noticed a man at the driver's door, and she was smiling that must be Judah damn. I noticed the guy to the left of him peeking trying to get a good look at me. Lord have mercy if that was Lorenzo I need to take my panties off now

The FEDS watched me my whole life while this nigga was doing whatever he wanted to do. Live your life our kids are grown Shon and Layla are happy. Hopefully, Malone will experience that with Sphinx." Shaolin had some valid points, but I wasn't looking for love. I knew this Lorenzo nigga wasn't weighing up to Big Shon nobody could compare to my husband.

When I say they don't make them like him anymore, I mean that shit. Yeah, I dated a few niggas in the past, but they didn't hold my interest. Maybe it was me and not them. I would compare every man to Big Shon, and there's no comparison. I've been in this fucked up world for a long time.

I have yet to meet a man that could snatch my soul the way Big Shon snatched my soul. If God blessed me with two soul mates that would be amazing until then I'll stay down until I could be reunited with my husband. I ain't afraid to die because when I do the only man I want to see is Big Shon I can't wait to jump on him. Shaolin finally pulled up at the spot. Damn this house looked like a big ass castle.

We grew up together he's divorced, and I'm a wIDow. We're going to a party Big Vell's wife is throwing. We couldn't get in this party without Judah and Lorenzo. It's business and pleasure, but I'm handling my business in the process."

"Okay. I'm happy for you. You deserve it; I'm a little pissed as soon as we're reunited your moving back to Haiti."

"If you and Lorenzo hit it off you wouldn't have to miss me we'll be neighbors."

"Shaolin don't do that. I haven't dated in years. When I said I do and till death do us part I meant that shit. I'm good."

"Leilani stop it you deserve to be happy. I know Big Shon would want you to be happy and move on. Someone else is capable of loving you how he loved you."

"It's sounds good, but I don't want to find out they don't make niggas like they used too."

"I thought the same thing but look at me. I yearned for Big Vell for years, and he was in our country doing him. He never sent for us or anything I didn't even have a hint that he was alive.

"Leilani, I haven't been home in twenty years, that's the truth. Judah and I have been good friends for very a long time. He spoils me. We haven't seen each other in over six months. He owns the property, and we've kept in touch with each other throughout the years, and we're somewhat dating.

The last time we saw each other he asked me would I ever come back to Haiti to live and I told him yes if he made it worthwhile. He brought me the condo and everything that's in the garage. You know I'm nurse, so he's building me my own physician's office, so I can continue to practice medicine."

"Shaolin, you're moving back home? I can't wait to meet this Judah. Vell and Sphinx aren't going to allow that. So, where are we going?"

"I think I am. I'm in love with him, and I have been for years. Layla has met him already. If you get, Malone onboard Sphinx wouldn't be worried about me. Vell, on the other hand, he'll be all right. We're both tired of the long-distance thing. Judah and I don't have any secrets, but he doesn't want me involved with the streets anymore.

Leilani

Shaolin had me in the real trenches. I'll always have my girls back; she assured me that I didn't need to tote my heat. I'm not going anywhere without my heat. I'm in a foreign country these fools are foreign to me, and I'm foreign to them.

The rain came out of nowhere. I thought we were taking a boat. Shaolin flipped the light in the garage; it looked like a car lot. It was a brand-new Mercedes Benz, Bentley Truck and Porsche for someone not to come home a lot. You sure do have a lot of new shit. It's not my business, but I'll pry later I'm sure there's an explanation. I wasn't feeling this blind date. I really didn't care to date.

"What's on your mind Leilani you've been quite ever since we left?"

"It's a lot of things on my mind. I need you to keep one hundred with me? Bitch when was the last time you've been home? The cars housed in the garage are brand fucking new. What's up with this double date shit. You know I'm not feeling it all."

"Hell yeah, let's go now." Vell and Dino are trying to get my ass in trouble. I'm saving myself for Malone. Ain't nothing wrong with flirting and getting your dick sucked. If I fuck a bitch with a condom on technically, we didn't fuck. I'm going to try to be on my best behavior even though she curved my ass earlier. Malone knew voodoo she's been on my mind heavy since I heard her voice. I stayed thinking about her. I wanted to break in the prison so bad to see her, but she wanted space. I'll play cool for now but once she gets home, it ain't no space.

It must not be meant for us to go out and fuck off. Suddenly it was storming and lightening real bad outside. I haven't had any sleep-in weeks. I needed to catch up on my rest because there's no telling what's in store for me in Haiti. I needed a few shots to get me there because I'll be thinking about Malone all night and fuck around and not get any sleep.

Sphinx

My OG is up to some shit. I'm not feeling her going out meeting a man that I don't know anything about. I'll kill a nigga if something happened to my mother. Haiti was beautiful, and the bitches on the beach were too. I caught a few looking at me.

I'm single, and I'm not trying to get caught up. I couldn't help to think about Malone. I don't appreciate how she played me earlier. I missed the shit out of her. I can't wait until she's free, so we could make shit right between us. She must be with me what other choice does she has? I heard a knock at my door.

"Yeah."

"What are you trying do?"

"I'm down for whatever, where's Shon pussy whipped ass?"

"On the phone with Layla." Vell and Dino laughed.

"I figured as much. Y'all peeped those hoes at the beach?"

Our kids are grown and dating. Meanwhile, we're not. I'm open to dating. I just want to be happy and live my life. That's not too much to ask for.

"Come on y'all follow me." Sphinx, Vell, Shon, and Dino were looking at the ladies laid out on the beach. "Y'all can look all y'all want but don't touch." Sphinx was the only one single, but he didn't need to touch anything. I unlocked the door to the beach house. It was a ten-bed room condo.

"Damn momma this is nice, you have to many secrets. I could've been over here relaxing and getting my mind right."

"Vell, hush buy you one. Y'all take the upstairs, and we'll take the downstairs."

"What's the move Shaolin and whose Judah and Lorenzo?"

"Leilani, follow my lead pick a room and go get dressed. I'm single and your single."

"I'm loyal to my husband even in death I'm good. I will never love another man like I loved Big Shon."

"Shit, what about me?"

"Chanta, you've been smiling since Day dropped you off. Go get your husband back; the nigga already said he was catching a flight over here."

"Fuck you Shaolin and Leilani." Chanta knew we weren't lying. It's time for Leilani and me to get our groove back.

"Vell, why do you think Chanta and Leilani are here? I raised y'all not to brag or anything, but I can guarantee you I have more bodies on my hand than the both of you.

This is my country Big Vell may have been running shit, but he still had to pay me. I must move around out here in these streets to see what the fuck was going on.

I must make my presence known. I must pull everybody affiliated with the mob out of hiding. Anytime a mob is dismantled you must build a new one. I don't want anybody working for you that could be a threat.

Do you think these niggas will give y'all the same respect they gave your father? They don't know y'all. Yes, you're Haitian, but you're not born and raised over here. I'm sure they've heard of you. Y'all ain't put in no work in over here. Let me do shit my way." Vell and Sphinx had an attitude. Haiti is foreign to them. I'm giving the orders, and they're to follow suit.

***

I purchased a Beach house years ago on Wahoo Bay Beach it's beautiful. My house is about forty-five minutes from the heart of Haiti. The boat ride was nice. Our driver pulled up to the dock and assisted us off the boat. The Dominican Republic wasn't too far from here.

I only plan to be out here for a few days. I had to handle Big Vell's wife her mouth was a little to reckless for me. She had so much to say about her husband she'll be lying next to him.

"What's the move Shaolin?"

"I have a house not to far from here; we need to drop our luggage off to get settled. We can go out for dinner and hit the streets. I must meet up with an old friend of mine Judah and Lorenzo. Leilani you can come with me. I want you to meet Lorenzo."

"Momma who the fuck is Judah and Lorenzo? Hell, no my OG ain't going no damn where to meet some niggas I don't know fuck that. We're here to handle business that's it."

"Sphinx watch your damn mouth. I'm a grown ass woman I gave birth to you it's not the other way around. Meeting Judah is business I can handle myself trust me. Sit your ass in the house I don't need you out here fucking none of these women out here. That goes for all of y'all."

"Momma we don't want anything to happen to you."

Chapter 8

Shaolin

We finally arrived in Haiti I haven't been home in over twenty years. Everything is foreign to me. I should've came back home years ago to see what the fuck was going on. Big Vell was always too good to be true. When you love someone as much as I loved him you overlook the signs.

I never look for the bad in the person I always look for the good. I've been calling my cousin Jacinda for the past few days, and I haven't been able to reach her. I find that to be odd and she was the one who dropped the dime on Big Vell.

I couldn't dwell on that right now. I'm on a mission I need to let these niggas know it's a new sheriff in town and the bitch that's running the Haitian Mob any business y'all had with big Vell is severed. I don't trust anything with his name attached.

"You need to tell him now, stop waiting because he'll be mad as hell."

"I know I'll deal with the consequences."

"I know where you're coming from but tell him. The two of you are crazy. I can't even blame you for not wanting to tell him because he's a fool. Me personally I would've told his ass I was pregnant with his child while I was locked up because he would've been really stressed out. He's loves kids he didn't need any more but knocking you up with a set of twins is hilarious. You had his love children. Things would be a lot better if y'all be together and just try the relationship thing."

"I hear you loud and clear but I'm not ready at all." My time was up on the phone. I heard Layla and my mother loud and clear, but my life doesn't revolve around Sphinx. He has the right to know when I want him to know.

"I'm glad Shon is smothering you, and he has a child of his own on the way. Now he can stay out of my business. I bet you it's a boy God wouldn't torture your daughter with a strict ass father like Shon."

"Stop Malone. Enough about me, how are you? I want to come and see you if you'll allow me too. I heard you're expecting also is it true and when are you due?"

"Yes, it's true I'm due in January, but with twins, they'll probably come in December. I'm okay you can come and see me my visits are Tuesday, and they're letting me have one this Sunday."

"Cool, I'll come Sunday to see you. Twins are you serious? Does he know?"

"Who is he?"

"Sphinx who else."

"Yes, he knows, but I haven't told him I'm carrying two babies and they're his. Please don't tell him let me do it."

"Malone, he knows you're pregnant, but you haven't told him he's the father? Girl he's going to be so happy. Why haven't you told him yet?"

"Layla, because he's crazy. I'm trying to see if I could deal with him for eighteen years."

I'm not a criminal and I didn't want them to think going to jail and being behind bars was cool because it isn't. It's crazy because they refuse to give me a bond? Why not I've never been in trouble a day in my life and trust me if I were guilty, I would've been on the run, but I'm not. I had another twenty minutes before it was time to lay it down. It dawned on me I needed to call Layla to see what's up and how's the pregnancy. I completely cut her off because of Sphinx and shouldn't have because she has nothing to do with us. I hope she answers. She answered on the first ring.

"Hi, Malone, how are you?"

"I'm good holding my head above the water and you?"

"I'm okay at home bored, missing Shon like crazy. Your babies and Samaya are on the way over here. OG Lou said they're driving her crazy she can't do it."

"Girl she a damn lie. I was surprised she was watching them anyway. How's the pregnancy?"

"I know right but I need the company anyway I don't mind keeping them. The pregnancy is amazing, and Shon is smothering me like crazy I want a girl so bad. I can't deal with another Shon."

Malone

My mother really tried me when she put Sphinx on the phone my heart dropped. I tried to keep it together and not be so rude because I was on speaker. It is what it is. The last time we saw each other wasn't so pleasant. How could she do that to me? She knew he's the last person I wanted to talk to while I was locked up. He knew he was on my shit list, so why try your luck?

I wonder what business they had going on for them to be leaving the country. For some reason today, I was missing my babies like crazy. It's hard being away from them. I couldn't imagine spending my life in here and away from kids. I haven't even told Jah and Kennedy they have some new siblings on the way. Kennedy loved babies, but Jah didn't.

I was so glad to hear their voices. Tears formed in my eyes when they asked me when was I coming home? My voice cracked. I prayed everyday they set me free, so I could be reunited with them, I know it's kind of selfish for me not invite them up here to see, but I didn't want my kids seeing me behind bars.

"I'm good OG. Malone she's still playing hard to get. If she didn't have any feelings for me, she wouldn't even act the way she does. Her mouth says one thing, but her heart says something else. I cuffed her a long time ago."

"I want her to give him some too. They'll work it out." If Shaolin only knew Malone looks like me but she's stubborn like her father, and she holds grudges, but she loves Sphinx, and he knows that.

"Hey momma what's up? I miss you where my babies at?" Sphinx instantly turned around and came closer to the phone."

"Your grandmother has them. I'm going out the country for a few days."

"OG Lou has my kids or Linda Faye? Who are you going out the country with and why? Damn, they're letting me have a Sunday visit, and you can't come?"

"OG Lou has them. Me, Auntie Chanta, Shaolin, Vell, Sphinx, Shon, and Dino."

"Oh, tell Auntie Chanta and Shaolin I love them. Tell Shon, Dino and Vell I said what's up."

"You're on speaker phone they heard you what about Sphinx?"

"Who is that I don't think I know him?" She laughed. Sphinx grabbed my phone he didn't like that at all. Everybody could tell Malone was laughing.

"Malone, you don't know me anymore?"

"Good bye Sphinx. Y'all be safe." I felt bad for him, he was trying, but she shut him out.

"Look Leilani; I'm going to need Malone give my son some slack. He's sorry I feel bad for him. He made a mistake. He wants to right his wrongs."

Please don't let that nurse uniform fool you. I couldn't wait to handle business and get back home.

I miss my daughter, and I can't wait until they free her. Chanta and Day was talking about God knows what in that truck. I gave Vell, Shon, Dino, and Sphinx a hug. I couldn't be mad at Sphinx for too long because my daughter was in love with his ass.

If you ask me Malone loved that crazy nigga showing his ass. The game has changed I wish she would tell him her babies are his. Children are blessings. Every time he drops the kids off he makes hints to see if I would drop the dime on her but I'm not.

I'm already going against the grain by letting you keep her kids. I'm curious to see how this would play out because Jah loves living with Sphinx and Samaya and Kennedy are inseparable they're sisters. Yes, for now until their crazy ass momma come home and fights being a family with her new baby daddy. Speaking of Malone, she's calling me now. I put it on speaker to see what Sphinx would say.

"You have a collect call from an inmate at Dekalb County Correctional facility press one to accept the call."

Big Shon and I had that real hood love. I stood in the trap with my nigga sun up to sun down. We broke down pounds of Kush together. I cooked the dope up he bagged and weighed it up.

They still want each other I had his ass to pick us up and drop us off at the airport. I sat up front and Day told me to get my ass in the back. Chanta called me everything but a child of a God. I wanted her happy and Day was the only nigga that could do that. It took him losing her to get his shit right.

OG Lou already told her she wasn't going back to wherever the fuck she came from. She needed her to get her husband back, so he could get the fuck out her face. She needed a nigga, and she couldn't bring him home until Day was gone. I swear my OG Lou is too wild. We finally arrived at the airport. Shaolin her sons were posted up at the air strip waiting on us. I had Day pop the trunk, so I could get my shit out.

It was a four flight to Cap-Haiten international Airport. I ain't never been to Haiti but today will be my first time. I already know it was about to be some smoke in the city. Big Vell's other wife was with the shit not knowing Shaolin a damn fool.

Chapter 7

Leilani

Shaolin hit me up a few days ago she told me she needed my assistance in Haiti. I was looking at the phone like she was crazy. We had lunch at my house, and she gave me the rundown of everything that was going on. I couldn't believe my bitch was the plug for all these years.

Of course, I was down to ride because I wanted to get at them niggas also. I knew Shaolin, and I could handle it with our sons of course. I needed my sister in law OG Chanta on the track. I knew Chanta coming back to Atlanta was a touchy situation due to my husband her twin being deceased and her ex-husband my brother Day.

None the less she agreed to come and put in work. We needed her because she could hack computers and she could swing an AK like a guitar. I had to beg her ass to come because she didn't want to run into Day. If y'all ain't together and your over him what the fuck are you hiding for? I wish Big Shon was alive. I couldn't wait to die so I could see him again.

Here I am four years later ministering in prison I found myself inside of here hopefully I could reach some more people, so they'll find themselves also."

"Oh, that's pretty dope, but I'm not trying to find myself. I know who I am. I never committed any crimes. I'm in here because a female was jealous of me. I'll be out of here once I go to court."

"I never said that. You were judging me. I was giving you a little insight on who I was. I can read people well. I can look at you and tell that you've been hurt, and you love hard. Every man isn't out to hurt you. Don't push the right one away because of what someone else done. Allow the next man to love you and love the hurt right out you. You need a God fearing praying man."

"Now you're judging me. It was good talking to you Mr. Travis I'll see you around."

"Why are you leaving?"

"My time is up." I wasn't ready to lay my truth on the table with Mr. Travis's fine ass. Next thing you know he'll have me hypnotized. His voice alone did something to me. I'll be face down ass up somewhere. He'll be fucking the hurt right out of me. He had some valid points. No, he wouldn't see me outside of here. No, I wouldn't be attending the church he preached at either.

"You're good on men? No, I don't ask out all the females I run across you're the first one. I know you look at me like I'm a square ass nigga because I'm preacher. Before I got lost in the prison system due to drugs and gang violence, I was a lost soul.

I was out here running wild in these streets and blind to what's going around me. I caught a charge in 2004 I got caught with six pounds of Kush riding through Bartow County speeding. Prior to that, I was getting in trouble a lot catching a lot of misdemeanors.

Normally any juvenile convictions they're not supposed to use against you. When I went to trial, they used everything against me and hid my ass. They sent me way across country to a federal prison in California.

My mother died when I was prison I couldn't even make it to her funeral. My mother dying when I was behind these walls fucked me up. All I wanted to do was provide for my family and make my mother proud.

I sat in prison for years trying to figure out what was my purpose. God started talking to me out the blue, and I listened. I started going to church while I was locked up and studying the bible. It's like I could feel the scriptures when I say them aloud and I took heed to that.

"You can call me Horace I'm not that much older than you."

"Okay, Horace."

"Can I join you? What are you day dreaming about?"

"You took it upon yourself to sit here, so I guess so. I'm day dreaming about the day I walk out of here."

"When you walk out of here can I take you out on a date?"

"Why do you want to take me out on a date? Isn't that against your job description? When I get out of here, I plan to just focus on me and my children that's it. Dates and dating isn't part of the plan."

"I want to get to know you a little more what's wrong with that? You should come to my church **Praying Hands on You Baptist Church** in **Decatur, Georgia** I work for myself. I have a contract with the state, but if I wanted to get to know you some more, I would switch to another facility."

"Nothing's wrong with it. I'm good on men right now. I'm curious but do you ask out all of your inmates you run across."

Chyla wrote me every week and sent me some urban books. She knows I'm a sucker for Urban Romance.

The last book I read was **Real Sisters** by **Chyna L.** when I tell you that book was so good. I wanted to take a trip to Boston and find me a nigga in the Bean town if they were giving it up like that. My plans were ruined for the summer.

I hate I'm pregnant ugh no turn up. Why couldn't it be one baby? Why did it have to be two? Twins run in our family. My father has a twin sister my auntie Chanta. Shon my dad's name is spelled Chon, but he took it upon himself to change it too Shon.

The two of them were close my mom, and my auntie Chanta were best friends growing up. My auntie Chanta used to date my uncle Day back in the day. She's supposed to come and visit in a few weeks. I can't wait to see her.

"Hey, what are you over here day dreaming about?" I looked over my shoulder. It's the fine ass preacher who always makes it his business to talk to me. I ignored him. I always came to the library to clear my mind and use the computer.

"Ms. Adams I'm talking to you."

"Mr. Travis, I don't answer to hey."

His reach in the county was so long it made me sick. I had to tell all his workers to leave me alone, or I will personally give his name. He wrote me a letter, but I refuse to read it. I tore that shit up. My mother said he's been asking about me.

Funny where you thinking about me when you were nailing Deja to the wall and she plotting against me? No all he cared about was the pussy. She could have him, and he could have her. It's crazy because if somebody would have told me three months ago this nigga was psycho and he was my next baby daddy I wouldn't believe them.

Sphinx is the devil in disguise. I haven't heard from Leah for one I was embarrassed her engagement party was ruined Second because I didn't want to know what was going on out in these streets. When I touch down, I can't wait for the tea.

I'm claiming it if I ended up doing jail time behind him all hell would break loose I would really catch a case and murder that nigga. Chyla wrote me I couldn't wait to kick it with my girl. She said she ran into Gotti and he was whipping the white Audi A8 that he brought me. She said he was salty because he felt like I played him and that was far from the truth. More of the reason why I had my momma give the nigga the car back.

Malone

I've been in the Dekalb County Jail for almost three weeks now. I would be here for Mother's Day, and that sucked. I normally go all out for my mother, grandmother, and aunties. I'll have to spoil them when I touch down. It wasn't so bad, but it wasn't good either. Because I'm pregnant, so I wasn't housed with the regular females. I've been making the best of my time.

My mother comes to see me every Tuesday faithfully and the only time I get to speak with my kids is on the weekends.

Every time I would call home they were never there or always gone. I miss them so much they're the only thing that keeps me going and they're the reason I hold my head up high every day. I'm scheduled to go to court next week I hope everything works because I'm ready to go home and get back to my life.

Deja's evidence was concrete, but emails can be altered, and that's my attorney's argument, and I had proof that this was a setup do to Deja tagging me on Facebook with pictures of her and him. Yes, him I refuse to say his name.

"She knows we're going to Haiti my OG said she couldn't go. Tell her you're rolling with us.

"Alright cool, I'll see you, two niggas, tomorrow text me the location." We finished chopping it. I ain't never been to Haiti. My only focus is killing them niggas and making it back home." I kissed OG Lou on her cheek and eased my way to my car before she asked for her money. I hit the push to star button. I could hear her old ass yelling and beating on my hood.

"Shon run me my money, don't even fucking try it." I peeled off three one hundred dollars bills and handed it to her.

Dino was already there; he sent me text stating Vell and Sphinx just pulled up which was cool because I was coming down the block. I had to stop and get OG Lou some Lemon Pepper wings; she wanted them wet. I still had to pay her to discuss business at the trap. I pulled up and hopped out. OG Lou and my auntie Linda Faye were sitting on the porch. She snatched the wings out of my hand. Rude ass.

"Y'all got thirty minutes. Invest in a trap nearby because I can't shut my shit down because you need to talk about a few things. I got money to make and dope to shake." I swear this lady does too much. She got dope to shake okay. I headed downstairs to the basement Vell and Dino were playing pool and Sphinx was on his phone. We dapped each other up. I got straight to the point.

"I got the drop on the Haitian Mob I'm making a move on Friday I'm shooting to Miami are y'all pulling out?"

"Nah we got the drop on The Haitian Mob." Sphinx and Vell gave me the rundown. I couldn't believe this shit. Yeah, I'll touch down in Haiti and let my niggas in Miami handle the shit going on down there.

"What the fuck am I going to tell Layla I'm not trying to be gone from her for three days?"

I owe Mrs. Shaolin my life for protecting Layla and my unborn child. I know some niggas who know some niggas. Sphinx isn't my favorite person because my sister is sitting in the County right now, but I must give him his props he's stepping up by doing his thing with Jah and Kennedy. Vell and I never had an issue.

Sphinx and I never had an issue until he started fucking with my sister, but I must let Malone grow up and live her life. Layla and I was going to be together regardless she was my rider, and I was ready to make her my wife and do the Happy wife, happy life thing with her. I had to handle The Haitian Mob, so we could have that.

I didn't need to look over my shoulder worrying about when those niggas are coming it's time to eliminate those niggas. I had my own team of niggas, but Vell and Sphinx wanted in on this. I understood we must come to an understanding because of Malone and Layla, but we would discuss that later now isn't the time.

I had one mission, and that was to kill the rest of The Haitian Mob that's it. I didn't need to be in my feelings right now because of my sister and what her Sphinx have going on. Vell and Sphinx were supposed to meet me at OG Lou's to discuss business.

Shon

A nigga was out of commission for a minute. I got
to give it to The Haitian Mob they came for a nigga, but I
held my own. My momma and my OG Lou came through
in the clutch. I knew my mother was gangsta but damn just
sitting back and watching her move I couldn't believe that
shit. She got hit up a few times, but she was making a mess.

My uncle Day had to stop me from getting out the
van. I would lose my fucking mind if something happened
to my mother. The worst thing you can do is attempt to kill
me and not succeed. I know Mrs. Shaolin said that she
wanted to handle it. I can handle my own shit. I sent for
The Haitian Mob on the strength Cree had to go because
Layla was forever mine.

"Momma, who is this lady texting your phone talking crazy?"

"What are you talking about Vell?" He tossed me my phone. I looked at the text. I had to laugh this bitch was silly.

"Oh, that's your father's other wife, she's the least of my worries. She'll see me when I touch down in my country. I'm surprised she could see I swore I made sure she was blind on our first encounter."

"Momma what did you do?" I gave Layla the run down hoping and praying she wouldn't get any ideas. I'm sure she would. We finished getting everything together. I couldn't pass my organization off to my kids without fully knowing what Big Vell was involved in.

"Remember we're takers I'm going back to Haiti to take my shit back."

"My OG is the plug? I would've never guessed you were plugged in. No wonder the FEDS were watching your ass. Do you think Vell and Layla's daddy snitched on you? Damn you're going to charge us for the bricks?"

"Sphinx y'all ain't the only niggas getting money. I'm not going to charge y'all for anything. I'm going to give it to y'all but don't cut Layla out split it evenly three ways. My only requirement is for Sphinx and Layla. I've been running my empire for years no fuck ups.

Sphinx, all this hot shit, you've been doing in the streets it's stops today. Once I make the call and let it be known that you guys are over everything. All eyes are on you. Layla, I know you and Shon have this thing going on, BUT this is your business too. You must stand side by side with them you're their muscle behind the scenes. I don't know what your father had going on, but I'm making a trip to Haiti to see.

I'm leaving Friday. Layla, you can't come, but these two fools are rolling with me. I don't want you seen at all. All shipments go through you. Whatever dealings you have with San Juan let that shit go he's a competitor, and you're the connect. We have eight cocaine fields in Haiti. Sphinx and Vell will okay it. I need you to watch the books and some other things."

My father felt it was safe if I played the back and your father was the face of The Haitian Mob. I didn't really care because I wanted to live a normal life. Your father turned my organization into things that I don't stand for."

"Momma, don't you think you should've told us that you were The Haitian Mob? Our daddy wasn't shit. How in the fuck could you tax your children on drugs and dope when that's our shit? To make matters worse, he was about to kill his own child. Anything that's rightfully ours I want it if it's mine."

"Vell, listen to me I had no clue you guys had any affiliation with the Haitian Mob. I was under the impression since your father died my cousin Isa was running everything. Every brick that was sold I got 60%, and he got 40%.

I haven't been home in years once word got out your father was killed my phone has been blowing. Isa died fifteen years ago. Your father kept everything the same, so I wouldn't know he was alive. I have $80,000,000 tucked in a foreign account. It's drug money. How much were you getting the bricks for? We might can work out something?" I tossed Vell my trap phone.

"I should've, but I didn't. He wanted to get at Layla when she least expected it. If I would've gave y'all the heads up. He wouldn't have made an appearance. Trust me if he was in the shadows he knows how y'all move any switch up would gave him a red flag."

"So, who's running The Haitian Mob since he's dead?"

"I have no clue and to be honest I don't want to know because everything will fall on me and I don't want to be affiliated with anything that's associated with him. The FEDS are already watching me."

"Momma, so you're running The Haitian Mob is that what you're saying?"

"Yes, Sphinx that's what I'm saying. I don't want y'all affiliated with it. It's rightfully yours, and it's been in my family for years. The only reason your father was even affiliated with The Haitian Mob was because of me. My father was the founder of the Haitian Mob he started it and passed it down to me.

My older brother passed away; my father groomed me to do everything. I met your father we got married. I was in the streets heavy with him until I got pregnant with Vell. Things started to get real dangerous.

Shaolin

I've been out the hospital for a few days now the FEDS were still on my ass, but my attorneys wanted me to cooperate. I didn't know shit. Big Vell pulled up on me about to kill my daughter, so I had to kill him. It was self-defense.

I haven't been able to sit down and give my children the answers to the questions they have. I invited them over for Sunday dinner. They had my place surrounded. I caught the train to Civic Center I had to shake them.

I don't know if they have my house bugged or not, but I didn't try to find out either. Sphinx had his driver pick me up from behind a high rise and took me too his house. I prepared dinner at his house. I was just about finished. I started fixing plates it's been a minute since I've had all my kids at a Sunday dinner together. My kids grabbed their plates. Layla said grace.

"Momma I know we're eating but let's cut to the chase I want to know what's up?" Sphinx was impatient. I gave them the run-down of what I found out they were shocked.

"Momma you should've said something."

"I'm not I can tell you have some feelings for him, Malone. When you talk about him, your eyes glisten. I knew it was something going on between the two of y'all when he was laid up in the hospital bed with you. He was holding you like you was his wife and you were mad when I told him he could leave. I just want you to be happy."

"I will be when the time is right." Malone and I finished chopping it up visitation was almost over. I love my child to death, but she plays a lot of games. Why won't you tell him that you're carrying his children? She knows that changes the game.

I don't know who this preacher is, but he can't stop looking over here at Malone. He was speaking with a few of the inmates. He made his way over here, and I could see the lust written all over his face. He needs to back up because Sphinx wouldn't spare him at all preacher or not. I really want to see Malone and Sphinx make it.

"I agree, but Sphinx isn't your typical nigga he can't handle a woman playing him how he plays these hoes out here. No woman has ever done that, they accept whatever he's offering, and you don't do that. It's dangerous game, and it needs to stop. I heard about your spilled milk too. Don't look at me like that Malone. You're not that slick."

"I owed him one. I was tired of him playing with me. I had to let him know he's not the only one that's crazy."

"I bet you did. When are you going to tell him that the babies your carrying are his?"

"Soon, not right now though. He knows I'm pregnant with his child. He doesn't know I'm carrying two children of his. I just want to make him sweat a little that's all."

"You need to stop. He wants to come and see you. He ask about you every day."

"I don't want to see him. Next time he asks tell him I'm doing horrible, and I'll kill his ass when I see him."

"Momma I do care for Sphinx more than I would like to admit. I don't want to be with a man that has a slew of bitches can say they fucked. I don't want to be another baby momma added to the hit list. He can't turn down pussy after the whole Deja situation I'm done. He knew she was running her mouth about me, but you still fuck her. As far as my kids he has four other baby mommas. What I choose to do and who I choose to do it with is my business."

"I agree he shouldn't have fucked Deja. He was wrong for that. I laid hands on his ass too. Why not tell Sphinx that? Who gives a fuck how many bitches he fucked before you? I know you're not worried about that. How many bitches can say they cuffed him and locked him down? Any nigga can turn down pussy for the right one. Tell him that you want more if that's what you want. A close mouth doesn't get fed. I'm sick of you and Sphinx. Shaolin and I just got back cool but we maybe back to where we started because of the two of you."

"It's not me momma; it's him. If he wants to be a whore, he can be one. Don't get mad and show your ass because I'm doing me."

I know he's not about to let another man raise his children he hates to see a man in her face. The guard escorted Malone out. I was so happy to see her.

"Hey, Malone, how are you? You look good."

"I'm good momma. How are you and what are my babies up too? How's Shon and what did he say?"

"I'm good; the kids are doing great. Your daddy Shon wants to kill Sphinx, but he can't that's a bullet that he must bite. He's in love with Layla they're expecting, and he can't upset her or interfere based off things that you and your new baby daddy have going on. He'll be okay once you make it home."

"True, Sphinx and I don't have anything going on."

"Malone stop saying that. I raised you better than that. If you can't keep it real with yourself. You can't keep it real with nobody else. It's something there you're pregnant by him he's good enough to fuck but not good enough to love? Guard your heart at all cost. If you speak on how you feel I don't think Sphinx would hurt, you.

He's doing too much killing and running niggas off to do that. I'm not taking up for him, but you know who he is. Life is to short, and I'm never going to advise you to settle, but you're about to be a mother of four. Do you think he's going to allow another man to raise his kids?"

Leilani

Malone has been locked up for about week now. Today would be the first time I've seen her. She could only get visits on Tuesday's at 4:00 p.m. It's after, and I've been waiting on them to bring her out for a minute. I needed my full thirty minutes.

Lord knows I miss baby she's never been in jail or juvenile. She's facing murder. Sphinx handled his business. He called me to the funeral home to watch him burn Deja's ass to crisp he should've been did it. I'm still not a fan of his. I will give him his props he took Jah and Kennedy off my hands.

I don't know how Malone is going to feel about that. She'll cross that bridge when she gets there. Sphinx and Malone need to figure out what they're going to do because the love they have is dangerous and they're about to have two children on the way.

I didn't stop until I watched that bitch flat line. He could meet his wife in hell. Majority of the dead weight was handled. I need to get at Leilani to see what's up with Malone. Layla sent me a text stating Shon wanted to holla at me. I already know what about. I had people on payroll who worked for the jail.

They were supposed to let me know anytime my name was mentioned or Malone's. What the fuck was I paying you for if you couldn't inform me. I walked out the same way I came in. Biggs was waiting on me I jumped in the truck he pulled off. I took this shit off, so I could dispose of this shit.

It took me forever to get to the 4th floor, and it's just my luck the nurses station wasn't to pack. I cleaned the room right beside Marco's room first. I stayed in there about fifteen minutes. His room was next on the list. Nobody was in his room visitation hours were over.

"Housekeeping." I made my way toward the niggas bed he was calm looking at TV. I had the mop in my hand. I grabbed it like I was about to start mopping the floor. I made my way toward his bed. I could tell he was looking at me.

"Are you new? Don't I know you from somewhere?" I walked up closer to him. I wanted this pussy ass nigga to look in the eyes of his killer.

"Yeah, I think I do know you. It's Marco, right?" He shook his head. Yes, I pulled down the face mask covering my face. His eyes got big he already knew what time it is. Before he could even scream my fist connected with his mouth. I had on gloves my DNA wouldn't be on him. I grabbed the mop and used the handle to beat him in his chest and to puncture his stomach. He was hooked up to the heart machine.

The clean-up crew chopped Deja's body up and placed her in a duffle bag. Normally I would let them dispose the bitch, but I personally wanted to dump her ass in an incinerator. I did that at my funeral home. Marco had to go today.

My nigga Fast-lane his mother does security for the hospital. She was able to give us a few hospital uniforms for housekeeping, so I can get in the room and handle my business that was perfect this nigga had to go. Crim owed me one and the only thing I wanted was Malone and his two children that's it.

Ms. Regina said shift change was at 7:00 p.m. I need to be there by 6:45 p.m. ready with my clothes on to make my move. The doctors come back around to check their patients at 8:00 p.m. Marco was scheduled to be seen by 8:23 p.m. Everything was cool I was in route. I had something covering mouth I didn't need my face being recognized.

My dreads were pulled back in a ponytail I had a Do-Rag covering them with one of those hats the doctors wore. Biggs dropped me off at the back I met Regina she escorted me in and gave me the room number to get at Marco. I took the steps I couldn't risk being seen by any cameras you could never be too sure.

"Oh yeah so her bitch ass husband was pimping her, so she could finesse me?"

"Yeah but check this, I hit up Poncho to see if I could get any information on Marco. Poncho said Marco was at Piedmont in ICU. He got caught with his baby momma in Crim's house, and both niggas got shot up. The hospital called Poncho because he was listed as next to kin."

"Crim, the short ass nigga from down by Panthersville?"

"Yeah that's him Poncho said Dee-Dee was Marco and Crim's baby momma. Marco used her to finesse Crim because he owed Marco some money. Dee-Dee died in the house she didn't make it out."

"Alright Gates. Good looking out." I swear when it rains it pours. Normally I wouldn't even get at nigga when they weren't in their best state but fuck it. He put a hoe in my path to finesse me for some cash. I ain't Crim he'll die by my hands. I'll figure out a way to sneak in his room, and he's in ICU to off him. I needed to do this within the next few hours. When I get at the Haitian Mob, I need to be focused no if and buts about it.

***

Sphinx

Deja sucking me off did nothing for me. I had plans to fuck her, but she wasn't worthy enough to get this dick. I had to kill this bitch quick, so I could get at the niggas who thought it was cool to get at my mother. I've disposed of two bitches in less than twenty-four hours. Deja was spoiled milk too.

She had a motive, but she couldn't finesse me with her pussy I would never fall victim to it. I drug Deja's body toward the kitchen. The clean-up crew was coming to dismantle this bitch. The clean-up crew grabbed the Uber driver also he was the last one to see Deja, so if somebody was looking for her, he would be the prime suspect. My phone was ringing I reached in my back pocket and grabbed it. It was my nigga Gates I guess he had some good news for me.

"Talk to me Gates what do you have?"

"Man, where are you? You wouldn't believe who this bitch was married too."

"Who was married?"

"Tiffany, she was married to Marco, the nigga from Mechanicsville who runs with Poncho and Sampson."

"I can't fuck with snitches. I killed your baby daddy behind my bitch. You're speaking reckless and snitching on my bitch. She's in jail right now and charged with murder because of you bitch. I'll never hesitate to off a bitch behind my bitch. I live by and die by that shit."

"Please don't do this Sphinx." I cried.

"It's too late. I love Malone, and it's not a nigga or a bitch breathing that's going to come in between that. For that reason alone, bitch you got to go. Loose lips sink ships. I kept you around to see if you would hang yourself.

You hung yourself; the pussy was cool and available when needed. The head was decent. You played your part, and I played mine. Eat these bullets the same way you ate my dick." My eyes got big and bucked as he pulled his dick out my mouth placed the gun in my mouth and pulled the trigger.

"You look good where you been?" He asked and licked his lips.

"Out."

"Take that shit off and let me smell you." I stood up and started undressing myself. He stood right behind me and sniffed my neck. He grabbed a handful of my ass. I was smiling. He bit my shoulders.

"Stop." I moaned.

"You never been good at lying." He walked away and hopped in the bed. He must have smelled Dodi's cologne on me. Oh well. He sat in the middle of the bed and stroked his dick. He never lets me ride him raw maybe tonight would be different.

I climbed between his legs and removed his hands and replaced them with my lips. I was sucking his dick like my life depended on it. He grabbed my hair and was forcing his dick deep down my throat I kept swallowing taking him inch by inch with a little gag and a nice hum.

"Deja." He moaned. He called my name real low and raspy. I looked up and smiled. He had a gun placed at my temple.

Deja

Whenever he called, I would come running. I wasn't that far from the house for that reason alone. I could've made it back home hours ago. I wanted to see if he missed me and he did. I went by the house to see Dodi, and he had bitch in the crib, we argued, and he sent that bitch home.

He wanted to know where I've been, and I told him I moved on and he needs to do the same. He wouldn't let me leave he kept trying to fuck. I wanted too because Sphinx pissed me off with that Malone shit. I didn't give in I left he stuffed a few bands in my purse begging me to come back and to be a family.

Dodi wasn't getting to the money like Sphinx, going back to him was hustling backwards. I finally arrived at the house Sphinx, and I shared. The garage went up as soon as I stepped in the driveway. He was waiting on little ole me. I took my time walking to our bedroom. When I finally made it to our bedroom he was relaxed in the bed, His head rested on the headboard and his dreads hung in his face. He looked up at me and motioned with his hands for me to come here. I kicked my shoes off and climbed in between his legs.

I took my clothes off. I opened my drawer and grabbed a blunt and a few Kush bud's outs. I broke down the weed and started to roll up. My phone alerted me that Deja pulled up. We can make this shit quick and easy. She knew the routine.

"You I'm at the crib waiting on you. I smell you, but I don't see you. I told you I was coming home to you. You went back to that nigga ha?"

"Of course, not. I needed a little fresh air. I was in my feelings earlier because I saw the video of you fighting Gotti. Were you fighting over Malone?"

"Look you're worried about the wrong shit. It doesn't concern you. I came home, and you're not here. Do I need to leave and make other plans let me know because I'm on my way back out the door and you can stay wherever the fuck you're at?"

"I'm on my way."

"Okay." I had Deja right where I wanted her. I knew she was coming home to me. You're worried about was I fighting over Malone? You already knew the answer to that. I killed your baby daddy over Malone, and now I'm about to kill you behind Malone. I should've done it weeks ago, but the pussy was to good and available but today that shit didn't matter you had to go. I placed the gun under the pillow.

Sphinx

Deja is going to wish she never laid eyes on a nigga like me or even opened her mouth about what Malone did. If I did want to be with you, it'll never happen because you're a fucking snitch. You'll call the police, the first chance you get. I had Deja hid at my crib in Lithonia, but the hiding shit was over.

I had to handle my business because you're a problem and I don't have time to worry about you. I have bigger problems. It's a must I get at them niggas who thought it was okay to get at my mother. I pulled up to my crib in Lithonia I threw the car in park and hopped out fast as hell. I grabbed my Glock 40 from underneath the fire place.

The silencer fell out right next to it. I screwed the silencer on. I made my way to bedroom. Deja wasn't anywhere to be found. I could smell her perfume lingering through the air. I grabbed my phone and dialed her number she answered on the first ring. I could tell she was up to no good she was laughing.

"Hey, baby, what's up?"

Three months later I'm in jail and pregnant with a set of twins. I could lose everything that I worked hard for because of him. I blame myself also as soon as Deja was being reckless with her mouth I should've killed her. The ass whooping alone wasn't enough. That's what I get for letting bitches make it. It wasn't even about Twin I'm in jail because of Sphinx she wanted him.

I hung myself I should've silenced her weeks ago. I could only pray my mother makes some shit happen. I'm sure she would. My mother has had her kids for weeks, but she's been laid up fucking Sphinx just thinking about it has my stomach hurting. If you care so much about me why would you hurt me? God blessed me with a big heart; I guess I should just become heartless and not care anymore. Nobody gives a fuck about me and my feelings. I'm not even mad that I'm in here because I wouldn't have to see Sphinx. I'm mad I'm away from my kids but I'm leaving Atlanta for a while I'm over it.

Chapter 4

Malone

I made it to Dekalb County Jail in about an hour. The police booked and processed me in. My attorney was waiting on me. I didn't have to make a phone call because my mother already knew what was going on. I knew I would be here for a while, but I'm not sure how long. I told my attorney to tell my mother I don't want Sphinx to make any contact with me.

My life is crazy the past 60 days has been nothing but chaos. If someone would've told me I was going to jail for murder, I wouldn't believe it. I can't even fault Sphinx because I should've kept it real about the extent of the relationship with Twin.

Why did it matter so much if you were openly doing you? I don't wish bad on anybody, but I can honestly say I wish he never laid eyes on me. I curved him the first time we met, and everybody told me to stay away from him, and I didn't listen. He was cool, sexy, and I would be lying if I said I didn't care for him because I do.

"Thank you." God is good. I'm glad Shon made it through surgery. He had a bullet proof vest on, but he got hit in the back and the stomach the bullet proof vest could only withhold so much impact. The Haitian Mob was trying to take Shon out I'm glad he's still standing.

I walked to Shon's room Leilani beat me there. She was holding his hands I could see his eyes scanning the room I knew he was looking for me, but I wasn't going anywhere I wasn't leaving his side at all. You don't realize how much you love a person until you're about to lose them. I know my heart couldn't take losing him. Shon was my forever, and I wanted to keep it that way. I walked beside his bed Mrs. Leilani took a step back. Shon looked at me, and I looked him. He placed his hands on my stomach.

"I love you."

"I love you more Shon."

"I don't want lose you, Layla; I prayed to God that he kept you safe."

"I don't want to lose you, Shon." I climbed inside the bed and laid next to Shon and stroked his beard. This is the only place that I'd want to be right here by his side.

Layla

If it's not one thing, it's something else. I don't think I can take any more unwelcome news today. Malone going to jail for murder. If Sphinx and Malone had any chances of being together, it's officially a wrap. To make matters worse how are we supposed to tell Shon, Malone can't come and see him because she's in jail for the murder of your best friend?

Sphinx knows better he was never supposed to let Malone get caught up behind him. I hope he wasn't fucking Deja that's low. My mother didn't need the extra stress. She wanted to jump out the bed to stop Leilani from putting her hands on him, but he deserved it. I went to jail behind Shon because I fought a bitch.

Going to jail for murder behind someone you didn't kill is different. Sphinx must learn the hard way. I told him to stay away from Malone if he couldn't do right by her. She has two beautiful babies she has too tend too. He didn't want to listen to me. Things get worse before they get better.

"Excuse Ms. Baptiste. Shon has made it through surgery, and he's looking for you and his mother."

"It's for Malone she's been arrested for the murder of Twin. A witness dropped some evidence on her. I don't give a fuck how many bitches you fuck. You can fuck the world but don't ever fuck over my daughter. I'm her keeper since you couldn't handle it and pussy clouded your judgment I'll handle it. Do me a favor stay away from her if your intentions aren't good. I mean it. I'm sorry Shaolin and Layla, but I just got the call."

Leilani walked out, my mother and Layla looked at me. I couldn't even say anything. I had to leave. I don't play games, and I don't give a fuck how good Deja sucks and fucks me it won't stop me from killing her this time. She envied Malone that much she lied on her. I knew she was crazy when she kept telling me she wanted more. We could never be I shouldn't have fucked her, but she wanted the dick, so I gave it to her. She took shit to far.

"I'm glad to hear that I don't want you working anyway. I need a few answers you don't have to say it out loud because this room could be bugged. I need you to whisper it in my ear."

"Lateef let me handle it, please. You see The FEDS are outside of the door they've watched me for years, and I'm clean as whistle my kids are grown. I don't want them watching you at all. I can do FED time if necessary, but you have a lot of small ones who depend on you. I got it trust me I got it." I've never heard my OG speak the way she just spoke I felt that shit. I knew she had it, but I'm her son and her keeper. I don't give a fuck whose watching they can watch all day, but they may not live to report back their findings. Everybody has an expiration date. I heard the door open, and it was Leilani.

"Just the man I wanted to see."

"Hey, Mrs. Leilani, how are you?" She walked up on me and hit me in my jaw twice. Blood dripped from my mouth. My mother raised from her bed. Layla stood up. I wiped my mouth and spit the blood on the floor.

"What the fuck was that for?"

"What's her name, sir?"

"Shaolin Baptiste."

"She has a room; would you like for me to escort you?"

"Sure, you can." She eye fucked me and led the way to my mother's room. She was something to look at. Any other day I wouldn't mind bending her fat ass over and blessing her with this Baptiste dick but today wasn't the day. I had to check on my OG. My mother was on the 8th floor. The FEDS were posted up outside. I pushed passed them and made my way inside. I slammed the door; the FEDS didn't need to hear the conversation between my mother and I. Layla sat on the couch she jumped up and hugged me. I gave her a hug I ran to my mother's side and held her hands.

"Momma, how are you feeling? I should've been there to protect you."

"I'm okay Lateef I'm glad you weren't there. I'll be fine I got hit a few times in the shoulders my upper back and legs. The doctors said I should heal fine, but I wouldn't be able to work for a few months."

Sphinx

It took me longer than usual to clean up my mess. My doctor confirmed Tiffany wasn't pregnant at all. It's all good because I had my nigga Gates digging all into Tiffany's background. I wanted to know everything about this bitch and everybody she was related too. A few of her family members would be reunited with her before the month is up.

My driver Biggs came to scoop me. I couldn't drive to the hospital because I would speed and get locked up in the process. Jail wasn't the place for a nigga like me. I needed to be on the streets handling business. My daughter needed me I filed for full custody of Samaya.

Tania didn't want to be a mother she didn't have to be. She had to leave my premises and never come back. I pulled up to the hospital I stepped out my truck. Vell wasn't lying when he said The FEDS had this bitch swarmed FOX 5 Atlanta and CBS were out here.

If my mother wasn't laid up here, I wouldn't have come. I didn't need to be anywhere near them. I approached the emergency room and asked the receptionist did my mother have a room?

I had to wipe my eyes because I'm tired of crying. I'm at my fucking breaking point. Granted we're not together, and I've known who he was the entire time. Nothing he does surprises me. I'm not even mad that he fucked her. I expected that from him.

I'm mad because you won't let me be happy with anyone. You killed Twin and beat Gotti's ass. Gotti and I could probably never be because I made this baby while we were getting to know each other. I hate we have ties with each other because of the children we made. I would rather raise my kids by myself than deal with his selfish ass for eighteen years.

"Why do I have too, and you already know the answer to the question?"

"I love you Malone, and I'll see you in a few."

"I love you to momma, kiss my babies for me." I've never been in any trouble a day of my life until Crim, and I went our separate ways. Everything that I have I obtained on my own is at risk. I could lose everything because of Sphinx. I'm going to give it to God. Twin knows that I didn't kill him.

I logged into Facebook and Instagram I had a ton of notifications. My text messages started buzzing. It was a text from Leah telling me to check Facebook. I clicked my notifications, and Deja tagged me. What the fuck is this bitch doing tagging me?

I clicked the tag, and it was a video of her and Sphinx and a few pictures. I didn't want to look, but I had too. Sphinx was really fucking with this bitch. He was laid up with her she was naked, and he was too. He was laid between her legs, and her hands were roaming his body. I had to swallow my throw up. Oh, my God, I wish I never met him. I wish I wasn't even pregnant by him. I don't even believe in abortions, but I will abort his kids. I don't want to anything to do with him.

It's Lay Day I'm tired of these hoes trying you. I'm sending some bitches back to their creators. I'm going to yellow tape her whole fucking block and Sphinx gone feel me."

"Momma I'm good."

"You ain't good, you've never been in trouble a day of your life until that selfish black motherfucka laid eyes on you. He got me fucked up. I'm one bitch that a nigga doesn't scare easily. He'll regret the day he ever laid eyes on you. You can play with any bitch you want but don't fucking play with mine. On God that hoe ass nigga gone see me."

"Momma let me handle it. She sent for me, so I'm the one that's coming. I got it. Don't tell Jah and Kennedy what's going on. I know I maybe pushing it but check on Crim he got shot up bad. Tell Shon I love him and I'm sorry. Kiss Shaolin and Layla for me. I'm pregnant with twins momma."

"Fuck Crim, but I'll check on his ass since you asked me too. I'll relay the message. Please tell me you didn't let him get you pregnant Malone?"

"Momma not now be happy for me. My kids are the only thing that keeps me sane."

"You still didn't answer my question."

I done everything the officer told me to do. Crim was on a stretcher and in the back of the ambulance. His eyes were trained on me. I didn't need him worrying about me he needed to get better for the sake of his kids. My cellphone was in my clutch. I grabbed my phone and call my mother. She answered on the first ring.

"Malone, where are you? Everybody's at the hospital Shon got shot, and me and Shaolin got hit a few times."

"Momma are you guys okay?" I cried.

"We're fine Malone. Shon got hit a few times, but he'll pull through. He lost a lot of blood, but you know I'll save my son before I save myself. We're at Dekalb Medical are you on your way?"

"No momma I'm not. I'm on way to the Dekalb County jail. They just arrested me for the murder of Twin. I went to check on Crim he got shot a few times and they ran my name and slapped handcuffs on me."

"I can't talk to tough on this phone. Let me make sure Shon pulls through surgery, and I'll be there immediately. I'm calling our attorney, and he'll meet you at the jail.

 **C**hapter 3

Malone

I can't win for loosing! Tears flooded my eyes for the second time tonight. I swear this is the worst day of my life. I don't owe any loyalty to Crim. He was the father of my kids that's it. No matter what he did and how he treated me. I never wanted to see him down bad. I had to check on him. I owed it to Jah and Kennedy.

He was shot up bad I'm glad I got there when I did or else he would've died. I grabbed the money that was scattered in his condo and hid it behind the washing machine. I can't believe Dee-Dee played him the way she did. In the midst, of me going to check on Crim to make sure he was straight. I got arrested for the murder of Twin. I could never kill Twin I loved him forever, and I would never stop loving him. I knew this had everything to do with Deja.

She takes Loc's daughter to see him once a month in the FEDS and Loc is scheduled to be released in June, and he has hopes Deja and him will be together. I told him Deja was for everybody he didn't want to believe that shit.

Dodi called me yesterday and said the bitch hasn't been home in over two weeks. I wasn't surprised. Typical hoe shit, she was with another nigga. I didn't even want to say I told you so because Dee-Dee pulled the same shit and look she was with a nigga who had an issue with me.

The paramedics placed me in the back of an ambulance I couldn't keep my eyes off Malone. I wish this was a bad dream, but this is my reality. I'm praying for Malone our kids didn't need to be left out here without her.

I tried to jump off the stretcher because she didn't kill anybody. Jatwon was Twin, and she didn't have any dealings with him to my knowledge.

"I need you to calm down sir, so we can provide you with the appropriate medical attention. Ms. Adams has a warrant out for her arrest. The police couldn't take her in if they didn't have the proper paperwork, but they do."

"I'm straight Crim, just focus on getting better and I'll see you soon. I didn't kill anybody." I swear this day couldn't get any worse I called Malone to come and help me out, and she gets arrested in the process. Who told that she murdered anybody?

Twin was Shon's nigga, and I bet Deja is behind it, she's so conniving. Dodi has been my nigga for years, and we fell out behind the Lisa and Mahogany shit, he hit me up a few weeks ago trying to squash that shit. It's squashed, but shit will never be the same because my mother was wrong on all levels and they were too.

I told him don't fuck with Deja when he started fucking with her, but he didn't listen. Deja grew up on my block, but she was an undercover hoe.

Her first daughter ain't Twin's it's by my cousin Loc that's in the FEDS Twin wasn't my nigga, so I didn't care to drop the dime on her.

"Hi, the victim and the intruders are upstairs." I heard the paramedics making their way upstairs. Thank God I didn't tap out before they came I started to tell Malone to finish Marco's ass off but fuck that I'm a real nigga. If I, make it out here and he does too I'll kill the nigga myself. I owe him one for preying on me and my family and placing this scandalous bitch in my path. I lost everything because of greed and community pussy. The paramedics entered the room and placed me on a stretcher.

"May I have your name please?"

"Jah Crim."

"Can you explain everything that happened here?" I gave the paramedics and the police officers my version of the story. They loaded Marco up he was still holding on, and the coroner grabbed Dee-Dee and escorted her out. We made downstairs to the living room, and Malone was talking to the police officers. I heard them ask her name.

"Malone Sophia Adams."

"We have a warrant out for your arrest for the murder of Jatwon Smith."

"Malone, what the fuck is going on? I'm sorry officer there must be some sort of mix up." The officer read Malone the Miranda and slapped handcuffs on her wrist.

"Okay grab the money that's lying over there. I have a brick in the basement underneath the rIDing lawn mower. If I don't make it give it to Shon to flip for you and put the money up for Jah and Kennedy."

"Stop saying that. Can I kill this bitch please Crim?"

"Malone she's not worth it, she is dying a slow death anyway. I don't even want you to touch a piece of trash, and she's toxic trash."

"I know Crim, but it's not about what you want it's about what I want. I'm doing this for me. I didn't get the chance to touch her when your mother and her friends ganged me, but today if the bitch was dying I'll be glad to finish her off." Malone stomped Dee-Dee in her chest and neck. I didn't even want to watch, but it is what it is. The reason we're in this position is because of her. Dee-Dee was dead her eyes were lifeless, and I watched her take her last breath.

Malone moved around the room and gathered the money. I noticed Marco looking at her, as she left the room and headed toward the stairs. I wish he would try to attempt to contact Malone he has life fucked up. I heard the ambulance pull up I hope Malone made it down the stairs in time to hide everything.

"Malone I'm upstairs," I yelled. Dee-Dee's eyes were trained on me, she could barely open them, but she wanted me to see her.

"It's always her, all of our years of being together I had to compete with her. Even on my death bed, I'm still in competition with her. Why her Crim why wasn't I enough?"

"Dee-Dee now isn't the time to be asking why. It should've always been her. I gave you everything I should've given her. In return what have you given me? Nothing I could lose my life right now because of you. Malone would never cross me, but you betrayed me the worst way. Right now, she didn't even have to come to my rescue, but she did." Malone made her way into my bed room and shook her head from side to side.

"Oh my God Crim." She cried.

"Shh! Malone stop crying. I'm glad you came. Call the ambulance for me, please. I love you and if I don't make it let my kids know I love them too."

"Damn Crim you've been hit up pretty bad. I called the ambulance they're on the way. Do you have any drugs or money I need to move? We don't have much time because the police our on their way also anytime it's a shooting."

She deserved the world, and I didn't want her to have it. I wish I wasn't a selfish ass nigga, but I was and in return and look at the outcome. If I didn't make it out of here alive and she didn't come to my rescue, I wouldn't even be mad because she didn't have too. She didn't owe me any loyalty, but I owed her everything. Dee-Dee's breathing was faint. Where are my kids if we both died they would be lost in the system?

"Dee-Dee where are my children?"

"With the nanny Crim, if I don't make it let my kids know I love them."

"Where can I find the nanny?"

"Grab my phone my home address is in there." Her home address bitch last I checked you lived here, but you have home. She was pregnant again it was a possibility I could be the father but if you were fucking this nigga and Mr. Otis ain't no way. Jayla and Jayln look like me, but I couldn't be sure with her track record lately. If I, make it out of here alive I'll be sure to get the twins tested.

"Crim where are you?" I heard Malone, but I'm scared if I yell I'll bleed out even more but fuck it. It was worth a try.

Crim

My whole life flashed right before my eyes. Marco had his gun trained on my face. I kicked him in his leg, and he fell to the floor. He fired a few shots one landing on my chest. He shot me, and I shot him. One of the shots that were intended for me hit Dee-Dee. We were both hit up a few times and bleeding out.

I called Malone I needed her to call for help and clear my safe and hide my money because if the police came and I had $70,000 in cash lying around I'll fuck around and catch a case, it's supposed to be in the bank. I had to re up regardless of the circumstances and how shit looks. I looked in front of me, and Dee-Dee was bleeding out. I didn't shoot her, but Marco did. If the ambulance didn't come quick, she wouldn't make it.

I can't believe she played me and she was setting me up and giving this nigga my money. I didn't want to believe it, but It was true. It was a fact I heard their whole conversation. God doesn't like ugly I guess this was my karma for treating Malone the way I did, and she didn't deserve it all.

"Ms. Angel are you sure Mr. Baptiste had nothing to do with it?"

"I'm positive."

"Okay, we'll make an arrest. We have more than enough evidence to bring her in. Thank you for cooperating." I feel so accomplished. Malone would rot in jail and Sphinx, and I could ride shot gun. The detectives escorted me to the front. Tomorrow I would go get my babies and bring them back to Sphinx's house with me. I had over a hundred missed calls from Dodi he's called me everything but a child of God. He'll be okay I'm moving on to improve.

I've could've made a phone call, but I didn't want them tracing my phone to Sphinx's address. I came in person. I couldn't get my man cased up. The lead detective who was working Twin's case he wasn't in. He was out in the field handling another case.

"Ms. Angel, I have another detective that can see you. Come this way and follow me." I followed the detective down the dark gray hallway. It was a police officer following behind me. I could feel him staring at my ass. I put a little pep in my step. The police officer behind me he brushed up against my ass.

"The door on the left," he stated. I looked over my shoulder, and he was smiling at me. I've seen him a few times in the hood. I guess he remembered me from around the way. I opened the door, and it was female detective and a male.

"Have a seat Ms. Angel how can we help you?"

"I have a few helpful tips regarding the murder of my fiancé Jatwon Smith."

"Tips?" I explained to the detective everything that I found, and Sphinx wasn't the subject it was Malone. I pulled out my phone and showed the evidence. I pulled it up on their computer and printed it out.

Mercedes Benz emailed me the GPS coordinates of Twin's vehicle, and I had the Sprint cell phone records and GPS signals in my email. I would forward this information to the detective that's handling Twin's case, so they could make an arrest.

I made it a habit every night to sleep in one of Sphinx's shirts. I tossed his oversized white Givenchy shirt on the floor. I pulled the covers back and hopped out of bed. Sphinx brought me a cute Givenchy jumper that I could wear to the Police station. I took a shower earlier because I was waiting on him to come home. I wanted to be fresh for him. I grabbed a towel to wash my face. I brushed my hair into a knot bun. I applied Amber & Argon body cream to my body. He knew my scent, and he loved the way it smelled on me. I coated my lips with a Red matte lip courtesy of Rihanna. I slid my nice pedicured toes in my Givenchy slides. I hit the Uber app on my phone. My Uber would be here in thirty minutes.

***

I made it to the Dekalb County police station in about thirty minutes. It was swarmed on a Friday night. I saw a few females I knew. They threw their hand up I nodded my head to acknowledge them.

He lied and said he was still figuring out what he was going to do. He couldn't kill me because he couldn't keep his hands off my ass and titties and his dick out my pussy.

I've been caged up at his house in Lithonia for a few weeks. Leilani had my kids, but I was coming out of hiding today. My first stop was the police station to clear his name. I would clear Sphinx's name without a doubt, but Malone had to go. Tiffany wasn't a threat, and Malone wasn't either, but she crossed me, and this was just the beginning of her feeling my wrath.

I could see Sphinx and I being in a relationship. I could tame a nigga like him. I think we would be the perfect match. It's crazy how we met our sexual chemistry is amazing. If Malone was feeling him, she wouldn't after today. I had a few videos and pictures of Sphinx and I that I couldn't wait to leak and hurt her feelings.

Sphinx was mine, and every bitch that's in my way would know that. It was after 1:00 a.m. It didn't matter what time of day it was I could clear Sphinx name at any given moment.

I couldn't believe he was tripping this hard behind her. It makes perfect sense why he wouldn't want me to come. It bothers the fuck out of me. I understood his situation with Tiffany. I wasn't going to spare Malone at all.

He was supposed to kill me, but he didn't. He couldn't resist the pussy that I threw at him. The first night we hooked up we fucked until the sun came up. I made sure it was worth it. I matched each stroke he gave me. It didn't stop after that; he would come by every day just to check on me.

Sphinx thought I was going to escape, but I wasn't. I liked what we had going on. I loved being in his presence. I loved the fact, that Dodi was tripping because he couldn't get in touch with me. I knew he was feeling me because he was buying me shit and every time he came over. I would be laid across his bed naked, and it didn't take him long to strip and baptize this pussy.

I knew I had him right where I wanted him. The other night he came over to spend the night with me, and I refused to fuck him, he was mad. I told him I wanted more than what he was offering right now.

Deja

Life is a beach, and I'm just playing in the sand. I laid my back up against the headboard of the bed Sphinx, and I shared. My tiny hands massaged my scalp. I've been waiting on him to come home for over an hour. My phone was buzzing with notifications about Vell and Leah's engagement party.

I wanted to show my face, but Sphinx was tripping. He was scared I was going to ruffle some feathers, he should be. I was going to do everything he thought I would. I couldn't wait to walk up in there and make my presence known. I couldn't wait to let Tiffany and Malone both know I was fucking him. Everybody in the hood knew I couldn't hold water. I finally bagged the Trap God.

I couldn't wait to let Leah know the bitch she sips wine with Mignon was fucking Vell too. Rocky had Vell on camera dropping off Mignon. My cousin Malaya works at The Marriot in Decatur they meet there twice a week. Videos and Live footage were in rotation. Sphinx and Gotti had a fight because of Malone? I hated to even look at this shit, but I'm nosey.

I'll never question my mother or any of her actions because she made the right decision, but I wanted to know did she know our father was alive and why didn't she say anything?

I feel played because my life with Cree was a lie, he knew my father was alive, and he laid next to me for years and didn't say anything. I can't dwell too much on that because I'm back where I wanted to be with Shon, and nobody was going to take that from me.

I'm pregnant, but I'll still put in work on the strength my mother got touched every Mob could be defeated, and The Haitian Mob wasn't exempt. I don't care what Sphinx and Vell has to say. My mother was put in this position because of me. It's only right I help to dismantle it. Cemay and Caineath couldn't let shit go, but it is what it is.

I didn't give a fuck about killing them. It was personal it didn't have anything to do with Cree. It was because San Juan cut them, niggas, off and I wouldn't give them any work on consignment. Shon didn't want me touching that shit at all. I understood where he was coming from. They felt some type of way because I wouldn't give them any bricks. Truth be told they were stealing from Cree for years, and he knew it he just didn't want to believe it.

I don't regret having sex with Shon again at all because I wanted it. We wanted it, and now we created a new life. I wanted him to fight for me for years, and now he's finally done that.

What I do regret is that Cree got killed in the process. I should've came outside when Shon told me to come on. It was going to be consequences anyway because Cree wouldn't let me leave him just because. Now that I think about it Cree's intentions couldn't have been good for me either. If my father ran The Haitian mob, Cree knew my father was alive the whole time. I'm glad he's gone.

My father had to know about our dealings he chose The Haitian Mob over his family we didn't matter at all to him. It's been years since I've saw my father, but I would never forget how he looks. He hasn't aged a bit. Looking at my father was like looking at Sphinx in the flesh. Vell looked more like my mother.

I was a combination of my mother and father. Sphinx and my father were identical, and I could tell just by father's whole demeanor Sphinx is the way he is because of him.

Chapter 2

Layla

Leah and Vell's engagement party was a beautiful event that was ruined by Sphinx. I swear I didn't think this night could get any worse. My fiancé is fighting for his life. My mother killed my father right in front of me. The FEDS are waiting to take her into custody. I don't know how much I could really take.

I don't want to lose Shon or my mother right now. I'm pregnant, and it's hard not to stress because my child's father is fighting for his life. My mother was dealt a bad hand and maybe going to prison, and she didn't do anything wrong but protect her child at all cost. I know they say things get worse before they get better, but I need things to turn around immediately.

Shon lost a lot of blood. I'm covered in blood, and I refuse to take a shower or get cleaned up until he makes it out of surgery and I get the okay that's he's going to be okay. I blame myself for everything that happened. God doesn't make any mistakes and things happen for reason.

"Okay that's fine Layla, and I will handle everything and make sure he's on his best behavior because they wouldn't mind taking in the Trap God himself he definitely doesn't need to be anywhere near here."

"I checked him." Vell and I finished chopping it up. I was happy for Leah, but this is the beginning of a storm, and it'll be awhile before we'll be able to weather it.

April showers bring May flowers. I'll be in Miami soon, and I'll take a boat to Haiti, this shit was far from over. I know Shon will pull through, but I must touch them niggas and anybody affiliated with them. I know my son could handle it, but Cree's pussy ass should've handled his business. Big Vell signed off on the hit, but every nigga that orchestrated the hit had to go.

It's about to be some smoke in the city for real because if the FEDS were in town, they had something solid and they wouldn't be leaving anytime soon. Which means all Traps would be closed and we couldn't make any money until they leave. Dino was on the way, but I didn't need him to come up here. I didn't need anybody affiliated with our business coming to see Shon because they would be a target.

Now that I think about it, after Shon's surgery he'll be moved to the house because I don't need them questioning him about anything or investigating him. I'll protect my kids at all cost. The United States justice system wasn't created for African Americans to win and I refuse to have my child lost in the system or to stand trial just to be convicted.

"Mrs. Leilani are you okay?"

"I'm good Vell; I need you to clear it. I got the hospital I'll make sure your mother is good, but I need you to hold court in the streets and shut down shop. I don't need them looking at you or taking you into custody."

"I feel you, and I appreciate it, but Sphinx he's on the way and then I'll leave once he gets here."

We had the same blood, so he could have all of mine to live. I know God didn't bring us this far just to get to this point. Layla has been right by his side every step of the way.

The doctors had an issue because she wasn't his wife she was about to be, and she was carrying his first child. Layla was the reason Shon was fighting as hard as he was. I needed her to keep the faith. It was like Déjà vu because Shon looked so much like Big Shon. I held Big Shon in my arms when he took his last breath.

He's in surgery now I'm praying for the best. Layla's blood pressure was high she was upset because Shon got hit up bad. I need her to focus because the baby didn't need the extra stress. Shaolin got hit up and to make matters worse the FEDS were posted outside of her room. OG Lou and Day cleared the waiting room quick. I swear that's the funniest shit. I yelled "OG Lou" in the waiting room, and the FEDS were looking she gave me a menacing stare. Normally I don't talk to the FEDS, but I was making an exception tonight. They had a list of charges for Shaolin how can they take her in and it was self-defense he was trying to kill her.

Of course, he was down. Shaolin and I were close growing up. We stopped being cool because of Shon and Layla I understood exactly where she was coming from because we were about to stop being cool again because of her son and my daughter. I would always be there for her no matter what our children are grown, and they don't have anything to do with us.

I was surprised to see OG Lou as the driver and Linda Faye in the back loading the pump up. I'm glad she was because my team was making a fucking mess. We lost a few niggas tonight, but it's all good long as my son is amongst the living. The Haitian Mob they lost a lot of niggas including the head nigga in charge. I got hit up a few times, but it's all good. I'll do that shit again to save my son. Big Vell was a sick nigga to even attempt to kill his own kids behind The Haitian Mob, shoot your wife over a nigga that's not even blood related but to him.

Big Vell had shit confused. I don't know why he thought Shaolin wasn't about that life never under estimate anyone. She didn't hesitate to pull the trigger behind Layla, and neither did I. Shon isn't looking to good he got shot a few times and lost a lot of blood.

Leilani

The game is to be sold and not told. Shaolin hit me up a few weeks ago and told me about her run in with Big Vell. I wasn't surprised at all. I knew that nigga wasn't dead I said it, and I always trust my first instinct. My sources were always on point.

I told her to watch him and keep a close eye on him. I knew he was coming for Shon, but if he knew me, he knew I was coming for his ass. I'm willing to die for mine. If he was in the states, some shit was bound to pop off.

I knew all about Big Vell's affiliations with The Haitian Mob. Fuck the Haitian Mob they bleed just like me. I made it clear to Shaolin I know that's your husband but if a nigga fakes his death and has a created another life he can't be trusted, and I'll kill his ass, she agreed. Long as we had that understood there wouldn't be any problems.

Shaolin called me right after Sphinx showed his ass at the engagement party. She told me The Haitian Mob had The Venue surrounded. It was music to my ears, and I was on my way. It's been years since I've been in a real live shoot out. I hit up my brother Day and told him. It was time to ride and strap all the way up.

My mother is everything to me and it ain't nobody safe fuck the FEDS they can take me now everybody affiliated dying. It's about to be war in the streets you can touch anybody but my mother I got an issue with that.

If they didn't know they'll find out real soon. It'll be a while before I get any sleep because any motherfucka that had the balls to try me behind my mother wouldn't live to tell about it. I can't believe I have to dispose Tiffany's body. I need this autopsy and pregnancy test ran on her first. I grabbed my phone and shot my doctor a test and told him 911 and sent the address. He stated he was on his way.

"What, a nigga touched my momma? Who had the balls to touch my momma Vell? I'm on my way."

"Your bitch ass daddy and the Haitian Mob."

"My daddy dead what the fuck is you talking about?"

"He's dead now, but make sure your clean coming up here. The FEDS got this bitch swarmed they're taking momma in custody, for conspiracy and hiding a fugitive from justice."

"I'm on my way. Malone made a mess, and I got to clean it up. Did you give her the keys to my shit?"

"She made a mess? Yes, I gave her the keys."

"It's a lot of spoiled milk but give me an hour I'll be there," I swear to God the Haitian Mob must see me. My mother is precious cargo, and she got hit up by my father and the Haitian Mob. I'm killing everything this shit is not a game. They will die behind my momma, and I don't give a fuck what ties we have together none of that shit matters to me.

I'll lay my life on the line for my momma. Lord Have Mercy on These Haitians niggas soul because they know it's hell when I come through. Big Vell was my father, but I don't really know the motherfucka.

Every bitch that claimed I fathered a child of hers a DNA test was performed when the alleged child was born. Whatever games Tiffany was playing eventually she would've ended up lying in a ditch.

I swear to God Malone loves to try me, she won't be satisfied until I fucking hurt her. I knew she was fucking with somebody. She disrespected me by bringing Gotti to my brother's fucking engagement party. I damn near tore my house up and killed her ass. I'm glad she took her ass on. She is pregnant with my child, she can talk all that bull shit, but she knows what time it is. She ain't crazy to let another nigga knock her up; she knows what I'm capable of.

My phone was ringing. I couldn't answer shit until I get this body moved out of here and call my doctor to run an autopsy and pregnancy test on Tiffany. If Tiffany was trying to finesse me, it had to be a nigga behind it, whoever the nigga was he would see me. My phone was constantly ringing. I grabbed it, and it was Vell.

"Yeah."

"Meet me at Piedmont right now, Momma, Shon, Leilani has been shot. They hit up bad. Shon might not make it he lost a lot of blood." He cried I never heard my brother cry it must be serious.

Sphinx

I was pacing back and forth through my house looking at Tiffany's lifeless body; her eyes were wide open. Malone had me shook. I swear I didn't think she would pull the trigger on Tiffany? I can't believe she had the gun trained on my face. I started to grab it I wanted to see what she would do. Now I know I guess she was fed up with a nigga.

My dick went limp instantly. In my twenty-nine years of living a bitch has never pulled a gun on me. I didn't even get to bust down her throat. Who gave her the keys to my fucking house? I can't believe Tiffany played me. If I could bring that bitch back to life and kill her again, I would. She wondered why I treated her the way I did; the bitch couldn't be trusted. I will kill her whole fucking family starting with her sister Ashley. A bitch can't play me and get away with it anybody related to her will be held accountable.

If any bitch has the balls to play me, they deserve to die. What cash was she getting? I wasn't coming up off any cash but a few hundred here and there.

"I want to put my hands on you so bad. I know you're pregnant with my child and the only reason I'm letting you go is because I don't want to make a mistake and hurt you. I want a DNA test I'm not taking your word for shit. For your sake and not mine the child you're carrying better not be by Twin or Gotti."

"I'm telling you I'm not pregnant by you. We don't need a DNA test. Take my word for it. I'm carrying someone else's child."

"Are you ready to die? Who is he?"

"Being in your presence alone feels like death." I didn't even say anything else to Sphinx. I wish the babies I'm carrying weren't his. I'm pregnant with twins again. I don't want to deal with him at all. I ran to my car and pulled off.

"If it's not your child would it make a difference? If it's your child, I'll have an abortion, and clearly, I have no plans of getting an abortion. I don't want any ties to you." Sphinx grabbed me by the neck and forced me to look at him.

"I don't put my hands-on females, but you're fucking pushing it. Stop playing games with me. Are you carrying a child of mine?"

"Why do you have to put your hands on me? It doesn't feel good to be played, does it? Worry about the bitch that's upstairs who lied like she was pregnant and finessing you for some money. No, it's not yours." He smashed his hands up against the wall. I jumped instantly. I tried to run from him; he grabbed the back of my dress to hold me in place. My phone rang interrupting our conversation. He grabbed my phone and looked at the caller ID it was Crim. I totally forgot I had to go check on Crim.

"What the fuck is he doing calling you?"

"Does it matter, that's my baby daddy. I have to go." I snatched my phone from him. He grabbed my wrist. I turned around too look at him.

Malone

Tears seeped through the corners of my eyes. My life flashed right before me. I wiped my eyes with the back of my hands. I was barely able to catch my breath. My elbows were covering my chest. I couldn't believe my heart was beating this fast. My heart wanted to jump out my chest. Sphinx and I looked at each other. I can't believe he really choked me out and gave me CPR at the same damn time.

Sphinx is crazy, and it's best that we stay away from each other. My back was lying against the wall. My ass sat on the plush white carpet. He hovered over me and looked me in my eyes. He grabbed my face roughly and made me look at him. I smacked the shit out of him. I tried to get up, and he pushed me back down. My face was beat red, and my make-up and hair were ruined dealing with him.

"Malone I'm not letting you leave here until you tell me if it's my baby that you're carrying."

Cuff Me Please...

Contents

Listen to the Cuffed By Trap God Playlist

https://itunes.apple.com/us/playlist/cuffed-by-a-trapgod/pl.u-38oWXd5u1oGzaV

If you're looking for us meet us in **Nikki Nicole's Readers Trap** on Facebook we are live and indirect all day.

S/O to My Pen Bae's **Ash ley, Chyna L, Chiquita, T. Miles,** I love them to the moon and back head over to Amazon and grab a book by them also.

To my new readers I have three complete series, and a standalone available.

Baby I Play for Keeps Series 1-3

For My Savage, I Will Ride or Die Series

He's My Savage, I'm His Ridah

Journee & Juelz 1-3

Giselle & Dro

Join my readers group Nikki Nicole's Readers Trap on Facebook

Follow me on Facebook Nikki Taylor

Follow me on Twitter WatchNikkiwrite

Like my Facebook Page AuthoressNikkiNicole

Instagram @WatchNikkiwrite

GoodReads @authoressnikkinicole

Visit me on the web authoressnikkinicole.com

email me *authoressnikkinicole@gmail.com*

Join my email contact list for exclusive sneak peaks.

http://eepurl.com/czCbKL

It's time for my S/O **Samantha, Tatina, Asha, Shanden (PinkDiva), Padrica, Chamyka, Trecie, Quack, Mauris, Shemekia, Toni, Amisha, Tamika, Valentina, Troy, Pat, Crystal C, Crystal L, Missy, Angela, Shelly, Latoya, Helene, Tiffany, Lamaka, Reneshia, Charmaine, Misty, Toy, Toi, Shelby, Chanta, Jessica, Snowie, Tay B, Jessica, Blany, Neek, Sommer, Cathy, Karen, Bria, Kelis, Lisa, Tina, Talisha, London, Naquisha, Iris, Nicole, Koi, Haze, Drea, Rickena, Saderia, Chanae, Chenelle, Shanise, Nacresha, Jalisa, Tamika H, Kendra, Meechie, Avis, Lynette, Pamela, Antoinette, Crystal G, Crystal W, Wakesha, Destinee, Daerelle, Ivee, Kimberly, Kia, Yutanzia, Seanise, Chrishae, Demetria, Jennifer, Shatavia, LaTonya, Dimitra, Kellissa, Jawanda, Renea, Tomeika, Viola, Kelsha, Gigi, Dayna, Regina, Barbie, Erica, Shanequa, Dallas, Verona, Ming Lee, Stacey, Catherine** If I named everybody I will be here all day. Put your name here_____ if I missed you. The list goes on S/O to every member in my reading group, I love y'all to the moon and back. These ladies right here are a hot mess, I love them to death. They go so hard about these books it doesn't make any sense. Sometimes, I feel like I should run and hide.

I had to dust my shoulders off because sales and trends don't define me. I refuse to water down a book to please anyone just to make a few coins.

I was comparing this series to my previous series. I refuse to be the author that's boxed in. I write because I have something to say. When I first started writing I didn't have an audience but that was okay because I still had something to say. I don't mind staying down and true to myself until I come up. Book 12 it's special to me because this is the first book that I've written from home. It's bittersweet to say goodbye to the crew. I'm going to miss them.

I dedicate this book to my Queens in the Trap. I swear y'all are the best y'all go so hard in the paint for me it's insane. Every day we lit. I appreciate y'all more than y'all will ever know. The Trap is going up on a Thursday. I can't wait for y'all to read it.

Acknowledgments

Hey Queens, how are you? I'm Nikki Nicole the Pen Goddess some of you may know me and some of you don't. I'm introducing myself. Every book that I pen, I'll write acknowledgments. My supporters are everything to me. I do this for each one of you. I may not know each one of you, but if I haven't found you yet, because I will find you. Make it your business to find me.

I appreciate each one of you for supporting me. Thank you for believing in me. I can't believe I just completed my 12th book. Out of all the books I've written Cuffed By a Trap God Series it's different it's real. It's hood, raw, urban and street lit. Sphinx and Malone they're the new kids on the block trying to make a name for themselves.

I love this series because nobody is afraid to take hit. They're open and they'll do whatever I want them to do, and they haven't shut down on me once. After I released Book 1 I was a little skeptical about Book 2, because it didn't get the response I wanted it too.

Cuffed by a Trap God 3

The Finale

Written By: Nikki Nicole